The Book of Autumn

The
Book
of Autumn

Molly O'Sullivan

kensingtonbooks.com

This book is a work of fiction. Names, characters, businesses, organizations, places, events, and incidents either are the product of the author's imagination or are used fictitiously. Any resemblance to actual persons, living or dead, events, or locales is entirely coincidental.

To the extent that the image or images on the cover of this book depict a person or persons, such person or persons are merely models, and are not intended to portray any character or characters featured in the book.

KENSINGTON BOOKS are published by

Kensington Publishing Corp.
900 Third Avenue
New York, NY 10022

Copyright © 2025 by Molly O'Sullivan

All rights reserved. No part of this book may be reproduced in any form or by any means without the prior written consent of the Publisher, excepting brief quotes used in reviews.

Without limiting the author's and publisher's exclusive rights, any unauthorized use of this publication to train generative artificial intelligence (AI) technologies is expressly prohibited.

All Kensington titles, imprints, and distributed lines are available at special quantity discounts for bulk purchases for sales promotion, premiums, fundraising, educational, or institutional use.

Special book excerpts or customized printings can also be created to fit specific needs. For details, write or phone the office of the Kensington Special Sales Manager: Kensington Publishing Corp., 900 Third Avenue, New York, NY, 10022. Attn. Special Sales Department. Phone: 1-800-221-2647.

KENSINGTON and the K with book logo Reg. U.S. Pat. & TM Off.

Librry of Congress Control Number: 2025937907

ISBN-13: 978-1-4967-5409-7
First Kensington Hardcover Edition: November 2025

ISBN-13: 978-1-4967-5411-0 (e-book)

10 9 8 7 6 5 4 3 2 1

Printed in the United States of America

The authorized representative in the EU for product safety and compliance is eucomply OU, Parnu mnt 139b-14, Apt 123 Tallinn, Berlin 11317, hello@eucompliancepartner.com

*For Chris.
And for the quiet kids—
you don't need to come out of any damn shell.*

Note to the Reader

When Dr. Robetresse first asked for my help, I was hesitant, to say the least. But the deeper I dug into the case, the more I thought it might make an interesting research study, so I kept notes in a journal of everything I noticed and everyone I talked to. I even had a title for the paper, "The Floating Girl," that I intended to publish in *New Magic Quarterly*. However, for whatever reason (the most likely being that someone else—and I'm fairly certain who—got to the journals before me), my paper was rejected. Despite the rejection, I still believe this text serves as the most complete record of what happened here. I'm sharing it so that no one makes the same mistakes I did. You'll notice I've left notes throughout to highlight spots of interest. There's so much to tell, so many instances where if I'd handled things differently, maybe things wouldn't have ended up the way they did. And if you're to read this story—whether you've practiced Magic or not—you need to understand the things I tell you. The others have left footnotes of their own throughout the text, which will be labeled, though the majority will be from me. Read them. There is valuable information there. Information to help serve as a warning, so it won't happen again. So we'll all know better for next time.

—MPG

The Book of Autumn

CHAPTER ONE

Some places never let go of you. They slip inside your pores, cling to your neck like a leech. And though you fight like hell to break loose, there's no stopping it. The place is part of you now. It's in your blood.

Seinford and Brown College was in my blood. That had to be it. Had to be how, despite a whole host of circulating nightmares over the last five years, it still had me here. Driving down this road, slowing as I reached the sign welcoming me to Marble County, New Mexico, which was nearly rusted off its hinges. Beside it was a spray-painted one that read JESUS HEALS.

I sighed and patted the steering wheel of the old pickup. "I dunno, Jesus, that might be a bigger job than you bargained for."

My husky, Bear, barked in the seat beside me and stuck his head out the window.

Marble County, New Mexico, sat between the southwestern tip of Colorado's border and the Sangre de Cristo Mountains. Everything in the county was parched. Mesas towered over rust-red earth covered in creosote bushes and sagebrush. Stray dogs nosed the dirt for something to chew on, finding nothing but bits of tire from the surrounding farms.

In the distance, a wooden sign flapped against the gate of Ludlow Ranch.

I swallowed, talking aloud to keep my thoughts from racing. "This is going to be fine. One job, enough to set us up for a while, then we can move on. For real this time." Bear howled with excitement at a cracker he found wedged in the seat, flipping it from side to side to lick off the salt.

The conversation stuck like a splinter in the back of my

mind. I hadn't even jumped when I saw Max standing outside the café two days ago, cowboy hat tucked low over his face, only too proud of himself for finding me again.

I blew out my cheeks, shoulders slumping. "I guess I should just give up on you people ever leaving me alone."

"You're a Magician, sweetheart," he said, grinning and leaning against a wall. "This shit you can do isn't going to just go away. And you're too damn talented to drop off the face of the earth. Besides"—he tapped the envelope he was holding—"I think you're going to want to see this one for yourself."

I glanced down at the letter, now folded in the seat beside me. "Bear!" I wiped it with my sleeve, trying to save it from Bear's drool. It had been a long drive from Portland, and we were both looking a little worse for the wear. There wasn't much to it. Only:

Cella,

There's been an incident at school. I need your help and knowledge of Object Theory in the investigation. I can't include many details here; it's something you'd best see for yourself. Please come. I promise I'll make it worth the journey.

Dr. Thea H. Robetresse
(P.S. Sorry about the choice of courier—Max insisted.)

Object Theory* said everyone had a comfort object. A warm blanket or spot on the couch, a favorite book, a hammock under an old, creaking tree. Once upon a time, I was an expert in the theory, a budding anthropologist who loved her

---

* A fundamental theory in Esoteric Psychology and a founding theory of the Three Arts. First originated in 1952; expanded upon in 2014. See also M. P. Gibbons, "Object Study: Advantages and Disadvantages of Base Materials in the Conveyance of Magic," *New Magic Quarterly*, Issue 427.

work and pushed hard for discoveries in the field. Now one of my own objects, the leather cord from an old journal, was wrapped so tight around my finger it could've snapped the bone in two. I'd jumped from job to job after leaving New Mexico, from working in a museum to a retail job to where Max ultimately found me, working at a coffee shop on the outskirts of Portland. Didn't really matter what I did, as long as there was no Magic involved.

But no matter how far I went, Magic always found me. It leaked out of my fingers, flooding the exhibits and scaring the shit out of the museum's visitors, or fried the cash register, or broke the espresso machine at work.

I couldn't seem to escape, and so now here I was, trudging back to this damn place with my very last bit of gas and a grand total of thirteen dollars in the bank, and holding onto that leather cord for dear life. I swore to myself this was the last time, the very last time I'd be back. I just needed enough to get myself on my feet again, to repair the truck and cover a month's rent or so, and then I would vanish for good, so far away they wouldn't be able to bother me again. Far enough away that I could start fresh, that Magic wouldn't get me fired from every job I had—far enough that even the nightmares couldn't reach.

My truck rolled under the sign for Ludlow Ranch. Rust-colored dust kicked up behind us, coating a bull skull. What was once Ludlow Cattle Ranch was now Seinford and Brown College of Agriculture—though it was really Seinford and Brown College of the Three Arts.

"It *is* your alma mater," Max had said that day, so quietly I nearly didn't hear him, "and you're still on the council. You must care at least a little about what happens there. We wouldn't have asked if it wasn't important. A student is unwell."

"But why me?" I asked, aware of how close my pitch came to whining. I cursed the day I agreed to be on Seinford and Brown's Advisory Council. Apparently, they all considered my appointment a life term, despite the fact that I hadn't been to one of their stupid meetings in years. "I'm no doctor. My objects have nothing to do with medical aid. There's little I can do for a sick student."

"Not that kind of unwell," he'd said quietly, and a prickle of unease slid down my shoulders.

Now the bump of my truck along the dirt road snapped me back to present. Bear barked at a group of students walking to class.

I gnawed on my lip, shoving the bangs out of my face. They'd ballooned in the heat, and I was rapidly giving up hope of taming "the Wall," the lovely nickname my mass of brown hair had been given in middle school. I cast a glance around me. "Yep, this place is definitely cursed."

There it was, Ludlow House, the sprawling adobe ranch house at the front of Ludlow Ranch. Built in 1883, the house was once home to the cattleman William Jameson Ludlow, his wife, Josephine, and their twelve children. After he went mad and pitched himself into the canyon, the house passed through a smattering of hands. None outside the family held it for longer than a year. There were complaints that the hallways stretched and twisted in on themselves, that in the low light, the red clay tile floors looked bloody. The ranch was more or less abandoned until the early 2000s, when Thea Robetresse bought it for a fraction of what it was worth. On its sprawling acres, she built a school.

Though Ludlow House wasn't the largest of the academic halls, the other buildings could do little but linger in its shadow. Its adobe walls blended into the red hills and mesas at its back as though it had been painted there. Iron lanterns and Spanish doors gave it a darkness that stood in defiance of the sun that baked the acres beyond it.

Behind it stood the rest of campus: three dormitories, the auditorium, the library, and the academic buildings. Greek fraternities and sororities were housed in smaller adobe buildings clustered near the fence's edge at the far side of campus. Over to the left was the main parking lot, on the ridge of a steep canyon.

They didn't have any cloaking enchantments over the college—too expensive—just relied on good old-fashioned geography. Sixty acres in the middle of a desert that reached 125 degrees before noon was ample-enough deterrent.*

Behind the Granary, the massive barn converted into a cafeteria, was the infirmary, where I was to report. A squat, pueblo-style cottage, the infirmary was one of the many dwellings that had belonged to ranch hands who used to work the property. This one was now home to the school's nurse, Maritza.

The cottage's door swung open as my truck sputtered to a stop.

I snuck one last glance in the mirror. Peeking out beneath the Wall were two rapidly blinking brown eyes. Bear was scarfing down his cracker as fast as possible.

I took a deep breath. "Everything is going to be fine."

As I stepped out of the truck, fingers clenched around my leather cord, I couldn't help but wonder how this place had pulled me back, yet again, nearly five years since I'd abandoned my PhD program. The sensation was so familiar, like falling into a deep, dark well.

---

* As a rule, we Magicians did try to hide and downplay the existence of Magic. We knew it was best not to draw attention to ourselves, but it wasn't easy keeping too many secrets in the age of the internet. It turned out not to matter much. If you went around screaming you could do Magic, people usually just gave you a polite smile and walked away quickly.

6 • Molly O'Sullivan

The Girl

Maritza walked out, wearing a white apron covering a long linen dress, and brushed strands of dark hair from her face. She looked slighter than usual standing next to the priest, in his black cowboy hat and boots. Every so often, her eyes would dart around him and back to the door, to what she'd left behind.

Bear leaped out of the open window, tail wagging. "Stay here, boy," I said, shielding my eyes from the harsh New Mexico sun. "And try to stay out of the sun." Bringing a husky down to New Mexico might not have been the best decision, but I wasn't about to leave him behind. I didn't know if I could do this without him.

I cleared my throat to temper my nerves. For an anthropologist—or almost-anthropologist—I wasn't terribly good with people, though it wasn't for lack of trying. I'd read all the self-help books, had planned to dedicate my career to understanding them, and still always felt on the outside looking in, like humans were some species I was studying but didn't quite belong to. "It's nice to see you, Maritza."

It wasn't great being here, exactly, but Maritza had always been kind to me. Nurses brought this inner warmth to the sterile environment of a hospital. It was a nurse, not a doctor, who held me after they said my brother was gone. It was a nurse who helped me gather his things, who walked me through everything after.

The feeling wasn't reciprocated, though, I guess, because she gave a curt nod and slid her gaze away from me and back toward the house.

I looked at the priest. The student must've been pretty bad off if they'd called him already. "What's, um, what's going on? I wasn't told much."

Why they were so insistent on my being here early, hours before the council meeting, was still a mystery to me. I had no medical training to speak of, had a difficult enough time taking care of myself and Bear, if I was being honest. Max's cryptic hints hadn't been any more illuminating. All I knew was there had been an incident with another student. A girl had wound up dead, and another was "unwell." Whatever that meant.

The priest stepped forward. "Perhaps it's best if we step inside, and you see for yourself."

I nodded and followed the priest inside, Maritza trailing after us.

"I must warn you," the priest said, "particularly if you're of delicate affections . . . this may bother you."

I'd been in the cottage before. I'd been admitted for exhaustion from spellwork more than once during my time at school. It had always smelled fresh and clean, like sage and soap and the dried red chiles hanging from Maritza's doorway. The floor was smooth red tile; a Zapotec rug lay in the corner. A handmade broom leaned against the wall, below wooden cubbies full of bottles of herbs and ointments, and stacks of bandages and gauze. In the kitchen was a small stove and a wide copper sink.

Now, although the lights were on and the drapes only partially shut, it was like someone had extinguished all the light. It smelled damp and dirty, like something inside hadn't been washed in quite some time. I resisted the urge to gag and followed Maritza and the priest deeper into the house.

I nearly asked why it was so dark, but the words died in my throat. There was a hushed, sepulchral silence to the room, and it felt somehow wrong to disturb it—like it didn't want me to disturb it. I felt the hair rise on the back of my neck.

I stopped when I caught sight of the bed, my breath catching in my throat. A girl levitated above it, her hair hanging beneath her. An old nightgown went down to her shins.

"We can't get her down, and the police haven't been able to question her about her motives or what happened."

The girl's eyes were closed, her skin mottled and covered in scars. She had scratches down her arms and chest, and something told me there were more beneath her gown, on her stomach and legs.

I swallowed. "She won't speak to them? Why? Is she in a coma?"

"No, she's awake," Maritza said, her eyes shifting downward, making the sign of the cross across her chest. Crucifixes were all over the wall around the bed, and the bedside table had been crammed with statues of Jesus and the manger, along with protective figures from folklore and Magic in a strange blend of mysticism, Magic, and Catholicism. "She hears everything we're saying, too. She'll speak every so often, but we can't understand her."

Seeing my puzzled expression, the priest explained, rubbing his fingers nervously. "She's not speaking English per se."

"She's speaking in tongues," Maritza blurted. The priest threw her a glance. I noticed leather straps had been tied to the bed, but they were released now. A shudder went through me.

"They said you had some experience with languages," the man said.

"Spanish, Latin, and Duolingo Italian, but something tells me they aren't going to help with this . . ." I glanced back toward the exit, not wanting to let it out of my sight. Whatever left that student dead was no illness. The priest's use of the word "motives" stuck in my head like a needle. A student had been murdered, and this girl had more to do with it than Max had mentioned. My guess, a lot more.

I looked back up at the girl. Her eyes were no longer closed. She had turned her head and was watching me with a curious expression on her face, her mouth twitched with bemusement. My limbs felt shaky, as if I was standing on the edge of a steep cliff. I opened my mouth to speak to her, finding my throat dry as the desert outside.

"Don't speak to her," Maritza hissed. "The devil will take your soul."

"She's just a girl," the priest said, keeping one eye on her, the other hand snaking to the cross at his chest. He cast a pointed glance at me. "We're at a loss," he said more quietly.

"We're just supposed to watch her here ... 'until something changes,'" Maritza said.

"Nothing ever changes," the girl said in a lifeless voice, staring back at the ceiling. I flinched at the sound. Her vocal cords sounded rough and deep, as if they were threaded with something unnatural. Something ancient.

The priest drew back.

Maritza screamed. At her scream, a man poked his head inside the cottage. He hovered at the door, unwilling to step inside the house. "Maritza?" he said. "We brought another carving."

Maritza shook her head. "I can't spend another minute in this house," she cried and stormed out the door. Outside, two men were hauling a wooden manger out of the flatbed of a truck.

The priest leaned forward and gestured to the girl, whose eyes were now closed. "That's the most she's said in days. They made the right call contacting you."

I pulled my arms close to my chest and inched closer to the girl, feeling that same strange pull in my gut. A sense of decay, and of deep, deep water.

She hears everything we're saying, Maritza had said.

I hesitated. "Can you tell me your name?" My voice had lowered to a choked whisper. I didn't know if I really wanted her to answer, if I even wanted her to hear me at all.

Her eyelids fluttered but remained closed. She was motionless save for the breath in and out of her chest.

Maritza came back into the cottage, hands clasped hard around the cross on her neck.

My eyes flicked to the priest, who nodded encouragement.

"What about the name of the other girl?" I tried again, directing my question to the hem of her nightgown hanging down above me instead of looking at the girl head-on. My heart pounded, voice wavering. "Were you two friends? Lovers? Why did you—can you tell me what happened?"

I was no detective, no police officer, didn't know if the questions I was asking her would set her off, trigger some sort of episode. But with the way the priest and Maritza watched me, I thought that was what they wanted. For something to happen, for something to change.

After a few minutes of silence, the only sound in the room the girl's steady intake of breath, Maritza's face fell. "That's enough for today. Perhaps you and Max could visit her again tomorrow, once you've both settled."

I winced. For some reason, the sound of my former partner's name sent the nerves in my gut churning faster than the terrifying girl in front of me did.

"Sure. Maybe," I said quietly, focusing all my attention on the door. I wanted out of the cottage, away from the smell, far away from the strange, levitating girl.

"Where's Dr. Robetresse?" I asked once I reached the doorway, one leg safely planted on the dry earth outside. I was here at the request of the president of the school, so why hadn't she filled me in herself? I was someone who liked to understand everything there was to know about any situation I walked into. If you're ready for all possible scenarios, nothing can surprise you. And if nothing can surprise you, then nothing can hurt. That was the thought, anyway.

"She's preparing for the meeting tonight in the main house."

I nodded, eyes searching the horizon. I kept waiting for her to offer more of an explanation—of anything, of why the priest was there, of what had happened to the girl—but none was forthcoming.

"Where's the manger?" I blurted instead. A nonsensical question; the house was crammed with religious and protective ornaments and didn't need more, but my head was still reeling.

Maritza stared at me. "It's outside. My brother won't come in here."

"Oh."

"Dr. Robetresse will fill you in on everything later tonight. The staff prepared your old room for you." She handed me a stack of fresh linens. "You remember the way?"

"Can't seem to forget it," I said.

The priest stood in the stray beam of sunlight that pierced the gloom. He touched the brim of his hat in farewell.

I bit my lip, a sudden surge of anxiety swelling in my gut as I thought about what "later tonight" meant. "Will you be at the meeting tonight, too, then?"

He shook his head, white-blond eyelashes fluttering like a moth in the light. "No. I need to stay here."

Behind him, the girl's eyes flickered open. Her cheeks spread into a wide, grotesque grin. She winked, as if it was our little secret, and I felt a chill crawl down my spine.

The door slapped shut behind me.

I shook my arms out, my feet moving as fast as possible back to the truck. The New Mexico sun rushed in to burn the dank, wrong feeling of the cottage from my skin.

Bear sniffed my legs, investigating the foreign smell for himself.

Dirt and clay kicked up in my eyes as I made my way to the dormitory buildings. Campus was curiously empty. The few stragglers who were around appraised me cautiously.

"Come on, boy," I nearly whispered. I'd never liked having attention on me, never enjoyed crowds or large groups of people, but now that I was here, my brain screaming *dangerdangerdanger*, I had an overwhelming urge to stay out of sight.

CHAPTER TWO

I reached the girls' dormitory, House Torlaine, an old, converted ranch house with a cattle skull hung out front, and pushed open its heavy, creaking door.

There were a lot of memories in this building. Few of them good, mostly . . . not good, but things were different now. I forced down the thoughts of Aaron and his funeral, of my catastrophic meltdown in the second year of my PhD program, of every single thing this place had taken from me. Mentally, I erected a giant metal barrier between myself and Marble County. I could do this. I'd left this place before. I would do it again.

I walked down the empty hall, rotating the bumblebee studs in my ears. The walls were painted a deep rust, and the red tile floors were covered in textiles. The lighting had been added last, dim fluorescents lodged in the low ceilings that cast eerie shadows.

The building was curiously quiet for a college campus, even if House Torlaine was one of the more mild-mannered of the dormitories. An all-girls' hall, and one of the oldest on campus, it had a lot of rules that the two other coed dormitories didn't have. No guests after eleven, a strict one a.m. curfew. The only way in was to call the resident assistant, who'd wring you out for waking her. Since off-campus housing was limited in the tiny town of Los Huesos, all years of undergrad students and even some postgrad students lived in the campus dorms or in Greek life housing, if they belonged to one of the fraternities or sororities on campus.

I stopped when I reached room 22. My old room. An old

iron key was already lodged in the door; one of the staff must have put it there earlier. I pushed the door open.

A clean white quilt lay on top of the bed. Bear promptly jumped up on it and made himself at home.

I dug the rest of my objects out of my bag. Besides my leather cord, there was the mug my younger brother Aaron had given me for Christmas with HOLLY JOLLY printed on it, and a small jar of water from a lake where my family used to camp in Colorado. I touched both of them, drawing what comfort I could from their familiarity. Object Theory wasn't just about comfort, though. Students at Seinford and Brown College practiced the Three Arts, a limited form of Magic channeled through three objects that meant the most to you, in any way you could think to combine them. Casting through objects wasn't so different from the old fantasy stories of wizards with their staffs or powerful talismans.* Objects were a protective mechanism, a way for excess Magic to be absorbed, rather than going right through the person. It wasn't the only way of practicing Magic, to be certain—there were still traditionalists and pockets of the community that rebelled against the "new age fad," people who believed it was simply survival of the fittest if you cast a spell that was too powerful for your abilities and died in the process—but it was the safest. And it was the Magic that I'd practiced, back when I still considered myself a Magician.

I started unpacking, trying to keep my mind occupied, but I couldn't help the way my mind strayed back to the girl hovering

---

* Not all schools taught this, and not all Magicians practiced the Three Arts, either. Britton College of the Arcane in Montana was an experimental school well-known for its alarming number of student deaths. Students at Britton were taught never to hold an object they cared for while casting a spell, because then they'd be bound to that object, and Magic would go through it instead of them. While people who practiced the Three Arts considered this protection a benefit, others considered it a flaw of the design.

above a bed just like this one. Had Max already seen her? He'd said things were bad—was she what he'd meant?

"Nothing ever changes," the girl in Maritza's cottage had said. As I looked around the plain dorm room, the dark walnut armoire in the corner, a single white lamp on the matching bedside table, I couldn't help but agree. It had been five years now since I'd been in this place, but it looked just the same. I scratched behind Bear's ears and peeled back the lace curtains to look out the solitary window. House Torlaine was the last in the row of buildings directly behind Ludlow House. My view was of the eastern edge of the ranch, sunbaked fields covered in creosote bushes, cacti, and patchy grasses, and the peaks of the mountains beyond.

There was something else, though. More than what the girl had said, it was how she'd said it. It was her voice, like two rocks grating against each other. An unnatural sound, the kind that stopped you in your tracks.

It reverberated over and over in my head, and a small part of me wondered if I'd heard the voice before. If, deep in my bones, I'd known it all my life.

Ludlow House hadn't changed a bit.

Fires roared in great dens that had been converted into common rooms and student gathering spaces, expanded with Magic to be so large your voice echoed from one end to the other. Rustic wooden beams ran across the ceilings, above dark walnut furniture and ornate, high-backed chairs in the Spanish style mixed with large, worn leather chairs with students sprawled across them. Towering windows boasted views of the Sangre de Cristo Mountains and the canyon beyond, with the Cimarron River rushing beneath it. Inside, lantern-style lights emitted a warm glow on oak carvings of great beasts and men standing on moonlit mountaintops, of crosses and the hushed utterances of God, though many of the religious carvings had long been covered with concealing spells. This included the crosses over the doors of the twelve bedrooms of the Ludlow children, since converted into classrooms or smaller offices for Admissions or the Dean, though the illusion was slipping. Bits of a crucifix peeked out.

The house had been charmed at one point, worked over by a Magician with a background in architecture, though the architect must have royally screwed up the enchantment because Ludlow House seemed to have a mind of its own. Hallways meandered and corkscrewed like in some old, abandoned castle, turning on themselves while you were going down them, leaving you stranded. There were all kinds of rumors that the house had eaten a student or two in the twenty-odd years it had been a Magic university, but I'd never seen any proof of that.

I walked down one narrow hallway, keeping a stern eye fixed on the walls ahead of me, and stopped at a portrait of the Ludlow family matriarch, Josephine Ludlow. I used to study in her old powder room. The painting showed dark circles beneath a pair of sharp, glittering eyes and chestnut hair piled above a dainty neck. A beautiful woman, but there was something off about the portrait. It betrayed a hint of madness behind her eyes.

"Well, I'll be," rumbled a deep voice behind me. "If it isn't Cella Gibbons, damn near back from the dead."

I knew who it was without turning around; I didn't even need to hear his voice. I could tell by the change in atmosphere as he entered it, as if the air itself crackled with wildfire smoke. A part of me always called to a part of him, no matter how much I fought it.

Max Middlemore walked toward me, black cowboy hat slung over his head, jeans hugging his hips, boots thudding against the tiles. He took off his hat, as if to get a better look at me, his face breaking into a wide, boyish grin. Those navy-blue eyes settled on me and didn't look away.

"Would you stop looking at me like that?" I murmured.

"Sorry. Just can't believe you're here, is all. You actually came."

Max had a way of doing that, of making me forget everything that had happened between us with just a look. He was taller than me, not quite six feet but close, with shadows skittering along his jawline, perpetually in need of a shave. I'd heard little of him since I'd left town, outside of the few times he'd found me when he volunteered to relay messages for Dr. Robetresse. I'd heard reports he'd been getting into trouble, that he'd gotten fired from Philmont Ranch after a nasty fight. His mom had called me, worried about him, scared that, without Magic, he was aimless, one mistake from ending up in a ditch.

Now my eyes narrowed in on an unsightly scar on his finger, flesh curling back from his thumb. Before we found each other, he'd been desperate to access Magic, resorting to some of the wickedest books he could find. Spells that hurt, that split his flesh down the middle. I wondered if he'd gone back to his old habits since I'd been gone.

"I won't be here long," I said quietly.

"I figured."

"How are you?" I asked, fidgeting with the cord in my pocket.

He looked down, a quiet smile flashing across his face, eyes twinkling. "I'm good. Bought a couple new colts, tending them back at my parents'. Hopefully I'll have enough for my own place here soon."

I knew that when I'd left, abandoning my PhD and our research on Object Theory, he was forced to do the same. He wasn't able to continue our research without me and wasn't able to finish his own PhD without Magic. But at least he had his horses to fall back on.

"Good," I said, clearing my throat. This was fine. I could do this. Talk to him like everything was fine. Like he hadn't smashed my heart into a billion pieces.

I still remembered the last time we'd really spoken, besides when he'd found me outside the café in Portland. I was out celebrating a friend's birthday when my phone lit up with a text that just said:

heyyy.

Who is this? New phone.

Come on now, don't be like that.

Fine. What do you want, Max?

What are you doing?

Out with friends.

Can I call u?

Under other circumstances, I probably would have said no, but after three shots and two vodka tonics, my decision-making skills regarding ex-boyfriends were severely degraded. He was on his porch nursing a beer, while I sat on the curb outside the bar. That low, rumbling voice of his took me right back. I could hear the distant bray of a horse in the background, a little more peaceful than the whoops and screams of the bachelorette party taking place behind me.

"Hey, you remember that time . . ."

And that's always how it starts, isn't it?

We talked for hours about our old breakthroughs and about nights spent at that little bar outside of town with the whiskey that burned all the way down your throat. We stayed on the phone through my cab ride home, in between me washing off my makeup and climbing into bed, nearly passing out on the phone with him before saying goodbye.

I felt like such an idiot when I kept checking my phone in the days after, thinking he would call again. Wondering if he thought I was too drunk to remember the conversation. Then when a month passed without word from him, I checked his social media, found out he was dating someone new, cried for a week, and then blocked his number all over again.

"You heading to the meeting?" he asked now, trying his best to fill the static between us. No doubt he sensed how out of my element I felt back here, like a rabbit caught out of its den. His gaze followed me gently, carefully, as if afraid of spooking me further.

I nodded. "Same conference room?"

He grinned. "The one and only."

I turned back down the hallway, which had now sprouted a string of doors to the left that hadn't been there before. Best to stick to the main corridors. The ones the house added at random were never permanent and always dependent on the house's moods. Ludlow House was old, and sensitive to its inhabitant's emotions.* And me, all full of nerves—I had the walls rattling.

Max scratched the back of his neck as one of the wall sconces surged with light and burst. "Best we get off this wing."

I nodded. "Good idea." We turned off the corridor, and I looked ahead, eyes darting from wall to wall. Max, though, never took his eyes off me.

There were far fewer people around than should've been roaming the halls this time of year. Even outside, no one played soccer or Frisbee on the west fields; no one dozed on blankets overlooking the Agricultural and Earth Science Lab's apple orchards. The orchards enabled students in the Agriculture and Earth Sciences major to put their lessons in Magical methods of water conservation and soil enrichment to good use. All I'd seen were a few people huddled outside dormitories, smoking and talking in hushed voices.

"Where is everyone?" I asked Max.

---

* Most scholars of Magic tend to agree that houses are chock-full of some of the most powerful Magic in existence. There's so much power in a place filled with memories. A place that holds the people and things you love most is the very definition of Magic. Unfortunately, houses could be wickedly temperamental. They made terrible objects because a mold or termite problem consumed all of their attention, and they'd redirect the flow of your Magic toward fixing it, leaving you with only the dregs of your power left for spells, spurting out like from a clogged drain. For more, see L. Perez, "An Analysis of Magic in Dwellings and Residential Areas," *Annual Arcanum*, Issue 36.

"After what happened with the girls, Dr. R canceled classes for the week and told everyone to stay in their rooms."

The closer we got to the conference room, the tighter my lungs got in my chest. I pressed my palms against my eyelids. Just a short trip. In and out. I could do this. I could.

Max stopped outside the door, watching me carefully. "Why don't we sit here for a sec?" he suggested quietly. "They're always late anyway."

I nodded and slid down the wall, struggling to calm my breathing. Max subtly shifted himself in front of me, using his body to shield me from any curious passersby. Great. All I needed was for one of my old professors to catch me having a panic attack.

He offered me a hand as I stood up, and I paused at the touch. His hand was warm, dry, a little rough at the calluses. "Ready?"

I held my breath as he opened the door.

CHAPTER THREE

The council meeting room was in an oft-neglected part of Ludlow House. Over a plush rug sat a long, rough-hewn wooden table. On the walls were old black-and-white photographs of Ludlow Ranch from when it had operated as an actual ranch: cowboys herding cattle, horses grazing in front of the mesas. Sconces laid a warm yellow glow onto bookshelves filled with books of Magic.

A woman was already seated inside, knitting needles floating in the air behind her, lazily completing the sleeve of her cardigan—Dr. Amy Nguyen, Professor of Comparative Literature and faculty president of the knitting club. Streaks of white hair ran through her messy bun.

"Ah, the dimidiums.* Was wondering when we'd be seeing you again. The other half of you, at least."

Max didn't just happen to know what I was feeling in the hallway by chance. We weren't each other's objects; people couldn't be objects, but our Magic was inextricably bonded, like two halves of a whole. Alone, we could barely manage the simplest of spells. But together, as dimidiums needed to be, our Magic had garnered itself a bit of a reputation. It was the reason he'd volunteered every time Robetresse had asked me to come back. Because if I came back, so did his Magic.

Max smiled and touched the brim of his hat. I said a brief hello before letting the thick strands of the Wall envelop me in my own private cocoon.

---

* Latin for the world's most annoying Magical cage. Or, I suppose, in a more accurate sense, Latin for "half."

We were an odd pairing, I knew. The quiet, studious girl from the country and the lovable cowboy. I was the half that didn't fit, the person content to fade into the background, typing up our research, while the beautiful part of our duo flashed his smile and made the crowd swoon.

The door opened, and one by one, the rest of the council members trickled in. A man in his seventies with a long, white, frizzy beard grunted in our direction.

Dr. Ellendale de Vries, Dean of the Numerology and Mathematics Department, and more frequently nursing a foul temper than a good one. He took a seat at the far end of the table from Dr. Nguyen, for they harbored a long-standing, mutual grudge, and took out his abacus, scribbling down notes on a piece of paper.

Behind him trotted bookish, mild-mannered Lucas Perez, head of the Archaeology and Arcane Artifacts Department. In his spare time, he ran an antiques shop with his wife where they studied the objects of people long dead, trying to determine if Magic could persist through death. I looked down as his eyes zeroed in on mine. He'd offered me a fellowship right before I left town.

A dark-haired teaching assistant I didn't know sat behind Ellendale, and shortly after came Maritza.

Last to enter, sweeping into the room in her signature lavender, steel-toed boots, was Dr. Thea Robetresse. She wore a huge handsaw* on a strap across her back and had amber tips to her box braids that looked a little like wood grain itself, going from ebony to oak to light ash. She had a good-natured laugh and was known to her students as kind, with a philanthropic spirit uncommon in the Magic community. However, since opening the school, she'd become more withdrawn from the public eye. It seemed the years of attention and rumors

---

* One of her objects. She won dozens of awards for an invention she made with it, a sort of prism carved of wood that she used to reflect her Magic.

of a past with experimental Magic at Britton College of the Arcane had taken their toll. These days, she preferred to concentrate on her foundation, which was focused on discovering Magical ability in underrepresented communities and recruiting more Black Magicians across the country to attend S&B.

In all, there were eight of us in the room—eight of the arguably most capable Magicians alive.[*]

"On the evening of April first," Robetresse began, "Maya Hagood was found on the floor of her dorm room with thirty-six stab wounds across her body. Lacerations covered nearly forty percent of her: face, arms, chest. The detectives who saw the body said it was one of the most brutal acts they'd seen in Marble County in over a decade.

"I've called you all here to discover why one of our students is responsible, Danica Stewart." Dr. Robetresse turned on the projector at the front of the room and put up a picture of a smiling young blond woman.

"And what—or who—made her end up like this."

She put another picture on the screen, and there were sharp intakes of breath throughout the room. Maritza looked away.

It was a picture of the floating girl, now. The tendons in her neck were strained as she arched into an unnatural position, her lips chewed raw, an angry flare to her nostrils as she caught sight of the camera. Dark circles created shadows beneath her eyes so that she looked not quite human. Whatever she was now, it was a world away from the girl in the first picture.

"Jesus, Thea," Ellendale said, averting his eyes.

Dr. Robetresse continued as if she didn't hear him. "We

---

[*] Contrary to what movies and books might tell you, just about anyone can do Magic. It's not like we have some extra gene or something. There were a million people that could've taken my place in that room, if given the opportunity and the right teacher. Maybe they wouldn't have made the same mistakes as me. Maybe they would've been better.

were able to temporarily hide the levitation by strapping her to the bed. We told the police she was too violent to move. She also wasn't speaking in any tongue we could understand, so they were inclined to believe us. A religious bunch themselves, they weren't too keen on bringing her to the station. Said it was best to keep her here until she calmed down enough to take her in for questioning."

She looked around at us. She had this way of looking right through you, like she saw everything you were trying to hide. Her gaze landed on the empty seat at the end of the table. Apparently, someone was missing.

"In the meantime, they've sent the priest from Saint Mary's to offer his assistance, though I don't know what assistance he has in mind other than the exorcism he's been champing at the bit to perform."

I grimaced. It was certainly no good having a priest around, particularly one who belonged to a small-town parish. People in small towns liked to talk.

"An exorcism?" Max asked, eyes wide. "They actually do those?"

"I don't have to remind you why something of this nature would be bad for all of us if it got out," Dr. Robetresse said.

"I can just picture the headlines now," Ellendale said, throwing his hands up, causing strands of his hair to wobble like they were tiny springs. "'Possession at college where students dabble in dark arts.' 'Angry mob demands investigation of Devil school!' Doesn't matter if most of the world has relegated the idea of Magicians to con artists and stage performers; they'll be at our gates with pitchforks."

Ellendale's abacus clicked. "Basile," he barked at the teaching assistant behind him, "pay attention."

Dr. Robetresse nodded. "Which is why I'd like to get Danica's condition reversed as quickly as possible. Truth be told, I fear the Marble County Police Department will be supportive of the priest's wishes, and I don't know how long I can hold off the police and the Church. Once she's back to normal, we can just say it was shock that caused her condition . . . and not what we know must be of Magical origins."

Maritza opened her mouth to protest, but Thea raised her hand. "I will not be entertaining any thoughts to the contrary." She lowered her voice. "We've discussed this, Maritza."

Maritza leaned back in her chair and crossed her arms. "The Devil's boots don't creak."

Dr. Robetresse gave an exasperated sigh, and Max sat up suddenly. "We can do it. Give us a few days; we'll fix her right up."

I slid down a little further in my chair. A few days? We didn't even have the slightest clue what was causing this, but that was Max. He liked to give people good news. I was always the one who had to fix it later, like a little storm cloud coming to rain on people's hopes and dreams.

Robetresse seemed to share my doubts. "I appreciate your enthusiasm, Mr. Middlemore. Graduation is at the end of the month, a little more than three weeks from now. If we don't have the culprit identified by then, we lose our window of opportunity. Though, in truth, I doubt we'll have that long. It's not just the matter of the police. Ms. Hagood's parents will certainly want answers before they lay their child to rest. They're on their way here as we speak," said Dr. Robetresse.

"I just can't imagine why Danica would do this," said Dr. Nguyen. "I had her in class. There was no indication she was a ruthless murderer."

Dr. Robetresse flipped to a new photo on the projector, one of the same blond girl, this time hugging a brunette. Both had bright smiles. "The two girls had something of a romantic relationship, as I take it. Apparently, Dani was quite devoted to her."

"It was probably a botched spell," Max decided, overconfident as always.

But I frowned. It didn't make any sense. That was the whole point of Object Theory, the entire reason we practiced the Three Arts at Seinford and Brown. Magic wasn't all sprinkles and fairy rainbows. It had bounds within which you needed to operate and very real consequences. People died all the time. It was why students at our school practiced a safer, limited Magic using their objects. Objects acted as a protective mechanism, protected you from the worst of Magic's toll when you made a mistake. Even so, few students hadn't attempted something past their skill level at one point or another and ended up sick in bed, vomiting out excess Magic.

But never had I seen someone as bad off as Danica.

Dr. Robetresse's mouth twisted. "I don't believe it was a spell Danica cast, but one that was cast *upon her*. She was at the top of her class, according to her advisor, and headed to MIT's graduate program in the fall. Attempting a spell with such disastrous consequences strikes me as out of character. And not only that—all our preliminary questioning suggests nothing more than a girl who loved Maya Hagood, who would do anything the other girl asked. No, it is my belief that Danica Stewart was hexed."

"A hex? But who would do such a thing?" asked Dr. Nguyen.

"That's just what I hope this investigation will uncover," said Dr. Robetresse, turning to me.

"I've called in some help. You all remember our former students and council members, Marcella Gibbons and Maximilian Middlemore. I'm sure you're all familiar with how much their contributions to the field of Object Theory have enhanced our knowledge of objects and Magic use. I would like the two of them to use their expertise in Object Theory to investigate the objects of anyone relevant to the case. Figure out who hexed Danica. Who would have cause to hurt these girls. We've done some preliminary questioning of the students, but haven't made much progress. Objects, at least, lack the ability to lie."

"And if they can't figure out what has happened?" Ellendale asked.

"Let's give our dimidiums some credit," said Dr. Robetresse.

"These two know perhaps more about objects than anyone in the world and are some of the strongest wielders of Magic alive.* I'm confident they're up to the task."

Ellendale snorted, and I sank farther into my chair. Max's brow got that furrow it did when he was trying to figure out what I was thinking. Our connection was close, but we couldn't read each other's minds. There was at least some justice in the world.🤠

In spite of myself, the more they explained about the case, the more intrigued I'd become. The whole thing was a murky mystery, a puzzle whose pieces lay shrouded in fog. I thought back to Danica, floating in that dark room. All those scars, like she was being torn apart from the inside. Something was wreaking havoc on her body. Levitation wasn't common. It took an exceptionally large amount of power, otherwise we'd all be flying around.‡ It was most typically presented as a loss-of-control effect from Magic. But a hex . . .

A hex was something else entirely. A malevolent spell, one of the most violent things a Magician could do to another. The range of side effects made them especially difficult to recognize. Not to mention cure. Whoever did it must've had some grudge.

I cleared my throat, curiosity outweighing my nerves. "Could someone else have been in the room? Maybe they did it and put the hex on Dani afterward to cover their tracks."

"We've already spoken to the girl working the front desk on

---

* I should clarify here. She meant specifically wielders of the Three Arts, the Magic that we practiced at S&B. There very well may have been an army of Magicians at Britton Arcane who could, under no uncertain terms, kick my ass. But they didn't practice the Three Arts and were liable to get themselves killed in the process.

🤠 (Max): Ah, I wouldn't worry. It's mostly just static up here.

‡ There are some exceptions—the Wicked Witch of the West, for example, is believed to be based on a real woman who channeled the ability to fly through her objects, one of which was a wooden broom.

the night of the attack," Ellendale said, a little more forcefully than necessary. "No visitors entered or left the dorm that night."

"Someone living in the dorm, then?"

"It's possible, though not likely," said Dr. Robetresse. "As it was the holiday break, most students were gone, home for the weekend."

Ellendale scoffed. "The last thing we need are the Arbiters* getting wind of this and coming down here at the request of one of the students' parents. Suits swarming the school, investigating a malignant practice of Magic. If you think enrollment is down now, I shudder to think what that will do. Not to mention what people at Britton will say. They'll have a field day! I can just hear them now: 'They use objects and look where it got them! Their students are practically possessed and murdering each other!'" He shook his head. "Danica will be back to herself in a few days' time. The police can question her then."

Murmurs traveled around the table. *He's got a point. Don't want the Arbiters.*

A spark of annoyance flared in my chest. They'd dragged me back here, forcing me to relive memories I'd spent years trying to forget. I could feel Aaron haunting every step I took on this campus, reminding me of every way I'd failed him. And now they had me actually willing to sit here and listen, and some of them wanted to dismiss the whole thing.

"No offense, Dr. de Vries," I said, adrenaline making me stumble over my words. "You're one of the world's foremost experts on the Magic inherent in numbers, but this is not your area of expertise."

I meant to say it as gently as possible, but I guess it didn't come off quite right because Ellendale looked like he might like to stab me himself. Ellendale's teaching assistant guffawed and spiraled into a coughing fit to cover it up.

"Sorry, that came out wrong—" I murmured. I suddenly wished I could melt into jelly and slip right under the door.

---

* Officials in charge of investigating Magical misuse.

The others ignored me entirely. Dr. Nguyen turned to Max. "What do you think?"

Max leaned back, manspreading in his chair. "A hex that strong, their object is gonna be acting all kinds of screwy afterward. It'll be obvious who did it. The Magic will tell on itself."

"That at least makes some sense," said Ellendale.

I squinted. Magic didn't tell on itself. To be honest, a lot of what Max said was nonsense, but that didn't seem to matter. I'd dubbed it the Max Middlemore Effect. The others nodded sagely at him, as if it made all the sense in the world. The only one who paid me any mind was Robetresse.

I didn't blame them. I sat there in my Bee Kind shirt and pink jellies, with my hair ballooning to epic proportions, and wondered if anyone would notice if I left. After all, Max had been getting by just fine on his own for the last five years. He'd bullshit a little, get help from some starry-eyed freshman, and stumble into a solution, like he always did. No reason for me to even be here.

I was pulling up the route home on my phone when I realized Robetresse was talking to me.

"The priest said she spoke to you. What did she say?"

"Oh." I hesitated. She also smiled creepily at me and winked, but I wasn't about to tell them that. "She said, 'Nothing ever changes.'"

I heard the mutterings of the others in the room trying the words out. "Nothing ever changes," they repeated.

I looked around the table at the inquisitive glances, as if they'd just noticed me sitting there.

"Maybe it would be better if someone else . . ."

"You'll keep trying, won't you?" Robetresse asked. "That's the most progress we've had in days."

My eyes flickered past them and landed instead on Max, who met my gaze with an unabashedly hopeful look of his own.

I tucked a piece of hair behind my ear. "Oh. Um, okay." I tried to look more confident than I felt. I'd never had cause to doubt Dr. Robetresse's judgment before. If she thought we could do it, I wanted to believe her. "We'll do our best."

As I was leaving, Dr. Robetresse asked Max and me to follow her to her office.

Dr. Robetresse cared deeply about propelling Magic into a new era, one where it wasn't hoarded among the wealthy in private institutions or kept locked behind expensive tutors. She'd left her career at Britton Arcane to open the first public university of Magic, where Magic was safer to use and open to all—and taken a lot of criticism for it. She'd done a lot for me and a lot for Magic, and though I hadn't wanted to take one step into Marble County again, I found it hard to say no to her.

She sat down behind a huge, wood-carved desk. "Thank God for you two. Ellendale and Amy will never be able to agree on a course of action; they disagree with each other for sport. And we don't have the time for it."

She pulled out a checkbook, and my eyes zeroed in on the little numbers she filled in with her pen. "Half now. Half when it's done," she said, before handing one to each of us. I could've cried tears of joy.

"That's why I'm giving you two full rein over your investigation," she continued. "Ellendale says there's too much potential to draw the Arbiters, but there were rumblings of an inappropriate relationship between a council member and a student long before all this. I don't want anything overlooked."

"Was there anyone who had a problem with either of the girls?" Max asked. "Anyone who might've wished them harm?"

"Not that I was able to find, though there were some issues with a previous roommate of Dani's, Joselyn Hart. I take it she moved out some months before the incident."

She glanced quickly at a telescope in the corner. "I also have one of Danica Stewart's objects here . . . though I hesitate to touch the thing. The other council members objected to even having it in the room, so it's been here since the incident. According to Ms. Stewart's advisor, her other object is Polaris, more commonly known as the North Star. Obviously, we don't have physical access to a celestial body, but Dr. Strauss will know more."

Just looking at the lone brass telescope, dark and looming in the corner, I understood her discomfort. There was something unsettling about it. Its tarnish had faded to a dusky ochre, and the Magic around it felt hollow and expectant, like a mouth open wide.

"What about the third?" I asked.

"Undiscovered, according to our records."*

I nodded. "We'll learn what we can."

"Good. Well then, I trust you two to keep us apprised of the situation. I'm confident in your strength as dimidiums, in light of any potential threat." She hesitated, clearly uncomfortable with said threat, but we understood her meaning.

If, by some chance, Dani attacked us, the Magic of two people combined would always be stronger than one.

"One last thing." She handed me a small blue journal. "The staff found this in Dani's room. I've looked through it myself, but I couldn't make sense of it. Maybe you two will find something I couldn't. Good luck," she said and then swept off down the hall.

---

* Many students at S&B only discovered one or two of their objects. This restricted the spells they could do because you needed to hold at least one of your objects to perform a spell. Once the third object was found, it opened countless more possibilities and combinations, all limited only by the caster's imagination. For more, see my series of studies on Object Transference. They were removed for a compliance mishap with one of the labs, but if you look, you should still be able to find them on the web.

(Robetresse): I debated with myself over this, but it was only natural to bring Cella back. I was too close to it—how could I possibly investigate my own staff objectively? These were people I'd hired, people I'd had deep, lasting friendships with. Marcella Gibbons had been far enough away from it all, but still retained her council seat. It was the best way to contain the situation, the only way. Because the last thing I wanted was for all of this to get out.

FROM THE JOURNAL OF DANICA STEWART

February 3ʳᵈ [two months before the murder]

And a number of those who had practiced magic arts brought their books together and burned them in sight of all. And they counted the value of them and found it came to fifty thousand pieces of silver. (Apostles Acts 19:19)

Facta arguebantur, dicta inpen errant.* Eh, Augustus?

---

* Latin. As best as I can translate, "Deeds were liable to accusation, words went unpunished." This suggests Dani is referring to the Roman emperor Caesar Augustus. He was known for many things, one of which was his interpretation of the Roman Law of Treason. He was the first to claim defamatory writings or criticisms against him, as well as a body of literature, applicable to the law of treason. He ordered many book burnings of the time, including the burning of nearly two thousand Magical scrolls.

CHAPTER FOUR

The air at midday was already stifling, and so dry I could barely breathe. It figured that I would be in Hell for a heat wave. Max and I trudged across the campus grounds, cracks running through the earth where it had been baked by the sun. Max adjusted his hat to keep himself shaded. Short brown hair peeked out beneath it, curling where it had gotten a little too long.

Already I had the crushing feeling that I was out of my depth. I knew what Robetresse hoped for in my coming back here. That I'd settle into my old routines again, take back up my research on how people used their objects, and finish my PhD. Take my position on the council. Practice Magic with Max. But I didn't have it in me to return to anthropology.

For a long time, I had loved my discipline, lived in this sense of awe of humanity, how we persisted through all the changing ages of the world. I admired our grit and determination, reveled in humanity's capacity for love and art, culture and language. But over time, my study of humanity just took me further from people. The more I saw, the more I started to experience a nagging sense of powerlessness in a world that felt like it was falling apart, a lingering hopelessness every time I turned on the news. I wanted to love people, but how could you love a world like this?

Max turned toward me, the corners of his mouth tugging down. "Already wanting to bolt, huh?"

I knew that he wasn't happy with me and that, while I didn't miss anthropology or Magic, he certainly did.

My mind kept returning to the girl in Maritza's cottage.

The dead look in her eyes, the bemused twitch of her lips. The whole thing sent dread squirming to the bottom of my toes. I wanted to grab my stuff, grab Bear, turn around, and drive back home.

I hugged my torso. "Let's not pretend this is your run-of-the-mill research project. Danica Stewart didn't just kill Maya Hagood. She had *thirty-six* stab wounds. Whatever this spell is, it made her brutalize her. It just makes you wonder . . . if she did that to someone she cared about, what would she do to us?"

His eyes said everything his mouth wouldn't. *It's what you always do, isn't it? Run away.*

I willed my fingers to stop shaking. I knew it would come to this, that we'd have to talk again. But as I looked around at this place, at the rusted metal Art building, and the creaking old barn they'd repainted and converted into the cafeteria, I couldn't stop all the memories from rushing back. The fights with Max, his brow furrowing in confusion after he finally said, "I love you," and I said nothing. The silent accusation that always accompanied it. *Why isn't it enough?*

The day Dr. Robetresse called me into her office to explain that my brother had taken his own life—that guilt had followed me everywhere I went. I was Aaron's big sister. I should've protected him. Everything in this place just kept reminding me of him. Showing Aaron around during his first week of college, moving him into his dorm room, us piling into my pickup to drive home for Sunday family dinner.

Then afterward—the RA telling me I needed to pack up his dorm room so another student could move into it. Sitting around the empty dinner table after he was gone.

And, of course, the night I lost control of my Magic.

It had taken only a second, one stupid moment where I couldn't keep it all in anymore. Whenever I closed my eyes, I was drenched in the acrid, horrible scent of the car on fire. The panicked look in the girl's eyes when she realized she was trapped inside. And how they all looked at me afterward, like I was some kind of animal.

Shadows flitted under Max's hat in the midday heat, darkening a tiny divot above his eyebrow. "You've got to forgive yourself. No one's mad anymore. No one even brought it up."

"Easy for you to say," I said, wrapping my arms around myself.

It didn't matter what Max said; I knew the facts. There were still people on this campus who thought I was dangerous. There were more than a few people—including some who had been sitting in that council room today—who'd called for my expulsion back then. I knew they hadn't forgotten.

Max reached a tendril of his Magic out to calm me. My mind filled with his Magic: the sound of warm rain, the rough feel of a saddle. Coarse horsehair brushed against my cheek, but it was too close. Too intimate. I shoved the Magic away.

"Look, you can stop pretending, okay? Stop pretending you want me here for any other reason than getting your Magic back. We won't last for two seconds in the cottage with that girl if we're not honest with each other. She'll eat us alive."♕

He took a step back, wounded. "If you'd consider it for a second, Cel, I think you'd see I'm not the only one who misses their Magic. Have you even seen your folks yet? There's a reason you came back here."

"That's not—"

We were interrupted by a voice behind me. "Cella! It's good to see you again."

"Dr. Simmons, hi," I said, turning around and pushing aside my bangs. He belonged to the Experimental, Esoteric,

---

♕ (Max): The truth was, yeah, I was in hell without Magic. Magic was what made me something other than some dumb cowboy from the middle of nowhere. And, yeah, maybe I did put a word into Dr. R's ear about bringing Cella back. But that wasn't the only reason. Five years was plenty long to be gone. I missed her; we all did. I wanted her to see that, no matter what she believed, this was still her home.

and Molecular Medicine (EEMM) Department. Even for a school of Magic, he was a little on the eccentric side. I wondered how he knew where I would be. I didn't remember seeing him in the room with us.

Max swallowed, the pained look on his face carefully painted over with his usual, relaxed charm. "I'm going to see if I can get someone to open the girl's old room." He hesitated. "See you in a bit?"

I nodded. "Yeah."

Dr. Simmons happily took the vacant position at my side. "I wonder if I might chat with you a little about your abilities, if you ever find yourself with a free moment. A dimidium on campus, the full pair! What a rare treat for those of us in the arcane studies."

"Oh, uh, I don't know if we'll have time for that. We'll only be here for a few days, helping with the investigation and all . . ." I fiddled with the bumblebee stud in my ear, rotating it back and forth.

"I wonder, when he feels pain, do you as well?"

I kept walking toward the campus dormitories, sidling away as the professor took a step closer. "It's a little more complicated than that. When we're close, our Magic is magnified, and so is our sensory input."

"You feel what the other feels."

"More or less."

Which was why it was hard to keep secrets from each other. Which was why I had moved to Portland, nearly fifteen hundred miles away. Which was why a whole lot of things, none of which I particularly wanted to explain to Dr. Simmons.

"And your objects are the same, of course, so that you may combine your Magic together."

"Sort of," I gritted out. Max's objects were the leather bit from the rein of his favorite horse, the first drops of a summer rain, and a porcelain dog figurine his dad had given him as a child. The same base materials as mine (leather, water, porcelain), but unique to him. Everyone did Magic differently, even us dimidiums. Max's Magic, for example, was sunny and a little rough like saddle leather; it felt warm like summer rain on the back of your neck. Whereas whenever I did Magic, I always ended up sopping wet and in the dark.

"Extraordinary," he said. "Much like the law of gravitational force. The closer you are in each other's orbit, the stronger your pull to each other. I often wonder how much progress I would make on my work if I had a powerful partner to help. You must be quite relieved when he's around!" He chuckled.

"Yeah. Well, if you'll excuse me . . ."

By now, I was used to the uncomfortable questions. As dimidiums, Max and I were two halves of one Magical soul. Dimidiums were a relatively recent concept in the Magic world, discovered only in the last century. There wasn't a whole lot of concrete information on them. There was, however, an abundance of speculation and misinformation. It didn't surprise me that Dr. Simmons implied that I needed Max more than he needed me.

Funny how whenever anyone talked to me about our abilities, they always found a reason to bring up Max. *You two were in a relationship, weren't you? Your emotional ties are quite strong; I wonder about the impact on you.* But whenever questions were posed to Max, they always centered around his strength, his accomplishments, our publications. I barely entered the conversation.

Max walked outside when we reached the front of House Torlaine, to investigate the prickly sensation I was feeling himself, and Dr. Simmons slunk back into the shadow.

Simmons nodded in the direction of Maritza's cottage. "Well, I'll leave you to it then. I'd loan you some holy water and crosses, but I'm afraid I don't have any to spare." He chuckled half-heartedly and nodded his goodbyes.

"What'd he want?" Max asked after he walked away.

"Just the usual dimidium questions. Can I experiment on you, et cetera." I shook my arms out, trying to shake loose the lingering ickiness.

Max grimaced.

I'd come here based on a desperate need for cash, and because Dr. Robetresse had asked for my help. It didn't change how I felt about Max, but if I stayed . . . we could use Object Theory to actually help people. It was what we'd dreamed of when we'd first started our research on objects. And if we could actually save someone like Dani? It would make all of this worth it. It would certainly silence Object Theory's critics, who'd been growing in recent years. My own, too.*

We walked into House Torlaine's cool, air-conditioned hallway, shutting out the bright sun outside. Now, inside with Max, everything felt too quiet, too close. I thought we could probably both hear my heart hammering away.

"Look," I said, unable to meet his gaze, "if we're going to be working together here . . ."

"So you're staying?" he asked. I didn't have to look up to hear the excitement in his voice.

"For now. But if we're going to be working together here, I think we should set some ground rules."

His posture relaxed, and he leaned back against the rust-colored wall, smiling good-naturedly. "Oh, this should be good."

"As you know, I've given up my Magic. I understand that while we're here, we may be required to . . . access said Magic. But I don't want you doing big spells and using up all my energy and leaving me drained. Granted, with an approved request, we may—"

He arched an eyebrow. "With your approval, I can access my Magic that you withheld for five years when you left without a word?"

I ignored him. "With a request that we both agree on, we

---

* I'd had no dearth of hate mail for my work on the theory, mostly from faculty and students of Britton Arcane, including a self-cloning letter that wouldn't stop reproducing in my recycling bin for a month.

may access each other's Magic, as needed. I won't be here long, so you might as well use the Magic you need. I think in this way we may be able to work together." I finished somewhat anticlimactically, blundering ahead despite the increasingly incredulous expressions he was making. Despite his attempts to hide it, he was definitely still a little pissed at me. Well, I guess that made two of us.

"What? No list of demands?"

"That's it." I cleared my throat, wondering if I should have added more, then shook my head. "Do you accept?"

He smiled, a spark of mischief in his eyes that I knew well enough to nearly make me regret the whole thing. "Ah, Cella," he breathed, his voice dropping to a growl. He took a step closer, pressing me to the wall and making my heart do an Olympic sprint. His hands splayed out above me, and he leaned in close to say into my ear, "You know that, for you, I'd do anything."👹

I fought to get my breathing under control, and that lopsided grin of his tumbled out. "Nice to see I can still get your blood pumping."

"You caught me off guard. Anyone would—" Damn our connection. Damn it to hell.

He walked away, still grinning. "Uh-huh."

👹 It was strange, being near her again. She'd been gone so long I didn't rightly know how to act. Every time I looked at her, I remembered the day she left, standing there all cold and sterile, her own perfect impression of Spock. Then she'd walked away while I stood there like a goddamn idiot. But there were the good bits, too. The stuff the liquor refused to wipe away. Fleeting bits, like the way she smelled. Musky, almost, cut with citrus, like her lemon shampoo. The look in her eyes when she found something interesting, the way they popped like stars all bursting. And how it drove her absolutely nuts that I knew her better than anyone else in the world.

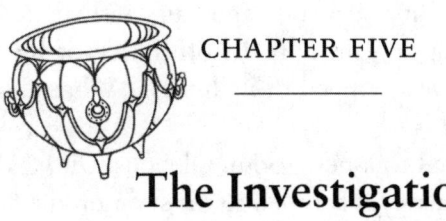

CHAPTER FIVE

The Investigation

"So, this is where . . ."

"Where it happened," she said. The girl,* short, with her hair dyed bright blue, was on work study, working as the resident assistant of House Torlaine. She'd let us inside Maya's room. "I wasn't here at the time, so I didn't hear the . . . Well, um, there weren't many people on campus at the time. It happened over Easter break."

Maya's dorm room was coated in the sharp, sterile scent of artificial lemon, probably a by-product of all the cleaning products they'd used to scrub the blood off the floor. In the center of the room was a spot as long as my arm that was lighter than the surrounding areas. If I focused on it, I could almost see the faint stain of blood, could almost smell its cloying, metallic scent. The room must have been filled with it.

On the bed, a pink-and-white quilt was layered over the plain white blanket supplied by the school, along with a matching pillowcase.

"We couldn't bring ourselves to start packing her things up just yet."

I reached for a stuffed bear leaning against the pillow. The bed was covered with stuffed animals and flowers, framed photos, handwritten notes folded into little triangles, and cards. There was clearly a lot of love here.

---

* Name has been redacted for privacy reasons.

"The girls on the hall wanted to do something. She had a lot of people here who really cared about her."

I picked up one of the pictures of Maya. The photos all showed a pretty, smiling girl, tall and tan, with light brown hair and a wide, angelic grin. On the other side of the room, the other twin bed was stripped of its linens. "What about the roommate?"

"She's been moved to a new room. Obviously, it was pretty traumatic for her." Her eyes traveled to the stain on the floor.

"Was she the one who found her?" Max asked.

"No, thank goodness. She was home for the holiday. Most students had cleared out, gone home to be with family. Dani and Maya were in here late. One of the staff heard screaming and ran in to find them. Dani had collapsed. They took her to Maritza's straight away, where she . . . Well, I don't know for sure, but I heard she got pretty violent before becoming the way she is now."

"And she hasn't moved since then?"

She shook her head. "Just been levitating for days. I heard from Dr. R they put an enchantment to keep her in the cottage, but I don't see her getting down anytime soon. To be honest, I don't know how she manages it, with the state she's in. Barely conscious and can still hold the spell to keep herself up there. I couldn't even levitate more than two inches fully conscious, if I tried." She looked down guiltily. "A lot of the girls on the hall have tried."

Over time and through questioning the girls on the hall, we were able to compose a fairly telling portrait of the two women. Maya was from a wealthy family down South, where she'd lived in a big, antebellum-style house in Charleston with her parents and two older brothers. They went boating a lot, and Maya had gone to a private girls' school. After not getting into her university of choice, she spent a couple of years at a trade school, but didn't tell anyone she knew; we found this out by looking through her records. Then she enrolled in the undergraduate program here.* She wore pearl earrings, laughed loudly, hugged freely, and apparently "was really cool about lending her curling iron."

Danica, according to the girls on the hall, was a thin girl from the Midwest with "fucked-up" eyebrows and stringy blond hair. "I think she's from Idaho," one of the girls said. "No, Kansas or something? Is that near Nevada? She said something about the Grand Canyon once." We later confirmed via school records that she was from Ohio.

It was harder than I thought it would be finding someone—anyone—who actually knew Dani. Plenty of girls on the hall beckoned us into their rooms when we knocked, pulling us close to whisper some bit of gossip or scandal or their own theories.

"I heard she went to class once covered head to toe in animal blood—"

"Her hands turned to claws. That's why there were so many marks on the body. The only reason they caught her was that, when she tried to get away, she couldn't fit her hands around the doorknob."

Or: "Dani and Strauss did it together. She promised if he helped her kill Maya, she'd finally sleep with him."

"Dr. Strauss, the physics professor?" I asked. And her advisor, according to Robetresse. "Why do you think that?"

The girl lowered her voice, leaning closer. "It's obvious, isn't it? He's a sexual deviant. Why else was he removed from the school's Advisory Council?"

---

* Acceptance to S&B wasn't as glamorous as one might think. There was no all-powerful Magic sensor in the president's office. There were no letters delivered by owl. Most students who attend are local. I wrote an essay, filled out a few questions so they could make sure I wasn't batshit or chasing the Illuminati, and a few months later, I got an admissions packet in the mail with a tidy letter of congratulations. This was coupled with directions and a list of "things to do" in the area. Mostly a joke considering the closest store is one on the corner that sells cheap tobacco and flat sodas.

Her roommate came up behind her chewing a Twizzler. "He's not a deviant, he's a god. A certified sex god."

The other rolled her eyes. "Please. You have not had sex with him. She has not had sex with him."

But none of what the students said could be confirmed, and none was firsthand, only repeated second- or thirdhand, sometimes even fourthhand accounts.

"Did you, um, did you actually know Danica, though?" I asked more than one of the girls on the hall. The answer was the same every time.

A blank look followed by, "No. She never spoke to us."

That didn't stop the people we talked to from adding their own opinions on the matter. "She was a fucking freak," one girl spat.

"Quiet and weird," another girl agreed. "Maya was too good for her."

"Maybe she was just shy," I murmured, but then shook my head quickly at their outraged stares.

The only one we found who had a kind word to say about her at all was Maya's roommate, Grace, and that had only been through a secondhand accounting of things Maya herself had said. We met Grace in her new room, sitting on the bed, her freshly washed hair wrapped in a towel.

I sat down at the desk across from her. Max settled against the opposing wall. Despite how I tried to resist it, Max and I quickly fell back into a familiar dynamic, one we'd used for past case studies while interviewing people about their objects. Max kicked off the questioning, working his charm to put subjects at ease while I observed them, their tics and nervous habits, their objects. I tried to look for the truth behind it all, what they were really saying. Or trying to hide.

"What can you tell me about Dani and Maya?" he asked, voice rumbling and deep. "How was their relationship? Was there ever any indication that Dani wanted to hurt her?"

"They dated on and off for, like, the majority of junior and senior year, but I've never seen two people more different. As for why Dani did this," Grace shook her head, voice shaking. "There was no indication. None. I thought she loved her. She had us all fooled."

Grace stared at her hands, and I realized how hard this must've been for her. Maya was her roommate, someone she'd slept only feet away from every night. Someone she saw probably every day. She wasn't even fully moved into her new room yet; there was a box in the corner of things left to unpack.

His voice softened. "You've never seen people more different—how so?"

"Dani had this stutter that came out sometimes that she was self-conscious of, so she didn't, like, put herself out there, you know? And Maya was exactly the opposite. Always hugging everyone, kind of loud. Everyone liked her."

"Lot of people knew her. She must have had some enemies," Max said. "Can you think of anyone who would want to hurt her?"

Grace shrugged. "No. Stuff like that was really important to Maya, being liked." She pulled out her phone and pulled up Maya's Instagram. "I mean look at this, not even one mean comment. Sometimes I think she spelled her page so people could only say nice things. If anything, people loved her too much."

"Could I take a look at that?" I asked.

Pictures on Maya's Instagram showed the same beautiful girl, light brown hair and startlingly blue eyes, artificially enhanced with some kind of filter. She had the same pose in most of her pictures, one that made her waist look thinner and hid the scar on her thigh.

"Over thirty-five thousand followers. Not bad for a college student."

Grace nodded. "She collaborated with brands sometimes. Posted their content or recommended stuff."

There were pictures with her various workout routines, some posts recommending vitamin supplements and tea infusers.

A quick skim of the comments showed a whole lot of heart eyes, "queen shit," or creepy comments from guys. I couldn't figure out why she did the ads. It was clear she'd come from money and wasn't hurting for it. A good portion of the photos and videos were her sailing or on boats with friends, a beer in one hand and a fish she'd caught in the other. Pictures at school were similar. She and friends in the backs of trucks, laughing and dancing, drinking whiskey or what looked suspiciously like moonshine. Photos from various parties, selfies with friends.

Something itched at me as I scrolled. I continued down, all the way down, finally finding what I was looking for.

There was one picture with Dani, only one. I recognized the pale skin, though not as pale as now. Even here, there was an uneasiness about her. The people in the picture seemed to hover just around her, not quite comfortable in her presence, though I don't know if this was because they simply didn't know her that well. Her blond hair fell in limp waves around her face, and though she was beautiful, the effect was unsettling. There was a haunted look in her blue-gray eyes, like an ocean at midnight.

Already gone, even then? Or were the effects of whatever this was just starting to take hold?

Max teetered on the desk opposite us, offering Grace a gentle smile. "They were pretty different then, huh?"

Grace looked up at him, cheeks coloring under his gaze. "Yeah." She unconsciously squared her shoulders to him, offered a small smile reserved only for someone like Max.

It wasn't the first time I'd noticed Max's effect on people. All of a sudden, I felt a little like the Dani to Max's Maya. For the most part, I was perfectly content to sit in the background, happily typing up my notes and research, looking up calculations or referencing textbooks, while he drank the attention awarded the two of us like nectar. After our first paper on Object Theory came out, something we'd worked on together, our peers at the conference circuit turned to him first with their questions. And I was happy to let him talk to them, let him explain our methods, and have them all gush at his brilliance—our brilliance. Besides, I would've butchered it anyway, bumbled through awkwardly, and said all the wrong things. I'd been grateful for him, really. If not for Max, I don't think our research would've gotten anywhere near the attention it did.

Still, sometimes I did wish I was more like him, bobbing happily through life, lifted by other people's smiles instead of their bewildered looks. I did sometimes wish that when people saw us, they would say, Look, it's Cella and Max! instead of Look, there's Max! Oh hey, Cella, didn't see you there.

I wondered if Dani had ever felt the same.

"Maya kind of did whatever Maya wanted to do, and everyone else was just along for the ride," Grace said.

I cleared my throat. "Do you think Maya loved her?" I directed the question at Grace, but my eyes had drifted to Max.

Grace stared at her fingernails, picking at flaking remnants of peachy pink. "To be honest, I think she took Dani for granted a little. Kissed her at parties and when she was drunk for attention and stuff. They were always breaking up and then getting back together again. I don't know if Maya was really as comfortable as Dani with having a girlfriend. A lot of her friends were in sororities, and I just kind of got the feeling that maybe she didn't think they'd accept her if she was actually serious about Dani. I don't know. But even when Maya came in sobbing after having messed around with some jerky guy, Dani was always there. She worshipped her. But did Maya love her back? Maya was . . . well, Maya was Maya."

Her voice had begun to shake. It must have been hard to admit these things about her friend. My heart went out to her. I wanted to comfort her, but I didn't know how. With my luck, I was more likely to say the wrong thing and make her feel worse, so I stayed quiet. Max was the one with the charm. I had observation.

"I think she loved her," she said carefully, "in the only way she knew how."

Max's gaze met mine and held it like an anchor.

A lesson better learned sooner rather than later, I thought. Sometimes the most someone could give you wasn't enough, and you had a choice. Make yourself small to accept that love, pretend it was all you needed, or realize you were worth far more and leave to find it.

Max typed a note on his phone. "And what about Dr. Strauss? Was there ever anything to suggest Dani and he had a relationship outside your everyday one between student and professor?"

She shook her head. "She never mentioned anything, but you can't really ignore his reputation, can you? I wouldn't be surprised if he tried."

I knew of his reputation from when I was a student, of the handsome twenty-nine-year-old professor with a voracious sexual appetite. Word was he'd slept with a large number of the staff and more than a few students. He cut quite the controversial figure on campus. He had a lot of supporters, was even on the council.* And there were plenty of stories of him going above and beyond for his students, reaching out to colleagues in the field for internships or job placements, hosting networking events, finding scholarships and grants for his students. But he had his critics, too. There were rumors that he engaged in sex Magic (which I had strong doubts even existed), that his preferred spot for trysts was right there in his office. I'd even heard that he could get broody and morose, that if you rejected his advances, he'd fail you. But rumors had a tendency to run wild in a place like this, and I thought it best to not put too much stock in them.

Max appeared to think a little differently. "Yeah, I know about him alright." He looked at me and pointedly raised his eyebrows as if making sure I was hearing this. *Subtle*.

"What about Maya's objects?" I asked Grace.

We learn in Object Study that you can uncover more about a person in the three things they hold most dear than in a decade's worth of knowing them. People had so many walls they put

---

* At least I thought he was. I didn't see him in the meeting.

up, but they couldn't hide their objects, or what those objects revealed about them.

"One was her phone, but besides that, I'm not sure even she knew. She took the Meditation 101 class,* but you know how tough that sort of stuff is. Especially for someone like Maya, always bouncing off the walls."

We had Maya's phone, but with her dead, it hummed dully, the last dregs of Magic fading from it even now.

"There's this, too," Grace said, pulling a pink bound notebook from a box next to the bed. "I just found it going through my stuff from the move. They must have packed it by mistake. It's Maya's."

Max and I both perked up.

It seemed to be a planner. Inside were birthdays to remember, Maya's parents' anniversary. Meetings with her advisor, and different teachers, Lisa's 21st!!!!, Homecoming. Then, two days before her death, there was a note:

Mtg with RO. LAST TIME.

"Last time" was underlined three times.

I flipped through the pages, going back several months. There were maybe four or five entries involving RO: *Coffee with RO, Drinks with RO*. And, once, *Dinner with RO*.

"Who's RO?" I asked Grace.

Grace lifted an eyebrow, confused. "No idea."

"I see," he said. "Thank you, Grace. This has been really helpful."

"I hope you . . ." Her mouth twisted, fingers knotting together. "I hope you find out who did this."

---

* One of the fundamental classes of the Three Arts. Every incoming freshman takes two blocks of it. Meant to be an exploratory class to guide you through your sense of self and help you discover your objects.

Afterward, Max and I went to the vending machine in the courtyard behind Ludlow House. He shook up a bag of gummy worms and offered it to me.

"What do you make of all this?" Max asked. "Not exactly something that falls in our usual purview, murder investigation and all."

I took a handful of worms for myself, but it wasn't the candy going sour in my mouth. I looked again at the single photo of Dani on Maya's page. Together for two years, and that was all she got.

"All these people at this school, and not a single one of them liked her, except for the girl she killed. They're all ready to burn her at the stake, and they didn't even know her."

"You can hardly blame them," he said, throwing a handful of candies into his mouth. "She killed their friend."

"Yeah, but none of them are even giving her the benefit of the doubt. They're not even stopping for a second to think maybe none of this was her fault. Especially if she was hexed."

Maya had been robbed of the rest of her life, and that was a wrong and terrible thing. But no one we spoke to spared a shred of sympathy for Danica. I just couldn't stop thinking that if Maya was alive, she'd want people to help the girl she loved. Try to figure out where it all went wrong in the first place.

"Or maybe you're ignoring the possibility that she did kill Maya in cold blood," Max said quietly.🝮

I whipped my head up. A sheen of sweat covered his throat. "You can't honestly believe that."

His eyebrow lifted. "Can't I?"

"Please tell me your explanation, then, for why she's speaking in tongues and scaring the crap out of Maritza."

🝮 This line of thinking by Cella worried me, to be honest. I didn't think it would help our credibility with the council to say this wouldn't have happened if everyone had just tried to get to know the murderer. I knew why she said it, though. Cella always had a soft spot for people on the outskirts, people who didn't quite fit. Always seemed to get her into trouble.

As I looked at him, his sea-blue eyes burrowing into mine, the realization dropped like a stone in my stomach.

"You think it's an act?"

"I think that if I killed my girlfriend on a college campus and I didn't want to go to jail, I'd think of something fast. And that something might be to pretend it wasn't me who did it at all."

I thought back to Grace's words. *She had us all fooled.*

But then there was Dani. Her blond hair, limp around her face. Her eyes, so unnaturally dark. And the feeling in that room, like sinking thirty feet underwater. "You didn't see her, Max. You didn't feel the energy in that room. I mean, they called a priest."

I shook my head. "You can't fake that. She's not acting of her own free will. Someone did this to her."

We sat on a concrete bench beneath a mesquite tree, and sunlight filtered onto my hand through the fernlike leaves. A warm wind blew from over the canyon, swirling up red dirt into a miniature dust devil.

The inescapable smell of burning rubber crept under my nose. Everywhere I looked I saw the polka-dotted bra, the pink fingernails tapping on a phone, and every time I closed my eyes, I heard her screams. I shut my eyes tight, forcing the memory down.

Max looked at me. "Then who? And what kind of spell could do something like that?"

I shrugged. "I don't know. Hexes are tricky. Difficult to pull off, difficult to keep someone hexed for that long. Whoever it is, whatever it is, is powerful."

He looked down at his phone. "I say we talk to this advisor of hers, Dr. Strauss. Six of her eight classes were with him. Maybe he knows if someone had a problem with her. Maybe someone was harassing her?"

"Good a place as any."

CHAPTER SIX

The Teacher

The Physics, Astronomy, and Astrological Divination Department was a two-room block at the back of Ridley Hall, one of the oldest buildings on campus. A small building, it was composed of fat russet bricks, arched windows, and a white domed observatory at the roof. Inside, the walls were covered with star charts, old maps, and prints of Copernicus, Galileo, and Newton.

I filled my Christmas mug with stale coffee from the break room and wrapped my fingers around it. The AC from the rest of the building shunted all the cold air down this wing—another sign of a Magic building that needed an architect. But I couldn't tell if it was the chill or anxiety that was responsible for the twisting of my stomach. The hallway was completely empty. As our footsteps echoed down it, I had the feeling of walking into a crypt.

When we reached the classroom, Dr. Antony Strauss was hunched over a lab table, back to us. Max knocked lightly on the wall.

"No office hours today," Strauss said without turning around. "Funny how the sign on the door supplies information. All you have to do is read it."

"Afraid we're not here for help with our physics homework," Max drawled.

Dr. Strauss's head flicked up, a lock of pale hair falling over one glassy, chilly eye. He slid in front of what he'd been working on. But not before I caught sight of it—a badly damaged miniature recreation of the Sir Isaac Newton statue at Cambridge, dressed in draping fabrics and holding a prism. The thing's head and legs had been lopped off.

His mouth folded into a smirk, as if more bemused than annoyed by the interruption. "And how can I help you?"

Dr. Strauss was as handsome as I remembered, tall and fit with short blond hair and a clean-shaven face. When he looked at me, I got the same giddy feeling from when I took his class years ago. Though he wasn't all the same. There was an unsettling intensity to his eyes that wasn't there before. And beneath the rolled sleeves of his button-up, his skin had an ill, feverish look to it. He yanked his sleeves down when he saw me looking.

Max stepped closer to me.

"We were hoping you could tell us about Dani," I said.

"Certainly," he said, not dropping his wolfish smile. "Anything I can do to help."

"Six of her eight classes were in here?"

I let my hair fall around me like a curtain, blocking out the feel of Strauss's eyes on me. Something about his glacier-blue eyes reminded me of a predator watching as I stumbled blindly through the woods. My fingers wrapped around my Christmas mug, drawing what comfort I could from it, from Aaron.

"Not in here. Up there," he said, pointing to the floor above us. We followed him up the creaking stairs to the observatory.

The observatory opened as wide as a whale's mouth. A twenty-foot white telescope stood in the center of the room, beneath a dome already partially open to the sky. Smaller telescopes were positioned around it and pointed skyward. Taped on the walls were sheets of paper filled with equations.

"You two must have been close, considering how much time you spent together," Max said.

"I make myself available to all my students during office hours, but I wouldn't say we were close, no."

I frowned. When I was a student, Dr. Strauss also served as Dean of Student Affairs. He was beloved by students and staff alike. I wondered if Dr. Robetresse ever regretted the position she'd put him in, if he'd ever used that power and popularity to try to weasel his way into her job. There was certainly the question of why he was no longer on the council.

"Did Dani ever do or mention anything that seemed odd to you? Any spells she asked for your help with?" Max asked, keeping his voice light, though I could tell from the tightness in his shoulders that he didn't feel entirely comfortable with the man either.

Strauss arched an eyebrow. "It's divine astrology; we don't do spells. And here I thought you were supposed to be some kind of genius." He didn't drop his smile, though it lacked any warmth.

Max halted. If there was anything he hated, it was condescension. There were so many times over the years when I'd wondered if academia was really not the place for him, and why he did it at all. If it was just for me.

Still, Max kept his expression carefully neutral, carefully friendly. "Ah."

"Though there was a time, shortly after Danica first entered my classes as a freshman, when she seemed . . . distracted. Obsessed with finding a book of some sort—one of Magic, I assumed—though it seemed, after a few conversations, she determined I didn't have it. I never heard any more of it, but several of her papers that first year had a fervent quality to them, some underlying obsession with arcana and the pursuit of knowledge. I admit much of it didn't make sense, and she had to rewrite them."

Nothing really out of the ordinary there; plenty of students came to this school looking for spellbooks. And there were plenty of them to be found, but the majority were fake, filled with junk spells. The real Magic texts, the old books that hadn't all been destroyed in the Inquisition and book burnings, were few and far between. Whenever any were found, they were kept in a locked room until they were approved for study.*

The wooden floor creaked as we walked. I tried to see it all from Dani's perspective, to imagine what it must have been like working up here. The observatory smelled like the dry, hazy air blowing across the mesas, tinged with smoke. Incense, maybe? I imagined I could spend a lot of time up here myself.

I ran my hand along the length of a telescope. "You don't do spellwork because you divine Magic streams from the paths of the stars, like in the old days of astronomy."

"Very good, Cella," Strauss said, his voice liquid and deep. "Magic of the gods is what they called it. Though now, of course, we all know it's not gods that are responsible for Magic. It's a force in its own right, like the wind or tides. Many of my students' objects lie outside of their reach. So we study. We look for the paths of the stars coming down, the threads of scattered Magic to find the best way we may channel those objects."

That seemed to be the one constant of Magic—many hours of study. Magic was complicated. There were few people who truly understood the intricacies of it, and fewer still Magic books had survived the ages to shed light on the subject. It was a lifetime of study, thousands of hours of practice, of meditation, of finding the texts. That was why many students here, despite being at a Magic university, didn't attempt much other than trivial spells. They weren't willing to spend days sweating over a spell, practicing until their lips cracked and their voice went hoarse. Until their fingers bled from clutching their objects and their minds felt like jelly from concentrating for so long. They took their discipline: mathematics, physics, language, biology, and hoped that they'd pick up a few things in Magic, too, to help them along. Spells to keep their coffee

---

* Most didn't make the cut. The ones that did were written in confusing and cyclical language to guard their secrets from prying eyes.

warm, or to find lost car keys, or to jot down notes in class. They kept their objects near, but the more difficult spells, the complexities where Magic really shone, they mostly gave up on.

The only thing the students really needed to understand about Magic was that it was always there, hovering beneath the surface. Just like the ocean: you enter at your own peril, because it wouldn't care one bit if you drowned in the process.

Strauss stepped toward me. "I had you in one of my classes, didn't I? Phys 303."

"Yes," I said, blushing. I was surprised he remembered.

He tapped his temple. "Never forget a face. Especially yours. One would be remiss to forget the dimidium pair who took the world by storm."

"For a time, at least."

He considered me thoughtfully. "Sometimes the brightest candles burn the quickest."

To my embarrassment, I found myself grinning like an idiot. The man frightened me, but there was something exciting, too, about his attention. As if by gaining it, you became somehow more significant in the world. I shook my head. It was a silly thought.

Max scuffed his boot against the ground, the cord bulging in his neck the only indication of a hitch in his pleasant demeanor. "What about her classmates? Were there any students Dani disliked or fought with? Anyone who had reason to hurt her?"

"These kids are applying to some of the most prestigious graduate programs in the country. MIT and Stanford only take a handful of PhD candidates a year. Joselyn, one of our seniors, was crushed after just narrowly missing a position at MIT. My students don't have time to waste on grudges."

"Uh huh. And these are spots they're competing for?"

"They're better suited to focus on their own applications."

They both smiled with their teeth at each other, Strauss with his icy Scandinavian looks, Max with his golden tan and dimples. The two fought to keep up the friendly façade.

"Ah, come on. They've got to be competing." Max shrugged innocently. "Only got so many spots, right?"

"In the strictest sense of the word, I suppose you could call it that," Dr. Strauss admitted. "But I would never let anyone harass any of my students. At any rate, Dani kept to herself. She was kind, and well on her way to becoming a brilliant physicist, but reclusive. She was most at ease up here, working."

"And what about you? *You* hold any grudges against her?" asked Max.

I nearly spewed coffee down my shirt. His meaning certainly wasn't lost on Dr. Strauss. I remembered what the girls on the hall and Grace had said. *You can't really ignore his reputation, can you?* Strauss's smile grew even wider, and I had the distinct impression of a wolf baring its teeth.

I quickly stepped between them. "You know, I think we've bothered you quite enough for today, sir." I prodded Max out the door with my elbow. "We can't thank you enough for your help."

"Cella," Dr. Strauss said, the light touch of his fingers stopping me before I made it into the hallway. My stomach swooped dangerously. "It wasn't so long ago that you yourself were enveloped in rumors. I'd hate to think you'd let something so silly influence your opinion of me."

I bit my lip. "Um. Yeah, of course," I said. I couldn't deny he had a point—how badly had I once wished someone would give me the benefit of the doubt? I nodded before disappearing into the hallway.

When I shut the door behind me, Max was there, leaning lazily against the wall. I shoved back my bangs. "You shouldn't have done that."

Max shrugged. "What? Ask him some questions? Seems like that's the whole reason we're here."

"We're not Arbiters. We're just trying to gather information, not accuse him of anything."

"You heard what he said. Dani spent hours up here. Six of her eight classes were in that building, she was with him all the time. If anyone had noticed something was wrong with Dani, it would've been him. It's obvious he knows something he's not telling us."

I scoffed. "Like what, her favorite ice cream flavor?"

Max sucked his teeth, waves of annoyance rolling off him that I knew he was trying to hold back. That was the tricky part of being a dimidium. You never could quite hide how you were feeling. "You always do this. He doesn't need you to protect him, Cella."

My eyes narrowed. "I don't think I am the one doing anything."

"You let people manipulate you. If he did nothing wrong, I see no reason for him to be in the least bit fazed."

"I don't let people manipulate me—"

He started walking away, long strides lengthening until he was out the door.

"Oh no, you do not!" I said, having to run just to catch up with him. "You don't get to just accuse me of things and then walk away."

A vein bulged in his neck. He finally stopped and lifted his shirt to mop his forehead, eyes dropping to my lips before cutting away. "He's hiding something, Cella. They all are. Tell me—why didn't the council call the Arbiters? Why would they have two inexperienced alumni 'investigate' and have us report all our findings to them, when several of them want to squash the whole thing?"

"Because we're experts in objects, and we're already on the council. It makes sense that they don't want Britton hearing about this and using it against us. Robetresse doesn't need any more criticism of the Three Arts. We have enough to deal with already."

"Maybe . . . but I don't think I've met a single person here who isn't holding onto some kind of secret. And if you care at all about these students, or about Danica Stewart, then you'll help me find out why that is."

I stopped, letting his words sink in. There were no cattle anymore on the ranch, hadn't been for years, but every now and then when the wind blew, I could've sworn I heard their low braying on the wind. I thought back to what the girls had said on the hall. *He's a sexual deviant. Why else was he removed from the school's Advisory Council?*

The empty seat at the council meeting must have been Strauss's. "If he was on the council, and they removed him just after the murder . . ." My head spun. "They could be covering for him."

Since we'd left Grace's room, I had a sense there was more to all of this, but I couldn't get my head clear enough to see it. Like the way forward was muffled somehow, covered by thousands of feet of water, and I was just grasping at bits of sand and sediment that slipped deftly through my fingers.

Max tucked his hands in his pockets, looking at the hills in the distance. "Could be." 🝳

"Look, I'm sorry," Max said, eyes softening to a clear, liquid blue. He grabbed my hand. "Really. The last thing I want to do is fight with you, but the council's been acting fishy ever since they invited us on. Something's not adding up."

For a moment, he rubbed his thumb in the center of my palm, just like he used to. His scent drifted under my nose: worn leather and baked earth and tobacco leaves. A jolt went through me, and I blushed furiously.

He seemed to realize his mistake and let go quickly. It all happened so fast I couldn't tell if the butterflies that went

---

🝳 I knew Cella and I had our problems. Knew if she could, she'd run as far away from me as she could get. But I had my own motives around this thing. I wanted my Magic back—but I also wanted to prove to her that I could do this, that we could work together again. Because more than Magic, I wanted to be her dimidium again. And, my God, I wanted her to stop looking at me like I was gonna rip her heart out and swallow it whole.

through me were my own, his, or simply our Magic burgeoning at the connection. His eyes shot straight to the ground.

There was so much tension in the lines of his face. Crow's feet around his eyes that hadn't been there the last time I'd seen him, stubble lining his jaw, a deep crease running across his forehead. This was all clearly bothering him.

I rocked on my feet. "Well, we have one of her objects," I said, thinking of the telescope. "I could see her spells—we could, I mean. If you want."

"You're right, you know," he said, "I should trust your instincts, too. The only way we're going to get through this is if we work together."

He looked hesitantly up at me, and I smiled. There was a lot of pain between us. A rift had split down the middle of us until it was as wide as a canyon. That wasn't going to sew itself back together anytime soon. But maybe I could throw him a rope. Just this once.

"Let's do it," I said.

FROM THE JOURNAL OF DANICA STEWART

FEBRUARY 16TH [A MONTH AND A HALF BEFORE THE MURDER]

Autumnúsque gravis, Libitinae quaestus acerbae.*

—Horace

---

* Translation: "Grave autumn, the harvest of cruel Libitina." What the full weight of this is, I don't know. In Ancient Rome, Libitina was the goddess of funerals.

CHAPTER SEVEN

We sat down in my room, and Bear promptly climbed into Max's lap, licking his face as readily as if he was his long-lost father.

"I don't know, Cel, he might have to come home with me. Would you like that, boy?" Bear shook with excitement, and I side-eyed my supposedly loyal companion.

I opened a locked folder on my laptop. It was filled with our old publications that had been published in *New Magic Quarterly* and *The Annual Arcanum*. The most recent item was an email from one of our editors asking for clarification on a few points in my most recent piece, "Object Study: Advantages and Disadvantages of Base Materials in the Conveyance of Magic." It was part of a series we'd been working on, a practical guide on the Magical properties of objects and the relationship with their casters.

When we'd written it, I'd been fascinated by Object Theory. I liked learning about the girl who couldn't cast through anything except the quilt her grandmother had made for her when she was a baby. The one that was threadbare now, but still smelled like home. Or the boy who collected rocks with his dad as a kid, and now had a geode collection to rival most museums, who cast some of the most wondrous Magic through them, all crystalline and quartz. Or the girl who could only access Magic when she was on the phone with her mom, while her mother whispered affirmations in her ear. "You can do this, honey. You've got it. Keep going." I loved hearing about the stories around people's objects, because an object only could become an object when it impacted its owner in a strong way.

Weirdly enough, it was studying things that brought me closest to people.

Max scratched behind Bear's ears and gestured to the telescope. "I didn't know you could see what spells someone did last."

"It was something I worked on before I left."

In my second year of postgrad, after I'd started drifting away, flocking toward ginger-haired Jamie and the others, a new group of friends that filled the hole Max left, who'd cared as much about Magic and the progression of the science as I had. I'd worked on it without Max. "Oh," he said, too quickly. "Right."

The silence afterward was filled with too many things that threatened our fragile new truce.

"Not spells, exactly," I said, stumbling to get my words out. "I developed an analytical model to assess an object and determine the emotional state of the Magician who last cast through it."

"Huh. Well, damn, that's pretty cool."

I smiled, an unexpected surge of pride going through me. While the process worked best with the actual Magician present, you could tell quite a lot just from examining your own response to an object. Where are your thoughts drawn when you look at it? Does it inspire different ideas when you touch the object versus only seeing it? What about smell?

And what about the object itself? Is it coarse or smooth? Does it emit a smell? A sound? Every Magical object I'd ever come into contact with had produced what I called "notes." They weren't audible, exactly, and maybe they were just in my head, but this was what I looked for above all.* It was a

---

* I discuss this more in Issue 298 of *New Magic Quarterly,* "The Heartbeat of Magic: An Object's Notes," a paper oft-cited by my critics. There are many in the field who believe I made up notes entirely because not everyone can hear them. Chief among them was Dr. Blythe Cromme, whose scathing review seemed almost personal, but I understand the concerns. It took me many, many hours of practice to even know what to listen for.

little like tasting wine. Harsh, sharp, or tangy notes implied a caster full of unease, anxiety, dread. But something softer, more buoyant or joyous, implied the Magician had been experiencing calm. Contentment. Joy.

My eyes traveled to the brass telescope between us. What I was most curious about was how Dani had been feeling before she turned into this . . . thing. If she'd been frightened, if she knew what was happening to her. I didn't know what kind of headspace she'd been in to do what she did to Maya, but every nerve in my body rebelled against reaching out to this object and experiencing it myself. Object Theory was an inexact science. I was terrified Dani's object might pull me under the same malevolent spell that had taken over its owner. If the next time I looked in the mirror, I would see the same blood-red eyes, the wan cheeks.

If I would have to be strapped to the bed, too.

Touching Magic like this, you become aware of the threads in the room. The thrum of Magic beneath my feet, the warmth of Max's body behind me. All at once, I was aware of his eyes on the back of my neck. Without meaning to, I pulled a cord of his Magic to me, smelled the saddle leather of his horses, felt the wind on my neck, the sun on my face, warm rain on my skin. Just a glimpse, just for a second. I dropped the thread.

"Sorry," I said, swallowing hard.

"It's alright," he said, warm eyes meeting mine. "We're dimidiums. It's bound to happen."

I buried my head back in my notes. Usually, I'd conduct a full interview with the Magician to figure out how the object fit into the broader scope of their life before even looking at the object. Though with Dani's state, an interview was clearly out of the question. As I jotted down thoughts, my eyes kept flitting back to the telescope. The presence the cold metal took up in the room was visceral, notes swirling around it like a steady, beating pulse.

The thing was old, but still lovingly maintained. From its age and appearance, I'd guessed Dani had gotten the telescope here at school. Which meant Seinford and Brown meant something to her. Maybe this was the first place she'd found belonging or had fallen in love. Maybe she'd found a passion in her studies, just as I had.

The thrum of the telescope got sharper the more I tried to ignore it, swelling until it drowned everything else out.

Max's lips moved, a crease forming on his forehead. "Cel, something wrong?" Bear whimpered and nudged my knee.

I could barely hear them.

I shook my head, shifting my focus to the telescope. That must've been what it was waiting for, because all at once the notes swelled until they sounded like they were coming from every direction. They turned to whispers inside my head, though I couldn't separate them to determine what they were saying. I felt myself falling through time and space. The air around me went still and lifeless.

When I opened my eyes, I was walking through a forest at night. Only the dimmest glow of stars guided me, the trees' canopies swallowing all light. Massive pine trees blocked my way, branches scratched at my face, but there was something else, too. The prickling sensation that while I traipsed through the chill undergrowth, scarcely able to see my hand in front of me, someone else was here, watching me. The breath tightened in my chest until I was gasping for air. I slammed my head back, loosening the telescope's grip and breaking whatever spell it had pulled me under.

Strong hands caught me before I hit the bed frame. Max's nose was inches from mine, his breath hot on my cheek. "Can you hear me?"

A thousand memories rushed through me. That same hot breath on my skin in his dorm room, dancing on the roof of the Math building after our first journal article was published, our drunken laughter after getting kicked out of a conference because he'd actually tried to *duel* someone who'd offended me. Nights spent at that bar in Albuquerque and ending up tangled in the sheets with him afterward.

Then I blinked, and he cleared his throat.

"What happened?" he asked, as we untangled ourselves from each other.

I sat back, breathing hard, and Bear set to work licking me back to health. "I'm okay. I must've—I must have done something wrong. I've just never experienced anything that visceral with objects." There was no denying I was a little rusty.

Max arched an eyebrow, unconvinced. "You sure you're alright?"

"Yeah." I swallowed and flipped through the notebook Dr. Robetresse had given us. Dani's notebook. Filled with equations and neat, tiny handwriting, each entry dated. Nothing like the furiously scribbled lines and mad circles in my own note taking, nor the large pink bubble letters of the writing in Maya's planner. Not surprisingly, the last entry was an equation to increase the clarity and distance her telescope could view. Nothing out of the ordinary. Something I might expect from someone whose object was a telescope.

"What'd you find out?" Max asked, keeping a careful eye on me. "Her mind must've been some kinda screwy to pull you in like that."

I thought back to the strangeness I'd experienced, but the cold feeling that had gripped me was already slipping from my grasp, like waking from a dream, where, in the cold light of day, it doesn't feel quite so scary after all.

And what had I seen, really? Just a forest. Had it really been so different than other objects I'd reached out to? After all, I'd gotten her emotional state before the incident. She hadn't been frightened or hiding. All I felt was a singular determined focus, though the intensity of it felt a little frightening on its own. She'd wanted something the trees had obscured from her—very badly, I think. To see the stars or something in the night sky? So we at least knew that she was driven. She'd had a goal, though if that goal had been tied to what had happened to Maya or was unrelated was still unclear.

From her equations and notes in the notebook—everything

listed in perfect detail, written in tiny, scrupulous notes—I had the impression that Dani knew what she was doing.

"We'll have to go through these entries more in depth later," I said, and Max agreed. "But from what I can tell, she's got a disciplined, scientific approach. Her Magic is rational, precise. Almost surgical. There's nothing to indicate she was running from something, or out of her mind with fear."

"Nothing to indicate she knew what was coming," Max said, and I nodded.

"So we're back to square one." Max stretched, back cracking so loud I nearly jumped. "I'm starving. I say we hold off for the rest of the night, and get started back up in the morning. I'm gonna get dinner." He hesitated. "As long as you're sure you're okay? You're not gonna fall into some other object while I'm not looking?" Beneath the brim of his hat, his eyes were shadowed. He was still a little worried, but his mouth crooked into a grin.

"I'm fine. Promise."

Max stood, and Bear stared at him like he'd just got dumped in the rain. "Aw, don't worry. I'll be back soon, buddy."

Max was tired, but I only felt energized after the work, and if I was being honest, a little on edge. I hadn't been around Magic in ages, and I could feel every thump of it now, every whip through the air, racing through every crevice in the ground. I couldn't stop now—what if another discovery was just looming around the corner? I jumped up, my hip accidentally smacking into the bedside table. "Ow. I'll go with you."

"Oh . . ." he said, slowly, putting a hand on the back of his neck. "I meant with Julia. My girlfriend."

The world seemed to move too fast and in slow motion all at once.

Ah. The girlfriend. Her Instagram showed her as a pretty blonde with freckles who wore sundresses and laughed in every picture. She was exactly the kind of person I'd imagine him with. I bet his mom loved her.

The uncomfortable squirm of his shoulders as I invited

myself to my ex and his new girlfriend's dinner popped any bubble of excitement I'd been floating in.

"Oh. Right, of course. Ignore me, I'm an idiot."

A crease appeared between his brows. His voice softened. "Cella Gibbons, you are many things, but an idiot is not one of them."

I couldn't take the pity in his voice, so I started vomiting words.

"Okay, well, good idea. Dinner, eating, good, all of it. Well, have fun eating. Have a good time, I mean. Have a good dinner. I'll, uh, I'll see you in the morning."

He bit his lip. "I'll text you when I get back on campus."

"Sure, yeah. Super."

My chest sagged as soon as he was out of the room. Bear turned to glower at me, as if I was responsible for his playmate leaving. I heard Max's boots thud against the floor and the main door creak open down the hall. *Super?* I whispered to myself.

Whether I wanted to admit it or not, I would always feel the lack of his presence, my Magic mourning for its other half, one half of a rope stretching toward its missing piece. My mind flashed to that night we spent lying on a blanket in the bed of his truck, looking up at the stars, thinking we'd be together forever, that the universe had all but decreed we were meant to be.

But that was stupid. And Magic was stupid, and it was all stupid.

The truth was we weren't soulmates.

We weren't lovers. We were just two people whose Magic worked better together, and I'd been fighting a long time to make it so neither I nor my Magic gave a shit when he left the room.

I turned back toward my room and shut the door to the darkness.

CHAPTER EIGHT

I woke the next morning surrounded by last night's dinner: a bag of chips I'd gotten from the vending machine and half a bottle of green tea. Bear wasn't at my feet. Usually, he slept right on top of them. But when I squinted around the room, half-blind without my contacts in, I could just make out a hazy blob standing with its front paws on the windowsill.

I was freezing. The desert got cold at night, so before bed I'd wrapped myself in blankets. But sometime in the night I must have kicked them off. The white quilt dangled loosely from my ankles.

I'd had strange dreams.

Dreams of dark forests and long corridors, a single light flickering down a hallway. Of Dani's eyes finding mine. Of her neck straining as her back arched into a horrible position. So many things here bothered me. The closeness to Max, the horrible things people said about Dani. The horrible things Dani had done.

That a spell could take someone over so fully that they'd kill the person they loved—and not just kill, stab thirty-six times—made me shudder. But even more was the lingering question of who would cast such a thing.

The meetings with "RO" loomed in the back of my mind. And I couldn't stop picturing Strauss yanking his sleeves down when he saw us, and the glimpse I got of the skin underneath right before he did. It was mottled and scarred. Just like Dani's.

Then there was Dani herself. Unlike Maya, she clearly didn't have many friends here. Maybe she had more enemies than we knew.

I ruffled through the pages of her notebook, still open on the covers beside my phone. *What are you hiding?*

The bells outside chimed nine a.m. If I wanted breakfast, I'd have to hurry. I took a deep breath and stretched my arms overhead, brushing the top of the headboard.

I winced, drawing my finger back. A drop of blood welled on my fingertip, courtesy of a fat splinter. My eyes drew up to the dark walnut headboard, and I lurched back, knocking over my lamp.

There, just above my pillow, someone had carved words into the wood. Words that spelled:

HELL IS HERE

My eyes flew to the door and window, but both were locked. I scrambled for my phone and whipped back the covers to look under the bed. I peered into the bathroom, but there was nothing.

No one in my room but me and Bear.

Was this some kind of sick joke? A "welcome home" present from one of the people who'd sent me death threats after my all-too-public meltdown in my second year of postgrad? Max said that no one cared anymore about me losing control of my Magic, but I wasn't so sure.* Or maybe it was Strauss? Or another council member who opposed my involvement so much they'd decided to scare me off themselves?

Cautiously, I reached a hand back up to the wood. But I would've noticed if someone had been looming over my bed, carving menacing words right above me, and Bear would've been barking his head off.

This couldn't be fresh.

Whoever was responsible must have done it some time ago. Probably the last occupant of my room, one last "fuck

---

* People had slipped letters under this very door after it happened, telling me to get out of their school. And someone had called the Arbiter on me. Maybe it was the same person who did this.

you" to the school before graduation. I must have just missed it yesterday.

The staff could've at least given me a warning, though. Pillows had even been placed strategically to hide it.

I resolved to ask the RA of the hall who'd been the last occupant of my room as soon as I saw her. Most likely she already knew about the vandalism, and it was the reason my room was empty in the first place. Still, I'd feel better if I at least had a name.

I took the world's quickest shower, fed Bear, and made my way down to the breakfast hall.

Wordlessly, I sat down next to Max, who was staring at a fixed point on the table and furiously shoveling Froot Loops into his mouth. Neither of us were morning people, but I did wonder what offense his breakfast had committed. His hat was on the table next to him, and he had a mixture of hat hair and bed head, chestnut curls sticking to his forehead.

"You know they have other cereal," I murmured.

He grunted in response. "Rough night." He grimaced over at his phone; it kept pinging with texts I could only imagine were from his girlfriend.

"Ah." I shifted. We weren't really good at this, the talking about our feelings bit. Suddenly, I preferred the creepy carving in my room.

"I'm going to need one of those request forms," he said abruptly.

I blinked. "What?"

"For the Magic."

"Oh . . ." I shook my head. "Oh, right. I was kidding. You don't need a form."

He looked down. "It's for my dad."

"Oh." Max's dad was this barrel-chested rancher, a real bear of a man, strong and buoyant and joyful, but an accident years ago had damaged his back and left him in intense pain. He was on medication and in bed most of the time, and I know it had been rough on all of them. Suddenly, I felt like the world's biggest jerk for posing stipulations on our Magic use. It was as much his as it was mine.

"Just a few spells around the house will help my mom out a lot." His voice quickened. "I can do it myself, you don't even have to come in—" 👺

"Of course I'll help," I blurted. I imagined his mom in that big old farmhouse, trying to take care of everything by herself. "Whatever you need. Seriously."

He nodded, and looked out the window, deep in thought.

I chewed around the edges of a piece of toast, my mind wandering, taking in the buzzing conversation of students flitting in and out of lines. Thankfully, Max had chosen a table on the other side of the room than the one Aaron used to frequent. I tried to not look to that corner, but my eyes kept getting drawn to it. Light filtered through the leaves of the desert willow outside. The leaves undulated like water.

When I was seven, my mother took me to Hillcrest Beach. It was a small little cove with wicked rip currents, sharp rocks, and no lifeguard. While I played, I noticed a figure out in the distance, bobbing in the waves. The more I watched, the more I realized the figure's body wasn't plunging above and under the surface voluntarily. He threw his arms up, only managing to lift them for a moment before the current sucked him back under.

I looked around for my mother or another grown-up to help the swimmer, but no one seemed to notice. I pointed at the man. "Look!" I shouted. Two adults ran out to him, diving

---

👺 I projected all this confidence, but the truth was, I didn't know what the hell I was doing most of the time. I wasn't smart like Cel, and Magic was the only way I knew to help my family. Sometimes, I was envious of her. Even while falling apart, Cella knew that, to save herself, she had to get out of this town. I wish I had the strength to do the same, instead of fighting like hell for things to just Magically fix themselves.

under again and again, but they never came back up with the man.

In later years, I would return to that day and wonder if I'd noticed him sooner, or if I'd tried to swim out myself, we might have saved him. They found his body eventually, I heard, though Mom turned off the TV quickly whenever news of it flashed on. Didn't want to scare me more, I guess. Or maybe she felt guilty that she'd missed it, too.

I still have dreams about that man, only our positions are reversed. I'm the one flailing in the water, lungs filling up with water. A little girl watches me, her voice not loud enough for anyone to hear or care. "Look, look, she's out there," she cries, eyes filling with tears, but no one even looks up. Slowly, my lungs fill with water, and at long last, I slip silently beneath the waves.

I grit my teeth. Some part of me wondered if Dani ever felt like this, too. Everyone just leaving her to slip beneath the surface, as if no one cared enough to even look up.

I wondered if Aaron felt like this.

Max had moved onto angrily slurping up his milk while I slathered more butter on my toast.

Maya's Instagram was still open on my phone, and at random, I started scrolling through it. I looked through her "likes" to see if there were some accounts that frequented her posts more than others, but there were too many to keep track of. That was when I started noticing the pictures.

In the background of many of them was the same person. A woman, perhaps a few years older than Maya. Pretty, with brown hair, shiny white teeth, and tanned skin. She looked a little like Maya herself.

Maybe a sister or cousin?

I kept scrolling down, and again and again, there was the woman. Sometimes, she was laughing along to whatever joke was shared, and sometimes, she was just standing there, off in the shadows. She wasn't tagged in any pictures; I don't think Maya would've even known she was there at all.

"Max . . . do you know who this is?"

He craned his neck to look at the phone. "That's Dr. Oswold, associate professor. Just joined staff at the beginning of the year."

I looked up her bio on the Seinford and Brown website. Dr. Rose Oswold, Associate Professor of History.

"What's wrong?" he asked.

Rose Oswold . . . Could she be our RO?

CHAPTER NINE

The "Friend"

We found Grace outside her accounting class.

"We were wondering if you ever saw this woman around Maya?" I asked, showing her the picture of Rose.

"Dr. Oswold? Oh yeah, Maya and her used to hang out. They were pretty good friends for a bit."

"For a bit?"

"I hadn't seen her around much lately."

"She came to her room?" I asked.

"Bit unusual for a teacher, huh?" Max said.

"I don't know," Grace said. "She's pretty young. Only a year or two older than us, I think. She's a lot like Maya. They got on well."

After Grace left us to go to her next class, Max turned to me, voice low. "What are you thinking?"

"I'd like to talk to her. She's all over Maya's planner. Drinks, coffee. Young or not, I still think it's a little weird that she was spending so much time with her."

Max rubbed callused hands against his jeans. Ranch work had done a number on them. During the investigation, he had to run back home to direct the hands working on his horses. It was his dream to own his own ranch one day, but until then (and since getting fired from his last ranch job for fighting), he made his living training horses. "Maybe she and Maya were sleeping together. She finds out about Dani, gets pissed, casts a hex on Dani to get her out of the picture. She gets revenge and skirts the blame. Two birds with one stone."

I considered it. "The body does resemble something that would occur from a crime of passion. Maybe Maya felt guilty, tried to call it off 'the last time.' Maybe Oswold didn't like that one bit."

Dr. Oswold was in her office. My first impression of her was that she was pretty, with dark, loose curls tied up in a bun, and soft brown eyes. My second impression was that this wasn't the girl in the pictures. That girl could've been Maya's twin, with the same tanned skin and blue eyes. And yet, there was a definite resemblance here. Same bone structure, same posture. Still, the contrast was jarring.

"Dr. Oswold?" Max asked, ambling inside.

"Yes?"

"Dr. *Rose* Oswold?" I asked.

"That's me," she said brightly. "How can I help you two?"

Something about the new look, the perfectly tailored, mature professor in tweed trousers and brown loafers, made her look years older than Maya, and years older than the Rose Oswold in the pictures, even though they were only taken a few months ago.

Max didn't seem to notice anything amiss, though. "We're here to ask you just a few questions about Maya Hagood, if that's alright."

"Certainly. Though I didn't have her in any of my classes, so I'm not sure how helpful I may be."

"It's just standard procedure, ma'am; we're asking most of the faculty. Just want to cover all our bases."

"Of course," she said, and it was handy that I could listen to people's objects because though Rose looked completely at ease, if a little annoyed at the interruption, I could hear her objects loud as day. And they were not nearly as calm and collected as the woman sitting in front of us.

"You were friends, weren't you?" Max asked.

"I wouldn't really say that."

"You're in quite a few pictures with her. You met on several occasions outside of school. Do you make it a habit of spending that much time with all of your students?"

One of her objects was in her pocket; the other I could tell was in a drawer, but I couldn't tell what they were, which was unusual. Her third object, the Etch-a-Sketch on the shelf behind her, was doodling away, but seemed at war with itself; every time it started drawing something, it deleted it halfway through, shaking itself up in frustration.

Her objects betrayed a frazzled mind, the likes of which I'd never witnessed before. It seemed like they couldn't quite decide what they wanted to be, frantically flitting from one thought to the next like bugs about to be squashed. All of this was at total odds with the calm, collected professor in front of me who seemed perfectly at ease with herself.

My second impression of Dr. Oswold was that she was a skilled observer. From the moment we walked into the classroom, I noticed her watching each and every thing we did. How Max stepped aside so I could take the chair closest to the door, every slight movement and decision on which we didn't converse with each other because we knew each other so well. It was subtle, the way she mirrored our movements to put us at ease. Max leaned forward on one elbow, and she matched him. When I tucked a strand of hair behind my ear, she did the same thing.

"Maya and I were from the same hometown, so we knew some of the same people. We liked the same kind of music, both cheered through high school. I was terribly sad to hear of her passing."

"Did you two have a falling out?" asked Max.

"No, I wouldn't say that," she said, her shiny teeth gleaming at us. "We never got close enough for that. We were more acquaintances than anything."

"Kept it strictly professional, then," Max said.

"Exactly."

"Anything odd you noticed last time you were together?"

She shrugged innocently. "Not that I can think of."

"And when was that, about?"

"Oh, I don't recall the exact date. It had to be some months ago. I believe we went out for celebratory drinks. A mutual friend was getting engaged."

"Another student?"

"Yes, in the graduate program."

Max nodded. "I see. Well, we won't waste any more of your time, ma'am."

I frowned.

Rose smiled warmly. "I'm sorry I couldn't be of more help. You two have a lovely day."

"That was weird," I said, once we were safely out of earshot. "Thought we would've asked her more questions, but I guess—"

"Well, we can cross her off the list," said Max.

"What?" I balked. "What are you talking about? There's something very off about that woman. Look at these pictures; she looks like a completely different person. And she lied about when she last saw Maya."

"Frankly, Cel, I don't see it. I thought she was perfectly nice."

I squinted at Max. I didn't think the woman had put a spell on him, and at any rate, her objects seemed to be in too much disarray to be able to do much of anything at the moment. Sometimes, a shiny smile was just as powerful as any spell. Max didn't think she was capable of a heinous crime.

Maybe he was right.

But I looked back at the pictures from only months prior and thought of how quickly Dr. Oswold had been able to make us trust her. About how quickly she'd shed her skin.

A little like a chameleon, I thought, able to adapt and change form to whatever her environment required.

Whatever it was, I knew I had to do more digging.

FROM THE JOURNAL OF DANICA STEWART
February 20ᵀᴴ [a little over a month before the murder]

what is being always, and has no becoming,
what is becoming always, and never being?*

your love

---

* From Plato's *Timaeus*, though I admit I'm a bit lost. It feels a little like another of Dani's entries, from months prior: "Sometimes I feel like I'm dangling at the edge of the universe. One strong gust, and I'll go flying right off."

CHAPTER TEN

Max and I decided to spend the day gathering everything we could find on hexes. It had been three days since we started investigating, and I was starting to get a little worried about our progress. We looked at hexes throughout history, their limitations, the length of time they lasted, and how much energy it would require to cast one like Dani's. But like any research on Magic, our progress was slow-going and painful, the texts clunky and unyielding. The most useful was a page from an old reference textbook.

> *Hex: any spell cast on a person without their consent. Can be fatal, though does not persist after death. See also: Curse.*

Potential Symptoms
- Sprouting of additional limbs, eyes, or heads
- Speaking to persons unseen or known to be dead
- Constricted pupils that may seem much smaller than normal
- Nausea or vomiting
- Fever
- Marks on skin and scarring (may or may not be flesh-colored)
- Tiredness and weakness
- Bleeding
- Speaking in languages unknown to the person
- Levitation (less common)

- Seizures (less common)
- Death

But it didn't tell us what to do in order to break a hex or give any useful way of telling who the caster might have been, so we were more or less back where we started.

"This is hopeless," I said, rubbing my eyes.

"Ah, we can do this, Cel. We can. We've just gotta put our heads together."

I raised a brow at the earnest determination in his eyes. When there was something he cared about, Max was like a dog with a bone. Though his motives weren't such a mystery, I knew he wanted to keep me happy, because if I stayed, so did his Magic, but I couldn't help but smile at his unwavering conviction that we could do this, that we could fix this whole mess. I doubted he'd ever had a problem he couldn't flirt or charm his way out of. I just didn't know how to tell him this wasn't one of them.

I still remembered the first time I saw Max after I'd learned he was my dimidium. I'd happened on the concept by luck, in the second half of my sophomore year of undergrad. In one of our classes, we had a reading that included a mention of dimidiums as a reason for "inefficiency of spells." Dimidium, roughly translated as "half"—one half of your Magical soul. Legend said it meant you had a broken soul. Supposedly there was one person, and only one, who was the missing piece to fix it again. People in the Golden Age of Magic* spent their whole lives searching for their dimidiums.† The search for a dimidium used

---

* There is some debate about this among scholars. Most agree it fell at some time in the fourteenth century.

† The common lore was that in order to be a dimidium, you had to have the same number of freckles and birth marks, birth date, birth hour, and the same base material for objects. For example, if your object was a glass perfume bottle, your dimidium's object could be a glass vase or the window of their bedroom. It all checked out for us, at least—32 freckles each; born June 22 at 10:06 a.m.; porcelain, water, and leather as the base materials.

to be more of a thing back then, but when Magic got shoved to the occult section and relegated to the musings of the mentally unstable or those on their way to it, people in the community decided a search for your Magical soulmate was a little too on the nose, and it entered into a rather extensive period of being out of style.

I didn't know if that was what was wrong with my Magic or not until my advisor called me in to talk to him. Apparently, the school kept a record of every student's objects, as well as entries for dimidiums.

And there he was listed, plain as day: Maximilian Middlemore.

"*Max?*" I yelped. "You're telling me my dimidium is Max?"

I'd never spoken to him, but I knew him by reputation. From the guys, how fast he could rope cattle; from the girls, how he was smoother than a shot of whiskey. Half the girls in my year were obsessed with him.

I'd fretted over it all week. I had no idea how to broach the subject, didn't know if he would laugh in my face or simply ignore me. I found him in the courtyard, wearing a tan cowboy hat, tattoos peeking out of his shirtsleeves. He was perched on a retaining wall beside an acacia tree, biting into an apple.

I walked over to him, every ounce of my body bristling with excitement. As I got closer, I decided: the hell with it, I didn't need a script to talk to him. We were two halves of the same soul. We were mystically connected. He'd know me as soon as he saw me, I was sure of it.

"I suppose you've been waiting for me," I said, hands on my hips, striking a Wonder Woman pose in front of him. "Well . . . here I am."

He cocked his head. "Come again?"

"Your dimidium, of course." I mean, obviously he'd done the reading. I'd checked his schedule; we were in the same class. Any dimidium of mine would naturally have completed the assignment.

He squinted. "This some kind of sex thing?"

"What?" Surely he'd done the reading? "A sex thing?"

"Yeah, I recognize you," he drawled. "You're in that sex group, right? Fighting for free sexual expression, and everything? More power to you, though I don't think I'm exactly up for it . . . ? You might try my friend Cody. He's a bit more adventurous in that regard."

Sex group? All the air fizzled out of me. "I'm not in any sex—you must have me mistaken with someone else."

"No, it was definitely you. You know! From the party in the courtyard."

I wracked my brain to figure out what the hell he was talking about. "Are you talking about the Women's Rights Collective? It's a reproductive rights group, not a sex group. And it was a *rally*."

"The hair!" He snapped his fingers. "I knew I recognized the hair."

"Not a sex group—" I paused, looking at the expectant look in his eyes, the raised eyebrows, the resolute confidence. "Oh my God, you think I came over here to proposition you, don't you?"

"And I have to tell you, I am so flattered."

I threw up my hands, outraged and thoroughly embarrassed. This—this person couldn't possibly be half of my soul. "There has to have been some kind of mistake," I muttered. "There's no way I could be tied to some narcissistic, self-obsessed, blockheaded cowherder who didn't even do the reading." I stormed off across the courtyard before he could say anything else.

Unfortunately for me, there was no mistake. I checked the database three times. Then I double-checked with both of our advisors. So two days later, there I was, dragging my feet across the courtyard back to him, cursing the universe for not just tying me to some dead scholar. Or, like, a dog.

His eyebrows raised when he saw me. "Sex girl! She's back! Lovely to see you again."

He stood up, and I lost all my resolve. I had to look nearly straight up to speak with him, and for some reason my eyes were drawn straight to the muscles in his shoulders, to his forearms. He was standing closer than was perhaps appropriate; I could feel the heat radiating off his body. It made my stomach do strange little backflips.

"Still not a sex group." I cleared my throat. "Yeah, so, slight misunderstanding the other day. I'm not here to *proposition you*. We're—well, don't you know what—"

He took a bite of his apple and watched me with a bemused smile. "Use your words."

I blushed furiously, trying to explain.

His lips spread into a slow, devilish grin. "You know, I was thinking about our conversation . . ."

My mouth fell open. "Oh my God, no. It's not like that! We're—"

"Dimidiums," he said. "I asked my advisor about it. Marcella Gibbons, right? I'm Max. Pleasure to meet you, honey."

I sank down onto the wall. "You could've said something."

"Ah, but I'm just a narcissistic, self-obsessed, blockheaded cowherder. What could I do?" He grinned sheepishly, then pulled out a book of spells. "I was thinking we could start with this one. If you're still up for it, of course."

My mouth opened and closed in quick succession.

The corner of his mouth quivered. "Deep breaths." He seemed to enjoy watching me squirm (some things never change, I suppose).♨

"*Yes*," I managed at last. "Now, let me see that."

♨ To be fair, Cella is an adorable squirmer.

CHAPTER ELEVEN

I was chasing down a tip that only ended in another dead end while Max tried to sweet-talk a lady in the Admin office into letting him see the security-camera footage near Strauss's office. On my way back, I slipped into one of my favorite classes back when I was at school, Ancient Magic and the Roots of Christianity, taught by Dr. Perez.*

I'd always been deeply interested in religion, but my relationship with Christianity was tremulous at best, unlike the people of Marble County, who lived and breathed God. The evidence was clear on any building, on any street corner, with a cross embedded above the door, in the malign gaze of any townsfolk who spat in the direction of the demented college kids. Even with Magic, our disguise as an agricultural school wasn't exactly infallible. The school couldn't afford farming equipment, so we had no tractors on campus, no granary, no animals. Only the workers on the far side of the property, a few apple orchard groves and what they could tease out of the dry earth. Even to my eyes, our disguise was a bit lacking. The people of Marble County weren't fools; they knew there was something unnatural going on at our school. The relationship between town and school had been shaky for decades. But

---

* Dr. Perez's book, *The Root of All Evil: Religion, Magic, and the Struggle for Power*, expands on the class. From an anthropological perspective, I particularly enjoy the chapters on ancient Magic. One thing Dr. Perez taught me—Magic is cultural. It's impacted by cultural thought and the social context of the time, which is why they teach this course in the Anthropology Department.

then, Magic and Christianity had been at each other's throats for thousands of years now, so that was nothing new.

Dr. Perez had short salt-and-pepper hair and alternated his attire between gray suits and emerald or sapphire-blue cardigans. On his pinky, he wore a stout emerald ring—one of his objects was a gemstone. Dr. Perez was a quiet man, but when he got going about anthropology topics, he could get quite spirited. Now his voice boomed through the lecture hall.

"Tell me, class, what is the difference between a miracle and Magic?"

"No? How about another? Why is Jesus not referred to as a Magician?"

The classroom was silent as students shifted uncomfortably in their seats.

"After all, any classic study of what he did—turning water to wine, exorcising demons, healing the sick—to me looks a lot like what Magic can do." He came out from behind the podium, walking in front of the first row of students. "Nothing? I want to know. Is it optics? Is it that he didn't wear a pointy hat and carry a staff?"

A guy laughed. "No, he . . . it was just different."

"Different?" he challenged, "Why? After all, it's not as if Magicians are absent from Christianity. Simon Magus ring a bell? A Magician referenced in the Bible, Simon levitates, even heals people, like Jesus, and yet Simon Magus is depicted as a bombastic drunkard, a charlatan. Why? Why is Simon Magus called a Magician, as if it's a dirty word, while Jesus is something else entirely: a performer of miracles, a wonder-worker? Why has the Church gone to such lengths to create a contrast between miracles and Magic, to contrast the good Christian miracle workers against the evil-doing Magicians in cahoots with demons?

"Because," he said, turning quickly back to the board, where he wrote and underlined *Magic is in the eye of the beholder,* "the similarity between Magic and Jesus's miracles wasn't lost on ancient people. In fact, in the third century, a pagan philosopher made the very charge that Jesus was a Magician and compared him to a marketplace charlatan. A Roman emperor said the apostles practiced Magic. But Jesus couldn't be Magic—no, no, no. Jesus's power was divine, not demonic."

Dr. Perez's eyes darted across the classroom, looking for someone to challenge him. I looked at all the students ducking their heads down, pretending to be diligently taking notes. How different my life had turned out than I had thought when I myself first sat in this class. How thoroughly off the rails it had all gone.

"Christianity waged a battle for religious authority for thousands of years. Magic was used as a weapon, a spearhead for the Church to attack its enemies and a way to target outsiders. Rival religious groups were labeled sorcerers working with demons. The charge of Magic became a way to attack political opponents and other rivals.* Magical books were targeted in book burnings, reducing our history to ashes. Who knows how much of our history and knowledge of Magic was lost when that literature was destroyed?

"Roman emperors decreed that private soothsaying was akin to treason; secret rituals and cults were viewed as a threat to their rule. Those guilty of the Magic art were to be either crucified or thrown to the beasts. Magicians were to be burned alive.† People with books of Magic had their books publicly burned, and they were exiled. People like us withdrew into private mystery schools or cults for protection, passing their knowledge in secret or hoarding it among themselves while the Church attacked Magic mercilessly until the very idea of performing Magic was considered as evil as a pact with the Devil himself. Until it was hounded to the very edge of its existence.

---

* Like the orator Demosthenes, who slandered an opponent by claiming he was part of a mystery cult.

† According to *Lex Cornelia de sicariis et veneficis*, or the Cornelian Law of Assassins and Poisoners.

In this class, I want you to understand what happened to us, and the lengths they went to for power, for control."

"And then what?" a brave student in the front row asked. "I mean it's not as if we can erase everything that happened."

Dr. Perez smiled, looked around at the rest of the room, a storm brewing in his eyes. "And then, we rebuild."

As I was leaving the classroom, I stopped.

A woman walked toward me down the hallway. Her black hair draped long and thick down her back, and large brown eyes, the kind that didn't miss an inch, cut across the floor before homing in on me. Her lips were the color of a desert rose against her light brown complexion, and a tattoo of a juniper tree covered her bicep. She seemed to have gotten prettier in the years since I'd seen her, if that was even possible. I'm sure she was every bit aware of that fact.

I stopped. "You."

"Marcella Gibbons," she said slowly, rolling my name around in her mouth like a curse. "The bitch that set me on fire."

"Not you. Your car," I said weakly. A sharp tack of pain hit me. I hadn't seen her in years, not since I'd left town. Not since my catastrophic meltdown . . . in which Luce Montgomery had had a starring role.

The scent of burning rubber still wafted in my nose whenever I least expected it. The frightened look in her eyes as her fingers scrabbled to open her car door that I'd . . . that I'd what? I always seemed to block this part out. That day, rage had bubbled over until I saw black, pushed to my limit by seeing her in her polka-dotted bra in Max's bed and Max stammering in the background. I could still hear her shrieks as her car lit up in flames, could see the horrified faces of everyone looking at me like I was some sort of animal.

"Uh huh." 🍄 Luce's eyes trailed down my legs, squinting at my shoes, then back up again. "No surprise they put you on the council. Not like you deserved it. Just like you didn't deserve the valedictorian spot."

I guffawed. "I suppose you thought that extra half point in my GPA—what, appeared out of thin air? I beat you fair and square. Give up, you lost."

"Oh, honey, don't flatter yourself. I never lose."

Luce brings out something immature and angry in me. We'd been fighting over everything there was to fight about since we met sophomore year in the Anthropology Department. Thankfully, she'd switched majors, but the seeds had been sown. Four years later, she made sure my life went up in flames before she walked out of it. Quite literally.

After it had happened, I'd tried apologizing dozens of times, but she never wanted to hear a word. I didn't blame her. I could barely look at myself in the mirror afterward. Still, I had a sneaking suspicion she was the one who passed around the petition to get my seat on the council revoked, and the one who reported me to the Arbiters as well. 🍄

Now, she brushed a stray hair from her face with a single green finger, all fuzzy and mossy, like it was the most normal thing in the world.

"Another failed experiment?" I asked.

🍄 (Luce): Sure, technically it was my car, but I don't see that as relevant considering I was *in the car* at the time. Had her Magic under control, yeah flipping right. I didn't care what anyone said, she was dangerous. She had no business being back here.

🍄 Damn right I did. She had no right being back on the council. But, of course, who gives a damn about what Luce says! She's not some all-powerful elderfrigginwitch, and there are two of them, you see, and only one of Luce, and we need their Magic, their research . . . Even though I've published three times the research papers Tweedledee and Tweedledum could ever dream of. But because my field of research wasn't all flashy, about objects and the nature of Magic and all that, somehow mycoforestry was less important.

A shadow crossed her face, and she looked away. "Like them calling you here, to save the day?"

I snorted. "Well, I notice they didn't call you to come in and fix it."

"No, but Maritza asked if I knew any fungal properties that could help the scarring on Dani's skin. I've been looking into it since I was going to be on campus anyway for a field study." She picked at her nails, and the fuzzy green algae blooming under the polish. "Sounds like they're not too confident in you and your little Disaster Twin."

I hated it when she called us that, the Disaster Twins. But I suppose that's why she continued doing it. "For the one millionth time, we are not twins. One hundred percent not related."

I was surprised at the jab that went through my heart at the mention of her research. While I'd been gone, she had not only finished her PhD, but had traveled all over the world, making breakthroughs in her field left and right. And now she was teaching at S&B.

"How is that nice hunk of man meat, hmm? See all the girlies on campus swooning over him? I could've sworn this freshman was ready to drop her panties for him right then and there."

"He's not interested in that," I clipped.

"Oh? And why not?"

"That's not what I meant," I stammered. Luce arched an eyebrow, mouth twisting like a cartoon Grinch's. "I just meant, we're working here, and whoever's . . . panties he drops," I choked out, "is no concern of mine."

Luce grinned, her teeth so bright she could probably blind someone. "Sure, Cel. Whatever you say."

"He's got a girlfriend, anyway," I muttered.

Her eyes widened in surprise. "*Quelle surprise*! So he's acquired a few brain cells after all and moved on from you. Honestly, I never thought he was going to get his balls back." She slow-clapped, she actually slow-clapped. "Good for him."

"Well, as illuminating as this conversation has been, I have to get going. I'm busy with the investigation and—"

"For sure, I totally get you! See you in the next council meeting."

I stopped, and she watched as I digested the information, savoring her victory and the stupefied look on my face.

Luce put a hand to her chest, shocked. "Oh, you didn't know? I'm on the council, too."

She paused, waiting for the information to sink in, and I felt my knees almost buckle beneath me. The empty seat, Dr. Strauss's empty seat . . . was now filled by Luce Montgomery.

"I just want you to know, Cella, that whatever direction you decide to take this investigation in . . . I will be behind you *one hundred percent*." Luce was going to make my life hell, that was clear enough. She'd make this investigation even worse, block me every chance she got.

"See you in a few days." She blew me a kiss and walked away, whistling.

Too many things were tumbling into me at once, and I felt overstimulated and raw, as though my nerves had been sliced open with a razor. I'd never wanted to hurt anyone. And I never again wanted to be the person who lost control and did just that.

Just the thought of doing Magic again put me into a cold sweat. Max had been asking since the first day I'd come back. But I just couldn't do it. It left me so vulnerable, so wide open. Stripped me of every ounce of my hard-earned independence of Max.

Because no matter what I wanted, when we did Magic together, we were connected. We were, just like the stories said, one half of each other's Magical soul. And that terrified me. I was terrified to give him more power over me than he already had, power I'd been fighting tooth and nail to get back over these past few years.

I stumbled across the grounds while the sun sank below the Sangre de Cristos and the sky bled scarlet.

Back at Ludlow House, the double doors of Josephine Ludlow's old powder room opened onto a balcony off the back side of the house. From there, I had a view of the other buildings on campus, including House Torlaine. I watched as a group of girls walked in, the hinges of the door groaning as it closed behind them. My eye caught on something above their heads. There was some sort of marking on the cattle skull over the door. Graffiti? I'd have to get a better look the next time I went to my room.

I've added here the notes of Dr. Luce Montgomery, assistant professor at S&B and mycologist, who, ~~with some hesitation and quite a bit of prodding,~~ generously granted me her field notes for admission to the investigation's record. She noticed things of interest during the time she'd spent here searching for an elusive fungal species in the Sangre de Cristo Mountains and looking for fungal properties that could help the scarring on Dani's skin.

Field Journal of Dr. Luce Montgomery

April 7th

My dreams were becoming strange. Massive cityscapes, hundreds of stories tall, all glassy and shiny, with mushrooms spilling out of their windows. Fuzzy green moss and lichen growing up the sides like on the back of a tree trunk, black mold weaving through the cracks in the walls.

In my waking life, the fungus had already found its way down to my palm. It sprouted from my fingernails, a fuzzy green moss that crept down my fingers. Quite possibly the dumbest thing I've ever done. Sure, Luce, let's go with the cheap gloves when experimenting with aggressive fungi.

Even so, I couldn't let it distract me from my real mission—what could be the biggest breakthrough of my career. Because I'd found it. After countless hours of experimentation and years of research, I found the thing that would save Lela, my four-hundred-year-old juniper dying in Carson National Forest. Something that could save old-growth forests across the Southwest, across the world even.

Agaricus cataphractus. Fungal armor. A fungus that existed nowhere else on earth except for the dry deserts of New Mexico, that showed resilience to fire and heavy metal toxicity, erosion, and disease, and that could help insulate trees against the rising temperatures. Dr. Rochester doubts such a thing could exist. No surprise there; it feels like all I ever get is doubt. I'm used to people sneering, thinking I'm the pretty Native American girl who couldn't possibly be a real scientist.

Well. I'm also used to the shocked look on their faces when I prove them wrong.

And this time, I will prove them wrong. This fungus exists, and

I'm going to find it. I have a map, thanks to the help of the local mycological community (what little one exists here), and all I have left to scour is the last quadrant.

It's here. It has to be. It's the only place I haven't searched.

April 8th

My search today yielded much of the same. Signs of fox activity around the crumbling structures of the campus perimeter, rodent skulls littering the canyon—might be a source of organic material? The only thing of real interest was the person I ran into behind the Phi Kat house, Dr. de Vries's TA and Marble County's own mini-celebrity, Basile Samir. His father's the Egyptian real estate mogul Amir Samir, who owns one of the largest development companies in the state. As a forester myself, that makes him my mortal enemy, but his son . . . perhaps there's still time left for him. Doesn't hurt that he looks the way he does, either.

Basile has this easy way about him, utterly relaxed in trousers and a breezy linen shirt, like he should be lounging on a sailboat in the Mediterranean. With his father's strong, regal Egyptian nose and his Italian mother's dark, glittering eyes, he looks like he belongs in a smoky jazz club, sipping a bourbon, with Louis Armstrong or Billie Holiday playing in the background rather than on a college campus. ~~Or better yet, in my bed.~~ ♇

I know him more from his Instagram and TikToks. Some of his eighty-thousand followers are there for the thirst traps, hoping to catch a shot of him with his shirt off, but a lot are there for the math shit, too. Supposedly, he came up with a mathematical proof of the existence of parallel realities, worlds that live alongside this one. Naturally, it was a magnet for controversy. Some people insisted it proved that Heaven and Hell existed. Other people thought it could be taken further, to examine multiverses. If there was another reality out there like this one, how many were there? Could you get to them? A whole host of mathematicians and physicists had come

---

♇   Scratch from the record.

forward to weigh in on it; about half of them dismissed his work as pseudo-science metaphysical bullshit conducted by an amateur grad student. The other half were cautiously optimistic.

He had a right to be suspicious of me snooping around behind the Phi Kat house, especially with everything going on. Campus was on edge while they underwent an investigation. I recently learned it was being led by Cella Gibbons, the bitch that *set me on fire*. But that's a whole other can of worms, and I won't waste what little time I have on it here.

Tomorrow, I'll continue my preliminary search of the western half of campus. So far, it's mostly just a lot of charred wood. Not firewood, but it looks like it's been burned deliberately, in some strange, swooping pattern I'm not familiar with. Could be indicative of some sort of cult activity. I'll report it to Dr. Robetresse. Magicians historically do have a proclivity to cults, if for no other reason than safety, but the practice is strictly forbidden at S&B.[*]

---

[*] Cult activity and extremist sects were, unfortunately, all too common in the Magic world. For a thorough and entertaining history on the topic, I recommend *A History of Magical Revolutions*, by Harris T. Gormand.

CHAPTER TWELVE

The library was the same as the day I'd left. Same burgundy carpet and dark wooden furniture, same enchantment that stretched the room's inside wider than its outside.*

I pulled a text at random, flipping through the yellowed pages, savoring that old-book smell, when someone cleared their throat behind me.

"I hope you've got your library card."

I spun around to see the man standing there, mouth crooked in a sly grin. His hair was whiter than the last time I'd seen him, and he wore his pants high up around his waist, the way men of a certain age tend to do.

My mouth stretched into a smile. "Vern!"

Vern had never enjoyed copious displays of warmth, so I stopped just before I threw my arms around his stooped neck. He offered a firm handshake.

"Good thing you made it back; these bones don't have much juice left in 'em." Vern *would* use his age to guilt me for not coming back sooner. He was only sixty-four, but liked to pretend he was going to kick it any day now.

---

* The effect was a little wonky; sometimes, if you turned too fast, it felt like you were inside a fishbowl. The enchantment wasn't installed by an actual architect, but by a visiting professor who'd learned the spell "in his travels." We found out later he'd been involved in an exotic animal smuggling ring, casting beautification spells on them—tigers with pink-and-white stripes, iguanas wearing lipstick. But by that point, it would've been too costly to get the spell reversed or worked over by a proper architect, so we made do.

"Well, of course, I had to come back, if only to haunt you after you're gone. I've still got a few books checked out."

He tapped his nose. "I know. Lucky for you, they're not particularly popular, or I'd have sent someone after them years ago." He shook his head. "Portland," he scoffed. "I suppose it's changed you forever, huh? Living with all those West Coasters, off having juice cleanses and getting your nipples pierced."

"Vern!"

"What? I watch the news. Bunch of lunatics, if you ask me. You should've never left home; you have everything you need right here." He tapped the book in my hand. "I'll bet you no goddamn bookstores out there have all three copies of *Willowson's Foil*. We've even got the Greek edition."

"I missed you, too."

"I suppose you're back for that nasty business with the girls." He shook his head. "Dani was a sweet girl, used to study in the west corner. Checked out nearly all the astronomy books at one point or another. Very bright. Didn't know the other girl; dreadful sorry about what happened to her. Her poor parents."

"Sad all around," I agreed.

"So they called you in to help? I thought I wouldn't see you back here in my lifetime, with the way you split out of town. And with Max and all . . ."

I grimaced. "I wasn't exactly jumping for joy at the opportunity. Well, not with Max, anyway. But we're . . . making it work."

He lifted an eyebrow.

"We haven't bitten each other's heads off yet," I admitted. "It's really good to see you."

I rubbed a hand down the walnut shelves. There was so much of me here. I was surprised to find a book I'd tucked into my own little hiding place near a crevice in the wall. I smiled, leafing through its yellow pages. The note from Max was still stuck to the front.

Thought you might like this –M

After we learned we were dimidiums, Max and I spent

nearly all our waking time together, practicing, studying, learning how we cast together, how we worked apart. Whenever we were forced to break for classes, I'd return to find that Max had left books outside my room with bookmarked pages or notes on the cover. Sometimes he'd ink little notes in the margins that Vern would have a fit about and that I'd have to use an illusion charm on to erase. Sometimes, though, I'd cast the countercharm, just to read them again.

Notes like: *Lmk what you think. You know what, scratch that. You're probably on your way here to tell me as we speak.*

Or: *Easy, killer. I know you hate this theory, but you hated me too, at first. And look how I've grown on you ;)* I could picture him chuckling to himself as he penned them.

But as we grew closer, I started to get scared. I could barely take it when he came over, with that sweet, earnest smile on his face, a new book in hand or some new theory he wanted my opinion on. And I could take it even less when his sad blue eyes dropped to the ground after I made up an excuse.

But I knew guys like him. Knew that I could never mean half as much to him as he meant to me. Knew I couldn't get attached because of how vulnerable, how miserable it would make him to know every ooey-gooey way I was falling for him, every time my heart swooped at those little notes, how my pulse quickened when I saw him coming toward me, how even now I still had every one of those stickies tucked away in a box under my bed. How embarrassing, how utterly exposed being a dimidium left me.

So I started to pull away. Started making excuses why I couldn't study with him, why I couldn't meet up.

But, of course, Max, being who he was, would never let it die a slow, natural death.

He stopped me one day, brow furrowed. "Did I . . . do something?" For once, uber-confident Max was unsure of himself.

And, for a second, that look of vulnerability made me nearly take back everything. I almost told him how crazy I was about him right then and there.

His throat bobbed. "I understand if there's someone else—"

"There's no one else," I blurted, and almost laughed. *Someone else?* How could he possibly think that he wasn't good enough for me?

"Oh, good." He breathed a sigh of relief. "Then what is it?"

And oh God, how many times have I regretted the stupid shit I said that day. "We're breaking ground in this new science, right? We're practitioners. The Magic is everything. We shouldn't muddy up our alliance with emotion. I'm sure you agree."

His smile dropped. "Oh. If that's . . . what you want."

"It is," I said. And though I spent the next I don't know how many hours regretting that statement, there was still truth in it. It wasn't his fault, of course. He wasn't even aware of it— of how he swallowed all the light, how anyone next to him fell into his shadow. Everyone loved Max; it was just who he was. He smiled, and the world unfurled for him.

But I knew that if we were in a relationship, that was all I would ever be. To him, to anyone else. I'd be dependent on him, just the little dog running after his heels. And I hadn't worked as hard as I had for my male colleagues to consider me Max's flavor of the month. I wanted to be whole, to stand on my own two feet, to not sink into the inescapable void that was Max Middlemore's shadow. Falling in love with him meant letting go of that tight grip of control that kept me grounded, the tether I'd relied on my entire life. I was logical, I was an academic. Love was uncharted territory. Love was something that could harm me.

And I'd worked too hard and built too many protections around myself to let that happen.

Vern snapped a heavy tome shut, jerking me back to the present. "So, whatcha need?"

I blinked, coughing a little at the dust swirling in the air. "You have anything on hexes?"

"Do I?" He grinned and turned to the shelves. "Back in a jiffy. Don't you go disappearing on me," he called as he shuffled down the aisles. "Hate to grab all these books and then not see you again for another five years."

Robetresse stopped me in the hallway on the way back.

"Cella," she called, "how is it going? I'm sorry to pry, but the council is feeling the pressure, so to speak. Maya Hagood's parents have been calling my office nonstop. I've managed to convince them to wait for the results of the internal investigation before going back to the police, but they're not going to wait forever. They want answers. And the students are getting antsy. We need something to tell them."

I shuffled on my feet. "I'm not sure we have anything concrete to announce, but we have some definite directions . . ." Her face fell, and my pulse spiked. "But we should have something soon. For sure. Hopefully, within the week."

Her eyes brightened. "That's reassuring. I hope I have no need to remind you of the dire circumstances here. Or of the extreme physical toll this Magic is causing on Miss Stewart's body."

I winced when I thought of all the scars and scratches on Dani's skin, like she was being torn apart from the inside. The sickening angle of her neck when she lifted into the air. Her eyes, so unnaturally dark, like she'd fallen into a shadow. And I couldn't shake the feeling that if I didn't help her, maybe no one would.

"That reminds me. The RA who was working the night shift at the dorm on the night of Maya's murder has been out of town. Death in the family, I believe, but she's back now. We've had a look at the logs from the night of the murder. Nothing out of the ordinary there, but you might speak to her. See if she noticed anything unusual?"

"We'll do that."

"Great, well, I'll leave you to it—" Dr. Robetresse started.

"Dr. R? One other thing. Dr. Rose Oswold, how long has she been on faculty here?"

"Dr. Oswold?" Robetresse frowned. "She transferred here during the middle of the term last year. A bit unusual, I don't usually accept staff members in the middle of a term, but not completely unheard of. This is the first year she'll be holding her own classes."

"Um." I wiped my sweaty palms on my jeans. "I'm aware of the transfer. I was wondering, has anyone ever looked into the reason why she transferred?"

Dr. Robetresse's fingernails tapped against her coffee cup. "Ah. I see you've been busy."

"It just surprises me, is all," I said quickly, "that a member of staff would be hired with a restraining order against her citing harassment and attempted impersonation. And from one of her former students, no less."

Dr. Robetresse nodded. "We're aware of the incident, and Rose has explained her side quite in depth. Given her presentation of facts, I have no reservations regarding her character nor her teaching abilities at S&B."

I raised an eyebrow. Usually, I wouldn't push against Dr. Robetresse's judgment, but this to me seemed like a glaring oversight. One I couldn't just ignore. "So, chalk it up to a misunderstanding? Is there a specific reason she's given you to trust her?"

"Everyone has their past, Miss Gibbons. I would think you, of all people, would understand that. If you'll excuse me."

CHAPTER THIRTEEN

Max and I headed to the front desk of House Torlaine in the afternoon, which ended up being staffed by a bored-looking student twirling a pen in her fingers.

"Dr. Robetresse said we might have a look at the logs for the days preceding the incident with Maya Hagood," I said.

"Sure," she droned, barely looking up. She pulled a clipboard from a locked drawer and handed it to me.

"I'm also curious if anyone visited Dani's room as well."

"Those are the logs we have for all the rooms."

Dr. Robetresse was right. There was nothing unusual in the logs the day of or before the murder. No one had visited either girl's room that week. However, at least twice in the month leading up to the incident, an "A. Strauss" was logged as visiting Dani's room after hours.

"How are these logs taken?" I asked.

She looked at me like I was an idiot. "I write down who comes in. And when."

"And the times, are those always accurate?"

The girl smacked her gum. "I mean, yeah. Who comes in, where they're going . . . and what time."

I peered at one of the entries. "And Antony Strauss, do you remember him coming in on the night of the February 15th?"

"Uhhh, I don't remember off the top of my head . . ."

"Dr. Strauss, the physics professor, you don't remember him coming in at nine p.m.?" I asked, growing irritated. "You'd think a professor coming to visit a student after hours would be noticed."

Max shot me a look and took off his hat. He flashed her

a smile, all dimples and pearly teeth. "We sure hate to be a bother, but anything that jogs your memory would really help."

The girl stared at Max, and for a second, I thought she'd drowned in those baby blues. "Yeah, I remember," she said at last. "Well, it's not, like, that unusual. He had stuff he was bringing her. A stack of papers, I think?"

I squinted. The 9 had been written over with a 3. "And the logs here, it looks like the time was changed. Do you remember changing it?"

"I didn't change it, but he probably got one of the other girls to. They love him. I'm sure if he asked, they wouldn't even question it. No one's gonna risk getting on his bad side."

"His bad side? What do you mean?"

She looked at me knowingly. "You went here, right? Then you know how he is. Oh, people can try to speak out against him, but until a whole lot of girls come forward, it doesn't matter. The last girl who tried to start shit against him doesn't even go here anymore. Then there's the fact that, because he's hot, some girls don't mind the attention. I don't know if this girl Dani minded or not, but I guarantee if it did bother her, she probably didn't think there was much she could do about it. Someone like Strauss, who's that popular around campus, he's basically untouchable."

Or was, I thought. Strauss wasn't on the council anymore. Maybe someone finally took a stand against him. Maybe he wasn't as untouchable as we all thought.

The handsome, charismatic, twenty-nine-year-old professor on top of the world, taken down a few notches. Removed from his position of power and obviously pissed about it. Maybe he'd wanted revenge.

Maybe he'd gotten it.

Before heading in for the night, I looked up at the bull skull over House Torlaine, trying to spot the graffiti mark I'd seen from the balcony. It was harder to see in the dark, illuminated only by the flickering floodlight above the door, but it was definitely there. I had a better view from the building's west corner if I carefully avoided a prickly pear cactus buried in the loose soil. Now I saw it wasn't just a graffiti tag, but some sort of odd symbol, a circle drawn in black ink on one side of the bull's snout, with a triangle formed by ten dots inside it (one dot on the first line, two on the second, three on the third, four on the fourth). Beneath the other eye socket, the number 191. The way the roof sloped, the only way you could see them was if you were standing at this exact spot or on the balcony on the back of Ludlow House.

191?

A room number? The dormitory rooms only went up to 36. I thought of the nearby buildings, wondering if any of the classroom blocks went to 191. It was a small campus. Did we even have 191 classrooms? I wasn't sure.

I wanted to study it more, but then the RA was shuffling me inside. I went in and closed the door.

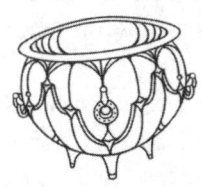

CHAPTER FOURTEEN

Max walked into the library around noon. I shouldn't say that, because of course that's not how Max moves. He saunters. He sauntered into the library, big, bright smile on his face, hat drawn over his head, hands in his pockets, the perfect cool guy. Meanwhile, my hair was a wreck, eyeliner smudged down my cheeks. It'd only been a couple of days, but I felt like I hadn't bathed in weeks.

He sat down at the table and pulled two books from my unread stack. "*Marboli's Hex and Other Curses from the Ancient World? Curse Tablets, Dolls, and Spells That Bind?* Looks like we've got our work cut out for us."

I propped up on my elbow, eying the notebook across from me. "I've been thinking . . . There's something else we need to try. Or *someone* else. But you're not going to like it . . ."

He looked at me, and I looked at him. He'd already started backing away. "Oh no no no no, Cella, no way. Come on."

"We need to talk to her, Max . . ."

"No, come on, there are tons of other leads still." For his size and general—let's go with woodsy nature—you wouldn't think Max was scared of anything, but he could be the biggest chicken. Spiders sent him running into the next room, complaining about headaches or poor air quality as he scurried out the door. Heights were also a particularly sore topic. I was all but forbidden to mention the time we went to the county fair and he very nearly had a heart attack on the kids' Ferris wheel.

"Look, we're not going to be able to fix her if we never see

 Is it just me, or is she implying I smell?

her, and she might be able to give us something concrete that points to who did this to her and how. Our council meeting is two days from now. Do you really want to show up empty-handed? We have to talk to her eventually."

He grumbled, shoulders sagging. "I know. I was just hoping it would be later rather than sooner."

When we stepped into Maritza's cottage, everything felt about ten degrees colder than the air outside. Dani was lying in the bed, and Maritza was at the stove, brewing tea.

"How is she?" I whispered.

She shook her head. "She is getting worse. Whatever this is, her body can't take it for much longer." She held up a rag near the copper sink, nearly soaked through with blood. "Started last night. I've had to change the bandages on her arms and legs twice already this morning."

"Would it be okay if we speak to her?"

Maritza bit her lip. "She's not good today. You should come back tomorrow."

Max turned around; that was all he needed to hear, but I took a step closer.

A feeling of wrongness swirled up around me. She wasn't this bad the last time I'd seen her. "We only need a few minutes."

"You heard the lady, Cel," Max said. "We can come back tomorrow." He lowered his voice. "Or never . . ."

Dani was bound to the bed with leather straps. Her fingernails had scratched down her palms, leaving jagged cuts where she'd tried to get at the binds. A groan built in her throat.

I took another step closer. I could practically hear Max's heart beating from where I was standing, his aura spiking with alarm. He held the rein bit that was his object, clenching his fingers stiff against the leather. If I concentrated, I could almost hear horses nervously stamping the ground.

Max's voice lowered to a whisper. "She can't get out of that, can she?"

Maritza shook her head. "The binds have held so far, and the room is enchanted. Even if she does get out, she can't escape."

"Oh, okay, so then we're trapped in here . . . with her." Max scratched the back of his neck. "That makes me feel loads better," he whispered.

Dani's eyes were ringed in black circles, and her blond hair stuck to her cheeks and neck. She looked so helpless and frail—something about it struck me as familiar. She looked like Aaron had in the hospital, after they'd tried to resuscitate him.

Blood flowed freely from the bandages on her legs. "Will she need a tourniquet?"

Maritza shook her head. "A cut from Magic is not like a normal cut . . . It will bleed for a bit, then stop, off and on throughout the day. If it keeps on much more, we will need to take her to a hospital."

"You didn't do this, Dani," I whispered. "I know you didn't." I touched her hand, and Max's shoulders stiffened.

"Cella," Dani rasped suddenly.

"I'm here." She tried to sit up and coughed herself hoarse. "I think she needs water."

"Cella, help me," Dani rasped.

"Of course," I said, sitting down next to her. "Just tell me what to do. I want to help in any way I can." I looked over at Max. "I knew we should have seen her sooner."

Her gaze took on a hopeful, hungry look. "Please." Her hands twisted in the restraints as blood trickled down her wrists.

"Are these really necessary? She's clearly in a lot of pain."

"Yes," Maritza said firmly. "And you shouldn't get so close."

"I agree with Maritza. Come back over here," hissed Max.

"Please," Dani rasped, her fingers stretching out toward me. "Please stay. Don't leave me here alone." She shot a frightened look at Maritza.

"How can I help?" I asked, my voice quickening, my heart thumping in my chest. "How can I make you more comfortable?"

She squirmed in her binds, her wrists twisting this way and that to get out of them. "They burn."

My teeth ground in my skull. How could they just leave her like this, tied up like some kind of animal? "She's in pain! This is barbaric!" As soon as we got out of here, I was going straight to Robetresse's office. Just what kind of school was she running here?

"Please stay," Dani rasped.

I ran down the list of symptoms I'd read for hexes. The scarring of her skin and the blood were consistent with what I'd read. I peered into her eyes, looking for constricted pupils. But her pupils were the opposite of tiny; they were blown wide, like she needed to drink in every inch of her surroundings, everything that entered or left the cottage.

"Dani, I want to help you. I need to know who did this to you. Was it one of the other students?" My voice dropped. "Another teacher? Was it Dr. Strauss?"

Something flashed over her face, but it was gone in an instant. Her voice took on a more urgent plea. "Please," she said, "they burn."

Blood pooled around her wrists and dripped down her palms.

"They're so tight," I pleaded. "She's rubbing them raw."

Maritza gave me a hard look. "Cella, step back."

I reached a hand toward Dani. "Help me figure out who did this to you. If you give me their name, I promise it won't get back to you. We can get you out of here—"

"Now," Maritza said, forcefully pushing me out of the way. I fell back into the sharp corner of the table and opened my mouth in protest. They couldn't treat students like this, like chattel. They couldn't abuse people, this wasn't right—

But then I saw the look Dani shot Maritza. It was the cruelest look I'd ever seen, eyebrows angled down, mouth twisted into a gruesome snarl.

I hadn't even noticed she'd gotten a hand out of her restraints. The bloody thing swiped at Maritza, fingers outstretched like claws. I took a step back in shock.

"I'll kill you, you fucking bitch—"

Then, apparently remembering she had an audience, Dani turned back to me, her face slipping back into its innocent expression. "Cella," she said, voice sugary sweet. "Cella. Cella, please," she pleaded as my footsteps slid backward. My eyes widened.

"Cella, Cella, Cella, Cella!" She screamed and shook the restraints, beating her limbs wildly. Her spine jostled up and down, rattling the bindings. With her free hand, she reached for the binding over the other wrist.

With a tug, I felt a rush of Magic leave me. Max was holding onto his rein object with eyes closed. A soft wind circled his ankles. I could smell fresh grass on the wind, hear a horse whinny in the distance. And I realized what he was doing. The leather binding lifted itself, snaking back over Dani's wrists.

She snarled.

"Your Magic, Cella!" Max hissed.

I frantically reached for my leather cord and the small jar of water in my other pocket. I let the Magic brush up against me. When I accessed Magic, I went somewhere else, in my mind, at least. I always landed in different bodies of water—lakes (the worst were in Florida, the alligators were as big as sedans), community pools, the Mediterranean Sea at midnight. More often than not, I was just dropped somewhere in the Pacific.* The first few times I was terrified I was going to drown or get dragged under or eaten, but I got used to it after a while.

This time, I plunged into water circling me, deep as the Mariana Trench and just as cold.

Magic swirled and sucked around me, drawing me into a vortex. I gargled water, my lungs tightening in my chest, and felt myself sinking farther down. With a gasping breath, I wrenched myself from it.

---

* Some scholars may take issue with this depiction of Magic as a place, and with Max's Magic described as horses running, but that's what it felt like to me. Whatever was actually happening, my mind filled it into this place that was both with and without Max.

"I can't," I gasped, shaking. "*I can't.*"

Dani smacked the leather snaking over her hand away.

Dani roared, then turned back to Maritza. She started writhing, her hips beating against the straps, moaning and panting like a dog. "You'll fucking pay for this, you whore. I'll fuck you like a dog. I'll wrap my hands around your throat until you feel the life seep from your veins—"

Max grabbed me by the waist and dragged me to the door.

His back was shoved against the door, trying to pull me out and open it at the same time, but my feet were planted to the floor. My heart shrieked in my ears, telling me to move, get out, before she wrapped those bloody fingers around my throat and squeezed. But I was in utter shock about what I was seeing, about how quickly things had turned.

About what might have happened if I had removed her restraints, as I'd wanted to.

Maritza shoved her sleeves up and furrowed her brow in determination, speaking the words of a powerful sleeping spell. Even as Dani fought it, I saw the first of its effects crash into her. Something to knock her out and calm her.

"Go," Maritza shouted at us, angry now.

My voice seemed to regain its sound. "Can you—will you be able to hold it on your own?"

"Yes," she said furiously. "You've done enough damage. Now *go.*"

Dani looked at me one last time, her eyes heavy with sleep that she could no longer resist. I saw her mouth try one last time—"Cel—"—before my name died on her lips.

Max threw his hands up once we were outside. "Well, that was just about the stupidest thing we've ever done!"

"It was necessary," I said rotating the studs in my ears. I paced back and forth, rubbing the sweat off my palms and onto my jeans.

"Necessary?" he balked. "In case you forgot, she murdered

someone not too long ago. Was it necessary for us to nearly get maimed, too?" His voice went high. "I don't know, Cel, I think that's debatable—"

But I needed to see what had happened to her, and whatever he said, I'd made up my own mind about the situation. For better or worse, I felt a connection to this girl. Someone had done this to her, had hurt her, had made her hurt other people. And now I had the sinking feeling that no one else cared to make sure she was okay. Sure, they wanted to know who was responsible, but did they really care about fixing Dani?

The council had brought me here, but it was more than the promise of money in my pocket that was making me stay. She needed someone. She needed my help.

And I needed to be ready. I'd been too afraid in there, unwilling to face my Magic head-on, too terrified to try, and it had nearly drowned me.

That couldn't happen again. Not if we were to save her.

Max walked away, still loudly complaining to shrubs, random passersby, and what he thought was me dawdling behind him. "I swear you've got one hell of a death wish. One of these days, you're gonna get me killed right along with you."

As I stood at the door, I swore it on my objects, on the mug and the leather cord that were all I had left of my brother: This wasn't going to be another Aaron. I wasn't going to let another person I was supposed to protect slip out of my grasp. *This time, I'll be there. I'm not going to leave or miss anything. I won't let you slip away into the darkness. I'll figure this out and fix you, I promise.*

I pressed my hand to the door, whispered my silent oath against the wooden frame. "I'll find out what's happened to you if it kills me."

FROM THE JOURNAL OF DANICA STEWART

March 25th [one week before the murder]

You Promised. You PROMISED ME. YOU LIED YOULIEDLIEDLIEDTOMELIED

March 26th

TRUST NO ONE.*

---

* The script this is written in is strange—big, swooping letters formed with circles.

CHAPTER FIFTEEN

The Rival

"Back again, I see?" Vern said.

The next day, I was at the library. Back when I was a student, I was here all the time. I used to go just to talk to Vern. Tell him about problems I'd had with Magic,* and he'd suggest this or that textbook. He'd tell me about his children, grown and moved away now, and his wife, Sonia, who worked part-time in the cafeteria. He missed his children, but he was proud of the people they'd become. He always said he just wanted to work long enough to be able to leave them "a little something." He was patient, and kind, and sensitive, and I loved how after thirty-five years of marriage, he'd still fret over what to buy Sonia for her birthday. He was my friend in this hellhole, and I loved him fiercely.

"I hate to ask . . ." I said, biting my lip, "but do you have anything else?"

Vern raised an eyebrow. "Must be some curse if you haven't found what you're looking for in the entire library."

"I've found hexes, but none that seem to fit the effects of

---

* Vern had Magic himself, though he was very self-conscious about it. He could find any library book in an instant, especially ones that had been shelved improperly. But it didn't come in handy for much other than his job at the library, so he didn't like to talk about it.

Dani's. The scarring, the" —I swallowed—"the behavior. It's unusual, to say the least. Whatever it is, the spell is very old."

He lifted a brow.

"What?"

"I'm just glad to see you doing what you love again, is all. You and Max back in here, it feels like old times."

I sighed. "I don't know. At least before, there wasn't a chance of anyone dying if I didn't get my notes on Object Transference in on time."

He waved me away. "If anyone can do it, it's you two. To be honest, Max seems on cloud nine since you came back. I have half a mind to think he cast the damn thing himself. Haven't seen him so happy in months."

I snorted and grew intensely interested in the inner workings of my pen.

Vern skimmed the stack. "As far as books, you've got yourself a good sampling here. Except . . . you'd be remiss to not have Brueste's *An Analysis of the Black Magicks*, little-known companion text to the *Ars Notoria*."

"You have that? It's got to be ancient."

He pressed a key on the computer, which made a less-than-encouraging *chug chug clunk* until he beat the sputtering thing with his palm. "*Tck*, don't have it. A student had it last, but hasn't returned it yet. Joselyn Hart."

"Joselyn Hart . . ." I said, the name ringing a bell. "Dani's old roommate?"

He scratched his head. "Could be. She's in the physics program, is always checking those books out."

"Dr. Strauss said she just missed out on acceptance to MIT's graduate program."

"I wouldn't doubt it. Last semester, she cast a spell so a blaring alarm clock followed a student through the halls after he kept a book past due that she had a hold on. Apparently, she kept the spell on the lad for months afterward, even after he returned the book. Messy affair, nearly sent the boy to a nervous breakdown. I tried to get her on staff. Anyone who's that passionate about books deserves a job, I said, but turns out she just wanted the book. Had some kind of test on it."

"She admitted to that?"

"No, I happened to see the confrontation when I was trying to catch The Fish." The Fish, also known as Vern's archnemesis. Before he left, one of the seniors had charmed one of those animatronic singing bass to life. Every few weeks, it would appear out of a shelf, singing Billie Eilish and telling really bad fish puns before knocking down *The Old Man and the Sea* or *Moby-Dick*. The thing drove Vern nuts.

"I swear I was *this close* to catching it when the damn alarm went off and startled the entire library. I peeked through the shelves to see the boy running off in tears, the feet of the little clock chasing like mad after him, and Joselyn standing there, book in hand, looking victorious. Wouldn't want to get on her bad side."

"Do you think it's possible she'd do something more serious?"

He raised an eyebrow. "Now, don't you go twisting my words. I never said I thought she did anything to that girl."

"Sure, sure," I said, the excitement mounting in my chest. "But why would she have a book on curses?"

"Well now, it's not only curses. There's lots of history in there, too. Early natural Magic, the movements of trees, water, and the like . . ."

Vern realized he'd said something that would lead to a confrontation and quickly tried to backpedal. But this wasn't something I could ignore. Not if he was right and Joselyn did have something to do with it.

"Dr. Strauss said himself that the physics majors are very competitive. And they are competing for the same spots—they basically kill themselves to get an edge. And they were roommates, too. All that festering tension from being together all the time . . ."

I was talking very fast now, my thoughts racing ahead of me. Suddenly, I stopped and smacked my hands down on the desk. Vern jumped. "If I didn't know any better, I'd call that a motive."

Vern faltered, voice weak. "I mean, I suppose it could be possible . . ."

I threw my stuff in my bag, shouting over my shoulder. "Thanks, Vern. I owe ya!"

An hour later, I'd got the rankings for the physics majors. "Dani and Joselyn are within only a few percentage points of each other. Joselyn is third in the class. Dani is second."

It was a slow afternoon in the library; exams had been postponed. Only two other students were inside. "Not this again," Vern said. He chewed on a ham sandwich and a bowl of goldfish crackers. Every so often, one of them would float up and up and try to swim toward the Marine Biology section, and he'd have to snatch it out of the air and push it back into the bowl. He released a string of expletives under his breath.

"It's a potential motive. I can't just ignore it."

"Say that's all true and she did go and off her competition. Why not go for the first in the class?"

"Maybe she was making her way up into it," I said.

Vern sighed, setting down his sandwich. "Now, I know you've gone and given up on people. 'There's no hope for humanity' and all that, but you can't always look for the worst in everyone. She's just a kid."

"It's not that I've given up on humanity. I just . . . would rather not study them, or allow myself to get disappointed by them any more than I already have."

He raised an eyebrow. "Uh-huh."

"Whatever. I don't see the worst in everyone. I don't see the worst in you."

He snorted. "That's because I am a goddamn delight."

I took a bite of his sandwich and continued. "Hey!" he said, reaching for it.

"Someone hexed Dani, Vern. How do you explain that?

Max and everyone else would be fine if I just ignored it, if I concluded that she simply did all this to herself. But who's looking out for Dani?"

Vern took off his glasses and set them on the table, rubbing his temples wearily. "Just be careful, is all I'm saying. You're messing with dangerous business here. If Joselyn or someone else really did do something to that girl, I don't think they'd take too kindly to you looking into them."

I nodded. "I know. But she's got nobody but me, Vern. And she's running out of time."

I'd protested, but the council hadn't called Dani's parents yet, said they didn't want to "cause them unnecessary panic," though I think it was more likely they didn't want another set of parents harassing them for information they clearly didn't have.

"Just watch yourself. Don't know what I'd do if you were floating there in Maritza's cottage. They'll be asking me to fix you next, and I'm afraid all I could do would be to throw a book at you, try to knock some sense into that brain of yours."

"Well, hopefully it'd be a heavy book. You know I've got a thick skull." I grinned and took another bite of his sandwich. "One for the road."

"Hey!"

"I'll see you later!" I said, rushing out, letting the door swing closed as I left.

Vern yelled after me. "And you'd better be bringing me a new sandwich when you come back, too!"

Max and I found Joselyn in the courtyard behind Ludlow House, on a stone bench in a rock garden housing bright orange poppies, yucca, and cacti in all different shapes and sizes. She had a line of stud earrings running up one ear and wore Doc Martens and a long purple skirt.

"Joselyn? My name is Max Middlemore, and this is Cel—"

"I know who you both are," she said drily, not looking up

from lying flat on her back. "You're here to ask me about the golden child." She brought her vape to her lips and took a drag. "She *would* get a full-scale investigation into trying to fix her after she murdered someone."

She was wearing thick black sunglasses that only cast our reflections back at us. I sat on the bench beside her. "Golden child? Why do you call her that?"

She waved her hand, the gold cross around her neck gleaming in the light. "She's Dr. Strauss's favorite, of course. The man is lodged so far up her ass."

"Mmm," Max said and smiled a country smile that veered just a little crooked. "And I take it that's why he gave her a recommendation to MIT and not you?"

While they spoke, I tried to ignore the ache lodged in my chest. This sun-baked courtyard was one of Aaron's favorite spots. He used to lean back on the benches, headphones over his ears; he insisted on using our dad's beat-up old Walkman. He always looked so peaceful like that.

At our last Christmas as a family, Aaron surprised everyone by using the money he'd made from cutting lawns to buy us all gifts with what little he had, including my Christmas mug.*

Max sent out a tendril of Magic that encircled my shoulders in a protective embrace.

She waved her hand. "He was too busy for me, of course, but who could deny the golden child? Even though I've wanted to work at NASA since I was five, and with MIT's work on

---

* It was why I hated the criticism from other researchers that Object Theory was promoting a culture of "things" and consumerism. (See B. Cromme, "Consumerism Culture in Magic: The Problem with 'Things,'" *New Magic Quarterly*, Issue 45.) That wasn't it at all. It wasn't as if you could bind to any old thing. You could only bind to the things that were most important to you. Maybe it happened by accident; you were holding something for luck or some superstition, and as you cast, your Magic flowed through the object instead of you. There was beauty in that; there was love in that. And that was what Magic was all about.

the Chandra Observatory, that program was the best chance for me."

"Did you know that she got accepted?" I asked quietly. I showed her the acceptance letter we'd found among Dani's things. She'd received it only one week before Maya's murder.

Joselyn pulled her sunglasses down and stared blankly at the paper. "And she's gone and blown herself up. What a waste. Hats off to whoever's on the waiting list." She mimed cheers-ing a wineglass, and I caught sight of the tattoo on her bicep: carefully curved letters that spelled *The Devil hides behind the cross.*

I stared at the tattoo until I realized why it felt so familiar. It reminded me of the HELL IS HERE carving on my bed. I made a mental note to ask around about who'd stayed in my dorm room since I'd been gone.

Max leaned in close and took off his hat. "Hey, look, I get it, believe me. Someone always getting in your way, throwing her clothes all around the room. Keepin' the light on all night, crunching her snacks in your ear. I wouldn't want to live with her anymore either. And then she goes and steals your spot at MIT, and you realize you've had enough, that's it. And you just snap. I mean, everybody's got their limits, right?"

Joselyn shoved up to a seated position and took off her sunglasses, eyes narrowing at him. "No. And let's get one thing straight. I never wanted to live with Dani. Our families were old friends after our dads were physicists at the same lab together for years. But that was before her dad stole my father's job. Sooooo, no. After that, I didn't want to keep up the sham that we were friends. Dr. Strauss's little pet project. Always getting the best marks on everything when she didn't deserve it. 'Oh Dani, what a great observation, oh Dani, how astute, oh Dani, *right there*, oh, how do you *do* that, oh-oh my God—"

Students walking into the School of Business looked over.

I cleared my throat. "They were sleeping together?"

She snorted. "He wishes. To tell you the truth, I wouldn't be surprised if he killed Maya in some botched attempt to get

Dani to love him back. I'm not the only one who noticed how obsessed he was with her." She took another drag from the vape. "Take out the competition and all that. Oh, that sweet, sweet unrequited love.

"To tell you the truth, Dani wasn't above using people to get what she wanted. Dr. Strauss worked with her a lot, on whatever questions she had. He was her window, her key to understanding more about Magic. It only made sense that he wanted something in return. For everything he taught her, for every way he helped her.

"But if you're asking all this because you think I had something to do with Little Miss Perfect going off and killing her girlfriend, I didn't. I was in the hospital and hadn't even left my room for days before that. Everyone says I just drank too much at the party, but I'm telling you, I was only throwing up because of that fucking pill."

"What pill?" Max asked.

"The pills with the shitty enchantments that are so popular right now. Go to any party with a drink in your hand and someone's bound to try it. Mine was slipped into my drink by local perv Grant Hafer. He should've been expelled years ago." She took another drag from her vape, exhaling toward the sky.

"An enchantment?" I asked. "How do you know it had a spell on it?"

"Why else would I be sick for so long? With my head pounding with thoughts of his jeans unbuckling? Just the thought of him alone is enough to make me want to puke, and I was having sex dreams about him." She spat on the ground, as if to get an awful taste out of her mouth. "I told Paul he was a creep, but, of course, he always stood up for him. Should've never trusted them. Bunch of fucking pagans."

I considered her statement. In the sky above us, a hawk let out a piercing cry and dove. "The enchantment sounds a lot like a hex. Is that why you have Brueste's *An Analysis of the Black Magicks*? Were you looking up hexes?"

Her eyes flashed with alarm. No doubt half the student

body by now knew we were looking for information about a hex. "I don't know anything about hexes. That book has one of the best compilations of the Magical properties of plants, and seeing how I'm failing my ecology course, I thought it would come in handy.✤ Dani was the same way about books, reading them all with this crazed desperation until she realized they didn't have whatever she was looking for. Could barely get my hands on any that she hadn't torn through like a psycho. All I know is Grant slipped me this date-rape pill. Grant Hafer, H-a-f-e-r, and I could barely get out of bed for days. Why don't you ask *him* about it? Maybe you guys will do something more than my advisor, whose stellar advice was that I shouldn't have been drinking in the first place. Fucking prick."

She got up from the bench. Before she left, Max called out to her. "One more question! Your tattoo, what's it mean?"

She looked down at the words on her bicep and smiled. "Even the Devil can quote Scripture. It means be wary of who you trust around here."

Max made a slow whistle after she left. "Wooh-wee. Don't know what idiot decided to mess with her. That bit she said about reading books with a crazy desperation sounds like someone else I know." He grinned over at me.

"Funny, because to me it sounded like you. I've never heard of a hexed pill before, though, have you?"

He shook his head, picking up one of the pebbles beneath a yucca plant and smoothing over it with his thumb. "No, but it looks like we've got another person to look into. Grant Hafer, H-a-f-e-r."

As we were walking back through Ludlow House, we stopped on one of the balconies that looked over the grounds. The sun was sinking in the sky. The ranch hands who worked the apple

---

✤ She would have been much better served by Lusinki's *Anatomy of Nature*.

orchards on the far side of the property were packing up and heading home. In the distance, I could see the faint outline of their trucks pulling out, bouncing and kicking up dust as they made their way down the dirt road. This was when the Land of Enchantment truly shone. The sky lit up cherry-red and tangerine against the mesas. Cicadas chirped as the sun drifted lower. A breeze rustled through the brush, trickling across the ground and lifting the roots of my hair.

I looked over at him. "Can I ask you something? And I swear to God, if you say, 'You just did' . . ."

He smiled. "Shoot."

"What would you have done if things hadn't happened the way they had? If I'd stayed and you could use your Magic whenever you wanted. What would you have done? Would you have taught?"

He snorted. "God, no. I'd probably be in the same place as now, taking care of the horses at Mom and Pop's and trying to make enough to open my own ranch. Though no doubt it would be easier with a little Magic."

I balked. "So then why do you care so much if I'm back? Why volunteer every time Robetresse wanted to find me, if your life would've been exactly the same?"

He looked at me for one long moment, then averted his gaze.

The look was gone so fast I might have imagined it, replaced by his cheeks brimming into a bright, mischievous grin. He gathered me up in a bear hug and squeezed, then smacked a kiss on my cheek. "Easy. So I can annoy you whenever I want."

I pushed him away. "Barf."

"You love it," he called over his shoulder, loping off for the cafeteria.

I shook my head as he walked away, grinning in spite of myself. "Dork."

When home isn't a place where you feel safe, it becomes other things. You attach the concept to people. Or to smells, or to places where you do feel safe and warm and loved.

Home for me was Max. Comfortable and familiar, and mine. I watched him from the spot on the balcony, his long loping strides, a hint of the gawkiness that remained from his younger days. He was looking at his phone and smiling about something. A dimple poked out on his cheek, and my heart twisted painfully in my chest.

Except he wasn't mine. Not anymore.

CHAPTER SIXTEEN

Our council meeting was the next day; they were occurring weekly now during the investigation instead of monthly, and I was dreading it. It had already been a week since we started, which left only a little over two weeks until graduation. Only two weeks until the students broke for the summer or graduated and we lost all opportunity to find the culprit. Though we had suspects with their own reasons for wanting to harm Dani or Maya, we didn't have evidence of how any of them might have gone about hexing her. Or even what they might have hexed her with, which meant we had exactly zilch to show for all our work thus far. I arrived at the meeting room without Max. He was trying to get the toxicology report from Joselyn Hart's stay at the hospital, and I hadn't spoken with him all day. Maybe he had some issues back at his parents' that he had to deal with. Or maybe he was just seeing his girlfriend and didn't want to tell me.

I walked in, found a seat at the long table, and proceeded to fidget until I had even more nervous energy, if that was possible. I sat on my feet, then readjusted to cross my legs. I put my hair up and then back down again until I finally looked up and noticed Dr. Perez watching me.

My cheeks reddened. "Oh."

He took the seat beside me. "Saw you sit in on my ancient religions class. Thought you might stay after for a chat."

"Oh, yeah, sorry. Lots to do, with the investigation and all."

His brow raised. "So you weren't avoiding me?"

I swallowed. "No."

"Really? Well, I suppose I'll have to take your word on that." He kept watching me, and I squirmed.

"Fine. I'm sorry I didn't come by to talk to you. Then, and now." I rubbed my thumb over my leather cord. "I didn't know what to say."

"You mean, 'Sorry I ran off and sent you a one-line email in response to declining the fellowship you spent several weeks securing a line of funding for. Sorry I never answered the phone when you tried to get a reason why?'"

"I didn't want to leave the position, honest. It's just . . . things were complicated."

He raised his eyebrows, looked around the room. "You're here now. Are they still complicated?"

I was distracted by Luce Montgomery walking into the room. I tried to send her a *hey, no hard feelings can-we-please-just-not-be-enemies* look, but what I got in return was such a stone-faced glower that I shrank back a little.

Okay, so still mad.

I stopped. "Wait, are you saying you still want me to work with you?"

He sighed. "Cella, you're one of the most gifted Magical researchers I've ever met. And I don't just say that because of the Magic. You see things other people don't. You're dedicated, kind, conscientious. There will always be a spot for you in my department, whether that's a year from now or five."

I smiled. Dr. Perez was one of the few people who'd always seen me, had read my research and understood what I was trying to do, independent of the fact that I was a dimidium. I suspect he'd realized not long after talking to Max that he couldn't have been the brains behind our work.

And yet I'd let him down, too.

"I appreciate that, sir. I really do. Though I don't want you to get your hopes up. I don't expect I'll be around long once the investigation is over."

He clapped me on the shoulder. "We'll talk about that when the time comes. For now, I think Thea has rather strong 'dibs' on your time. Far be it from me to insist my work is more important than your help with our current predicament."

In the corner, Luce snorted. Dr. Perez returned to his seat as Dr. Robetresse walked in, steel-toed boots gleaming. She brushed wood shavings off her jacket and took a long swig of coffee. "Before we get started, I want to let everyone know that the Hagoods have agreed to halt their impending lawsuit against the school. They seem, for the time being, appeased by my confidence in the investigation and the capabilities of Cella and Max, who I believe have an update for us. What have you found?"

All the eyes in the room swiveled toward me. Max still hadn't arrived. I swallowed and tried not to shrink down in my seat. "We're trying to get the toxicology report from Joselyn Hart's stay at a local hospital. There was a report about hexed pills at a fraternity party, so that'll be another line of inquiry. Otherwise, we have a few . . ." I looked down. If there was an easy way to imply that teachers of the university could be involved without offending said teachers, I wished I knew.

"There are other suspects involved with S&B who were close to either Dani or Maya whom we'd like to continue looking into, though I'd prefer not to say more until we have a definitive direction." I cringed at how soft my voice sounded.

Dr. Ellendale de Vries was in his usual lovely mood. "And did they provide some sort of reason that would make you suspicious? Anything you'd like to share with the class?"

"Give the girl a chance to conduct her investigation without you harping on her about every little thing," said Dr. Nguyen. She was wearing a bright yellow sweater with daisies on it, and a ball of yellow yarn was trailing off of it and darting behind her like a bee looking for a flower.

"I just don't want the two of them going around making accusations without adequate cause."

I swallowed. "There's nothing so far to tie them to hexes, but there are motives present for hurting either of the girls."

Ellendale was part of the reason I didn't want to go further into the details of the investigation. He'd already blocked his PhD students from talking to us, and it seemed like he was doing everything in his power to make the investigation more difficult for us. He'd had no classes with either Dani or Maya and, as far as I knew, no contact with them outside of school, but his disdain for the investigation was still an aggravating and perplexing obstacle we had to deal with.

"Dr. Oswold, you mean?" Dr. Robetresse asked. I knew she was unhappy about me looking into her, which was another reason I wasn't too thrilled about updating the council so publicly.

"A professor is a suspect?" Dr. Nguyen squeaked, the yarn unspooling behind her.

"But of course," Ellendale scowled. "The rumors this is going to cause, I swear, Thea. Who are the others? And where is Max?"

I wished Max was here almost as much as Ellendale did. If only because then I wouldn't have to go through the rest of this rapidly spiraling meeting alone. I tried to summon all my confidence, twist myself into someone they would want to listen to, into the version of myself that most suited everyone else. Someone braver, someone wittier, someone more believable somehow.

Just as I found myself cursing him for abandoning me to the wolves, the door opened, and there he was.

"Dr. Strauss would be the other suspect," he said, tipping his hat. "Excuse my tardiness, I do apologize."

He winked and touched the brim of his hat. "And there's no need to throw accusations at Cella. We're only doing the job that was asked of us by this council."

"Dr. Strauss? That's ridiculous," Ellendale sputtered, the hairs on his head shaking like tiny furious coils.

Dr. Nguyen shared a look with Robetresse, so quick and fleeting that I might've imagined it.

"What evidence do you have?" asked Ellendale.

My pulse beat in my throat. The light flickering from the ornate iron chandelier cast a hungry gleam on all their faces.

Dr. Nguyen's yarn flitted back and forth, frantically trying to catch the information flying by too quickly to process. Ellendale's TA had both forearms propped up on the table, watching the scene with keen interest. Dr. Perez frowned in the corner. And Luce looked like the only thing she was missing was a bowl of popcorn.

Max sent a tendril of Magic to calm me down. Gentle waves coursed through me, the smell of saddle leather, the warm breath of horses. I took a deep breath.

"I could walk you all through my process. Maybe that would help," I said.

"Please," said Dr. Robetresse.

I nodded. "So, with object analysis, we're looking for things that might raise suspicion or point toward who might be responsible. That generally falls into three categories: First, if the person's object has something in common with the hex. This might not be as obvious as it sounds. It's not straightforward how people shape their will around their objects. Magic is a tricky thing. In this case, we're looking for an object that might inspire violence. A weapon, perhaps, or something that might be used as one. Perhaps something that flies or levitates, as levitation is one of Dani's most visible symptoms. The object could also be scarred in a way that mirrors the scarring on Dani's skin."

"Something that might be used as a weapon?" Ellendale scoffed. "For God's sake, I could use a stapler as a weapon. I could use my abacus as a weapon. Does that make me a suspect?"

"Ellendale, please," Dr. Robetresse said.✤

Somehow, I doubted that Max would be met with the same

✤ Truth be told, I wasn't entirely comfortable with this whole thing either. I didn't blame Ellendale for wanting more control over the investigation, especially with Tweedledee and Tweedledum playing spin the bottle with their suspects and accusing members of the council. It'd be just my luck for Cella to try to pin the whole goddamn thing on me now, when I was on the verge of the biggest breakthrough of my career.

chagrin by Ellendale if he was giving this speech. I was reminded of all the conferences I'd been to with Max. Every time someone came up to talk to us and directed their questions at Max, assuming I was his assistant, or his date. Offering him a nice, firm handshake while I got a polite nod. Or a wave.

But I gritted my teeth and continued. "The second thing we're looking for is inconsistency. If the object behaves in a manner that's at odds with what its owner is saying or how they're acting, it could indicate there's something the person is trying to hide. Objects, intentionally or not, tend to betray their owners in one way or another."

I thought back to the notes coming off Dr. Oswold's objects: completely frazzled, exhibiting a total unsurety of even what they were—at complete odds with the calm, collected professor.

"And lastly, what happened to Maya was an incredibly violent act. I hesitate to believe the culprit intended it to go as far as it did. In which case, the person's object may indicate some degree of guilt or inner turmoil, even if the person is less obvious in portraying said guilt. This may manifest in damage to the object, such as cracks, splinters, smoking, or malfunctioning, a model airplane with torn wings, a kettle that refuses to boil, et cetera."

An image popped into my head of the little statue in Strauss's office, with its head and legs lopped clear off. He'd been trying to fix it—and hide from us the damage done to it.

"And how would you know all this about an object? It's not like they bloody well speak," Ellendale asked.

"Well, in a way, they do. I've studied notes in objects for years. You're welcome to have a look at my paper on the subject."

Dr. Robetresse nodded. "That's quite enough evidence for me. I thank you both for the update. I'm sure we all have quite a bit to mull over. As always, if—"

Max tilted his hat back. "One more thing. Why was Dr. Strauss removed from this council?"

Dr. Robetresse arched an eyebrow. "That is a private matter unrelated to this investigation."

"Pardon my French, ma'am, but the hell it is. We have a right to know."

Dr. Robetresse gave him a withering stare. "Again, I thank you both for your update on the investigation. As always, if anyone has any new information, I'd like to discuss it here."

Ellendale nodded in agreement.

"Yeah, discuss it here," Max murmured after the meeting, once everyone had cleared off, "so they can do damage control beforehand. So they can protect their own."

"Robetresse is protecting him."

"Yeah, and she's not the only one," Max said.

I nodded, catching his train of thought. "Ellendale."

CHAPTER SEVENTEEN

After the meeting, I told Max I would catch up with him. Then I slumped, going through my mandatory self-assessment after every social encounter. I mentally replayed everything I'd said and cringed, straining to identify how I could have better articulated this or that.

I caught sight of Ellendale's TA walking out and steeled the last remnants of my social energy. Maybe he had some insight into why Ellendale was so hell-bent on blocking the investigation. Or why he was so irate at our suspicions of Dr. Strauss. Maybe Ellendale had seen something . . . or knew something and didn't want to say.

"Hi. Basile, right? Can I talk to you?" I shoved out my hand. "I know you don't know me, but I'm . . ."

Basile was terribly good-looking, with dark hair that was smoothed back, a long, elegant nose, and kind eyes. He watched me, a furtive smile starting to build.

"The youngest council member of an arcane school in a century. Responsible for discovering an entirely new branch of Object Theory and Magic study. Countless publications—I know people who've been assigned the readings for class and can barely keep up. Set a car on fire when it wasn't even part of your objects! Not to mention, one of the strongest practitioners of Magic in a decade—and you just leave it all behind"—he snapped his fingers—"like that. Of course, I know who you are." He shook his head. "You don't give yourself nearly enough credit."

I snorted and played with my earrings. "It's not really me doing all that. I mean, Max . . ."

He opened the door to the world outside. It was still early, not yet noon, and a cool breeze drifted over my neck and arms. From a nearby building wind chimes sounded.

"Don't you let anyone here make you think less of yourself. If Ellendale left campus this second, Robetresse wouldn't spare a minute grieving him, much less beg him to come back. Actually, she might even cry tears of joy."

I chuckled. A group of girls walking by waved, skirting a cluster of agaves. "Basile!" one of them shouted, and he waved back, flashing a warm smile.

"That's part of the reason I stopped you, actually. Mind if I walk with you?"

"Certainly." I felt like a bobblehead standing next to a movie star. There wasn't a person we passed who didn't wave or at least acknowledge Basile. Many of them treated him with an almost reverent air. There was something intangible about him, some illuminating quality that I couldn't quite put into words. He had an eloquent way of speaking and a low voice as smooth as velvet. I could have sworn a girl pulled out her phone when we passed and started recording us. I slapped my hands over my face in the chillest way possible.

Basile looked over at me and frowned. "You okay?"

"Absolutely," I said, slowly removing my hands from my face. "Actually, I was hoping I could ask you a few questions about Ellendale."

He blew out his cheeks, dark eyes glittering mischievously. "Oh, boy. You're putting me in hot water here, asking me to rat on my boss. He's got such a bug up his ass about the two of you and this investigation."

I cast a glance at the students passing us. "That's what I'd like to understand," I said, lowering my voice. He gestured to a breezeway between two buildings, supported by rough wooden columns. We stopped in a spot that offered at least a little privacy, our backs pressed against stone. "Why is he so bothered by it?"

Basile's own voice lowered. "He finds out I talked to you, and I'll never hear the end of it."

I turned toward him, the air between us packed so tightly with heat I could barely breathe. His scent wafted over me, a delicious, smoky combination of anise and lime. Even the frizzy pieces of my own hair seemed to drift toward him, drawn to whatever product he must have used to slick his hair back. "But you don't think Ellendale had anything to do with this?"

"Of course not."

Along the border of the breezeway were poppies and scorpionweed, the same purple wildflowers that grew in fields nearby. Absentmindedly I picked one of them, running my thumb over the petals. "Then is it Strauss? Is he trying to protect him? Does Ellendale know something?"

He looked around, ushering me out of our hiding place as other people passed under the breezeway. We crossed the breezeway toward the Arts building, full of the chatter of students and the sharp tap of footsteps on stone.

"Ellendale and Strauss are old friends. I know there are connections to Ellendale's research funding with some of Strauss's colleagues at Harvard, but I don't know. I guess if he believed Strauss was guilty, or if Strauss said something, that would be a reason to not want your investigation to go further . . ." He shook his head. "But he hasn't said anything to me that would suggest that. This is all conjecture, and this conversation stays strictly between us, please."

While we walked, he shortened his stride so we'd keep the same pace, and I liked the way he squared his shoulders to face me when he answered my questions, his steady brown eyes meeting mine. He had a pleasant way about him, a gentle smoothness to his mannerisms. When he spoke, his voice was liquid and melodic. I found myself enjoying listening to it.

"What about your fraternity? Was Dani a member? Some guys on the hall said she used to hang around." One of the seniors had thought he'd seen Dani around them once. It was a lead we had to follow up on, but I wasn't exactly optimistic. The guy had complained he didn't like the frat's "shit taste in beer."

He thought for a moment. "Dani came to exactly one meeting, and then I think we scared her off. Too many guys slobbering over a girl who liked math. It sucks. I always wonder if she'd joined the fraternity, maybe we could have . . . I don't know, protected her or something. Maybe that's stupid."

"I don't think that's stupid at all. But how could she join as a female student?"

"We're a gender-inclusive group. We try to have a very welcoming environment."

"I see, and how was Dani at the meeting?"

"She was quiet. I think she was overwhelmed; the guys can be a little spirited once they get going, but she seemed normal. If you're wondering if there was any indication that she might go full *Exorcist* on us, then no. There wasn't." He looked away. "Sorry, the whole thing just makes me sad, you know?"

"Me too." I looked down. I hated this part, that I had to ask people over and over again to rehash minute details about something so horrible. "And she didn't come to any meetings after that one?"

"She put her name down for the list-serve, but no. I didn't see her again until they were taking her to Maritza's."

"Okay."

We'd reached the Phi Kat house at the far side of campus, an old Victorian structure that must've been built some years after the school's main house.* The staircase creaked, and the

---

* I was no expert in Magical architecture, but I guessed it must have been the home of the Ludlow children's governess or perhaps a village schoolteacher. The architecture program at S&B was woefully understaffed, and I knew Dr. R wanted someone desperately to help with some of the failing buildings. But Magic didn't necessarily mean great wealth or power anymore, and it definitely didn't command a great salary. The last few centuries had made sure of that, had made sure that few people, if any, wanted to identify as practitioners of Magic.

roof leaked murky water onto the porch. In the corner, a forgotten swing hung by one end while the other half rested on peeling floorboards.

"You know," Basile said, "I think our treasurer has the notes for that meeting still, if you want them."

"That would be great."

"Come on in," he said, beckoning me up the stairs. "You can wait in my office."

The inside of the Phi Kat house was less dreary. Walls were filled with old-school DnD posters and video-game apparel. Headsets and game controllers were set around a giant TV that faced a beat-up leather couch. Empty beer bottles cluttered up the coffee table. Very bachelor pad.

"Hey, what's up?" a tall, brown-haired boy said as he headed out the door.

"That's Paul," Basile explained. "He's Phi Kat's vice president. You might see him flit in and out of the council meetings. He's doing a work study with Dr. R."

"Excuse the mess," he said, directing me away from what looked like soccer equipment, waving to a couple of guys in the kitchen. "It's not exactly awesome living with undergrads, but don't tell them I said that." He chuckled. "But free room and board as president of the fraternity while I try to finish my dissertation? Not a bad trade."

I tucked my hair behind my ear, glad I'd washed it today, though I don't think the guys in the house minded one way or another. Their eyes ran appreciatively down my frame. I swallowed and tried not to trip.

He showed me to his office, which was little more than a converted broom closet. "Be right back," he said, and a few seconds later, I heard the thump of his footsteps up the stairs. "Hey, Grant!" he called from somewhere above me.

The office-closet was crammed with posters of mathematics and robotics competitions from the last couple of years, and a large poster of a symbol that looked a little like a misshapen integral. There was a typewriter on a desk that was so cluttered with papers it looked like a fire hazard.

"Here you are," he said, handing me a piece of paper when he returned a few minutes later. I still hadn't sat down, opting instead to stand against the door, and now he'd almost run into me.

"Your treasurer's name is Grant? As in Grant Hafer?"

"Yeah, you know him?"

I shook my head. "Not exactly. But thanks a lot for this." All of a sudden, I didn't want the conversation to end. He was another person my age at this school besides Max and Luce, another scholar, another person who lost himself in his studies like me. I blurted the first thing I could think of. "Kat is not a Greek character."

Basile's eyes lit up, and I flushed. "No, it's not. It stands for καθαρός, Katharos." He sat down at the chair behind the desk, thumb absentmindedly running over his bottom lip. "*Philosopho, katharí psychí.* Lover of wisdom, pure of soul. Truth be told, we're not as much of a frat as a glorified math club. We've won the tri-state mathematics competition for the last three years in a row, and we participate in this local outreach of robotics and mathematics programs for elementary and middle-school kids. Since we get a lot of donors and alumni looking to help out, the school let us have a house on campus. This poster here"—he pointed to the symbol on the poster of two intertwined snakes that branched in two different directions—"a graphic designer alum designed it for us a couple of years ago. It's a play on an integral. I know, bunch of nerds, right? We're lucky anyone comes to our parties." He chuckled.

I shrugged. "You don't strike me as the giant nerd type."

"What does a nerd look like, I wonder?" He smiled good-naturedly.

I blushed profusely. "God, that was so rude, I'm sorry."

He tucked his hands in his pockets and rocked back, dark eyes dancing with mirth. "There's no need to apologize."

I slipped a lock of hair behind my ear. "Well, I should really get going," I said, waving the paper around like an idiot. "This is really helpful, super helpful. Thanks—thank you for this."

He laughed and walked me out of the cramped office, which seemed to be shrinking the more I talked. I sidled past him in the confined space, our shoulders brushing against each other. I held mine rigid so we didn't accidentally touch again.

He laughed again, not unkindly. "Any time, and if you need anything else, don't be a stranger."

"*Blargh!*" I blurted the minute I was out the door and down the steps, trying to will everything dumb I'd said out of my head. What was wrong with me? I shook my head as I walked away, feeling a little like I'd woken from a dream.

In the interest of having a complete record, I've added several of Danica's shorter journal entries below. They do give some indication of her state of mind, I think, which seems to change radically in a short period of time. These take place roughly one month before the murder, from the period of February 25th to March 3rd.

FEBRUARY 25TH

when nyx was born, I became

nyktipoloi

when you were born, I became

whole

FEBRUARY 26TH

It's like you breathed me into life,

What was once monad, dyad

((((Your soul is immortal))))

March 2ⁿᵈ

Your name means ignorance, did you know that? It means the veil that covers our real nature and the reality of the world around us.

((((Your soul is imprisoned))))

March 4ᵀᴴ

Do I scare you? I know I do. I see it in the way you look at me.

CHAPTER EIGHTEEN

The next day, I was in the library, scrolling through my phone. The last page open was Basile's Instagram. He was all over TikTok, Instagram, Twitter. Anywhere people congregated online, he was there, stirring up publicity (and funding, presumably) for his theory, the Reality Paradox. And so were hundreds, thousands of other people, watching him. At first, I'd just watched a few of his TikToks. After our meeting, I'd wanted to know more about him, but the more I watched, the more I got sucked in. His eyes grew wide, swelling with passion as he spoke in his deep, velvety voice. He was different from a normal person, somehow more beautiful, more eloquent, like he'd been sculpted straight from stone. Many of his clips were set to the songs of a young rapper who'd died last year, at only twenty-one. The two worked well together, Basile's ideas that death wasn't the end, and the dulcet tones of the rapper, known for his melancholic verses that intermingled sadness with hope. Basile believed in reincarnation. He believed and spoke often of the world beyond this one, the one he'd supposedly proven with a rather complicated combination of physics and mathematics. I confess the calculations were over my head, and I don't think I was the only one. But his fans weren't there for that, their attitude reflected in a favorite saying among them: *It's not just math, it's a movement.* The fans loved his videos, seeing their pain reflected back at them. He spoke to a generation who felt lost and powerless, young people who were searching desperately for a shred of hope of an escape from this life, that there was something better out there.

A lot of them had strange spiritual practices, because, after all, if there were other worlds, what was to say they had to be Heaven and Hell? They shirked the traditional ideas of religion and embraced a polytheistic collection of gods, taking bits and pieces of religions from around the world. They worshipped the old gods, some very old, of the Orphic pantheon, bringing back the polytheism of Western culture that had long been buried.

I'd gone to his page several times now, whenever I was anxious or stressed, and found that just listening to him talk about other worlds soothed my mind, made it so my thoughts didn't come streaming in, bouncing all around my head. The idea was so intriguing to me. A world where things could be different, where you weren't judged for your past, where your colossal fuckups had never happened. The chance of a clean slate. It was almost too compelling to resist.

I returned from lunch to find Max methodically tearing up a sheet of paper into tiny little pieces.

I arched an eyebrow. "You okay? I can sense you from the door."

"I'm fine," he grunted, brushing the paper into a waste bin. He was wound as tight as a coil, his aura* hissing like spurts of electricity.

"You know, it's okay to have feelings. It's bothering me, too."

He always did that, acted like having emotions was somehow a burden to other people. Like if he wasn't perfect, shiny, happy Max all the time, all the love anyone had for him would get sucked through a window.

---

* There is some debate about this among those who have studied dimidiums. Because we can sense the Magic aura of our partner, their emotions, and the threads of Magic around them, it is believed dimidiums are more sensitive to the presence of Magic in general. That would perhaps explain why it's easier for us to sense the Magic around objects, and why I can hear an object's notes while other people can't.

He grunted again. "I'm gonna get a coffee. You want anything?"

I shook my head. I knew the investigation was getting to him. We'd been stonewalled ever since the council meeting. Strauss was avoiding us as much as possible, Dr. Oswold was conveniently out of the office for the next week, and other teachers wouldn't answer a single question about either of them. As for students, we couldn't find a single person on campus who'd encountered any kind of hexed pill.

Our time was dwindling down, an ever-present hourglass in my mind's eye. The police had already come sniffing around again—Dr. Robetresse couldn't keep them at bay forever. Dani's body couldn't withstand whatever this was for much longer. And graduation was looming. Dread made me sick to my stomach. If we didn't find the culprit before then, we might never find them.

As for Dani, no matter how hard I tried not to imagine her, I couldn't. She'd become a more regular occurrence in my nightmares.

They were strange dreams, watery and dark, where I wandered around and around, feet slapping against puddles, desperately searching for something down long and winding corridors, straining my eyes to make out something, anything, that would contrast against the dim. She was there, too, but she never said anything. Just stood there watching, her hair limp around her face. Lips bloodless, skin marred and bruised. Silent as the grave.

To make up for our lack of progress, I started spending more time in the library; Vern left out cups of black tea with honey for me that went cold as I hunted through the shelves. Night after night, I sat there, reading page after page on curses. How long they could last, any obvious effects on the caster. It got so bad I had to start carrying eye drops whenever I left the dim lighting of the library.

Sometimes Max was there, sometimes not. Half the time, he was running down Ellendale's funding sources, trying to find a link between them and Strauss's colleagues at Harvard. He had a theory Strauss had bankrolled one of Ellendale's research projects, and now, out of loyalty, Ellendale was trying to impede our investigation so we didn't discover proof of Strauss's guilt. Or he was at the hospital, desperately trying to sweet-talk a nurse into giving up Joselyn's toxicology screening. Truth be told, I think he wanted to prove to me more than to anyone that we were doing a good job, that we were making progress, despite the mounting evidence to the contrary.

I couldn't fault him for it; he was so damned determined about it all.

Sometimes, he had to leave to check on his horses or things back at home. Other times, I assumed, he was seeing his girlfriend. He'd come back afterward, eyes red, the faint smell of alcohol on his breath. I'd ask him what was the matter, but he'd just shake his head.

Once, he came in on a Saturday night because he'd left his phone. "What are you doing in here? I thought we said we were going to meet up tomorrow."

In truth, I think he was a little baffled by my work ethic. Max had always had people who cared about him. He never had to worry about being someone like Dani, wasting away in a cold room while everyone just hoped he would die and get it over with. He'd never had people gossip or think he was stuck-up because he was quiet or just had a face that people thought looked kind of bitchy.

But I did.

I knew what it felt like to be a Dani, to be an Aaron. To run yourself ragged trying to be kinder, or smarter, or more charming, or just *better*. To work your ass off and still be overlooked in favor of the charming, beautiful people of the world.

Max was part of me, but this was something he would never understand.

Field Journal of Dr. Luce Montgomery

I've been spending more time with Basile lately. He's been helping me look for the fungi and with testing a fungal salve for Dani's skin. No luck as of yet with either—though, to be honest, I think we're both just looking for more excuses to spend time together. He's an interesting creature, is practically running the math department since Ellendale is on some vendetta against the world. I feel terrible for him. Some part of me thinks Basile's drummed up all this attention for his theory just to get the attention of the one person whose approval he desperately wants. I don't have the heart to tell him I think he's fighting a losing battle. It's obvious Dr. de Vries has spiraled too far into the role of old-man-yells-at-cloud.

Key observations:

I haven't made as much progress as I'd hoped. The desert isn't exactly a haven for mushrooms, and my hand is getting a lot worse. There are spidery streaks creeping up my forearm that I didn't notice before.

Or are you just losing more of yourself?

Sometimes, I wonder if it's just another side effect of the fungi. Is this how a tree feels when the mycelium's hyphae slowly start to intertwine with its roots? Whispering in that earthy voice, light as wind rustling leaves, *It's a gift. We're here to help.*

I left Basile's late, slipped out of the Phi Kat house while he was sleeping. Even though it was dark, I could've sworn I saw one of my coworkers, Dr. Oswold, sneaking out of her office with a stack of papers under her arm. Not sure what business she had that necessitated the late hour; she certainly appeared to wish not to be seen, but it's certainly none of mine. I've got my own problems to worry about.

Ones that seem to be growing.

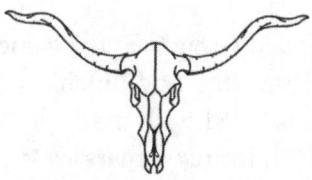

CHAPTER NINETEEN

After nearly three days of no breaks, Max came into the library with a strut in his step like he'd just won the lottery.

"Who's your Daddy?" he said, wiggling his eyebrows before slipping the toxicology report under my nose.

"Do I even want to know how you got this . . . ?"

"Probably not. The act's illegal on three continents." He winked, and I made a face.

"Kidding. My mom made her famous peach pie. Always a hit."

"God bless Mrs. Middlemore."

"And maybe a little help from our favorite jeans."

"Oh God, not the supertight ones? You still have those?"

He wiggled his eyebrows again. "What? Jealous I'm not wearing them for you?"

I rolled my eyes and reached around him for the report. "Give me that."

"No drugs in her system. Alcohol under the legal limit," he said.

"So she wasn't under the influence of anything. Anything non-Magical, at least," I said.

"I also asked around to some of the Chemistry and EEMM majors. Hexed pills are definitely possible, though none of them know anything about campus drug deals other than weed and some caffeine pills."

I raised an eyebrow. "You've been busy."

"And that's not all I found," he said, taking out his phone. "Grant Hafer's social media pages."

The picture showed a white guy with beady eyes and a short

black beard. He looked straight at the camera, unsmiling, like he was daring the cameraman to flinch.

Grant's page was filled with math proofs, offensive jokes, and a number of conspiracy theories reposted from other accounts.

"Gross."

He tapped his finger on the screen. "And look at this."

"What is that? A meme?"

"If it is, he's got a dog-shit sense of humor."

It was Maya's face photoshopped onto a person wandering down a path that split into two. The one on the right side went through a patch of green grass beneath a shimmering sun and a river of clear water. On the left was a darker path full of upturned nails and a river full of toxic sludge. A murderous clown hid behind a tree with a saw. Maya chose the worse path—stepping on rusty nails, heading right toward the tree with the hidden clown, a stupid smile plastered on her face.

Above the meme, a caption read: RECEIVE NOT A SWALLOW IN YOUR HOUSE . . . SHE COULDN'T SWALLOW FOR SHIT ANYWAY.

The comments were filled with a string of laughing emojis from other accounts.

"That's disgusting."

"Look at the date," Max said.

"Two days after Maya's death."

Our eyebrows raised, and I knew what we were both thinking without saying it.

Max nodded. "I'd say Mr. Hafer just moved to the top of our suspect list."

CHAPTER TWENTY

The Ex

When we went to the Phi Kat house to question Grant, he wasn't there. Basile was.

"It's good to see you again, Cella," he said and gestured us inside. "Grant's not here, I'm afraid, but I'd be happy to try and help if I can."

As we faced each other in the living room, beer bottles on the coffee table and the faint smell of sweaty soccer gear in the air, I couldn't help but notice the contrast between the two men. Max appeared to be nearly Basile's opposite. Where Max was rough, Basile was smooth, in his pressed trousers and airy shirts, unbuttoned at the top so you could just see a sliver of his chest. Max wore a hat because his hair was a mess most of the time, while Basile's was polished and perfectly arranged. Max smelled like rain and hard earth and the outdoors, Basile like expensive cologne. Basile had dark circles beneath his eyes and hands that were smudged with ink. He looked like he'd been grading papers until the early hours of the morning. As for Max . . . well, to be honest, Max always looked a little disheveled and feral, like he'd just had sex.

As if he knew what I was thinking, Max smiled roguishly.

"Can I get you anything? Coffee? Water?" Basile asked, directing the question to me.

"I'm okay, thanks," I said, trying to ignore Max raising his eyebrows and gesturing at his jeans. "We were hoping you could tell us about Grant Hafer. How did he know Maya?" I asked.

"Of course." Basile set down his cappuccino. "Before we

go in, if I could ask you to remove your shoes?" His nose crinkled at Max. Max had just driven over from the ranch and had dirt splattered across his jeans and caked on his boots. "We don't usually have workers trudge through the house. They're the original floors. I'm sure you understand."

A flush crept up Max's neck. "Sure thing."

We followed Basile and sat down on the sofa. "Grant and Maya were high school sweethearts. He actually proposed to her here, sophomore year. They broke up shortly afterward."

Max glanced at me, his expression as shocked as mine. How had this not come out earlier?

"What happened after that?" I asked.

Basile shrugged. "And then Maya was single for a while. Went to parties, enjoyed her time as a college girl."

Max lifted an eyebrow. "Huh. Guessing Grant wasn't too happy about that."

Basile rubbed the back of his neck; he tapped his fingers against his knee. A tremor in his statuesque calm. "No, he wasn't, but it's not as if she was terribly discreet or gave any thought to his feelings. I'm not saying it was right, but I understand why he felt the way he did."

"Her sophomore-year roommate mentioned threatening notes," I said. "Guessing that was Grant."

Max leaned back. "Sounds like your boy had a case of small-dick syndrome."

Basile's expression darkened.

"How far did it go?" I asked.

Basile grimaced. "He called her a whore. Look, I know how it sounds," he said when Max and I exchanged a glance, "but he's all talk. Grant's not dangerous. He'd never actually do anything—"

"But obviously he had some animosity toward Dani," Max said.

"Dani and Maya started dating nearly a year after all this happened. Grant was over it at that point."

"Doesn't sound like he was over it to me." Max showed

him the meme on his phone. "I'd like to know what you make of this."

Basile leaned forward to grab the phone, accidentally brushing against my knee. "Sorry," his lips murmured. I traced the cut of his jaw, his long nose, every inch of him regal and refined. I could feel Max's eyes on me and cut my glance away.

Basile studied the image for a moment and winced. "Obviously, it's not good."

"You're tellin' me. It was posted two days after her death. What's it mean?"

"Well, I should think there are some obvious implications . . ."

"We understand the reference," Max said, a little more sharply than was warranted. "We mean the first part. The cryptic 'Receive not a swallow in your house.'"

Basile sighed, his shoulders rocking back, legs spreading. "You must understand, we think of Phi Kat as a well-rounded organization, well-versed in culture, the arts, literature, philosophy, science, math. Renaissance men, if you will. I imagine it's in reference to some obscure bit of philosophy. Grant has the tendency to be a bit pretentious when he wants, and he likes to speak in codes. Though what the full meaning of it is, I couldn't tell you. He often finds rather colorful ways to insult people."

"He thought she was dumb," I said.

"Grant thinks everyone is dumb. But please, that has no bearing on the rest of Phi Katharos. It's just his nature. He comes from a very long line of Magical families, straight from Princeton. He's doing a split degree program to study under Professor de Vries on his way to his PhD. He'll probably spend his entire life in academia, sneering down at people. It's what he likes best. I'm not saying he's perfect, and he can be downright cruel when he wants, but please, believe me when I say this: He is not dangerous."

He looked imploringly at me when he said it, as if I was the more reasonable of the two of us.

"Uh huh," Max said. "Look, your Phi Kataros fellas—"

"Katharos," Basile said, correcting his pronunciation.

The cord stuck out in Max's neck. "Katharos," he spat.

While a part of me wanted to believe Basile—a very large part—I recognized this for what it was: damage control. Spinning it in a way that, while not looking exactly rosy for Grant, at least would absolve him from any wrongdoing or criminal action. But that made sense, too. Not only was Grant Basile's friend, but his involvement would also look bad for the entire organization, something that Basile had no doubt poured countless hours of his time into. He gathered volunteers for outreach projects. He put on conferences. Whatever he said, it was clear he cared about this fraternity-not-fraternity of his. I imagined he would do quite a bit to protect it.

I wondered if Grant was even gone from the house, as Basile had said. Or if he was simply in an upstairs bedroom, lying low until we left.

A bell sounded across campus, signaling the noon hour. Students came barging into the house, dropping bags, rummaging in the fridge. We stood to leave.

"Thank you for this, Basile. This has been really helpful."

"Of course. And I'll talk to Grant," he said, directing that same hopeful gaze toward me. He barely spared a glance at Max. "We'll get this all sorted."

Basile lingered a moment on the porch. "Cella? Could you wait up a sec?"

Max was already at the bottom, staring at the dirt as though he'd like to pummel it.

"I was wondering . . . we were wondering if you'd give a talk to the brothers on your research in Object Theory? You have a lot of fans here. I know I'm not the only one who's a little star-struck around you." He scribbled against the inside of my palm with a Sharpie. "If that sounds like something you're interested in, here's my cell. Anytime; the offer doesn't expire."

"Oh," I said, tucking a hair behind my ear. "I don't know if Max will want to do that, with everything going on and all—"

"Oh, no," he said, smiling. "He's welcome to come, of course. But we're really more interested in hearing from you."

Me? It'd been so long since I got to talk about my research. And longer still since someone had approached me about it and not Max. Maybe the world wouldn't come crashing down if I were to admit that I missed my work, just a little bit.

"Sure. Um." I peered down at the numbers scrolled on the palm of my hand. "I'll get back to you."

Basile smiled warmly. "Please do."

I was quiet as we walked back, shaking rust-colored soil out of my sandals, even though Max could've bored a hole through my head with his staring. I knew he was just dying to know what we'd talked about.

"Renaissance men," he snorted. "What a pretentious ass."

He looked over, waiting for me to agree.

My head was a jumble of thoughts. Someone wanted to talk to *me*, about my research. Not just as an opener for Max, not as Max's sidekick.

Though in the back of my mind, I couldn't help wondering if what Basile wanted to hear about wasn't my research, but my catastrophic meltdown. The worst moment of my life.

The day I was called into Dr. Robetresse's office, and she calmly explained to me that my brother was dead, that they'd found him in his room, limp and cold. Only the night before, he'd come to my dorm room, asking if we could talk. To ask me for help, I'd realized later, but did I help him? Did I talk to him that night? No.

I was too busy fucking studying Magic.

When I'd walked out of Robetresse's office that day, everything was too sharp, too bright. The Magic flowed hot and steady. I could barely control it, could barely get a handle on my emotions. That's when I saw Luce. I remembered her sitting in her polka-dotted bra in Max's bed, and the twist of my stomach felt like the twinge of a knife.

I only remember bits and pieces after that. The flames, the desperate thumping against the car door, Dr. Perez shaking me to get me to stop. And everyone's eyes on me. Girls pulling their friends out of the way, people staring like I was some sort of animal, ready to tear out their throats.

I wasn't naïve. That's what the brothers wanted to know; it's what they all wanted to know. Why I did it—and how I was able to do it in the first place.

And yet I couldn't deny I was intrigued by Basile, by everything he represented. I wanted him to like me, wanted him to teach me more about his Reality Paradox, about what it could do. A world where your mistakes were erased, where things could be different . . . where maybe . . . where maybe my little brother hadn't killed himself.

Since we'd met, I could barely tear myself away from Basile's TikToks. I hated watching them, but I also couldn't stop. In part, I'd blamed social media for Aaron's death. I never liked how everything you posted was attached to that little fear in the back of your mind—will this flop? Every statement watered down to some easily digestible segment that had already been stated days before by someone else precisely so it wouldn't flop. The entire system encouraged sameness, every thought and image subjected to peer approval. That wasn't even mentioning what happened when you didn't get their approval. How the suicide rate of girls was at an all-time high. How every single like and comment you didn't get on a selfie or swimsuit picture subtly scraped away at your self-esteem, your self-worth subject to a jury of your peers. You want likes? Dance for the masses. Show us your tits so we can judge them. And how it must have been for someone like Aaron, a shy eighteen-year-old who wasn't classically handsome or entirely comfortable in front of a camera, who grew up thinking his worth was in his follower count. The sick way social media companies were beholden to nothing—no code of ethics or responsibility to the mental health and well-being of the public except through what they themselves established and in spite of the countless studies conducted by their own researchers that found the platforms directly responsible for the decline in mental health of their users. And instead of doing something to fix it, they tried to make it more contentious by testing adding downvotes, so now unpopular takes and the people who housed them could be bullied into oblivion.

And then they said, *Hey, how about we make a version for children?*

Despite the guilt and shame I felt, how with each swipe and scroll and little double tap I contributed to the same system that made my brother and countless other kids feel worthless, I couldn't keep my eyes off of Basile's posts. With a frenzied, compulsive fervor, I started counting myself one of his many fans, just another in a sea of numbers. The difference between six thousand likes and six thousand and one. I, along with thousands of others, Basile, waited with anticipation for new content to drop, for you to fill us with new words so we could drink from your cup like a god.

I turned to Max. "Mind if we meet up a bit later? I forgot to eat lunch."

"Sure," Max murmured. I could still feel his eyes on the back of my neck as I walked away. Like he'd give anything to pry open my head and figure out what I was thinking.

It was fine. Normal, in fact. I was an academician. It was only natural for me to want to know more about any groundbreaking theory.

CHAPTER TWENTY-ONE

I didn't tell Max, but I went to see Dani the next morning. Ever since the day at Maritza's, Max had obstinately refused to see Dani, and I knew if he found out he might barricade me in my room to stop me.

This time, I wasn't as naïve as the last. I listened to Maritza, and I only entered when she told me it was safe. I walked in as she was sweeping a bundle of herbs over Dani's body.

"Rue and basil," she explained. "My mother was a *curandera*, a folk healer."

Behind her, there was a table of lit candles and a shrine with a photograph of Don Pedrito Jaramillo.*

She saw my look of confusion. Also on the table were crosses and figures from Magiclore, ancient mystics, and early alchemists.

"There is more than one path to God."

"What does it do?" I asked, gesturing to the herbs.

"It's to retrieve her lost soul." She stored the bundle on a shelf, then said quietly, "She is calmer today, but the sedative has made her sleepy. I don't know if she will hear you."

"That's okay, I just wanted to sit with her, if that's alright."

Was I hoping something would come out of it? That she'd rasp out who was responsible in her sleep, without resorting to any of the gyrating or trying to throttle me to death like last time? Sure. But I also thought maybe she'd want some company.

She seemed weaker today. I sat beside her and held her hand, just talking to her like I'd want someone to talk to me if

---

* Nineteenth-century Mexican folk healer who emphasized a holistic approach to healing.

I was alone and scared. She didn't say anything back. Every so often a breath rattled her lungs.

I thought of the only post of Dani on her girlfriend's social media during their entire relationship together and of Dani's prized possession, her telescope. The telescope that had not been given to her by parents, but by a teacher at school. The council still hadn't called her parents, but at the same time, Dani's parents hadn't called here wondering why they hadn't heard from their daughter. I wondered if they were just two more people who overlooked her. I squeezed her hand a little tighter.

All of a sudden, the bed creaked like someone had applied weight to it. Dani lifted into the air, back arching, arms dangling behind her. I jerked my hand back and stood, breath catching in my throat.

"It's okay," Maritza said.

"Does she do this often?" I whispered, afraid that Dani would hear me, that somehow, she'd wake and become that terrible thing she was last time we were here.

"Once or twice a day, then she floats back again. I imagine her body doesn't have enough energy to sustain it."

It shouldn't have scared me so much, the levitation. Though it was levitation that was happening while she was unconscious . . . which shouldn't have been possible. None of this should've been possible.

When I came out of the cottage half an hour later, Max was waiting for me. His hat was tipped low over his face, and his lips were pulled in a firm line.

"Thought we were supposed to meet up. I didn't realize you were going to see Dani."

I pretended not to hear the disapproval in his voice. "Sorry, thought I still had some time," I said, shifting my weight.

He cleared his throat. "So, uh, how is she?"

"Not much change, a little weaker. Maritza's not staying in there anymore overnight, just watching over her in shifts with Dr. Nguyen and some other staff. I just hope Dani will be alright."

He seemed to want to say something but hesitated. A trail of ants marched just behind him, crawling up and under the lip of the doorframe. Max rubbed his hand over the back of his neck. "You shouldn't spend so much time with her, Cel; she's dangerous. And we're not here to fix her. We're here to figure out what happened so no one else gets hurt. We're here for the students."

"She is a student."

He yanked off his hat, ran his fingers quickly through his hair. "Cel, for God's sake. The truth is we're speculating here—we don't know what happened. We have no idea what happened to her, and no idea the residual Magic that could still be on her. We shouldn't spend time with her unless absolutely necessary."

"Right, got it. You'd rather she just died and became someone else's problem. Not enough glory in actually helping her, huh?"

He rubbed his temples, his eyes a slate-gray. "That's not what I said. Not to mention we're supposed to be working together on this. That doesn't work when you sneak off without me and question her. I know you have no issues with leaving me behind, but what if something happened to you in there?"

Ah. So that was what was actually bothering him.

"I know you're used to me being at your beck and call. But this is too important."

The back of my throat felt hot and dry, and I was tired, so tired, and everything rankled me all of sudden. It was perfectly fine for him to escape for hours on end to be with his girlfriend, but I couldn't visit the person we were trying to save. I felt the same white-hot prickle of annoyance that was in his aura. It all swirled around and around until we were a mass of tangled threads, festering in each other's irritation.

He ran his tongue over his teeth. "I never asked for you to

be at my beck and call. But is it too much to ask that we conduct the investigation together. As a team?"

I scoffed. "When have we ever been a team? It's always been the great Max Middlemore and whatever groupie tags along after him. Look, I'm sorry that my ambitions for my life weren't to be your housewife, but you're just going to have to get over it."

He sucked on his teeth, an angry red flush creeping up his throat. "She's not Aaron, Cella! Dani wasn't bullied into killing someone."

My chest went cold. He could've slapped me in the face and I wouldn't have been more surprised. My tone turned icy. "No, he was just bullied into killing himself, but thanks for bringing that up. I love thinking about it. Great to be reminded that I wasn't there for him."

He ran his hands down his face. "Shit, Cel, I'm sorry. That's not what I meant—"

I only saw red. "I'm not going to abandon her just because you and everyone else here thinks she deserves to burn in Hell. I've felt like an outcast before, too. Hated by nearly everyone, including you."

His mouth worked furiously to backpedal. "Now, hold on here. I have never hated you. Come on now, wait—" 👺

I stormed off before I had to listen to any more.

I should've figured we couldn't do this together, that we

👺 That was stupid, stupid, stupid. I know it. But goddamn, it felt like an uphill battle trying to get her to trust me again, to stop pulling away from me. And I was worried about her. I knew why she cared so much about that girl. Dani reminded her of Aaron. And if you'd seen her back then, you'd know no good would come out of Cella going back down that path. This investigation had done at least some good in bringing her back here, and I could see the light come back into her eyes when she dove into her old studies again. But I had to find a way to make it clear to her. Saving Dani wasn't going to bring him back, no matter how far she was willing to push herself over the edge.

couldn't work together for two freaking seconds without fighting. There was too much between us that had been built up and torn down again, and I was getting sick of thinking of it every time I looked at him.

Tomorrow, I would go back to the library, and I would stare at those damn books until I found out what had happened to her. I would search through every ounce of information they had on curses, on levitation, on hexes. Anything I could find—everything I could find.

But for now, I would sleep. And try not to imagine throwing a brick at Max's face.

I got to my dorm and closed the front door of House Torlaine too loudly behind me, causing the hinges to rattle.

"Shhh," came an angry voice from the front desk. My chest flared all over again.

Here I was, back at school, even though I was twenty-nine years old and long since graduated. I shut my own door with a snap and resolved to direct my fury toward helping Dani.

I was going to find out what was wrong with her, and Max or no Max, I'd damn well fix her, if it was the last thing I did.

CHAPTER TWENTY-TWO

I woke to a pitch-black room. My phone screen read 2:55 a.m.
The hair on the back of my head was damp. My skin was covered in a sticky film from the heat. I rubbed my forehead and sat up.

What woke me?

Bear wasn't at my feet. I squinted through the dark to the other edge of the room.

"Come here, boy," I said to the dark thing in the corner. But Bear didn't move, didn't even grumble in annoyance. I flashed my phone at him.

Bright pupils stared back at me, strange and alien-like in the artificial light. He flicked his tail once, then turned his back to me.

I lay back down, and it all came back in flashes. Another nightmare. One eerily similar to the day I'd had.

I was at Maritza's cottage with Dani, just like earlier in the day. Max was there, too, and Maritza in the corner. Everything felt hazy somehow, the way dreams feel liquid and warm, shadows of the real thing.

We walked over to Dani's bed. A thin line of ants preceded us, crawling up the dangling sheets and over her nightgown. I reached for her hand. Only this time, her eyes weren't closed. They were open and staring straight at the ceiling. When I touched her hand, her head snapped toward me, and her fingers clenched around mine.

I startled, drawing back. I tried to wrench my hand from hers but couldn't.

Let go, I tried to say. *Let go of me.*

Panic rose in my chest, but when I opened my mouth to scream, nothing came out. I kept trying to scream. *Help, someone! Please!* But even as I fought, the only thing that came out was a choked whisper. It was barely enough for even Dani to hear.

She leaned in, the trail of ants still marching up her neck and into her mouth through the corner of her lips.

A voice whispered in my head, twisting and curling. *Go on with your Magic spells and sorcery. Perhaps you will succeed, perhaps you will cause terror.*

Dani held fast to my hand.

"Dani? Is that you?"

She released my hand and leaned back, her face nearly black with hundreds of squirming ants. I looked at Max, who wasn't moving. He stared at the place where our hands had been.

"What does it mean?" I asked, and he didn't look up.

"Max?"

My voice felt watery and dark. An echo, one very far away.

"Max?"

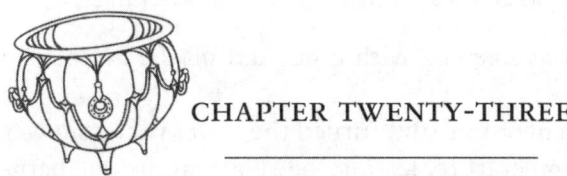

CHAPTER TWENTY-THREE

On my way back from breakfast the next morning, I passed Robetresse's office. The door was cracked, and I caught a glimpse of a huge wooden desk and hand-crafted oak chairs.* From inside came a man's clawing voice, raw with emotion.

"Please, I've already lost everything; you can't do this—"

Robetresse's own voice was strained and hushed. "It's too soon to reinstate you, Antony. The council would have a fit. Besides, you and I both know you're much too close to the girl."

"It was one mistake. Thea, please."

"I'm sorry."

I backpedaled at the thud of her boots and slipped behind a corner off the hallway.

Too close to what girl? To Dani? Was that why he was removed from the council? Dr. Robetresse had mentioned rumors of an inappropriate relationship between a council member and a student. What if it wasn't Maya, but Dani? She was excelling in her studies and was heading to MIT in the fall, glowing recommendation in hand. Dani and Strauss obviously

---

* Carved by herself, most likely. It was a known fact that when Dr. Robetresse left her career at Britton Arcane to start S&B under a new, safer kind of Magic practice, her old colleagues wrote her off almost overnight. I wondered sometimes if the saw and the knife she carried as her objects were something she'd chosen herself, as a defense against the jabs, against all the people who wanted to doubt what she was doing.

had a close relationship. And I hated to think it, hated to diminish her success in such a way, but the clock was ticking.

Maybe she *was* sleeping with him. And maybe . . . maybe she'd stopped.

I returned to my room and turned the water in the shower to the hottest temperature, letting the steam fill up the bathroom and shake loose the dust from my thoughts. I'd torn my nails to shreds these last few days, picked at them until the corners of my fingers were bloody and raw. I'd tried to kick the habit, but it always flared up when I was stressed out or wasn't sleeping enough. Which seemed to be about the only state I'd been in lately.

I pressed my hands to the wall, watching the rivulets of water streaking the glass. I liked to watch raindrops on windowpanes when I was a kid, how the tiny streams gathered droplets on their way past, picking up speed until they were barreling full speed ahead. Now one dribbled down, rolling past the letter H written in the condensation.

I stepped back.

Another letter was there next to the H. An O? This one was sloppier, as if waterdrops had splattered all over it. Then another, R.

I drew back and turned off the faucet. How had I not noticed the letters before? I wiped the water from my eyes, heart beating fast.

Unmistakable letters appeared now, all over the glass. Whether they'd been there all along or were just appearing now, I couldn't tell.

THROAT below the first word.

SLT(?) below that.

WINSTOS on the back wall.

HEL to the left.

BURN at the top.

And interspersed among all the letters was the number 1. Written over and over again.

I shut my eyes tight. "I'm tired," I whispered. "I'm just seeing things."

That was certainly more believable than the other option—that the last person who took a shower in here wrote a bunch of nonsense in the condensation. Not likely, seeing how the staff cleaned all the rooms at the end of each semester.

There was another option, though. One I didn't want to think of.

That someone had broken in and written words on the door to scare me. That someone didn't want me here. Someone who wanted to scare me so badly I'd leave. Strauss? Or maybe it was Rose Oswold. Ellendale? Maybe he'd bribed one of the RAs to open my room. He certainly hadn't made a secret of his disdain for everything I was doing here.

But that was ridiculous. Right?

I stepped out of the shower and toweled off. "I'm just tired."

Bear wasn't in the room. Max had started taking him with him when he drove back to the farm, said he liked the company. Bear seemed all too pleased with the arrangement.

I got dressed quickly, my movements jerky and nervous despite the pep talk I'd given myself. I yanked a comb through my hair, scanning the room every few seconds. I finally gave up and bolted out the door, jiggling the handle to make sure it was locked.

I looked up and down the hall to make sure there was no one there.

I was alone.

CHAPTER TWENTY-FOUR

"You've got a visitor," Vern said around noon. Max came in, ducking his shoulders, a guilty half smile on his lips. You couldn't stay mad at him, and he knew it. He nudged a small, plastic-wrapped item forward like a golden retriever apologizing for eating your favorite shoes. "Brought you a cookie."

I crossed my arms.

"I'm really sorry about last night," he said quietly. "What I said—I put my boot in my mouth. I wasn't there for you back then, when you needed me. And I can't take that back, but I swear, Cella, if something were to ever happen to you, I wouldn't survive it." He looked at me, his eyes a sharp cerulean, and my stomach did a little somersault. There it was again, that feeling of familiarity, of home. The feeling of his hands around my waist, that little jolt whenever we touched. The knowledge that I always knew what he was thinking, and he knew me, too. Knew all the secrets I tried to hide, all my insecurities.

And he knew exactly what sweet treat melted my cold, dead heart.

I unwrapped the plastic around the chocolate chip cookie and took a bite. "It's good," I said begrudgingly.

He beamed that classic Max grin, all blinding white teeth and dimples. "I picked the biggest one they had." He caught my gaze and held it. "I want to figure this thing out with Dani, too. Because you're right. Something happened to her, and we owe it to her to get to the bottom of it. All the stuff with us, and the past, is . . ." —he took a deep breath—"Dani. That's the most important thing."

"Well..." I slid him a pile of texts and took another bite. "If you're going to be here, I suppose I might as well put you to work."

He grinned. "Way ahead of you there," he said sheepishly. "I drove to Rose Oswold's old school this morning. And woohwee, the admins there sure love to gossip. You were right about her. Turns out she was fired for... drumroll please... casting a hex. Looks like dear old Rosie has a pattern of getting too close to her students, and things don't go too well when they don't return the sentiment."

I chewed the soft bits around the cookie, savoring its sweetness. "I found something, too." I recounted what I'd overheard this morning with Robetresse and Strauss.

"Robetresse probably told her not to come within a mile of here. Strauss, too," he said.

"We could look up the hex she cast, see if there are any similarities with the one on Dani. Then the council would have to listen."

Max nodded. The lines in his face were even more pronounced, black stubble shadowing his jawline. "I've been thinking, too. I want to go back and talk to Grant." 👺

"What makes you think he'll talk to us?"

"Because it looks bad if he doesn't. I know guys like this; they're going to be thinking two steps ahead of everybody. Or at least they think they are. He'll want to clear his name."

"Seems like the most logical next step. At the very least, he

---

👺 I'd fucked up with Basile last time. For so long, I'd been terrified that one day Cella was going to turn around and see how much of an idiot I really was. Think, *Damn, what did I do to deserve getting stuck with this guy?* Turned out she saw it anyway, even with how much I tried to hide it. But damned if I wasn't going to try and change her mind. I wanted to prove to her that, even though I fucked up things between us, I wasn't going to fuck up this investigation. Maybe, if we could solve this case, if we could figure this out together, she'd see that we weren't so god-awful together. Maybe this time, she'd stay.

doesn't have the council protecting him," I said, trying not to sound too eager to return to the Phi Kat house.

We found Grant rounding the steps to the Phi Kat house.

"Hey, there. Grant, right?" Max flashed that easy country smile and leaned on the staircase banister like he didn't have a care in the world. He didn't mention the investigation, of course, didn't bring up the meme. "Quite the commotion, huh? What do you make of all this?"

Grant took a hard look at both of us, then crossed his arms.

"Of my ex getting murdered, you mean," he said, and we were both stunned by the bluntness of his statement. But this wasn't a misstep. No, he looked at us both dead in the eye as he said it, looking slowly between the two of us to measure our reactions.

Grant wasn't what I expected. Where I thought I'd find sharpness, finely tailored clothes, and a curling lip, there was . . . not quite softness, but something else. A graphic T-shirt with an outline of Han Solo, hair that was just a smidge too long, eyes that were small and dark and penetrating. He was too short to be imposing and had an average build. On his face, he wore a carefully managed easiness that continued down his shoulders. Trying a little too hard, I think, to say, *Look all you want. I have nothing to hide.*

"I grieved the Maya that I knew and loved a long time ago," he said by way of explanation. "She hasn't been that person in years."

"So, no lingering feelings? No resentment, even after she left you?" Max asked. *And started dating a woman* lingered in the air. For a second, there was a tightness in his neck that passed just as quickly. It was so fast I could have imagined it. Max flashed him a quick, mollifying smile.

Grant raised an eyebrow, as if to say that would be nuts. "It's been two years. No, I'm not still pining for Maya."

I was tempted to believe him. After all, he seemed so calm, measured. Controlled.

But, all at once, the gruesome meme flashed against my eyelids, and the sick caption, and the reminder that here was the smart guy. He wasn't handsome or tall or particularly charming, but he was smart. And this whole buddy-buddy bit, lean in close and smile pretty, felt like part of the act. A way to get you to trust him.

"To tell you the truth, Maya rubbed a lot of people the wrong way. She always had to be the center of attention. Always had to one-up everyone. She always had to be having the most fun, the best time, have the best of everything. I know, don't speak ill of the dead and all that. I just thought it'd be better if you knew the real her."

And there it was. In just a few statements, he'd pivoted. *She'd rubbed a lot of people the wrong way . . . Anyone could be responsible; anyone could have held a grudge. But not me, look how easy I can talk about it all, look how over her I am.* My eyes narrowed.

"I always knew she was going to go too far one day."

The bluntness felt at first like he was simply being candid with us, that he was entirely open and only wanting to help. But no one's that open. Not with people they'd just met. And if Object Theory had taught me anything, it was that people were guarded.

I studied him, steadied my breathing, and reached out to his objects. I listened out for their hum.* Unlike Grant, they were not calm, cool, or measured. Their gentle buzzing was erratic—first quietly humming, then a series of loud pops like a car backfiring.

---

* By some definitions, the study of anthropology was the study of customary patterns in human behavior, thoughts, and feelings. One reoccurring pattern in humans: they lie. But objects were just things, weren't they? They had no reason for deceit. Luckily, most people carried their objects with them, so all it took was for me to quiet my breathing and listen for them.

Here was a guy pretending. The kind of guy who spent all his time bragging about how smart he was, but when you asked him to solve a problem that deviated even slightly from the standard set in the textbook he'd seen a thousand times, he was all mumbled excuses. The guy on Reddit telling everyone he could have done it. The one judging girls from behind a computer screen, turning them into soulless creatures with "an average face and small tits, 4/10."

But I was projecting. This was unfair. I'd known Grant Hafer for all of six minutes.

"Tell us about the pill you slipped Joselyn Hart," said Max.

Grant's jaw dropped, and I had to hide my snort as a coughing fit. Grant wasn't the only one who was clever, and Max's bullshit meter was one of the best I'd ever seen. Suddenly, I felt inexplicably proud of him. Proud of us. Who's young and incompetent now, Ellendale?

"Yeah, she told us about that chivalrous bit of chemistry. Tell me, is it often you find people have to be unconscious before they can stomach to be around you?"

Finally, a break in the calm façade. Grant blinked, and it was obvious Max had gotten to him. He took a steadying breath, trying to regain control of the situation. "I don't know what you're talking about."

Max leaned in. Grant tried to keep his easy posture, but I could see the tension in his shoulders, a tendon bulging in his neck.

"I didn't slip anyone anything. Joselyn's trying to shift the blame off herself. Have you even asked why they aren't roommates anymore? Or who was responsible for the threatening notes Dani kept finding on all her shit last year? All Joselyn, man. She's so jealous of Dani she can't even handle it."

"We confirmed with the girls on her hall that Joselyn was ill for several days after attending a party you also attended."

"Yeah, because she probably drank enough to sedate a bison. I was with my friends all night. I didn't even talk to her."

Max continued forward, using the crack in Grant's armor

as a wedge. "We believe Dani may have been hexed, and as someone with a passion for illegal medications, we thought you might be able to point us in the right direction. Perhaps Joselyn wasn't the only one you slipped a pill to."

"A hexed pill? What are you even talking about?"

"I suppose we could have a talk with your dealer instead..."

Just then, Basile opened the door. "Grant? Cella? What's going on?"

Max tried to hide the frost in his eyes, but the bite in his voice gave him away. "None of your concern."

Shit. I tried to grab Max's attention, tried to get him to relax, but there was that same dogged determination in his eyes. The need to prove that we could do this, work together again like old times. And maybe just a smidge of him wanting to prove to me and to the world that he was deserving of all the accolades and all the love it had given him.

Whatever it was, he wasn't about to let anyone get in his way.

Basile turned to me. "What is this?"

"We just wanted to ask him about the meme," I said.

Grant jumped at the chance for escape. "Last I checked, it wasn't illegal to make jokes," he gritted out.

"Only ones that don't lead to girls being killed," Max said dangerously. Foolishly, because now Basile's gaze flickered toward us, eyes wide with alarm.

Basile frowned, all paternal figure. A shining white knight rushing in to save his charge. He beckoned to Grant like a child, arms outstretched like he would shield him with his body. "I think that's enough for tonight."

Basile turned back after Grant was safely inside, propping the screened door with his arm. He hesitated on the doorstep. "If... if you would like to speak to him again, I think it best you go through our lawyer. I don't think the council intends to accuse any of its students of wrongdoing without ample evidence, and I don't think a simple meme warrants any of this."

When he shut the door on us, I sagged back against the railing, sliding down. "Well, that went well. You lost your cool."

His aura felt like a thunderstorm, hissing and swirling in a mass of dark clouds. "I wouldn't have if you didn't get all giddy when you see him, like some schoolgirl."

"Grant?" I snorted. "Yeah, the creepy incel is totally up my alley. I just can't control myself around him."

"Not him," he said, as we trudged back across the grounds. "Basile. Acting like he's some genius incarnate. Like he's Aristotle come back from the dead."

I swallowed. I thought I'd done a good enough job of hiding it, but there was only so much you could hide when you were tied together like Max and I were. "Actually, I'm more of a Plato girlie, myself. Aristotle's writings are an absolute menace to wade through . . ."

Max scowled and mumbled something about going to check on the horses.

"I'm kidding!" I said. But he'd already reached the parking lot and was climbing into his truck.

I returned to my room and took a hot shower. I'd scrubbed the shower door until my fingers were raw, and thankfully no new threats or bizarre words had appeared written in the condensation. I stared at my bare feet against the terra-cotta tiles, letting the water and steam wash all the stress and chaos over the last few days down the drain.

I didn't trust Grant. But Basile was Grant's friend, so what about him? Max didn't like or trust Basile, but I did. Not for the first time, our relationship as dimidiums led us in two entirely opposite directions. But something about Basile was different. I was convinced Max would see it too, in time.

I'd gone to one of Basile's talks on campus earlier in the week. It was amazing to see how he commanded a room with just his energy. People perched on the edge of their seat when he spoke, just to get a bit closer to him. He was a force all his own, and we were drawn to him like some myth straight out of the Greeks, with his glittering eyes and dark hair and his strong nose and sun-drenched skin. His face belonged on the back of coins, like some philosopher-king of old.

"Our world is subject to famine and disease," he'd said, loafers softly echoing across the auditorium stage. "It could perish in an instant. But we don't have to suffer that fate. There's another world. Changeless, eternal."

A woman leaned forward in the crowd, her eyes bulging wide. "Is it like Heaven? This other world?"

"Not exactly. Upon death, the highest level of sage will go there and live forever through his ideas. You see," he said, in his velvety voice, his eyes touching each member of his rapt audience, "our souls have always been immortal, and the immortal soul aspires to freedom even while the body holds it prisoner. But the purer your soul is, the closer you are to stopping the endless cycle of rebirth and death."

But while his face drew me in, it was his mind that held me. His discussions of mathematics, his thoughts on the world captivated me. It all just made so much sense. And I realized he was cunning, too, just like the crafty strategist Odysseus. Basile didn't use social media because he wanted to, but because it was the fastest, easiest way to reach an audience, and I couldn't deny that he deserved an audience. People needed to watch him; they needed to hear him speak. I watched him talk about how mathematics could unlock infinite possibilities, how we were so much more than this one life and all the mistakes we'd made while living it. I listened to Basile speak about how mathematics could change the world, and I believed him.

I believed he could do anything.

I'd never felt closer to death than during my time at Seinford and Brown. But watching Basile walk onto stage, hands pressed together, eyes pointed to Heaven, I'd never felt closer to God.

After the talk was over, he spotted me trying to slip out unnoticed.

"Cella! Great to see you, though I have to say I'm not surprised to see you here."

"I'm an academic. Curiosity comes with the territory."

"Of course. I only meant you're not the first person who's come to us grieving the loss of a loved one. Aaron was a kind soul. You both deserve a second chance."

I perked at the mention of him. I'd be lying if I said that very idea hadn't drawn me to the Reality Paradox in the first place.

"You think he's in that other world, then? That I could I reach him?"

"Whoa, now," he said, running a thumb over his bottom lip. "Let's not get ahead of ourselves. That's not something I can answer for you. I can only show you the way."

He watched me with his dark, glittering eyes, and I swallowed, licking my lips.

"But with the power that you already have as a dimidium, who knows what you could do? I hope to see you here again soon. There's so much that we could learn from each other."

CHAPTER TWENTY-FIVE

"Anything on curses taking place over the cycles of the moon? Could be something there?"

I'd looked up the hex Dr. Oswold had cast on the student at her former school, but it didn't have any similarities to Dani's. In fact, from what Max had reported from her previous school, Rose's spells were decidedly less serious. They included hexing her frenemy's phone to spam her contact list, making all their pink clothes bleed in the wash, a spell so their Starbucks order was always wrong. Nowhere near the same profile as the hex on Dani. That, combined with records confirming she was at a conference out of the country the week of Maya's murder, dropped her significantly down on our suspect list.

"Sure, maybe she's a werewolf," came the dry reply.

I'd recruited Vern's help, but he was exhausted, too. And when Vern was tired, he was even crankier than usual.

He looked sadly at the three-day old mascara smudged beneath my eyes and the threadbare sweater that, judging from the wide berth everyone gave me, was starting to smell. "I'll come up with another one if you tell me why you're killing yourself trying to do this."

"I'm not."

"Now you can pretend all you want, but it sure doesn't look like you've given up on people to me. All I see is you trying your damnedest to save that girl. Don't get me wrong; nothing warms my heart more than seeing you in your old studies again, but this is too much. You're pushing yourself too hard. One dead girl is enough, you should go back to your room. Rest. Eat. Bathe, for all our sakes."

Because I can't was what I wanted to say. There was a girl beneath the terrifying voice, and the levitating, and the blood, a girl who was probably alone and scared, and I couldn't bear to leave her. How different might things have been for Aaron if he'd had a friend? If there had been even one person who'd doggedly refused to leave his side?

My phone buzzed in my pocket. A blinking notification showed two missed calls from Mom. How she knew I was in town was beyond me.

I shoved it back in my pocket.

Vern arched an eyebrow. "You haven't seen them yet?"

I grunted.

"You can't avoid them forever. Seeing you would do her a world of good, Cella."

I blew out my cheeks. "Check on one more book for me, and I'll go get a sandwich. Deal?"

He only sighed and shuffled away down the aisles.

"What's that?" Max asked, sliding next to me. I stuffed the slip of paper in my pocket.

"Nothing. Got a headache."

I'd been finding notes at the table increasingly more often, strings of numbers that didn't make any sense to me. At first, I thought it was Vern, leaving Dewey Decimal codes for books to check or maybe even page numbers, but neither of those lined up. As far as I could tell, the numbers were gibberish. I considered briefly that it could be Max, but I couldn't take the way he'd been looking at me lately, a mixture of pity and confusion when he found I'd spent another night in the library. Somehow, I didn't think asking him if he was the one writing me nonsensical notes would help. I even hid behind the shelves a couple of times to see who was leaving them, but no one came into this corner of the library except for me, and I never saw who it was.

"Probably just the poor lighting in here," Max said.

"What?"

"Your headache." He cast me a funny look again. "You should get some fresh air."

I didn't want to admit how nervous I was, scared of all the things happening to me. I strived to be the girl with all the answers, but now I couldn't account for the dreams I was having, for the terrifying messages in my shower, for the carvings above my bed. Something was happening to me, and I was afraid.

"You know you can talk to me, right?" Max said, voice softening. "One of the perks of being a dimidium, you know. You don't have to go through any of this alone." 👹

"Why is everyone on my case today? Maybe you get too much fresh air," I snapped, hard enough for him to drop it.

👹 I was worried about Cella, and to tell the truth, I didn't like getting left behind all the time while her mind jumped from one thing to the next. I wished she'd just slow down so we could talk things out together, but she seemed hell-bent on racing ahead, leaving me behind in the dust.

Field Journal of Dr. Luce Montgomery

I went to see Basile at the Phi Kat house to ask if he wanted to go into the canyon with me. Every time I go down there looking for the fungus, I can hear chanting, loud enough to hear over the rush of the Cimarron River, though I can't pinpoint its location. Sometimes it seems like it's right around the rocks from me, but maybe it's just the way the sound echoes down there. Either way, I'm not eager to go alone. But when I stopped in to see him, he seemed preoccupied.

I was about to walk into Basile's bedroom when I heard voices. I hesitated, hovering outside the doorway.

"What were you thinking?" came Basile's smoky voice, low and deep and tinged with an emotion I hadn't witnessed on him before. I couldn't quite imagine his features all twisted in anger. "You know we can't afford this kind of negative attention right now. Not with the funding hanging on a string and Ellendale not taking an interest in anything."

"I didn't think they'd see it."

"You're right, you didn't think. You act like you're one of the greatest minds to ever bless our halls, but I swear you don't ever think."

"I'm sorry. I don't know what else to say."

"For how much shit you stirred, you'd better be."

I shifted my weight, and the floorboard beneath me squeaked loudly. Shit.

A pause, then, "Get out of here. I'll deal with you later."

I moved to the side of the door. Basile looked even more flustered than the boy who'd just walked out of the room.

I flicked my hair behind my shoulder and walked in. "What was that about?"

He sighed and rubbed his temples. "We have a meet in a few

months, and if we don't get any of Ellendale's funding, we'll have to do some serious fundraising of our own. I don't want to have to cancel; those kids have been preparing for months. And now Cella and Max are hounding us, thinking one of our members has something to do with that girl."

I quirked an eyebrow. "Well, do they?"

"No," he said emphatically. "Grant is just an idiot. Doesn't think before he talks, or posts. He's going to get himself into trouble one of these days."

He's lying.

It appeared as a whisper at the back of my mind, a voice I could no longer discern was the fungi or my own. Something about the way he turned his eyes down before looking at me or the way his heart sped up imperceptibly, something I shouldn't have noticed, something I shouldn't have been able to hear, yet somehow, I still knew . . .

Grant had done something, and Basile was trying to cover for him.

I left shortly after, resigned to going into the canyon alone.

Key observations: Perhaps my newfound spidey senses will help me locate *Agaricus cataphractus*? Lord knows, I've tried everything else.

CHAPTER TWENTY-SIX

The next morning, Max knocked on my door, swearing up and down he'd found a student who could turn the entire investigation on its head. I jumped up and grabbed my bag. "Then what are we waiting for?" We had little over a week left before graduation to figure all of this out, and I wasn't eager to waste any more time.

When we arrived at his room, the guy was hitting a bong with his friend and surrounded by a cloud of smoke. He fist-bumped us when we walked in. I looked dubiously at Max, who winced and clasped his hands together. *Just a couple minutes*, he mouthed.

"Honestly, if you're looking into anyone," Jack D was saying, after an exceptionally verbose explanation of his fish tank, the different species of fish inside, and what actors he thought they all looked like, "look into Grant Hafer."

Grant? That was the big revelation? I sighed. "We already talked to Grant, but we can't exactly question him without evidence."

"Evidence? What more do you need? The little dude was on an incel revenge trip. He was obsessed, man. He hated that Maya was dating a girl after him. Said she was loaning herself out to anyone who wanted it."

"Creepy and gross, but it's not exactly cold, hard proof," I said.

"Tell her what you told me about the party," Max said.

"Grant told me once that he wanted to fuck Dani to get back at Maya, that he'd 'fuck her straight.' Maya said he used to leave these freaky notes on her car."

I grimaced. "Still, I doubt Basile will let us talk to him without a lawyer."

Jack shook his limbs out as if he'd gotten a chill. "That whole frat gives me the creeps, man." His friend, who'd been sitting on a beanbag chair in the corner playing Super Smash Bros., nodded in agreement. "Creepy dudes, for real."

"What do you mean?" Max asked.

His friend spoke up. "They do fucked-up shit in the canyon. Cult shit."

"Cult shit?" Max repeated, voice lowering. "Like what?"

"You should talk to Emma."

"Who's Emma?" I asked.

Jack shook his head. "Emma Garcia. She lives in town, not a student, but hangs out sometimes. I told her not to hang around with them, bunch of fucking incels. Then, of course, what happened? They assaulted her at a party. She was so freaked out afterward that she stopped coming around. Wouldn't say a word about it, just up and left. Haven't seen her much since. She's supposed to be coming back soon; my buddy down the hall texted her, but she never answered."

Max clapped his hands. "You see?"

"See what, exactly?" I said.

"They're creeps, Cel! He's a creep."

"Please, not this again."

We'd been arguing about it for days. Max thought Basile was involved in what happened to Dani; I didn't.

It just didn't make sense to me that he would be involved. Even on the off chance that the two of them had had some sort of spat (though no evidence suggested they were anything more than passing acquaintances), someone like him didn't just go around hexing people. He didn't need to. With his allure, the way he could win people over, he was far more likely to recruit an enemy, to draw them over to his way of thinking, than to hex them. And I didn't entirely trust Max's judgment toward him, either. They came from different worlds, and I think Max was jealous of him, of his schooling, of the fact that he came from money. I wasn't sure quite what it was, but I wished he would stop. Basile could be an asset to the investigation, I just knew it, if only Max would give him a chance.

"Well then, let's settle this," said Max. "Let's figure out what happened to Emma Garcia."

As I climbed into Max's truck, I was hit with a wave of nostalgia. Bits and pieces of memories I'd been trying to hold back came surging in like a tidal wave. Strands of hair lifting and blowing out the open window, his hand wrapped over mine. A million forehead kisses set to the tune of Debussy's *Rêverie* or whatever other composer he was into at the time. How for three weeks in July, the air-conditioning was broken, so we only went out at night, cranked down the windows, and let the breeze ripple across our salt- and sweat-streaked skin. Kissing those same bits of salt and sweat off later, tumbling to the floor, sheets tangled around our ankles.

I squeezed my eyes shut, rolled the window back up, and cleared my throat loudly.

Driving through town hit me with another wave of it. That feeling of familiarity, knowing a place so well you could navigate it with your eyes closed, just by the sound of a neighbor's ranchera music or the smell of tires roasting in the sun at the old junkyard, the cheers and jostles coming from the rodeo arena that had seen better days even when you were a kid. Smiling, long-haired Thom, who worked at the video store, selling drugs on the side and steadily building his copper jewelry empire, selling pieces to whatever woebegone tourists found themselves lost enough to end up here, of all places.

Now it seemed like time had aged this place a hundred years.

Los Huesos wasn't a large town. A gas station greeted visitors with a big old-fashioned Coca-Cola sign as though the place was perpetually stuck in 1973. Below that, a sign advertised GROCERIES - ICE - FEED - LAUNDRY against the backdrop of a mesa. There was a post office, a couple of schools, and a tiny clinic run by a couple that didn't speak English. Max's Chevy rolled past chicken coops, trailers, stout, pueblo-style houses with colorful doors, front yards of sagebrush and clumps of dead grass, and a little farm with a rooster weathervane at the front. The whole place was a study in color, pale yellow grass and green sagebrush against rust-red dirt, the mesas a million different colors in the sun, blood-orange and bronze and streaked scarlet, russet earth and rocks tumbling down like fat drips of blood.

But even in town, it was like Emma Garcia was a ghost. No one we asked had heard anything of her. She'd worked at the gas station, but the owner said she'd stopped showing up for her shifts some months back.

"Not a big surprise," the man said. "Kids like that don't have much going on in their lives. They're in and out of jail, and that's if they're lucky."

"And if they're not?" Max asked.

"Whatever happened to her is the same fate that happens to countless girls here. Drugs, prostitution, maybe a drunk driver hit her and tossed her body in the ravine. Besides, girls from the rez, no one comes around looking for them."

My stomach turned at his words.

He called after us as we walked out. "You hear about someone who wants a part-time job, you tell 'em I'm looking."

Our drive back to campus was silent. I felt so awful after speaking to the gas station owner. His words echoed and twisted in my stomach. *No one comes around looking for them.*

We pulled into the parking lot at school, keeping a safe distance from the metal railing that marked the edge of the cliff, and I leaned my head against the window. Rain fell on the bull skull at the front of the ranch, streaking across the dust like tears.

Max stared straight ahead. Neither of us wanted to admit it, the hopelessness seeping in. We both felt like we were spinning our gears, reaching for thread after thread, only for them to all get tangled in a vicious knot.

But Max Middlemore was not someone used to losing. And he wouldn't let something like this investigation defeat him.

Suddenly, he turned toward me, eyes wide.

I sighed. "No. Whatever it is, no."

"You don't even know what I'm going to ask."

"Don't need to. I don't like that look."

"Let's just be honest for a second. Basile likes you a hell of a lot more than he likes me. To be honest, I might be offended if you weren't so pretty."

I blushed scarlet.

"If you were to talk to him, alone, maybe we could settle our little disagreement once and for all."

I balked. "Now you're offering me up as *bait*?"

"Well, if you're right, and he has nothing to do with this, then you'll be perfectly fine. If you're not, well, it's been a pleasure knowing you . . ."

I punched him in the arm.

"Kidding, I'm kidding. It's just one conversation, and I'll stay close enough to smell."

"God, I hope not." I pinched my nose. "What am I supposed to say anyway? Someone accused your friends of assaulting someone. Do you have any comment? If he wants to sue over Grant, I'm sure this won't be welcome."

"Don't make it about that," he said, stroking his hand over the stubble on his chin. He needed a shave; we were both looking a little worse for the wear. "Pretend like you need his help with something else." His mouth twisted, and for a second, he wouldn't meet my eyes. "Trust me, I don't like it either, but we need this. For Dani."

"But what if—?" My mind started to go haywire, imagining every freak accident imaginable.

"It won't." He grabbed my hand. "It'll be alright, I promise."

I blew out my cheeks. "Fine, but you owe me, like, . . . ten thousand chocolate cookies. And the good ones, too."

He flashed a boyish grin, all dimples. "When we crack this case, I'll get you a cookie the size of a car."

I pulled out my phone, still open to Basile's TikTok page. There were hundreds of comments from Basile's thousands of followers, and I felt myself shrinking down, a small voice in my head whispering, *What would someone like him get from hearing a speech by someone like you?**

I'd never been the type of person to glamorize all that. I'd always preferred gentleness and kindness to flashiness and charm, but now that I watched him, I couldn't look away. His charisma bled across the screen—the ease of his smile, the way everything he said made so much sense. How his theory could unlock an entire new world to us. And despite the whispers of caution at the back of my mind, I knew he was the only one who could help me learn more.

"It must take him forever to do this shit," Max said, looking over. "What a waste of time."

"Maybe he just wants people to like him."

"Don't tell me you fall for all that, the trousers and the shiny shoes and the hair? He's such a try-hard."

"Just because some people like to present themselves better than just having rolled in the barn . . ."

---

* Maybe this was the anthropology nerd coming out in me, but anyone who's studied the Ancient Greeks might draw a comparison to how influencers today are viewed similarly to how humanity once viewed the heroes of epics. The deeds of the ancient heroes were meant to draw marvel, wonder, envy. While today we put less value on battle prowess, our society is obsessed with status, beauty, money, popularity. When you have these things, you are elevated to hero status, seen as more beautiful than a real person, more exciting, more adventurous, more charismatic, more blessed. The poems and stories of old are now tweets and memes and videos, and we watch, and we read their posts, and we love and trust these people we've never met like they're gods.

"You used to not mind rolling in the barn with me." He grinned, and it was so devilish I had to smile.

His expression grew serious for a moment. "You know, for how much you used to hate all this stuff, you're sure spending a lot of time on it. You're getting sucked into this stuff again, just like with Jamie."

The mention of Jamie caught me off guard. It had been a silent truce between us that we wouldn't mention that final year before I left, our breakup, any of it. "This isn't like that."

"Isn't it? I feel like I'm losing you all over again." He reached out his hand and tucked a stray piece of hair behind my ear. His hand lingered against my cheek.

"You never lost me," I murmured. I hadn't meant for it to be such a weighted statement, and I flushed as soon as I said it.

It was quiet for a moment, his eyes intently focused on mine. "Good."

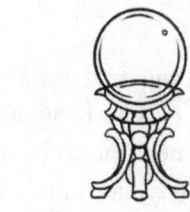

CHAPTER TWENTY-SEVEN

"Basile!" I waved to him in the hallway and jogged over. "So glad I ran into you!"

It was obvious it wasn't a chance encounter, given that I'd run into him outside the classroom where he'd just finished teaching a class, but he was polite enough not to say so.

He smiled. "How is the investigation going?"

"That's something I wanted to talk to you about, actually..."

"Oh?" His brow furrowed, probably bracing himself for another round of questions. I could imagine how annoying we were getting. "And how is it that I can help?" He was all polite gentleman, but there was a modicum of strain in his voice. A tendon cut right into the curve of his neck. I didn't blame him; he was trying to protect his friend. And we were trying to find evidence linking him to a crime.

"I was wondering if I could talk to you about something. Emma Garcia, did you know her?"

He nodded. "I did. She hung around the house some last semester. Came to the parties, dated Paul off and on after he broke up with Joselyn."

This next part was the hard part; I didn't know how he would react. The last thing I wanted to do was upset him. I squirmed and forced myself to remember why I was doing all of this. To help Dani. Saving a girl's life was worth a little discomfort on my part.

I swallowed. "There are reports that she was sexually assaulted by one of the brothers."

His eyes went wide, and his mouth tightened.

I started talking fast. I suddenly wanted to retract every word I'd said, but there was nothing to be done. They were out in the open now. "We'd talk to her about it ourselves, but we can't find a way of getting in touch with her. She hasn't shown up to her job in months. No one's heard from her."

As I spoke, the tendon in Basile's neck grew more and more pronounced.

"A sexual assault?" he asked incredulously. "Is that what they're saying? Emma went to *rehab*, that's why she hasn't been around. She didn't want everyone knowing about it. Although, I guess now the cat's out of the bag. There wasn't any kind of assault, except if you count the wall that she smashed a two-hundred-year-old chandelier through. The girl had a problem. If you ask me, rehab was long overdue." He shook his head. "It doesn't surprise me, the rumors people spread, silly stories to explain why she left. It does surprise me that you'd believe it. I thought you'd think better of us than that."

"I'm sorry. I had to ask."

"Yeah," he said, the toe of his loafer scuffing the ground. His glittering eyes were dark, lifeless coals.

"Seriously, I'm sorry." I ran my thumb over the leather cord in my pocket. "I'm just doing my job. It's what they hired me to do."

And I was sorry that I offended him, but I wasn't sorry for looking for who did this to Dani and for trying to get justice for Maya. I was only sorry about the look in his eyes, and the gut-wrenching feeling that I'd disappointed him.

He nodded, turning as the noon bell rang. "Is it?" he asked, before walking away.

As he said it, something flashed in my head. A voice, not Basile's, but carrying the same intonation, that same disappointed, questioning tone. *Can you really see the nature of your reality?*

Déjà vu?

It was an echo of something I'd heard before, only I couldn't place the memory. Something from one of Basile's videos?

I shook my head, trying to will away the rotten feeling spreading through my chest.

I went straight back to Jack D's room and shot off a text to Max, who was waiting in the Arts building.

> Found out Emma Garcia's in rehab. Back to square 1?

The words tumbled out as soon as Jack opened the door, welcoming me inside with a cloud of smoke. "Emma Garcia is in a rehabilitation facility."

He took another hit and shook his head. "Rehab? How the hell's she gonna pay for rehab? Who told you that?"

"Basile Samir."

"Of course he did."

"Sometimes what you don't know about someone will surprise you," I said. "People keep secrets better than you think." I knew that well myself. I had enough secrets you could bury me in them.

"No. Look, man, you didn't see her afterward. She was super withdrawn, would barely speak, had these huge purple circles around her eyes. Then a week later, poof. Never a word from her again. Now you tell me that's because of rehab."

Maybe he had a point. I tried to think what I would do if I'd been in her situation. I'd tell people. I would say my goodbyes. At least tie up loose ends.

I bit my lip.

"You see?" he said, slapping his knees.

"What am I supposed to be seeing, exactly?"

"That Magic isn't the only tricky thing around here. If I were you, I'd get out. Go back home where it's safe."

Home? I couldn't leave, not now. What would Max say, and Dr. Robetresse, and Vern? But more than that, I was always leaving. Every time something got hard, I picked up and left and never looked back.

I shook my head. "I can't do that."

Jack shrugged. "Suit yourself. But keep your shit about you, you know? This place . . ." —he shook his head—"it's not as safe as they'd have you think."*

---

* I don't know if *safe* was ever a term I'd use to describe Seinford and Brown. The intentions were good, and I trusted Dr. Robetresse, but there were secrets here, just like anywhere else. Maybe more than I thought.

FROM THE JOURNAL OF DANICA STEWART

March 30ᵀᴴ [two days before the murder]

No no no no no no non onnonononon. Remember. Cut not fire with a sword. Wear not a ring. Do not speak of things under the moonlight. Remember.

Remember.

REMEMBERREMEMBERJREMEVJBERREME BER

REMTMGER REMEMER MEMBER RER R

R

R

CHAPTER TWENTY-EIGHT

Dr. Robetresse seemed tenser than usual at the council meeting later on. Her posture was rigid, all business. I thought she was worried that our investigation had concluded, that we'd decided it was one of her professors and were ready to call it a day.

Only hours earlier, we'd walked past Dr. Strauss's office. A group of girls huddled around it, talking. One of them turned to me and whispered excitedly, "They found a pair of girl's underwear in his office."

My face must've betrayed what I was thinking because her eyes widened as she recognized who I was. "Oh, God. You don't think it had anything to do with the investigation?"

"No, no!" I said, quickly. Already I'd sparked the attention of the rest of her group.

One of the girls leaned in conspiratorially. "My friend works in the Records office. She said Dani had requested a different advisor, months before everything happened. Apparently, she didn't feel comfortable with Strauss, though she didn't cite specifics."

"Obvious what she meant, though," another girl said.

The group scooted closer to the doors of his office, trying to catch a glimpse of the man inside. Strauss caught my eye from inside the room. He looked like a haunted man, drained of color, like all the ego and power had been sucked right out of him. Red, splotchy scars crept up his neck from under his collar.

"I wonder if the underwear is hers," one of the girls said.

"How'd they find it?" I asked.

"One of his students did and reported it to the dean. That stuck-up Christian chick. Joselyn Hart."

Now, at the council meeting, Dr. Robetresse sipped a coffee, eyes darting around the room.

"Thank you all for coming. I apologize for not being available to meet sooner. I've had my hands full fielding questions from anxious parents, and getting hounded by local journalists trying to sniff out a story. If you all haven't exercised caution when venturing off campus, I urge you to start." 🐚

The meeting concluded quickly. The pressing need for security drew Dr. Robetresse's attention away, and the rest of us were left to stew in her warning.

I caught Maritza before she left. I touched her shoulder, and she spun, giving me a sharp look. I drew my hand back quickly.

In recent days, I'd stopped visiting her cottage. I was becoming increasingly aware of the way she looked at me. She had a distrustful eye, like she knew I was seeing things I shouldn't. ✝

"I've been meaning to ask you," I said. "Would you know who was in my room last?" I wasn't sure who to ask. Maritza

---

🐚 (Robetresse): This investigation had caused more of an uproar than I was ready for. I was having a hard enough time bringing money into the school without tales of demonic possession and the murder of a student. To top it off, someone kept attempting to break into the library and access the Magic books. It reminded me of when once, at Britton, a group tried to torch all the Magic books the school had. There was a rumor it was all just a ploy to steal one particular book, but we never found out what it was. At any rate, no Magic books were reported stolen.

✝ I didn't blame Maritza one bit. Maybe everyone else fell for her bullshit, but I knew something was up with Cella. I'd seen her research, knew all her accolades and blah, blah, blah, but I still couldn't shake the idea that she was hiding something. I mean, this doesn't even have to do with the whole trying to set me on fire thing. But clearly there's some undiagnosed rage there that she needs to work on. Someone does something like that, they obviously have issues.

was one of those people who, if she didn't know, would know exactly who would.

She frowned. "I'm not sure what you mean. Before you attended the school? I would have to look at the records."

"No, I mean recently. I assume someone's used it since I left."

"Room 22 has been empty for several years. There were a few boards that needed to be replaced after you left, so a crew was lined up to replace them, but they never showed up."

"So no one was in there after me?"

"No."

I hesitated. I almost asked if she could check the records; there had to be some sort of mistake. I couldn't have been the last one, but she nodded quickly.

"If you'll excuse me, I've got to be getting back." She spun back toward her cottage.

I started to think I was losing my mind. Shadows danced in the corner of my vision, just outside my reach. I noticed more of the symbols on the cattle skulls above the dorms, now on nearly every building on campus, each with the dot-triangle inside a circle and a different number inked on them: 46 above the Science building, 12 above the Arts hall. Tons of numbers that had no rhyme or reason to them, they didn't correspond to the number of rooms in the building nor number of doors, windows, lights. I even counted the fire sprinklers. Even more concerning, I was seeing words written on the walls—though these, I'm sure, were hallucinations.

The fact didn't bring me much comfort.

I stopped drinking coffee. I'd read that caffeine could spark hallucinations, and I'd always been pretty sensitive to anything stronger than tea. It made sense that it would affect me now, after the long hours I was putting in at the library. But even as I stopped drinking caffeine, I made up for it with more books.

CHAPTER TWENTY-NINE

When I came back to my spot in the library from the bathroom, my things were scattered across the table. Stuff was everywhere, books strewn open, pens all over the floor. Even blood. Sheets of notebook paper were smeared with it and stuffed in my backpack. I took a step back.

The sheet on top bore a message written in black ink.

If you're smart, you'll keep your mouth shut.

A shock of cold ran down my back. A threat? Someone was threatening me. My mind shot to one person: Grant. But why would he do such a thing?

Well, that was at least less opaque. To stop me from looking into him, from tarnishing his reputation. From telling the council that he had something to do with Maya's death.

My nerves were shaky and on edge. I went for a walk to clear my head but, on returning to the library, promptly fell asleep at a table. I woke with a start.

Hours later, when I saw Max again, I dug in my bag. "I want to show you something."

But the notes weren't there.

Max's brow raised. "What is it?"

I shook my head, digging deeper into the bag. "They're not ... they're not here." I shook my head. "He must have taken them back. Stolen the evidence."

"What do you mean? Who stole what back?"

"Grant."

At once, every muscle in Max's body seemed to tighten. "What did he do? Did he threaten you?"

"I'm not . . . I'm not sure it was him."

"Who, then? Basile?"

I shook my head. Was I even sure it had happened at all? What was happening to me?

I noticed the flare of Max's nostrils, the cord running through his neck. He'd been on edge lately, too, and just itching for a fight. And I didn't know what had really happened to the letters. Maybe they'd fallen out. Maybe the janitor came by and threw them away while I was asleep. I couldn't imagine spilled blood was exactly welcome in a school library.

"I made a mistake," I said. "It's fine."

His eyes met mine, all liquid concern. He cupped my chin in his palm with a tenderness that surprised me. "Are you sure, Cella? If he did something to you, I swear to God, . . ."

"Really, it's nothing."

He released me and started pacing.

"Max, tell me you're not going to do anything. Max!"

In his charcoal T-shirt, black hat, and jeans, he was the perfect impression of a thunder cloud. "Sorry, I was caught in a daydream in which I pulled every bone from Grant's body. What were you saying?"

"Please, don't do anything." I regretted saying anything at all, especially with him all worked up like this. With monumental effort, he forced himself to take a breath and nodded. "Fine. At the very least, we've got to tell Dr. Robetresse."

"No. She has enough to deal with, and I don't want him to think he's getting to me. He's just scared. It's his future at risk, and he's . . ." I swallowed. "He's just protecting it."

"And what if he does something else 'to protect his future'?"

"I'm not afraid of him."

He growled, his eyes set on a spot in the distance. "Neither am I."

Field Journal of Luce Montgomery

Basile was weird tonight, and for a moment, I thought about calling the whole thing off. It's not like our little rendezvous in the field were doing me any favors. I still haven't found the fungi, and I'm running out of time.

I stayed up after he fell asleep. I couldn't stop thinking about the way his hands kept creeping to my neck when we were intimate. Cradling it, wrapping his fingers around it like he could crush the life in his hands in an instant. I knew I was going to see a different side of him eventually, no one was that perfect, but this one was rougher than I expected. Crueler. His hands tangled in my hair and pulled so hard my eyes watered.

But every time I think about ending things, something stops me. He's not like anyone I've ever met. It's not just the theory that draws people to him. For all his fame and adoring fans, he doesn't seem all that attached to living. He talks about death a lot, hovers on its precipice, flirts with its borders. That seems to speak to a lot of the young people following him. "Why should I be afraid of death?" he asked in one of his videos, filmed standing on the railing at the top of a building, with the hazy glow of city lights below. He spread his arms wide. "A philosopher fears death least of all men. For, as Plato says, it's only in death that a true philosopher finds what he desires, the truth." Then he took off his shirt and bared the tattoo inked in black across his back.

Saluta mortem. Greet death.

The comments went wild.

CHAPTER THIRTY

I looked down at my phone, the blinking notification from a text I still hadn't replied to.

I had an idea.

One that Max definitely, unequivocally, absolutely would not like, but I thought maybe if I could talk to him about it in person, he'd be less likely to flip. So I got in my truck and drove to his house.

Max's family lived in a big farmhouse on the outside of town, with two pens for training horses and a greenhouse in back for his dad's tomatoes.

I got out of the car, popping the back on and off my earring—I'd swapped out my bumblebee studs for ladybugs. I'd been here so many times before, but every time I'd come as a friend, a welcome guest. Now I walked up the front porch and felt dread brew in my stomach. I swung open the screened door and knocked, wondering what his mom would do. Scream at me, tell me to leave?

As usual, the house was bustling, loud, and chaotic, with dogs barking and kids screaming. Mrs. Middlemore yelled, "Oh, quit!" to the dogs jostling to get to the door, until all eyes landed on me.

She stared at me for one long moment, and I half-considered turning around and pretending I had the wrong house. Nothing to see here, just slide back in my truck, when her face broke into a huge grin.

"Cella!" She rushed toward me, arms outstretched.

There was more hustle and bustle as chairs scooted and Cheerios were hastily moved. I was sat at the kitchen table and introduced to various nieces and nephews staying for the week. Mrs. Middlemore set a bowl of tomato soup and a heaping plate of mac and cheese in front of me. Both made from scratch, of course. Not for the first time, I wondered if Max's mom didn't have some Magic of her own in those cast-iron pans.

She started chatting almost immediately. I was grateful all I was required to do was nod every so often.

"And look, Jason's got himself a new leg brace and a walker. He's going to do just fine. Janie's not here, Max told you, I suppose. I swear, if the Devil himself had gotten into that girl, she'd be better behaved than she is now. Disappears for days, can't ever call her mama to let her know she's alright, has me worried sick half the time. But oh!" she cried, and turned to me suddenly. I jumped.

"I'm just so happy you two are working together again! You know his Magic was on the fritz, and we could really use the help around here. Between you and me, that girlfriend of his isn't worth a sack of salt. Ain't got a lick of Magic in her, and even then, she doesn't have the sense not to smooch all over a man in his daddy's house. She came over here last week, and I could just hear them in the upstairs bathroom. And you know I'm a Christian woman, I don't like to say nothing bad about nobody, but, well, Old Lou died, and she didn't even send a condolence card. Nothing! I don't know, I just didn't think it was very polite."

"Eileen said she got it. It just came in a little later than the others," one of Max's younger cousins said, sipping his soup.

She waved him away. "Are you all done, honey? You want some pie? Neighbor across the street made it."

I'd always liked coming here. It was so much sunnier than my own home. The creaking old farmhouse, filled with rugs passed down from his grandmother, the scent of the tomatoes from the greenhouse. His dad, cracking jokes from the den.

I stood up from the table and washed my plate in the sink. "No, thanks, Mrs. Middlemore. I should really see Max. Is he in the barn?"

"Sure is," she said, wiping up a spill from one of the little ones. "And, Cella?"

I looked up as I headed for the door.

"It's good to see you, honey. I wish you'd come around more often."

"It's really good to see you, too, Mrs. Middlemore." The screened door swung shut behind me.

I had so many memories from this place, sitting on the fence with Max's sister eating Twizzlers and watching the horses, riding a horse myself for the first time—Max taught me. Granted, I felt a little out of place now, worlds away from the girl I was the last time I was here. The girl climbing out of Max's truck with flushed cheeks, so carefree in her sundress and cowboy boots, not a problem in the world.

I wasn't sure I even knew who that person was anymore.

Max was in the barn, working the saddle leather.

"Hey." I popped open a bottle of Coke from their icebox.

"Just be a sec. This one here's a little difficult."

Marlon, the brown stallion, who was temperamental on his best day. "I know." I patted his neck, breathed into his nose. "Hello, Marlon."

"He always did like you."

I climbed up on the fence to wait.

I had flashbacks of another time here. Crickets chirping, lying in the bed of his truck, wrapped up in an old blanket. The truck had broken down at the back of the farm, and we were waiting for his sister to come and bring the cables, laughing and resigning ourselves to a night beneath the stars. He leaned over and kissed me. I'd had kisses before, but this one made it feel like this was the only kiss that had ever mattered. He looked at me, tilted my chin with his finger, and I was lost in blue, blue, blue.

Now he heaved the saddle off Marlon with a grunt. "If you're here, I'm guessing there's bad news."

I took a swig of the Coke, letting the bubbles crackle and fizz in my throat. "No."

I watched the muscles tense and flex under his loose T-shirt as he worked the oil into the leather. The aura around him was a tangle of stormy thoughts, but I didn't have to peek at his Magic to know something was up. He'd been in moods like this before. He had a lot on his plate, I knew, and for a moment, all I wanted to do was ease his burden. Hold his hand while the storm passed.

"Saw your mom."

He laughed, "Oh yeah? She's been asking about you ever since I got elected to the council. 'When are you going to tell Cella to get over here? I miss that girl,' yada yada." He smiled, then looked down. "Dad wasn't there."

"No."

I watched him work the leather, his hands applying more and more pressure.

I climbed off the fence, took a brush to groom Marlon.

"Careful of the—"

"Left leg, I know," I smiled.

We worked in sync for a while, falling into a groove, and it was quiet except for the bray of the horse, the buzz of the cicadas, and the gentle rush of the wind through the open doors. I didn't know what it was about this place that felt like coming home.

"I forget what a natural you are at this. Julia's terrified of the horses."

"How's that going?"

"Could be better," he said, looking down and scuffing his boot on the ground. Didn't want to talk about it, then. I continued brushing.

"Everything feels like it's kind of just . . . closing in, you know? You ever feel like that?"

I sighed. "All the time."

He looked down at me from beneath his hat, the sapphire glint coming back into his eye, if only for a second. His boot slid closer, sole scraping against the wet pavement after he'd hosed it down. He was so close I could see the sunburn on the back of his neck, the tan line beneath his shirt. "You know, I'm glad you're here."

That night, in his truck, he'd whispered promises in between kisses. "I know you're afraid, that you think I'll hurt you. I promise you, I won't. I won't." He'd whispered it into my ear all night. "I'll never hurt you, Cella." He breathed it into my neck, into my hair, into my heart.

All of a sudden that familiar pounding hit my chest. The feeling that reminds me to run, to get the hell out of here, to not let him get any closer. And a familiar voice, from a conversation years ago.

What are you so afraid of?

"Everything," I'd wanted to tell him, "everything."

Now I swallowed, his face drawing closer, the warm scent of him filling the space between us.

"I think I should go to the Phi Kat party tonight," I blurted.

He stopped inches before my face, still staring at my lips. "What?"

I glanced down at my phone, the blinking notification still at the top of my screen. The text from Basile I'd yet to answer.

Still coming tonight?

I'd felt so bad after our conversation, like the light of the sun had left me, that I sought him out to clear the air. He'd taken the whole thing gracefully and offhandedly had mentioned a party tonight.

"You should come. Meet the guys," he'd said.

I took a deep breath. "There's a party tonight at the Phi Kat house, and I think it's the perfect opportunity to dig more into Grant. We need more information, and what better way to get it than at a house party with all his friends? Maybe I could even sneak into his room, do some real recon."

Any trace of a smile dropped from Max's face. "He threatened you. He drugged Joselyn Hart. The guy is dangerous. And

I don't think going to a creepy rapist frat party is the right move."

"We need information, and we're running out of time. You saw the bloodstains at Maritza's. Dani's running out of time, and I won't abandon her, Max. I can't."

And while that part was true, that it was a way to get more information about the frat—it was also a way to smooth the waters with Basile. Because, despite the nagging warning in the back of my mind, I couldn't just give up on this, on the Reality Paradox, on the promise of everything he could teach me. I didn't know how exactly it worked, but he'd proposed theorems of how to reach this new world, and the promise of it, the idea of this . . . this untapped knowledge was too enticing to give up. For me, it was so much more than some theory. It was everything I loved about Magic, about discovery. It was an opportunity, a place where maybe I hadn't missed it all, where I hadn't fucked up so badly. A place where . . . where maybe Aaron was still alive.

And I saw it then in Max's eyes, the look of defeat. I wasn't going to back down, and he knew it. He exhaled a giant sigh. "Alright. But I'm coming with you."

"Sorry, but no, you aren't. I won't find out anything if you're tagging along after me like a bodyguard."

"You're joking, right? What if something goes wrong? If Grant corners you or finds you poking around and decides he doesn't like it?"

I put my hand on his, watched as he mollified. "They won't touch me. If it were me and I'd done something wrong, I'd be on my very best behavior. Maybe I'd . . . maybe I'd be so focused on that that I wouldn't remember the things I forgot to clean up.

"Besides, I'm stronger than them, and they know it. Even stronger with . . ."—I faltered—"with you here."

He smirked. "How hard was that for you to say?"

"I'll be fine, okay? I'll text you in the morning and let you know what I find."

He shoved his hands in his pockets and squirmed. "Just don't get too close to anyone. And don't let anyone near your drink, for God's sake."[†]

I quirked an eyebrow. "Careful, you don't want Julia hearing you express concern for your ex." I made a shocked gesture. "Scandalous!"

He laughed at that, and I let myself out the way I'd come in.

I climbed in my truck and put my palms against my cheeks to cool my flush. It wasn't just the summer heat or the stifling hot barn that was coloring my cheeks. There was something electric about being here. I felt like that time I'd drunk half a bottle of Mrs. Middlemore's homemade peach wine.

I looked back out the window, toward the grassy fields, the wooden fence penning in the horse pasture, the stables that I'd just left.

The thing was, if I let myself fall into these things, get comfortable here . . . if I let myself want what I wanted and reach for it, what was to say it wouldn't all be ripped from me again? That a chasm wouldn't just open up wide and take what was left of me? I couldn't do it. I couldn't let myself get hurt all over again.

I looked back down at the blinking light on my phone, the text I still hadn't replied to.

I shoved back the frizzy hair curling around my face and reapplied my lipstick in the rearview mirror.

On my way, I texted back, and pulled onto the highway back to campus.

[†] I didn't feel right about her going out there, but Cella was as stubborn as old Marlon. I couldn't think of anything I could say to stop her.

CHAPTER THIRTY-ONE

Later that night, I attempted to navigate through a sea of bodies around the Phi Katharos house. While nobody was vomiting in the corner or twerking on the back wall just yet, there were more people than I expected.

"Cella!" a voice said when I made my way in. Paul. I remembered him from our brief meeting my first time at the house. He was happier than I thought he would be to see me. "Come out to let loose, I see. Basile was hoping you'd show up."

"Hey, Paul, looks like you've been enjoying yourself." From his unfocused gaze, it was clear he must've been pregaming for a while.

"Libations are in the other room. Help yourself to whatever you like, but watch out for Alex's moonshine, it will get you fucked up. Me, I prefer to sail on stormy seas." He winked.

"I'll head for safer waters," I said with a grin.

Inside was smoky and electric. The stereo crackled, the bass boomed. Though I'd never been much of a partier, I was hit with a wave of nostalgia. The smell of beer and cologne and body spray, and the buzz of excitement. Hoping to see that person you wanted to see.

Then I blinked, and the song was over.

Someone was slumped over on the staircase. As I moved closer, I noticed they were wearing a T-shirt with an xkcd comic on it, jeans, and sneakers. Grant. But what was he doing? Everyone was moving around him like they didn't notice him there, even the brothers. A little early to be that drunk, I thought, but then his eyelids did that fluttering thing when someone just starts to fall asleep. All of a sudden, his head jerked back, and his eyes flew open. He whipped his head wildly from side to side.

"Are you alright?" I asked.

"Did anyone see me?" he asked, his eyes wide and terrified. "Basile, or anyone else in Phi Kat?"

"Sleeping? No, I don't think so."

He nodded, the tension easing slightly from his shoulders. "Good—good." Then he stood and quickly ran his fingers through his hair. Without another word to me, he hurried through the crowd.

A staircase didn't seem to me to be the best place to fall asleep, and I didn't know why anyone would be upset about it, but before I could linger anymore on the odd behavior, Basile caught my eye from across the room.

"You came!" His eyes were tinged hazy red, and his smile was completely relaxed, even warmer and wider than usual. "Do you have a drink? Can I get you anything? Paul's fired up the grill out back, though I cannot in good conscience recommend you eat anything he tries to cook."

I could smell the faintest hint of weed on him. I laughed. "I'm good." I shook the drink in my hand. "I just grabbed a beer from the cooler."

"You want something stronger? One of the perks of living here, the guys keep a stocked liquor cabinet." He looked around for a glass when raised voices sprung from the back of the room.

Two guys arguing loudly, two brothers I thought I recognized. One shoved the other, and Basile blew out his cheeks. "Oh boy."

"Go, it's okay," I said, waving him away. "I can fend for myself."

"I'll see you later?"

"Definitely."

He disappeared into the sea of bodies, and I looked around the house, drifting to the edges of the room.

The music was a mix of Top 40 and the odd nineties favorites; "Jump Around" by House of Pain was playing currently. I couldn't hear anyone, and they couldn't hear each other, and I was more than happy to drift through the crowd, nodding along to the beat, sipping my lukewarm beer, except I was here for information. I was here to talk, so I needed something stronger. There was a substantial bonfire out back now; I could see it in flashes out the window as the crowd parted, even though it was so hot outside I could have melted.

The light was on in Basile's office, and I skirted closer to it, my curiosity piquing. The door was cracked, but no shadows moved inside. Basile wasn't in there, but he wasn't in the back corner of the room anymore either, so I moved toward it. I could just slip inside while no one was looking . . .

I ran headfirst into someone's chest.

"Whoa," the guy said, looking confused and maybe a little pissed until he recognized me.

"Look who we have here! Come to try something a little stronger, I see," he said, and I laughed, because he sounded like one of those old circus performers enticing you to take a step closer. He leaned in close, his arm looping over my shoulder conspiratorially. "Can I interest you in some apple pie moonshine?"

"You must be Alex."

"Made it myself." He took a swig from a cup. "It's delicious," he said with a wink, "if I do say so myself."

One of his friends came over and roped his arm around my other shoulder. "Don't let this guy fool you, it is absolutely not delicious."

"Okay, not delicious," Alex conceded, "but it will for sure fuck you up. Want to try it?"

I looked at them all, with their warm, expectant smiles. I had to keep my wits about me tonight. I couldn't forget what Joselyn Hart had said about her last party with the Phi Kat members. And rehab or no, something had happened to Emma Garcia.

But at the same time, I needed them to trust me. To not suspect I was there for any reason other than a good time.

"What the hell, hit me," I said, taking a sip of the liquid that smelled like a cross between gasoline and paint thinner. The guys cheered.

The others were in a heated discussion about . . . lifting? One stopped another guy who had a plate loaded with hamburgers and hotdogs. I guess Basile didn't stop the grill after all.

"What're you doing, man?" Alex said. "You'd better not let the Mathematici see you with all that."

"I'm hungry." The edge to his voice caused that little voice in my head to whisper *danger danger danger*, or would've whispered *danger danger danger*, but it was more like *dang dune dimmer*, and that didn't really make any sense, so I ignored it.

"Who's the Mathematici?" I asked.

"Basile," Paul said.

I frowned. "Why do you—"

"Oh, shit! Did you see that?" I was drowned out by someone smashing a bottle, or maybe several bottles, near the beer pong table. It was loud enough to be intentional, and the guys swarmed to the sound.

I frowned. Why did they call him that, and why wouldn't Basile want them eating? Maybe there wasn't enough food for everyone and he wanted the guests to have food, though most of the people at the party looked to be brothers. They were . . . vaguely man-shaped, at least. The room had filled up quite a bit from when I first got here.

I hovered on the edges of conversation for a while, a pleasant buzz dulling my nerves, not quite sure how to bring up the subject of Dani and Maya without drawing too much attention. The brothers didn't seem to mind my hovering, even as their words echoed and warped in my ears, and I laughed a little too loudly at their jokes. They were nice to me. Paul came over and offered to get me a burger or a beer or water, and Alex looked over often, sure to include me in the conversation.

Part of me thought they were being nice because I was Basile's guest; he was flitting around the party doing damage control. Some sort of internal spat, it looked like. It was funny watching the other brothers interact with him, like he was some kind of god.

But another part of me remembered what Max had said.

They know your reputation, Cel, of course they're going to be nice to you.

And though I suspected Max had said it to dissuade me from getting too close to them, it had the opposite effect. It burnished my ego, a bit, knowing they wanted me here. Knowing they respected me, bumbling gremlin and all. Respected my research, the things I had done.

Sure, I had enemies at Seinford and Brown. People on the council, Luce being at least one of them. Maybe some of the students who disagreed with Object Theory, or those who'd heard about what I'd done, who remembered what happened at the end of my second year of postgrad. But I had followers, too. People who found my social media sites, who every so often would send messages begging me to teach them, to tell them how I was able to do what I do.

Magic didn't need to be a well-kept secret. Skepticism usually did the job just fine, but there were some outside the community who believed. Who found poor-quality videos on the internet and chased after it with an obsessive fervor.

How does Magic work? they asked hopefully, though they never started with this, of course. They'd start off like they were just trying to be friends, but I knew the question that was coming next. Always the same question.

How does it work? Can you teach me?

I always tried to stop it before it got to that point, because it only got more uncomfortable after I inevitably said no.

Please, I can pay.

I'll give you anything.

My friend knows an exec at Chanel; I can get you bags,

clothes. You want drugs? Coke? Molly? Fentanyl? I'll do anything. Anything you want, just name it.

But it wasn't something I could explain in a few sentences. I couldn't condense years' worth of study into a few simple, digestible lines. A few incantations, a spell written on a scroll. Hand it out like, here, here's the key to all your dreams.

That was too simple, it was something that could only happen in a story. The real reason Magic isn't pervasive, isn't widely practiced is because there isn't a formula. It was years of study, years of clawing your eyes over text you could barely understand, of practicing combinations of words and sounds until your lips cracked, until your fingers scuffed and bled, and that was not something people wanted to hear. I couldn't recite the steps to find your objects, to reach the level of understanding you needed to be able to access Magic. There was no easy way to make you understand that Magic was not there to be your equal or your subservient. It was there to be a part of you, and if you let it in, you had to be prepared to deal with it.

But people didn't want to hear that. They wanted me to write it out on a sheet of paper, a step-by-step recipe to follow to make all their dreams come true. Words that they could repeat over and over again to make something happen. And I got tired of telling them no, that Magic wasn't fantasy, that it was nothing like a fairy tale.

Luckily, there weren't many of those people. Most were just members of a silent audience, people who quietly kept tabs on Max and me, watching to see what we did next.

The group dissipated as the boys zeroed in on a group of girls who walked into the room, and I faded into the background of the party. The taste of moonshine was less harsh on my tongue than it was before, and I wondered why I'd ever thought it tasted like gasoline to begin with. A guy walked upstairs to grab something from a bedroom, and my eyes followed him up.

That was at least one good reason to be a fly on the wall at these sorts of things. My feet carried me to the stairwell and the door to Basile's office beside it, which had now been shut. I nursed my drink, looking at a picture on the wall. Next to the World of Warcraft and Call of Duty posters was a framed print of what looked to be an Ancient Greek philosopher, with a long beard and robe. He stood beside a stone table with a hexafoil carved into the front.

I tried the door handle, locked. Again, my eyes traveled up the stairs. Which bedroom was Grant's?

Another old song played on the stereo, following a string of Third Eye Blind hits from the nineties, and though I was here with the brothers, I was thinking about someone else entirely. Stuck in a different time, a memory I couldn't escape, lyrics pumping through the stereo making me remember things I would rather stay forgotten. Not because they were bad memories, but because they were just the opposite.

Bits and pieces of "How's It Going to Be" drifted over to me, and I was hit with a wave of nostalgia so hard I could barely breathe. Max's hands on my face, lips on my forehead, hot breath against my neck.

A scribbled lyric slipped into a book and left outside my door. He knew I'd liked them, had discovered it during one of those games you play when you're first trying to get to know someone.

> Favorite band? he'd texted one night.
>
> Too easy. The Offspring. No, wait! Smashing Pumpkins. No!
>
> Can't decide?
>
> Okay, okay. Third Eye Blind.
>
> Final answer?
>
> Final answer.
>
> Ohhh, straight nineties girl, huh? What a millennial. I'm a Randy Houser fan myself.
>
> Okay, somehow that doesn't surprise me at all.

Not only had he remembered it, but he'd listened to the whole album, and for the next six months had slipped the lyrics into our conversations.

"You might call that . . . Losing a Whole Year," he'd said, or "Gah. What a Semi-Charmed Life," in typical Max fashion.

Now I made it up the stairs—my compliments to an extremely sturdy banister—and slipped into a room on my left. The room was empty of people, but full of stuff. I rummaged through notebooks lying on the desk in the corner, looking for any indication of its owner, but I was getting dizzy and lightheaded. My pleasant buzz had veered off into something a lot less pleasant. The alcohol had hit me faster than I expected. Definitely harder than any mixed drink I'd ever had.

I quickly sifted through a folder of history notes when something caught my eye below the nightstand.

A loose slip of paper sticking out of a composition book. I picked it up and smoothed it with both hands.

It must have been the alcohol hitting me because when I tried to focus on the words, I couldn't make any sense of it, one side effect of my blood alcohol content veering off a steep cliff.

The note was only two lines long.

Cut not fire with a sword. When the wind blows, worship the noise.

Music reached me from the hallway and downstairs, and I spun to the door, not remembering if I'd shut it behind me. The room started to tilt a little on its axis, and I stuffed the note into my purse and stumbled to the door.

I'd made it back into the hallway when the ground did a swan dive and I fell flat on my face.

"Whoa," someone said, a hand falling on my back. "Are you okay?"

I jerked away. "Sorry," I mumbled. I just needed to get to the bathroom.

Bathroom, bathroom, where the fuck was the bathroom?

The upbeat melopop rhythm of Third Eye Blind shrieked

in my ears—why were they playing, like, their entire freaking discography—as my fingers braced against the wall.

Max's face popped up in my vision, singing along with the song playing. He'd downloaded them, and we sang along in the car. He looked over to see if I was pleased, pulling my hand to his mouth so he could give it a quick kiss.

I shut my eyes tight. Please, *please* play another song.

When I opened my eyes again, the ground violently swooped and swerved. It looked so far away and was shifting as though made of tectonic plates. I could see the floor down below, people partying and screaming to their friends. The party was so much louder now. I clutched the rail with both hands to avoid losing my balance.

I looked down at the Solo cup I was still miraculously holding. I'd only had one cup of the moonshine; this shouldn't have hit me this hard, this fast. Sure, I'd drank it fast, but it was still only one cup.

I thought back to any time I'd left my cup unattended, but I didn't know a single female who would do that— it was preached into us from a young age. Always get a new drink; never return to one you'd left on the counter. Because that was something that was normal, that we should worry about guys drugging us so they could fuck our semi-conscious bodies while we were too weak to move.

No. I hadn't left it alone. And I'd kept my drink covered with my hand. Most of the time, at least.

But—I swore inwardly—the cup that Alex had handed me, had I actually seen him pour it? There were other times it could have happened, too, when I was looking at the posters on the wall outside Basile's office, when Grant, moving stealthily across the room, had drawn my eye when someone else could have slipped something in. All it took was one quick movement, dropping it into my cup. I certainly wouldn't have tasted a difference.

I pulled out my phone to text Max, but the numbers blurred on the screen, and I kept typing in the wrong passcode. Images wafted across my vision, bits and pieces of another party, of another night, drunk and stumbling up the stairs to the bathroom. And, just like now, there in the memory is the dark teal green of the walls outlined by a squeaky oak banister going up the stairs.

I'd been here before?

Had I blacked out then, too, and it was only coming back to me now? God, what did they do to my drink?

A sick feeling twisted in my stomach. All my cleverly made plans, and for what? Was this what they did to Emma Garcia? To Joselyn?

But that couldn't be right. My memory was playing tricks on me. I'd never been here before. The fraternity wasn't even a fraternity when I was on campus. I half-climbed and half-crawled forward, fingernails digging into the banister that lined the upper level. I imagined my nails instead digging into Basile's neck and ripping out a chunk.

Another flash. Of me, another time, laughing, a red Solo cup in hand. "Attention, everyone, I have an announcement to make!" and laughing hysterically.

An echo popped into my mind, *What has happened once, happens again.*

What the fuck, what the fuck.

Miraculously I made it to the bathroom and locked the door, frantically looking for something I could shove up against it.

If they'd roofied me, I'd much rather pass out here, in the bathroom, without anyone able to drag me off into a bedroom. I ran the faucet, dousing my face in cold water.

Open your eyes. Keep them open. Keep them the fuck open, Cella.

I fought against the tunnel vision. My pulse, which should've been spiking in my neck, had slowed to a dull thud, and if I listened to it, I could almost feel the lazy way it thrummed. I was overcome with sleepiness, and looked down at the floor for somewhere to lie down. I was so, *so* tired, could no longer fight against the blackness overtaking my vision. Pressing in on me, my vision clouding with spots. I ran water over a hand towel and pressed it to my forehead, praying the cold would snap my eyes into focus. That was when I saw it.

Nearly invisible against the scallop-shell wallpaper. Someone had drawn it with black marker. A circle with a ten-dot triangle inside it.

"I have to tell Max," I said. It meant something, I knew it did.

Then everything pressed in too close, and I was falling. Cloth still in hand, head smacking hard against the floor.

Before everything went black, I imagined the lock of the door twisting to the side and I thought, hazily, I need to reach out. Put a hand out to stop it. But when my fingers stretched, I only caught the metal chain to the toilet. The shadows at the edge of my vision expanded until they blotted out everything. The floor was cool against my cheek.

CHAPTER THIRTY-TWO

My dreams were dark and watery. I walked down a series of staircases, one after another after another, over and over again, only I wasn't confused or lost. I knew exactly where I was going. I walked straight into the dark, the same dark space I entered when I called my Magic. But instead of the water that was usually present, Danica was there. Standing, smiling.

"Hello?" I asked.

She wasn't wearing the dirty nightgown I'd seen her in last, but jean shorts and a tank top. Everything else about her was the same, though. The bruised skin, the shadowed eyes, the grim smile. It was a sick juxtaposition, the outfit of countless girls I'd seen at the party mixed with her condition now.

"What are you doing here?" I asked again. It was so quiet, and Dani standing there, saying nothing, unnerved me. Her smile grew.

"Can you help me?" I asked, trying to steady my voice. I didn't know why, but I thought if she knew I was afraid, it was only going to be worse for me. "I don't—I'm not sure what happened. I need to get a message to Max."

Abruptly, she turned, and walked back into the black behind her. "The truth will set you free," she said, her voice echoing.

"What truth?" I asked, stumbling to keep up.

"The One truth."

"Wait, where are you going?" I called, following her into the dark.

My eyes opened. I was on the floor of the bathroom, and Basile's face stared into mine. I drew back quickly.

"Cella? Are you alright?"

His face was all smooth, stoic concern, the handsome lick of his hair perfectly placed against his forehead. I swallowed. I felt sick, heat sloshing against the sides of my gut.

My mouth tasted funny. My tongue was fuzzy and thick. A verse echoed in my head. *The Devil has been sinning from the beginning.**

My hands flew to my waist. I looked down at my flats, which were still on my feet. My pants were zipped. Shirt was on, underwear, bra, everything felt . . . fine. Except it didn't. Something had changed. Something had shifted.

"Did you drug me?"

"What?"

The door was ajar, and three of the others stood back, looking concerned. "You passed out in the bathroom," a guy said, as if explaining the obvious to a child.

Paul nodded. "We would've left you in there, but we've only got one shower, and some of us work early shifts."

Basile reached for me. "Are you alright?"

"You drugged me," I said, jerking away from his touch.

He leaned back, wounded. He whipped his head back to Alex. "You didn't warn her about the moonshine?"

"'I told her this shit would fuck her up.'"

"That's hardly a warning," I seethed, and the others shook their heads.

Another of the brothers clutched his stomach. "That stuff is not fit for consumption."

"So maybe I haven't got the proportions of it right just yet," Alex said.

"Yeah, you think?" said one of the others.

I shook my head. "Moonshine doesn't make you pass out

---

* 1 John 3:8 NIV.

like that." I shot an accusing glare at Basile. It didn't make you remember things that didn't happen. I reached up and felt a lump on my forehead. Must have hit the absolute crap out of my head on the way down.

"It does if you drank too much of it," Alex said. "I suspect you'll be feeling like crud for the rest of the day." He looked at me. "Maybe a couple of days. You'll be fine by the end of the week. By then I'll have it sorted and a new batch started."

"A new batch? You must be joking." Paul hit him in the arm.

Basile didn't take his eyes off me. "Look, you're welcome to question the guys, but most of them are just as hungover as you. If you're looking for someone who . . . drugged you, I assure you no one even noticed you were gone until the line for the bathroom started piling up."

"And what about you? A little convenient, hmm? That I came to look for information on a fraternity that didn't want me snooping and ended up passed out in their bathroom like some freshman who doesn't know how to hold their liquor."

Oops.

The room could've frozen over and it wouldn't have felt colder. "Sorry, I thought you were here to have a couple of drinks and hang out. I didn't realize you were spying on us."

"That came out wrong, I—" But I'd already put my foot in my mouth.

"Well, Cella, I hope you got whatever it was you were looking for," Basile said icily. "If you'll excuse me."

And then he left the room.

My path back outside was considerably more awkward than the few conversations I would've had to bumble through if I would've just stayed sober. Why did I even drink at all last night? There was shit everywhere downstairs—half-empty cups and beer cans and bottles of energy drinks, wine bottles and bits and pieces of clothes and what I really hoped were gum wrappers. And the floor was so *sticky*.

These were the people I was so proud to have impressed?

I closed the front door of the house behind me, shaking off the last bit of chill, though no one was around to send me off. A few guys were snoring on the sofa. I felt a little like I was coming down with a fever.

CHAPTER THIRTY-THREE

I woke to the last rays of the sunset out my window, and Max sitting at the edge of my bed, eating. Naturally.

"Scone?" he asked, and I covered my head with a pillow. I could smell the sickly sweetness of it from here, something with cinnamon. A little like those scented brooms in the stores at the beginning of fall. My stomach heaved dangerously.

"No," I groaned, pressing the fabric into my nose.

"What happened last night? I tried calling."

"I sort of, um, passed out. On the bathroom floor."

"Gross," he said, miming shivers. "I bet that bathroom is disgusting. What'd you get for all that acting?"

I shook my head, grimacing. "Nothing."

"Nothing?" he said, picking a crumb off his T-shirt and dropping it in his mouth. "That must have been the performance of a lifetime. Why'd you get so drunk?"

"Wait, no." The note from the room upstairs. "Hand me my bag."

I dug my hands into my purse, but though everything else was present—phone, keys, chapstick, hairbrush—the slip of paper I'd found in the room wasn't.

"Shit. It must have fallen out when I was at the party, or . . ."

Or maybe I was too drunk and it had never made it into my bag in the first place. I was getting really sick of not being able to trust my own head.

"I got nothing." I slumped down farther into the bed.

"Nothing but a headache," he said, nodding to the way I rubbed my temples. My stomach twisted. Maybe it was just a hangover after all.

"I peeked into one of the brother's rooms, but it wasn't all that groundbreaking. Normal guy stuff." What had the note said? Something I couldn't make sense of, even if I had remembered. Probably just gibberish. Maybe a spell he'd been trying.

"Get a look at Grant's things?"

I shook my head. "When I saw him, he was terrified that someone might have seen him fall asleep. It was weird. Like he was being punished or something."

"What, like sleep deprivation?"

"I don't know. Maybe. I just get the feeling that this is bigger than Grant alone."

Max chewed his lip. "Hmm. What about Basile?"

"His office door was locked. Though I think you're right. Things were definitely off. Basile is hiding something. It may not be big, it may not have anything to do with Dani or Maya, but it's certainly something he doesn't want me knowing about."

He beamed. "I'll try my best not to gloat."

I leaned back on my pillow. "Now what?"

"Well, lucky for you, while you were busy getting wrecked, I did find something."

"What? You were there?"

Max smiled and pulled up a picture on his phone. "You think I was going to leave you alone with those creeps? I figured if I was at least there, I could hear if you screamed, maybe. Or if you called, I'd be close by."

Was that a blush creeping up his cheeks? 👺

"I snuck around the back of the property after the party and took these. Guess those guys we questioned in the hall

---

👺 Are you crazy? Of course, I wasn't going to leave her alone around those creeps. I played it off, but I'd panicked when she wasn't answering her phone, and it took everything in me to not burst in there and run to her rescue. But I knew she wouldn't have wanted that, especially if I was overreacting and everything was fine. The last thing I wanted was for her to get pissed that I'd ruined her plan and have her go and leave again.

were right. Phi Kat is into some weird shit, Cella. I don't think you should go back there alone."

The picture was of the empty field a little way from the back of the house. The picture also showed the faded white boards of the house. On the ground were bits of ash and wood—and the charred remains of what looked like bones.

"Please tell me those are not human."

"They look to be cattle. Rib, maybe. Too big to be human."

"What are they doing burning cattle bones?"

"Your guess is as good as mine."

"There was a bonfire at the party . . .", I said slowly, then my stomach twisted. "You don't think they were burning it then?"

Max grimaced. "We should tell the council."

"Tell them what, exactly? That we found some burned cattle bones at an old cattle ranch? They'll laugh in our faces. We can't even prove this is from the party. It could've been out there for ages."✤

"It's still suspicious."

"Definitely," I agreed, "but it's not enough."

Max nodded, rubbing his palms together. A conspiratorial glint came into his eye. "Okay. We lie low; we don't confront them just yet. We gather information, we watch them. If they're up to something, they'll slip. Basile might have his ship shut up tight, but the rest of them are bound to trip up sooner or later. And we'll be there when they do."

"And in the meantime?" I said.

"We wait, and you sleep off what I expect is bound to be one nasty hangover. And potentially some rare incurable disease or staph infection from what I suspect is a truly gnarly bathroom—"

I threw a pillow at him.

✤ In my searches of the area, I never came across bones of that size.

FROM THE JOURNAL OF DANICA STEWART
March 30th [two days before the murder]

—the pages hold the truth—

—and the truth will set you* free—

*your soul

CHAPTER THIRTY-FOUR

My truck parked, I sat in the driveway, counting the seconds. I looked in the mirror, reapplied chapstick for the fiftieth time, looked out over the dash. *Home.* How long could I sit here before they noticed the car in the driveway?

The house was just the same. The grass was dying in a few spots. A blue Buick, roof faded from the sun, sagged in its spot in front of the house where it hadn't been moved in years. Dad hadn't worked on it in ages. They'd both be home. It had been months since Mom had shown up to her job at the real estate firm.

Just like at school, here were so many reminders of things I didn't want to remember. After Aaron died, my mother slapped me hard across the face for talking back in that very same Buick. Days later, she flew off the handle over something I didn't even remember. When I told her what a fucked-up childhood I'd had, she told me every family had its problems.

But there was love here, too. It had just . . . faded over the years, like the tips of the grasses, like the sunny yellow paint on the door, now a dull cream.

I got out of the truck and walked past the house, out into the yard. Our five acres were overgrown, like most of the properties out here. Sure, it might be worth something if people actually wanted to live in Marble County, but they didn't. Our horse, Willow, had liked it enough. My parents had sold her not long after Aaron died.

I stopped below the oak tree where we buried him. There was a path that had been made in the grass, trudged by someone walking there several times a day. Mama or Daddy? Did they come out here and talk to him when they couldn't sleep? Did they ask him why?

I hadn't been back here since it happened. Couldn't walk in our house, couldn't face it or him, couldn't face every single way I'd failed. Failed my brother, failed my family, failed everyone. I had been so busy, focused on publications, and research, and mastering Magic, and studying studying studying that I didn't notice that my brother was so sad he didn't want to live anymore.

I stood staring at his grave. A small stone marker, the plainest, cheapest one they had. Next to it, they'd placed the hiking stick that he'd used to walk in the hills, the knob at the top carved into the face of an old man. It was starting to warp from the rain and wind.

If I'd noticed more, I would have seen the bags under his eyes and known he wasn't sleeping. He had a few friends at S&B. Did they have any clue? I asked them after it happened.

No, they'd said. Aaron was so quiet. He didn't tell a soul.

Of course. No one looked at a kid like Aaron.

My own brother, and I missed it.

Missed it even more because he'd been trying to reach out to me for help, and did I even look up from studying? Did I even look up from my stupid fucking obsession with Magic?

"I'm so fucking sorry," I whispered.

I barely registered the soft footsteps in the grass. Mom came up behind me, wrapping her cardigan around herself to guard from the night's chill. "Saw the truck. Thought that might be you."

I wiped my eyes with my sleeve. "It was my fault. I missed it."

"Oh, honey, no." The knit of her sweater brushed against my chin. She smelled the same, like those incense sticks she bought from the corner store. She looked the same too, only her hair was whiter, the roundness of her cheeks thinned. "You've got to let go of that. None of this was your fault."

It hit me how much older she was getting. I'd been gone,

but here everything felt like it was moving at warp speed. "I'm so sorry, Mama. That I've been gone. That I didn't come back. That I left in the first place." My breath came short and fast, the tears hot on my cheeks. I couldn't remember the last time I'd cried. "I'm so sorry about all of it."

"Shh, shh," she said, and my mother held me and kissed my cheek.

After I'd settled, she hummed a song she used to sing on the radio and offered me a cigarette. We looked out at the old tire swing, still on the ground from the time Aaron and I tried to swing at the same time and snapped the rope, at the fence that was falling over.

"We all blame ourselves. Lord knows, I struggle with it every day." She paused and looked toward the sky. "But the last thing he would've wanted was you throwing your life away over this. Go back to school, honey."

She walked back down the grass path to the house, leaving me alone with my thoughts.

CHAPTER THIRTY-FIVE

I wanted to return to the library and our research, but since the frat party, Max had harped on me nonstop about practicing together. Other than the attempt in Maritza's cottage, I hadn't done Magic since I was back on campus, and Max and I hadn't cast together at all. Word had spread quickly of my actions at the frat party, and now it felt like every room I entered greeted me with an icy silence. The students took offense to my role as a "spy"—only had myself to blame for that one—and believed I'd name them as suspects if they said the wrong thing around me. I caught whispers of rumors that I was actually an Arbiter, and other, more disturbing ones, too. That the underwear found in Dr. Strauss's office was mine. That we'd had an illicit affair, and now I was looking to pin the crime on someone else to protect him. That I'd gone mad. I was the one who'd cast the hex on Dani and was looking for my next victim. I had to agree with Max. Being confident in our Magic use would make me feel a lot safer here. And I had to face it sooner or later.

"Nice boots," Max said.

"Picked up some clothes from home."

"No shit? That's awesome. I hope you told your mom I said hello."

We were sitting across from each other in a little-used courtyard outside the Science building. A peaceful spot, with a few old pavers buried in the grass, beneath the roots of a gnarled juniper that provided a little shade. Max put his jacket down for me to sit on. I stared at him for a moment, his throat bobbing, eyes focused on the ground. Felt the brush and dip of his Magic—he was nervous. I was nervous, too. It had been a long time since we'd trusted each other enough to do this.

I closed my eyes, waiting for his breathing to settle and match mine. My mind wandered. A bee buzzed past. I was reminded of another breakthrough Max and I'd had together, a short while after we'd found out we were dimidiums.

We'd been at it all night, practicing in an abandoned room in Ludlow House, and we'd finally done it. We'd actually cast together, and I could feel his Magic surging through me. It wasn't perfect; we still had a long way to go, and our Magic came out in small spurts, as though from a faulty hose, but it worked. After weeks of long nights and brutal days, pushing ourselves to the absolute brink of our strength, finally, it had worked.

"That was . . . fucking amazing," he'd said, breathing hard. He broke out in a fit of exhausted, giddy laughter. "I mean, that was *fucking amazing*, Cella."

"I know," I said, beaming. Our first touch of Magic, what a head rush. I felt electric, like all my senses were on fire.

"Fuck, we've got to celebrate. Unless"—a rare glimpse of self-consciousness in the usually so self-assured Max—"unless you had plans?"

I shook my head. "I was going to eat Twizzlers and sneak my dog into my dorm room. It can wait."

And he laughed again, that adorable, boisterous laugh where he gripped his sides. I loved hearing him laugh. Suddenly, I knew that if I could, I'd make him laugh, every day, for the rest of my life.

He took us to a small club near Albuquerque, dark and smoky, and the music pounded through my veins. After a couple of drinks, we could've been anywhere in the world and it wouldn't have made a difference to me, as long as I was with him.

We soon found out that Magic wasn't the only thing

that worked well as dimidiums. When we danced, we moved smoothly, his hips pressing against mine, perfectly in sync. He'd drunk just enough for a buzz, to laugh that warm laugh that melted me to my core. I took another sip and looked into his eyes.

He grabbed my hand and pulled me closer, letting my hand rest on his chest. "I love this song," he whispered.

I couldn't look away from him. His eyes were a clear, liquid blue. A thin line of stubble ran over his chin and down his neck. "Me too."

He put a hand on my waist and whispered in my hair, "Come here."

He cupped my chin in his hand and tilted it up to him. His lips were feverishly hot, parting slightly to invite me inside. We fell into the dark, the music pumping all around us. My legs tangled in his, his hips pressing me into the wall. A knee slipped between my legs, and my hands looped around his waist, pulling him closer.

My dorm room afterward was a blur of hot breath on lips, flashes of his chest, and the sharp line of his hip in the sliver of light shining through the curtain. We breathed together, and one by one, more pieces of clothing slipped to the floor.

I wrapped my hand around the back of his neck and yanked him close, greedy for the heat of his lips on me. His lips traced down my neck, my shoulder, to my collarbone, and down. All along the line to my stomach. And as we tangled together in a flurry of clothes and hot breath and sticky kisses, for once I felt clean, I felt whole, I felt safe.

"You fucking wreck me," he said, lips against my neck.

"Are you sure we should do this?" I whispered, in between soft kisses in the moonlight. Despite how good it felt, I was afraid of what people would say, afraid of rumors and of stupid people's talk. God, I was afraid of so many things.

And here he was, afraid of nothing.

"Fuck them. Forget about everything else except this right here. Because you and me, this is real. This is what matters."

Now the bell outside the Science building trilled four p.m. Max frowned.

"Did you want to go first?"

I blinked. "Sorry, what?"

"Did you want to go first pulling? Or should I?"

"Oh. I can."

I cleared my throat and tentatively reached out to his aura.

Our Magic brushed up against each other, as if we were reacquainting ourselves. In a way, his Magic balanced mine. On my own, my Magic was dark and watery—but when we cast together, I ended up in altogether nicer locales. Instead of at the bottom of a murky lake, seaweed clawing at my legs, I'd be on a sunny beach, splashing in tide pools, or floating down a peaceful, rolling river.

I pulled a couple of threads to me. First only two, then another and another, and gathered them in my palms. Even if my body wasn't truly there, my mind filled it in for me. I could feel the water trickling onto my feet, the wind lifting my air, the night sky blinking back at me. But I wasn't alone. In the distance—somewhere far, but not too far—were galloping horses. They were breathing hard, writhing to get free of the leather binding their bodies. To reach me.

I remembered all of a sudden what Dr. Simmons had said about Max and me when I'd first arrived. *Extraordinary, much like the law of gravitational force. The closer you are in each other's orbit, the stronger your pull to each other.*

I felt our Magic swirling and twisting and whipping around, a thousand tiny pieces of electricity firing on all my nerves.

Somewhere outside all of it, Max took a shuddering breath. "Cel."

Too much.

"Sorry," I murmured, my voice not sounding quite like my own. Because while my body was in the courtyard with him, *I* was here, in the Magic, on a short stretch of windswept, forgotten beach, tree roots tangled in the rocks behind me. I let some of the threads I'd pulled from him go and took a deep breath.

I scooped a palmful of water beneath me, watched with wonder as it stayed molded to the shape of my palm afterward. As if it had gone as solid as metal, the threads of Magic writhing beneath it, all lit up like stars.

"Cel," he said again, breathing hard. "Cel, it's too much. I've got to stop."

"I can hear the galloping," I said faintly. "What's wrong?"

Then, like a cold wind receding, I felt him tug his threads back. The stars in the sky above me blinked out one by one, until I was left in complete darkness.

I dropped my own threads and opened my eyes. "You okay?"

But he was looking at me with a scrutinizing gaze.

"What?"

"You weren't holding an object."

"Oh." I dug it out of my pocket. "Here."

Sweat shined across his forehead. He frowned, nodding before wiping the sweat off his face with his shirt. He wearily leaned forward, and his hands shook. "I guess I'm just not used to it. It's a lot of power; we really need to practice with it more regularly."

"Yeah."

He got up to get a drink of water, and I closed my eyes, willing away the cold, dark feeling I'd been left in when he'd gone. I felt it when he walked away. Just like I'd felt it every day when he was gone. Alone, in the dark. And I didn't want to be alone. Not anymore.

I realized out here under the dry, unrelenting New Mexico sun, I felt the first clarity I had in months. I knew what Vern would say, that it was because I was here with Max. Connected to my dimidium.

Maybe he was right, and maybe he wasn't. All I knew was that, for once, things weren't so overwhelming. For once, things felt like they were going to be alright.

Field Journal of Luce Montgomery

My hands are shaking so badly I can hardly hold the pen, but I've got to get this down.

I found something.

Something terrible. Something—I have to tell someone.

I was looking for animal trails using the map from the mycologists' network. There were signs of a small predator in the area, scatterings of tiny bones belonging to a bird and grass tamped down by scampering bodies. As I followed the trail farther, I noticed bits of fur and blood scraped across the grass. It wasn't as far from the school as I thought I would need to go. The rocks were loose, so I had to watch my footing, but I continued down to the bottom of the canyon.

It was there I found mushrooms.

It wasn't the right conditions for fruiting bodies, but food was food, and whatever nutrients this fungi fed on were sure to spark the interest of *Agaricus cataphractus* as well. I used the small hand trowel I'd brought with me and got on my hands and knees. I'd found plenty of decomposing animal bodies, dead birds, cats, coyotes in my line of work. I wasn't squeamish. But when my shovel hit bone and I caught a glimpse of long hair that didn't belong to any animal, my scream sent the birds scattering across the sky.

I dropped the trowel right where I stood.

My only question is what now? Where do I go? Who can I go to with this? And why do the voices chanting on the breeze sound like they're getting closer?

I'll make for the closest building to me, the Phi Kat house. I can see it now in the distance. In the upstairs window, a light is on.

FROM THE JOURNAL OF DANICA STEWART
April 1ˢᵀ [the day of the murder]

Danica DANICA DANICAAA DANICA Danica Dani Dani Deni Deneni Deani Deai Dead Dead DEAD DEADDEAD DAEAD DEADDEADDEAD

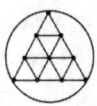

we're all a little bit monster nowadays, aren't we?*

---

* This appears to be written with the same strange, circular letters as in a previous journal entry.

CHAPTER THIRTY-SIX

I ran into Basile the next morning in the Business building. I made to walk right past him, pretend I didn't see him, but the building was old, and the floorboards beneath the ratty gray carpet needed to be replaced. I took one squeaky step, and he turned. "Cella?"

Something was different, and we both knew it. I'd deleted my phone's history, stopped watching his videos, stopped looking at his posts. The part of me that whispered warnings in the back of my mind was on red alert. I didn't know how to reconcile the two versions of him in my head. Basile Samir, the brilliant theorist, with this idea that could change the world . . . and Basile Samir, head of a creepy frat, who may have drugged me and who could very well be involved in Dani's death.

"I can't help but feel awful about how things went down the other night. Truly, I—you're really not going to look at me?"

I pulled my lip between my teeth and chewed, making a decision. "Don't worry about it," I said, and his eyes widened in surprise.

"Really?"

There was still something I wanted from Basile, information he had that I badly wanted, that I would've given anything for. Maybe he was a devil . . . but sometimes the devil was the only one willing to tell you what you wanted to know.

"Water under the bridge. Honestly, I'm a little embarrassed myself for accusing you all, when everyone was so nice to me all night. You gave me no reason to be suspicious, and I was a jerk. I'm sorry."

He tucked his hands in his pockets and rocked back. "I'll admit, I didn't expect this, but I'm glad to hear it. The guys were really excited to see you, you know. I think we have a lot we could learn from each other."

I smiled innocently at him. "My thoughts exactly."

Over the next few days, I spent time with Basile in secret, soaking up everything I could about the Reality Paradox. But no matter how much I learned, how long we spent together, it wasn't enough. He still seemed to be holding something back. He would trickle out bits of information, but always kept me wanting more, like a fish chasing after a shining, razor-sharp hook.

"Why do they call you Mathematici?" I blurted as we sat in the empty Auditorium.

He blinked, surprised. "It's just a joke, really. Because we're mathematicians. A lot of the guys are into the Ancient Greeks. Plato and stuff. You know, bunch of nerds."

"Yeah, you said that. What about the Ancient Greeks? How do they relate?"

"Well . . . Plato says to learn the truth, we have to go beyond words. That's what the Reality Paradox is all about. It's more than just its mathematical aspects; it's a belief system, a way of life. It's about finding the truth and about grasping the real nature of things. One way to do that is through mathematics. Numbers are something we can use to make sense of our world. That's what Mathematici means. It's a sign of respect, that I'm on the path."

"Hmm," I said, chewing on his words, still not quite satisfied.

"You seem unconvinced."

I tucked a hair behind my ear. "I just don't know about the whole divine origin of the soul thing."

"I know it sounds far-fetched at first. But the divine origin of a man's soul is not a new concept. In fact, it's extremely old, rooted in the Orphic religion. There are recordings of it even in the Derveni Papyrus.* *Of all things the soul is immortal, but the bodies are subject to death.*

"In truth, it's not all that different from the concept of Heaven. Except this way the scale is tipped back into the hands of those who've always felt powerless, who've always been overlooked. If you live a disciplined life, stay on a path of good, there's hope for you to make it to the world of Being, too."

"And the world of Being, that's the one you reference in the Paradox?" I asked. *The one where I could reach Aaron?* was my silent question.

He nodded. "The world of Being is where all ideas are created and all thought is first generated.† Where daimons and gods and the souls of men who've been perfected go. You'd have a hand in shaping every thought, every idea, for all of time. That's the thought, anyway," he said with a shy smile. "I know you may not agree with it—plenty of people don't—but that's what a belief system is, isn't it? This one gives hope to a lot of people. It promises there's more to life than"—he gestured around us—"than *this*. It's a way for people to feel like they can have at least a modicum of power in their own destinies. Some power in a world that's made us feel powerless. We all just want to be heard. Don't you?"

I sighed. "Most of the time, I'm just trying to get through the day. Did you come up with all this yourself?"

"No. My beliefs were introduced to me by our teacher."

---

* According to Dr. Perez, the Derveni Papyrus is the oldest surviving manuscript in the Western world and possibly the oldest surviving papyrus written in Greek. It contains commentary on an Orphic poem concerning the birth of the gods.

† After we spoke, I did a search on this "world of Being." It's adopted from Plato's theory of Forms, in reference to the unchanging world where the Forms exist. It says that our physical world is not as real as the changeless world where ideas and thoughts are generated—the world of Being. Though it's obvious Basile took some liberties with the original idea, expanding on it and changing it to fit his Reality Paradox.

"And who is that?"

"He's a brilliant man, though people have all sorts of disparaging names for him. Crook, swindler, con artist, chief of charlatans, you name it, but you're an anthropologist. You get it. One man's religion is another man's Magic, isn't it?"

He looked down at me, hand tracing along his smooth chin. "You know, Cella, if I tell you any more, I might have to make you a member of the frat. You've got to promise to at least come talk to the guys, about Object Theory. About how you were able to do what you did. It's not every day someone is able to cast outside their objects."

I bit my lip. "Oh. Yeah. Of course I will." I squirmed. I was so close now. Could taste the feeling on my tongue, of something good and real and right within my reach.

The truth was I would've told him whatever he wanted, done whatever he wanted, just to learn more.

Cut Not Fire With a Sword

I spent the rest of the morning in the library. I was heading out for lunch when I heard raised voices from a few buildings over.

"—and you tell your little buddy Grant that if I see him on this campus again, I'll kill him."

Oh no. Oh no no no.

I raced across campus as fast as my feet would take me, silently thanking whoever was listening that I was wearing cowboy boots instead of my jellies. Besides the scorching ground, there was broken glass everywhere.

Max was in the shadow of the Numerology and Mathematics building, finger prodding Basile's chest. They both looked as mad as I'd ever seen them.

"Max," I hissed, "what are you doing?"

"Teaching your little friend here a few things."

Shit, shit, shit.

People had already gathered to watch. I had flashbacks to losing control of my Magic all over again. I tugged his arm. "Stand down," I hissed. "I've got it under control."

He yanked his arm out of my grasp, and I got a whiff of the liquor on his breath.

"Are you *drunk*? It's the middle of the day. What is wrong with you?"

"Don't worry, Cel. I'll only hurt him a little."

"You're out of your depth, cowboy," Basile growled. His hair was in disarray, pieces falling from their perfectly set position.

Max's eyes rolled back as he laughed. "Wanna bet?" The leather wound its way around his wrist as Max reached for his Magic. I could almost hear the pound of horses' hooves on grass.

He'd pulled a lot of Magic—way too much.

I gasped as the Magic ripped out of me. Max's shoulders sagged like he'd been hit with a boulder. He gritted his teeth and straightened, but I knew it had drained him. It was not only his life he was being reckless with.

In response, Basile closed his eyes, whispering quick and harsh under his breath. I could feel the Magic rising all around us, hissing and twisting in the air.

"Stop! Stop! You're going to kill yourselves," I cried. "Look, you've proven how tough you are. Happy?"

Max tipped the bottle he held into his mouth and shrugged. "Not particularly."

"You're not worth my time," Basile said as he turned to walk away. "Cella, you should get a better handle on your dog."

Max tipped the dregs of the bottle into his mouth and smashed it on the ground.

Alright, he's gone now, you can all go home, I thought furiously, wishing the crowd would dissipate. I turned to Max. "What is wrong with you? Did you and Julia have a fight or something?"

He laughed a cruel laugh I'd never heard before. "Julia and

I broke up days ago because she couldn't handle how much time I was spending with you. I told her there was nothing to worry about until I was blue in the face. She didn't believe me." He crunched the last of the bottle with his boot.

"I'm sorry," I said quietly. "I didn't want you guys to break up." The lie spilled out of my mouth.

"You know what the funny thing is? I'm relieved. What girl would want to be with someone who has some mystical other half?" He laughed, that same mean laugh. I could barely look at him. 👻

I'd been jealous of him and Julia, there was no denying that, but that didn't mean I wanted to see him miserable. I didn't want to see him like this.

"Is there . . . anything I can do? Do you want to talk about it?"

"Don't worry about it." He looked at me suddenly, and I could see all the hurt swirling up in his eyes, such a dark blue they were almost black. "You know, sometimes I wonder what the hell I'm doing, chasing after a woman who doesn't want a damn thing to do with me. I don't even know why I brought you here."

I frowned. "The school brought me here."

"Forget it."

"Max, what do you mean 'you brought me here'?" I asked, catching the twist of his mouth, how he could barely look at me. "Dr. Robetresse requested my help on this case. The council—the council wanted my help. You found me because they asked you to. Right?"

"It's nothing."

"Wait." I paused, started shaking my head. "Max, you didn't." This whole time—forcing me to relive every single

---

👻 I've got to be honest, I feel pretty ashamed reading this account. I hated the way she looked at me then, but I felt all of it slipping through my fingers, my whole plan getting her to come back here, losing it all to that manipulative prick.

traumatic memory of my brother and Max and setting Luce's car on fire, and the fallout afterward, slowly and inevitably becoming a pariah, watching as my reputation went up in smoke—this whole time, he'd let me think I'd had to come back because Dr. Robetresse and the school needed my help.

He wouldn't meet my eyes.

"Tell me you didn't float our names for this investigation."

"They needed someone who knew objects, Cella. They needed us. Dr. R said herself Ellendale and Amy disagree for sport, that the council couldn't work together for three seconds."

"Neither can we! She's probably going to die, you know, because we couldn't figure it out! And that's on us."

He kicked the ground with his shoe. "Forget about it! Fuck, Cella, now I know how goddamn painful it is for you to even be in the same city as me. I'm sorry, okay? Is that what you want to hear?"

"So that was it, then. You needed Magic so badly that you couldn't stand to let me live my life in peace. What the fuck do you even need Magic for? You wrangle horses!"

He held my gaze, then looked away. "Forget about it."

"Oh no, you don't walk away from me, Max Middlemore!" I grabbed a rock and chucked it hard as I could at his back. It glanced uselessly off his belt; I fumed. "And after you embarrassed the hell out of me with Basile. I'm getting information from him! You need to stay out of it."

"Are you, Cel? Because it sure as hell looks to me that he's getting information from you."

I was so frustrated I wanted to scream. "What do you care about what I do or who I talk to?"

He threw his hands up. "Because it feels like I'm losing you all over again!"

Both of us stood there staring at each other, breathing hard. A blisteringly hot breeze swept through the grounds, lifting the branches of a creosote bush.

"Look," he said, "I'm not going to pretend it's somehow

the chivalrous thing to do to let you go and leave forever. I know you said you never wanted to see me again, but what about what I want?"

I cackled, aware of how maniacal it sounded, but past the point of caring. People were gathered to stare at us now. "When do we ever not consider what you want? We broke up because you couldn't ignore what *you* wanted."

He looked at me and shook his head, once, firmly. "That's not fair, and you know it. We were not together when Luce and I . . . Look, I know I've hurt you. But I'm going to fight for it. I just got you back, Cel. And I see you pulled into this shit again, somebody talks a big game and entices you with their theories and all these exciting ideas, and you jump in because that's who you are, and I love that about you, but damn, I hate when you leave me behind. You're getting sucked in again, just like with Jamie and the others. And maybe I'm not as smart as Basile or any of those guys, but I know what it looks like when you're pulling away." He shook his head. "You're just running, Cel. It's what you've been doing for years. And I'm not going to let you do it anymore. It was time for you to come home, to come back to your life and your career and your Magic. You know it, too."

Then he turned and left me there, staring after him, the sound of boots crunching against glass still ringing in my ears.

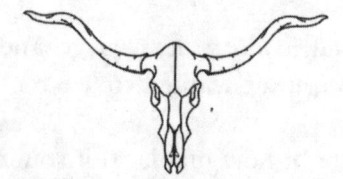

CHAPTER THIRTY-SEVEN

We didn't make up after the fight. The next day, Max shuffled into the library looking like he'd seen better days, dark bags under his eyes, face drained of much of its color.

"Hey," he said, tossing his hat down on the table.

"Hey," I said.

And that was that. It wasn't that I didn't want to breach the topic of our fight. Okay, maybe it was a little bit of that, but I was also still mad, and I'm sure he was too. That didn't change the fact that we still had a job to do. We wanted to save Dani, and we owed it to her to not let our near constant state of unrest get in the way of it.

So, for now, it was easier to just try and work around our own issues.

I nibbled a blueberry muffin and scrolled through the news headlines, trying to wake up. Wildfires on the West Coast,* the rise and fall of Hollywood's hottest celebs, and blah blah blah. But it was a header off the sideboard that caught my attention.

How Did Dean Morren Become America's Biggest TikTok Star?

A little younger than me, Dean Morren had become popular for his video-game content. He'd gotten into a bit of a

---

* Which Seinford, the wealthy Magician turned venture capitalist, was trying to alleviate. Seinford (of Seinford and Brown) was one of the school's largest donors, along with the Brown family, owners of the Southwest's largest agricultural conglomerate. Seinford was also trying to fix the drought in California through the use of a "curious new drilling" technique, which actually wasn't drilling at all, but Magic.

firestorm last May over a challenge that landed a kid in the hospital. Along with the story was a photo of him. My eyes traveled to the tattoo on his wrist, and I nearly dropped my phone.

It was a tattoo of the same ten-dot triangle, the same symbol I'd seen in Dani's notebooks, though not inside a circle this time. The triangle stood on its own, a version of the symbol I'd seen over the dormitories across campus.

I looked over at Max, opening my mouth, then closing it. He sighed. "Better tell me whatever it is before you pee your pants."

"Look at this!" I blurted, thrusting the phone under his nose. "Dean Morren, he's a TikTokker." I pointed to the tattoo on his wrist. "It's the same symbol that I saw in the frat house!"

Max frowned and looked down. "We can't talk to them again."

My face fell. "Look, I know everything yesterday was—a lot," I stumbled.

"That's not it." He dug a card out of his pocket and tossed it on the table.

I turned it over in my hands. "LP Lewis Associates, Attorney at Law. So, he really got a lawyer?"

"It's why Basile"—he spat out the name like a bug—"and I were talking yesterday. A girl said she saw Grant lurking outside House Torlaine the night before the murder. I went to go ask him about it, but the brothers wouldn't let me in the house. Threw me this fucking card."

I deflated and put my head on the desk. Yet another roadblock. "They did warn us, I guess."

He tapped his finger on the card. "It's not just some local guy, either. That's a private firm in Boston. The kind that doesn't come cheap."

"Could we get the council to intervene?" I sat up, an idea sparking. "Make him talk to us?"

"Not unless you'd like this lawyer to slap the school with a lawsuit. But we can ask Dr. Robetresse."

I propped my hand on my chin. "*Blargh*," I murmured,

thinking back on our last meeting with Basile and Grant. "So embarrassing."

Max opened his phone to send a text, then frowned. "Did you see this? They want us to come to a council meeting. Sent three texts already. Shit, we'd better go."

When we got to the meeting, Dr. Robetresse was pacing in front of the room. We sat down, and she dove straight in.

"Thank you for all coming on such short notice. Given the nature of the situation, I thought it best you all know immediately." She took a deep breath and gritted her teeth.

"Another person has been afflicted in the same manner as Danica Stewart. A member of our very own council, Luce Montgomery."

My chest turned to ice. Everything around me felt like it was moving in slow motion. Before my brain could catch up, Dr. Robetresse was already fielding questions from the rest of the council.

"No, she was found convulsing outside of Maritza's cottage. As I understand it, she had been ill for some time. An infection of some type. It is possible she was going to Maritza's for help when it happened."

"And where is Maritza?" The question was from Dr. Nguyen.

"We've set Luce up in the old Biology building. Maritza is splitting her time between the two of them, trying to treat them both. Though, obviously, it's a lot of pressure on Maritza. We're contacting medical at Britton Arcane and Maritza's colleagues in the Marble County medical community, those she trusts to be discreet, to help contain the situation."

"There's something else," she said, looking around at everyone in turn and pausing. "A strange thing that Maritza is reporting. After Luce was discovered, the effects on Dani's body seem to have changed."

"My God," Dr. Perez said quietly, "how much more can the

girl take?" From the sympathetic looks going around the table, it was clear many of them were thinking the same thing.

"Curiously, it seems to have had some stabilizing effect on her. She's got more energy herself, she's even able to sit up, from what Maritza tells me. Though something warns me this is not good news." Dr. Robetresse turned to me. "Have you any idea of how to stop this? Or who did it? Anything at all? I don't think I have to stress how short our timetables are. Not if we're to save them."

I stumbled. And now the moment when my failure was on full display for everyone to see, how absolutely out of my depth I was. I got to look all of them in the face and tell them that I had absolutely nothing to show for the three weeks I'd been here investigating. No culprit, no specific hex to point to, and no counterspell to undo the damage. Graduation was mere days away, and then everyone would break for the summer. Whoever did this would get away. And Dani would . . . I didn't even want to think what would happen to Dani. "I . . . We're looking . . . that is, we hope to have something soon."

I had to face the facts. We had no clue what we were dealing with, and every day we didn't was putting the entire campus in danger.

Dr. Robetresse's shoulders deflated, and I saw the faith she once had in me drain out of her. She turned to the rest of the room. "Does anyone else have any ideas? Any at all? Luce was working with Maritza on a salve to aid in the healing of Dani's skin, but I don't know if it has been effective."

I felt so useless, so utterly hopeless, all I could whisper out was that we were doing the best we could. We're trying, we're trying—it was all I'd been saying. But now it was quite clear: my best wasn't good enough.

CHAPTER THIRTY-EIGHT

Another person possessed with whatever was taking over Dani. The students were in danger; the staff was in danger. The thing I'd been called here to prevent had happened, and I couldn't do a damn thing. I felt worse than useless. What was I even doing here? Why had Max brought us here?

A light hand landed on my shoulder. "You can do this," Vern said, sliding a cup of tea toward me. "I know you can."

"Vern, I don't know what I'm doing—"

He put up a hand to stop me. "Now you listen here. You're here every day, killing yourself to save that girl. You're doing as well as anyone could. And now what? A little bend in the road, and you're just going to stop? A little stumble has never stopped you before. At least, it didn't stop the old Cella."

The "old" Cella. I huffed. The old Cella got her heart broken and smashed into a tiny million pieces. The old Cella flew into a rage and nearly killed someone. I didn't want to be the old Cella.

"Look, now, I understand," he said, in his gravelly voice. "You've been carrying around a whole lot of hurt. I know being here is hard, and it's bringing up a lot of painful memories. It's only natural to put as much distance between yourself and what's hurting you as you can." He put up his hands. "But what happened with Aaron was not your fault. Forgive yourself. Forgive Max. Take it from me—I've been around the block once or twice—if you don't let go of all that hurt you're carrying around, sooner or later it's gonna bury you."

I held my head in my hands. "I'm trying. It just feels like, no matter what I do, I keep sliding backward. I take one step forward and two steps back."

"Honey, that's what healing is. You're just starting to trust again, and that's hard. But you came back here, didn't you? That's a giant leap forward in my book."

He landed a kiss on my head. "You can do this." His gaze was fixed in such a determined stare that I nearly believed him. "You just need a cup of tea and a clear head. I'll leave you to it."

I sipped the tea he left for me, a rich, nutty rooibos with milk and a hint of peppermint, and took a deep breath.

I started slowly. I looked up Dean Morren's interviews with the press, watched his videos—a good portion of the nearly four hundred of them—until the sun went down outside the window. The breeze that drifted in was cool; an owl hooted. A group of coyotes barked and howled in the distance.

Dean Morren went to college, but not here, and he definitely wasn't a member of Phi Kat. As a matter of fact, he was pretty anti-Greek life, even made a video mocking college frats after news of hazing at a school on the East Coast.

I stumbled on a clip of him from one of those prank shows where the hosts run after you on the street and shove a microphone in your face. "What's your tattoo mean?"

Dean shrugged. "It's just some math thing I used to be into."

A math thing?

But still, even when it felt like it was right there in front of me, itching at the back of my skull, I couldn't find any connection to him and Phi Kat, nor any other math organizations around the country.

I had just put my head down on the desk when Max stumbled over with a mess of notes of his own, mind maps and arrows of jotted-down questions going every which way, looking just as frustrated as me. "This is hopeless," I groaned. "At this rate, half the school will be dead before we even land in the right direction."

He stared at his notes. "I think I have an idea."

"What?" I hurried after him, but when he was excited about something, that long loping stride was a force to be reckoned with. He finally stopped in front of Maritza's cottage.

"Dani?" I asked, "*You* want to talk to Dani?"

He was absolutely the last person I thought would suggest such a thing, given that every other time I suggested it, his answer had been an emphatic "Absolutely the fuck not." Lately, he didn't so much as stray onto that side of campus.

"I know, but Dr. R said she's stronger now. Maybe she'll be able to talk to us. She's the only one who knows for sure what happened, so let's come right out and ask her. Ask if she's seen this symbol before."

My hands instinctively wrapped around my torso. "I hope you're sure about this."

When we walked into Maritza's cottage, Dani was awake. More surprising than that, instead of on the bed, she was sitting at the round wooden table near the kitchen. A piece of paper was in front of her, a black crayon in her hand.

"Come in," Maritza said, "we're just having lunch. She seems to have regained some of her strength."

Her eyes were still ringed in purple and her arms and legs were still scarred, but color had returned to her cheeks. There was no blood dripping down her arms. I couldn't even see any bandages.

Max's eyebrow lifted, footsteps halting. "Are you sure about that? Is it safe, I mean? Considering last time . . ."

Maritza nodded. "It's perfectly safe. She's on a strict regimen of medication to keep her moods stable. Even more now, since Luce." She looked away.

"I'm glad you're feeling better, Dani," I said quietly. She let Maritza spoon soup into her mouth, still drawing with her crayon.

"She doesn't talk much," Maritza said. "Her new medication makes her more docile."

Dani stared straight ahead like a zombie. What she was doing couldn't in good faith be considered drawing; she was etching a thick black mark into the paper over and over again.

When I touched her, she flinched. It was only slight, but I was so surprised I nearly lurched back in alarm.

I sat down in the chair farthest from her, warning bells ringing in my ears.

"That's a nice drawing," Max prodded. "Cella draws a bit, too. Don't you, Cella?"

"Yes," I said, trying and failing to mask my nervousness with a cough. "Just doodles, really. One of my objects is part of a leather journal."

A hiccup of laughter escaped from the seemingly lifeless girl in front of us. My shoulders went rigid.

"Why is that funny, Dani?" Max asked, leaning forward. My breath squeezed in my lungs. All I wanted to do was get in my truck and never look back. But I forced myself to stay in my seat.

Dani didn't answer. She continued scribbling, running her crayon over and over the same mark on the paper.

I looked over at Maritza, who had retreated to the kitchen but was watching with keen interest. "Does she do this often?"

"No," she said, looking bewildered. "That's the first time she's laughed since she came into my care."

Dani dropped her crayon on the table and looked down at her drawing. What I'd thought were just random scratches across the paper I now saw were a series of interconnected and intersecting lines. It was nothing I could read, but it had to be deliberate. Again, I felt the flicker of something just out of reach, something I should've understood. I ground my teeth in frustration.

"What does your drawing mean, Dani?" Max asked.

No response.

He looked at me meaningfully. *Your turn.* I shifted uncomfortably.

"Dani, did you know the members of Phi Kat?"

No answer.

I opened to the picture of Dean Morren's tattoo and slid my phone to her. "What about this symbol? Have you seen it before? Or this one?" I swiped to a picture of the marking over House Torlaine.

Her eyes flicked over the phone, and her grip on the crayon tightened. She scribbled harder than ever on her paper, hand flying over the page.

I pushed forward. "It's all over campus. We can't make heads or tails of it, but you know what it is, don't you? It was in your notebook. Did you draw it?"

She held the crayon so tightly I could see tiny cracks running up its side.

Maritza's voice hitched up an octave. "Maybe that's enough for one day. I don't want her getting all riled up."

I bit my lip, a hazy memory surfacing of the dream I had featuring Dani, where she'd desperately wanted to tell me something. "What about . . . 'Perhaps you will succeed, perhaps you will cause terror'?"

Dani's eyes flashed, burrowing straight into mine. I saw what could only be called recognition in her eyes.

"What does it mean, Dani?"

Dani started rocking back and forth and muttering to herself. Her voice was too low for me to make out the words. Maritza backpedaled, knocking into the wooden manger scene.

The symbols on Dani's paper were larger now. Big sweeping letters with circles at the bottoms. Now I could see the pattern formed by the interconnecting lines.

"Ring letters," I said, tracing a finger over the lines. "I've seen these characters before. They say they're the letters of angels."

Dani stopped. Her eyes flicked up to meet mine so fast

I nearly fell backward. She laughed, a guttural sound. "Or demons."

Max took in a sharp breath. Maritza screamed, but we were so close now, so close to uncovering everything. If I could just—

"I know how the other students treated you," I said, the words flying off my tongue. "Did they hurt you? Did you try a spell to get back at them?"

She scribbled faster, her crayon flying across the page. Over and over, she traced the letters, carving into the paper until she went straight through to the table.

"Cella," Max warned.

"Tell me. Tell me what it means. Who did this to you?"

Her murmuring quickened. First just a whisper, then louder and louder. "Go on with your Magic spells and sorcery. Perhaps you will succeed," she hissed, "perhaps you will cause terror. These books are banned. They are forbidden. Stray not from the path; wear not a ring; cross not your heart. Look not from the light."

"I think that's enough," Max said, reaching for my hand.

"What do you think, Cella, would you like to join me?" she whispered, her fingers curling toward me. A grotesque grin spread across her face. Max lunged, wrapping an arm around my waist to pull me back.

"Cella, get out of here!"

"Do not speak of these things in the dark," she said, her tone guttural yet saccharine. "They find you there."

"What," Max said, once we made it out of the cottage, "in the ever-loving fuck was that?"

"I don't know, but I think we're finally getting somewhere."

"Getting somewhere?" Uncontrolled laughter burst from him. "Have you lost your mind? I was about ready for her freaking jaw to unhinge and gobble you right up."

"At least then we'd know what we're dealing with."

"I'm just going to pretend you didn't say that. Great, and she just leaves. Where are you going?"

"To look up the passage that she kept repeating. It's got to mean something. Maybe she was giving us a clue. Telling us where to look."

"Or she was just enjoying scaring the piss out of us. Cella, wait."

We reached the library doors, and I pushed them open, Max still on my heels. "Cella, I know you want to help Dani and all, but . . ." He shook his head. "You were right. We shouldn't have gone in there because whatever that . . . thing is, is not Dani. It's the remnants of the curse or hex or whatever was done to her. And let's not forget—she already, you know, *murdered someone*."

I nodded, roaming the aisles. I knew what I was looking for, but where would it be?

"I think we should forget it," Max babbled, "abandon this whole thing, get her sent to an asylum where she is locked up twenty-four seven and can't hurt anyone else. Just cut our losses now. Look, I'm the last person to admit defeat, but we should be reasonable here. The person that Dani was died when she killed Maya. There is nothing human left in her."

He stood, panting in front of me, waiting for my answer. But I was barely listening. Because I'd found what I was looking for and was already flipping through the delicate, yellowing pages.

"Are you even listening to me?" he asked, running his hands down his face.

"I'm not abandoning her, Max. Not when we've finally got a lead as to what's causing this."

"I'm not saying you should abandon her; I'm saying we should . . . rethink the whole 'saving her' bit."

"Besides," I said, beaming, "I've found the passage she was referencing."

For perhaps the entire time I'd known him, Max's mouth fell open, and no words came out.

I pointed to the page in front of me. "It's a Bible passage. I knew it sounded familiar, and with the mention of demons . . .* but I couldn't quite put my finger on it before. Then I remembered something from my old Ancient Magic and Christianity class with Dr. Perez. He was always picking out different passages for us to read and study the context. The full verse was in the context of foretelling the fall of Babylon, 'the daughter of Chaldeans.' It's something of a rebuke, deriding the wicked city and all those who practice Magic within its walls. Like if you're so powerful, see if you can prevent it."

> Keep on, then, with your magic spells
> and with your many sorceries,
> which you have labored at since childhood.

---

* Something strikes me that I hadn't realized in the moment. When Dani said, "or demons," she didn't actually say "demon." She pronounced it "daimon" (as in the Ancient Greek δαίμων and the Latin *daemon*). After a discussion with Dr. Perez, I thought the etymology of this term might be of note. As far as Western connotations, Homer used *daimon* almost interchangeably with the term *theos* (god), but particularly for describing the activity of a nonpersonified god or godlike activity. This is similar to Plato's writings, where Socrates speaks of his *daimonisque*, a voice or godlike activity that warns him against being led astray. In Plato's *Phaedo*, a daimon is shown as a helpful entity that lives with a person beginning at birth; upon death, it serves as a guide for the soul into the afterlife. For many thousands of years, the term meant something entirely different than the Christian connotation of "daemon": evil-doing or evil spirits. There's much to be said about why the change came to be. About how and why daemons came to function as an explanation for disease, for bad behavior, for disability, for disorder in ancient times, and why identifying Greek gods with demons started happening more and more. One would be remiss to ignore the war for religious authority occurring between Graeco-Roman cults and Christianity in ancient times (again, if you see this, thank you, Dr. Perez, for your insight on this topic). After all, it's so much easier to turn a population against a belief system if you consider one of their basic tenets, conversing with *daimones*—or even their gods themselves—as something inherently evil.

Perhaps you will succeed,
  perhaps you will cause terror.
All the counsel you have received has only worn you out!
Let your astrologers come forward,
  those stargazers who make predictions month by
    month,
  let them save you from what is coming upon you.
Surely they are like stubble;
  the fire will burn them up.
They cannot even save themselves
  from the power of the flame.
These are not coals for warmth;
  this is not a fire to sit by.
That is all they are to you—
  these you have dealt with
  and labored with since childhood.
All of them go on in their error;
  there is not one that can save you.*

Max made a low whistle.

I thought back to the way Dani's eyes burrowed into mine, and I shivered. "It's portraying Magic as a wicked deed.† What else did she say? 'These books are banned, they are forbidden.'" I flipped furiously through Dani's notebook, an echo of something from the night of the frat party swirling

---

* Isaiah 47:12–15 NIV.

† Nothing new here. This particular excerpt reminded me of something I'd run across in my readings in Dr. Perez's class. Emperor Constantius labeled augurs, prophets, enchanters, Chaldeans, Magicians, and sorcerers as reprehensible enemies of the people, and if they wouldn't stop their depraved art, they would be run through with a sword.

in my mind. *The truth will set you free.* The statement had seemed to be everywhere lately.

I found the journal entry from Dani. "That's it . . . 'The pages hold the truth, and the truth will set you free.' Some twisted version of another biblical passage: 'Then you will know the truth, and the truth will set you free.'" I slapped the book shut. "The pages . . . She's pointing us toward a book."

Max rubbed a hand over his chin. "That's what Strauss said, too, remember? That Dani was obsessed with some book when she first came to the school. Are there books that are banned from Catholicism?"

"Of course," I said slowly. "Well, not so much anymore, but centuries ago, definitely. During the Inquisition, they even went so far as to burn the home of anyone harboring the books."

"So maybe a book hunted to extinction. Something they really hated?" Max said.

Notes, notes. I needed my notes from the class. Vern came over as I opened Dr. Perez's course website.

"There it is," I said, looking through the course notes. "The *Index Librorum Prohibitorum*. The Catholic Index of Forbidden Books."

Max leaned forward. "Now what? How do we tell which one it is?"

I scanned the list, many of the works in Latin. *Candide* and many of Voltaire's other works, *Madame Bovary*, *Paradise Lost*, and the writings of Jean-Paul Sartre. Dr. Perez had broken the list down further into Magical texts and grimoires, supplemented with titles from his own research when possession of texts had been used as evidence in witch trials. *Lemegeton Clavicula Salomonis*, or *the Lesser Key of Solomon*, a demonology grimoire, and *Picatrix*, one of the foremost texts on astrological Magic.* Agrippa's *De occulta philosophia libri*

---

* An Arabic text whose authorship is unknown, believed to have been compiled in the eleventh century. Dr. Strauss refers to this text quite frequently in his lectures.

tres (Three Books of Occult Philosophy)—Agrippa's complete works had been banned.

"Well, let's look at the books on the list and see if there are any that reference any of the things Dani said, or the symbol we've been seeing around campus. There's got to be something," I said.

My mind raced, and my thoughts flew past faster than I could make sense of them.

We ended up eliminating many of the texts. For some of them, not a single copy had survived into this century. Others had been studied and were believed to be nothing more than the works of delirious alchemists poisoned from their own experiments. Our list dwindled to two: *Liber incantationum, exorcismorum et fascinationum variarum* and *Liber Autumnus*.

Max paused, running his eyes over the words of the first. "Maybe there's a reason these books are banned," he said quietly.

I bit my lip. "Vern?"

Vern looked at the computer screen, nodding slowly. "I'll see if we have either of them in the system. But . . ." —he spread his hands—"if these are indeed the old Magic texts, you need to watch yourselves."

I knew the danger these texts posed. There were so few real Magic books left in the world, and the ones that were genuine were written to be intentionally confusing to guard their secrets from untrained eyes, shrouded in symbols that could only be understood by followers or other expert Magicians. Spells were hidden between nonsensical statements. You could be reading a paragraph for hours trying to make sense of it and have no idea you were casting a spell. And all the while Magic would be dripping from your fingertips like a leaky faucet. If Dr. Robetresse knew what we were looking into, I half-think she might've tried to stop us. We were going against the entire system of Magic we'd studied. Everything about the Three Arts focused on control, on limitations, on not jumping headfirst into spellwork that had been written centuries ago and never studied to ensure its safety. Wild, reckless Magic like that was for students at Britton Arcane.

Or for people who ended up dead.

But while a part of me was afraid, I was also excited. If I could study one of the real Magic texts, not only could I possibly find the spell to cure Dani but spells I'd never seen before, that no one had been able to decipher in centuries. Who knew what kind of Magic was out there? Magic to return in time and fix your mistakes? To bring back the dead? To . . . I was getting ahead of myself. I sucked in a deep breath. My fingers shook.

Vern tapped the screen. "This first one is better known as the Munich Manual of Demonic Magic. It's a grimoire penned in the fifteenth century."

Max closed his eyes. "Lovely," he whispered.

Vern dug a key ring from his pocket and returned a few minutes later from a back room, holding a very old, very creepy-looking book bound in vellum. He set the book in front of Max, who visibly shivered when his hands touched it.

"But the other, *Liber Autumnus*, The Book of Autumn . . ." Vern said, returning to the screen. He looked back at the screen and shook his head. "That one's going to be a bit trickier."

Max still hadn't opened the grimoire in front of him, so I pulled it over to me. As soon as I touched it, I was overwhelmed with a sense of wrong. Magic books sound a little like objects, so many spells swirling around at once, and this one emitted a frantic *thump-thump-thump-thump*, like the heartbeat of a small, tormented creature. I closed the cover immediately.

"Vern, has anyone checked this out recently?"

He jotted in his notebook, and I could practically taste his Magic swirling around. The sound of old, yellowing pages flipping, the musty smell of old books. It swept the icky feeling of the grimoire from me. He shook his head. "No one's touched this book in many years."

I nodded. "I'm inclined to leave it that way."

Vern nodded and gingerly picked up the book to carry it to the back room. He locked the door behind him.

In the meantime, Max and I crowded around the computer. "So what about this other one . . . ?" Max asked slowly.

Liber Autumnus didn't yield any searches, but the translation, The Book of Autumn, got a few hits.

The first one was on an old forum site that looked like it'd been coded in the early HTML days. It was called the Dawn Underground, and it seemed like the sort of website for people who didn't believe we'd really landed on the moon. I clicked away.

"What are you doing? Go back," Max urged.

"Why? It's just going to be a bunch of nutsos."

Not only were real books of Magic dangerous—if you could find any—but so were the people looking for them. We'd been warned from our very first day at Seinford and Brown of people who not only believed in the existence of Magic, but were obsessed with it; if they discovered you could use it, they would do anything to get you to teach them.

"That's exactly what we need right now. People who're obsessed. People who are crazy in their pursuit of it. This forum is exactly the sort of place we need to be."

Under the site's title was a short description, "Everything You Might Ever Want to Know Pertaining to the Book of Autumn."

I hovered over the hyperlink, which took me to a short introductory page.

> *The Book of Autumn, believed to be one of the last alchemical and Magical texts to come out of the Hellenistic period*, was believed to be a part of the Magical Papyri. (Not to be confused with the Hermeticus Corpi, of which no connection has been found.)*

---

* The period of Greek history after Classical Greece, between the death of Alexander the Great in 323 BCE to the conquest of the last Hellenistic dynasty in 31 BCE.

Although there is plenty of evidence pointing definitively to its existence, as well as known references to the Book in the Emerald Tablet, which you can read more about <u>here</u>, all copies are at present missing. This site is dedicated to the discovery of any copies of the Book of Autumn still in existence, in either part or whole.

"No copies in existence . . . Max, they're looking for copies, anywhere . . ."

"And if Dani was trying to tell us about a book hunted to near extinction—"

Something tingled in my fingers, excitement bloomed in my chest. "Max," I nearly whispered, "what if this is it? The book that Dani was pointing us to?"

And maybe, inside this book, we would find the key to unlocking whatever had happened to her.

Below the introductory note, user *Ciceroisdead490* had put together a rough timeline of discoveries pertaining to the Book of Autumn.

3rd–4th Century BCE, Est. Written: Author ???

3rd Century CE, Referenced in Iamblichus's* On the mysteries: "Virtus dei autumnus" (Some disagreement regarding translation)

10th Century, Referenced in Ghâyat al-Hakîm fi'l-sihr: "Autumnus"

1542, Rome, Sanctioned in book burnings list.

~~*2003, Sighting in Harvard Bookshop*~~*: This information has not been verified. Have a tip? Know something we don't? Contact a mod.*

---

* Philosopher of the Neoplatonic school.

Then, in bold red letters near the bottom of the page:

UPDATE — 1745.

In 1745, it was obtained by a rare-books dealer in Turkey, after having been catalogued on a ship's manifest. There was a picture of the manifest, written on old, curling parchment, the ink fading but still legible. Beneath the image, the translation:

> *One stack of books: Philologia sacra, The Life and Histories of the Prophet Mulutak, Flora and Fauna of the New World, and Liber Autumnus.*

The more I looked through the forum, the more intrigued I became by the mystery surrounding this book.

"It seems to be an enigma," wrote one researcher in a news article from 1995. "No one knows who the author is, and I've barely found anyone in my studies of historical records who's even heard of it. Yet there are references to it throughout history, and not just from ancient history either, but from as recent as the eighteenth century. We're talking an influence spanning thousands of years. This leads me to believe, unequivocally, that it does exist, it has to exist, and that the book's simply been passed down secretly through the ages. The only question is . . . by whom? Who cares so much about this book to ensure that it exists through time? And if so, why keep it a secret now?"

There were so many theories about the book on the forum that it was hard to keep track of them all. Some people were convinced the whole thing was a hoax, that the book wasn't even real. Others believed it was real, but that it had been burned during the Inquisition and maybe even beforehand, and no copies survived. And still others believed that it was out there somewhere, just waiting to be found and unfurl the mysteries of the world to us.

It was this camp that I found myself falling into, heart beating fast, eyes flying through links and articles.

"What if Dani was leaving clues so we could find this book, Max? What if inside this volume is the spell that's responsible for what happened to her?"

But Max was bleary-eyed staring at the computer screen. "We've been at this for hours."

"You should take a break," Vern agreed.

"You go ahead. I'm fine." I couldn't leave it now, not when we were this close.

There was even a Book of Autumn subreddit, but it kept getting taken down by the mods, overrun as it was by conspiracy theories on how Bill Gates was implanting us all with microchips. Par for the course, I guessed. Conspiracy theorists and people who actually believed in Magic usually fell into the same circle. There was a strict code of rules pinned to the side and a strict one-strike policy for the Dawn Underground forum: ANY *discussion of topics not related to the information pertaining to the Book of Autumn, its contents, or persons relating to its authorship will be deleted and the user summarily banned from posting in the future.*

It was my first foray into the world of underground Magical theories, so I was somewhat new to all of it, but I happily raced through the excitement of their discoveries and marveled at these people who'd spent years analyzing photographs, searching ship manifests, and hunting through collections of rare books across the globe, just for a peek into our world.

CHAPTER THIRTY-NINE

Every Star Is a World

"Jesus, Cel, have you been at it all night? When's the last time you slept?"

"This book is it, Max, I know it," I said, not taking my eyes from the screen. I'd spent longer than I'd wanted glued to my computer screen, certainly, but there was a lot of information to get through. I knew how I looked. The wild eyes, the tangled hair. It had been so easy for me to join in the fervor with everyone else. Since a couple of hours before the sun had risen, I'd fallen into the threads dedicated to authorship. There were even proposed timelines of possible handlers throughout the centuries.

Still, other people on the site claimed the author was anonymous. There were so many threads on the topic that an entire folder was devoted to it.

Surely anonymous is anonymous, I commented, as there was an open chat window at the time.

You'd think that, user Aklarkson wrote—his bio denoted him a professor of Occult History at Brevard College—*but plenty of authors penned their works under sages or popular wisemen of their time, so the true authors of many of the ancient texts are lost to us. But there are ways of tracking them down, particularly through whom they reference in the work, which philosophy they subscribe to, and who their teacher was. The ancient world was not so large as we might think.*

So then who do we think it is?

You should read this. Aklarkson linked me to a sticky thread at the top of the chat.

It was a list of potential authors, with a prefacing note attached. *If we are correct in assuming the text was written in the Hellenistic period, then we may narrow down the list of potential authors to Magicians of the time, including wandering Magi and holy men who dabbled in the occult. There were many philosophers, particularly among the Greeks, who considered the practice of magia to be the practice of charlatans, but there were many who believed. Nigidius, for one, whom Cicero claimed was a "keen and diligent searcher after that which nature keeps veiled." Or Apulieus, who, in his Apologia, whilst defending himself against a charge of sorcery, claims that the practice of philosophy and magia are intricately bound together, that there was not one without the other.*

There were still other less-plausible theories of authorship (according to the forum's users), such as members of a mystery school of the Hellenistic period called the Order of Autumn and the writer of another, more popular grimoire, the *Ghâyat al-Hakîm fi'l-sihr*, or *Picatrix*.

"We have to find this book," I said suddenly.

"And how are we going to do that," Max said, rubbing his temples and sipping a coffee, "if even these people can't find it?"

"Because we have something they don't. We have Dani. She's pointing us to it, I know it. And all those symbols on campus over the dormitories—it's got to be related."

My temples burned, a memory flashing to the surface. The memory of the frat party, that strange feeling of déjà vu swimming through it, that I'd been in that house before, that I'd done all of this before.

Suddenly, I had an idea. "Vern?"

Vern shook his head. "I can't find books that aren't catalogued in the system."

"It's not in the library's catalog, but what if it was on campus? Could you find it then?"

Vern's mouth twisted. "I don't know, I've never—"

"I know you're always saying your Magic isn't worth anything, but finding something lost is a rare gift. You're always telling me I can't let a little thing like fear get in my way. Please, Vern. This could be the key to everything."

He put up his hands and shook his head. "I don't know, you two . . ."

"It'll be okay," I insisted, "we'll be here with you the whole time." I squeezed his hand.

"That's right," Max agreed. "And if it doesn't work, no harm done."

"All we're asking is that you try."

Vern bit his lip. "Well, alright. But I'm telling you, don't expect anything."

Vern pulled out his notebook and pencil. At the top of a fresh page, he slowly wrote *Liber Autumnus*. "Help me find it," he muttered and closed his eyes.

For several long minutes, nothing happened. His weathered hand rested on the table.

"It's okay, Vern," I said, standing up from the table. I was worried he was upset with me for making him try, for confirming what he'd already known.

"You're still the best damn librarian I've ever met," Max said, when Vern's eyes rolled back. His pencil started moving quickly across the page. At first, it was just lines; then I realized it was a sketch. Of a building, long columns on either side of a doorway and a sagging roof. Inside the building—a kitchen, living room, then stairs up to bedrooms. Beneath the stairs, an office. A more detailed drawing of the office, showing a small space cluttered with books and posters and a desk with papers all over it.

Vern finished his drawing and opened his eyes. He looked down. "Oh. Now that's unexpected. Last time I tried this spell, I set fire to the Health Sciences section."

Max rubbed his chin. "If I didn't know better, I'd say that's the—"

I swallowed. "The Phi Kat house."

CHAPTER FORTY

The Book

Max tapped his boot against the floor. "Well, I won't say I told you so, but . . ."

I squirmed. I was still doing lessons with Basile, but now it was hard to ignore the mounting evidence that pointed toward him. On the one hand, I felt a responsibility to Dani, to find out what happened to her, to get justice for her. She needed me, like Aaron had. But on the other hand, I still needed Basile. Every day, I got a little closer to the heart of his theory, to the heart of the world of Being.

"We have to tell Dr. Robetresse," Max said.

"Not yet," I said, biting my lip.

Max arched an eyebrow.

I had this under control. If I played it smart, I knew there was a way to get the book without making an enemy of Basile. "You haven't trusted them from the beginning."

Max arched an eyebrow. "True, but they did hire us to find out what happened to Dani and who's responsible. And we have."

"You said it yourself," I protested. "They've been trying to sweep this thing under the rug from the start. If this is one of the books of Magic, they might want it for themselves. You know how valuable these things are."

"So then what do you propose we do? We need the book. It's not like we can just mosey on up to Basile and ask him for it."

"No, we can't. But I have an idea."

I drafted probably thirty texts to Basile. In the end, I texted asking if we could meet up.

Cella! he responded quickly. *I would love nothing more. Coffee?*

Sure. Meet you at the house in a few.

When I got to the house, Basile was dressed impeccably in an airy white shirt, straight, dark jeans, and soft leather shoes. All charm, all smiles. It left a sour taste in my mouth. "Just one sec, I'll get my keys."

"Actually, maybe we could talk here? In your office maybe?"

He looked surprised, but recovered quickly. "Of course. Whatever you'd like."

He walked me through the house, casting a glance at me every few seconds as if to make sure I was still there. When we reached his office, he pulled a small brass key from a key ring.

This time, there were no papers on his desk. No book. It was like another person entirely had moved into the space; this time everything was tidy and neat, discrete math and physics textbooks meticulously stacked in a pile in the corner. Even his pens were lined up in a row.

Something twisted in my stomach.

"So," he said, slipping into the leather rolling chair across from me, a smile brimming across his lips. I noticed the armrests of the chair had been punctured, like someone had stabbed their fingers through them again and again.

Had I felt so confined in here the last time?

The walls looked much closer than I remembered. He hadn't turned on any more of the lamps, so we were sitting in the dim light from a single bulb hanging from the ceiling.

I squirmed in my seat, trying to surreptitiously do a scan of the room. I pulled my hair up, then tugged it back down again a second later.

"There's no need to be nervous, Cella," he said. Was it just me, or did his fingers clench around the pocket with his key ring in it?

"Actually, I'm quite happy you decided to come over," he said, running his thumb over his lip. "There's still a lot of ground we need to cover."

As my eyes ran over him, everything about him seemed too perfect. The tone of his voice, his mannerisms, his hair, clothes. All perfectly placed and considered. None of it authentic, none of it real. And yet it had all been perfectly set. The perfect trap to draw me in.

Well, two could play at that game.

I flashed him a blistering smile. "Definitely."

He stood up, traced his finger across the table, drawing closer to me.

He put a hand on mine, and I fought the urge to flinch. "Your brother would have wanted this for you. He believed in what we're doing here, too."

I frowned. "What do you mean?"

He slapped his hands against his sides, standing up from his chair. "But I'm getting ahead of myself. You wanted coffee. Sugar?"

"Sure, but—" I shook my head. This wasn't the first time Basile had mentioned Aaron. How did he know him? And what did he mean, he believed in what they were doing here? Had Aaron known about the Reality Paradox, too?

Basile smiled, and the light from the single bulb above his head cast eerie shadows on his face.

"All in good time," he said, walking out of the room, keys jingling as he went.

My phone dinged, a text from Max.

How is it going? Need backup?

I shoved the phone back in my pocket. I might have imagined it, but I could've sworn that the corner of Basile's mouth lifted, just a smidge, when I put it away.

He'd set the perfect trap. I knew I should be looking for the book, but another thought entered my mind. I was so close now that my fingers shook. So close to discovering everything I wanted. Each time we'd spoken, I was drawn to him as though to a heady cup of wine, clinging to every intoxicating word.

And yet.

Basile dangled my brother's ghost in front of me like a wriggling worm. Part of me couldn't help but fall for it, but another part didn't appreciate the manipulation. And this new revelation . . . was it just more of the same? Or did he actually know Aaron?

What did Aaron have to do with the Reality Paradox?

My Christmas mug pulsed in my pocket, the last gift my brother had given me. Sometimes phantom notes drifted up from it, like the ghost of Aaron's beating heart. I held it close.

And I realized that, in my heart, I knew what Aaron would've wanted. Aaron was a kind, generous soul. He cared for others over himself. If he knew there was a way that I could help someone else, someone like Dani, he would've wanted me to. I could just imagine the look of disappointment on his face if he knew I'd ignored a chance to help Dani and Luce.

And given all the strangeness lately, all my questions piling up one after another, I knew that, to uncover the truth about all of it, I needed this book.

My eyes shot toward the kitchen. I could hear Basile rooting around in the cabinets, the coffee pot boiling.

The only question was how much time did I have left?

I jumped up, my shaking hands rummaging through the drawers of his desk. I searched for hidden spots on the shelf, but where would you hide such a huge book in this tiny room? My heart pounded in my ears. At any moment, he could come back. What would he do if he saw me poking around his things?

"Did you say you wanted sugar? All we've got is stevia," he called, his footsteps walking back this way.

"That'd be great," I yelled.

Come on, come on. Where are you?

I quieted my breathing, trying to listen as I did with objects for the murmur of Magic. For one long, heart-stopping moment, there was nothing. Only silence, until a whisper.

A rush of water, the rustle of worn, bare footsteps on stone. The low chanting of priests, the breath of a flame, the steady choke of incense. And flashes of color: gold paint, a black hood, streaks of blood.

I followed the notes, thumping nearly as loud as my pulse in my ears, to a stack of books in the corner. Nestled in the center of the stack, buried inside the false cover of a discrete mathematics textbook, was a very old, thin book, bound in vellum. This was it. As I held it, I got the same feeling I had had with Dani, of being pulled under deep, deep water.

Basile's footsteps drew closer. I shoved the book under my shirt.

"I just got a text from Robetresse. She wants a meeting. Some kind of break in the investigation. I've got to go!" I yelled.

My limbs felt like jelly. The book safely under my shirt, I slipped out of the room and made for the door.

"Cella?" Basile asked.

I took off at a run out the door. Then I was racing across campus, dirt and clay kicking up behind my feet, the air outside so hot it was suffocating. One hand on my belly, like I was holding an awkwardly shaped baby, I sent Max a text with the other.

Got it !!!!! Meet @ my room ASAP.

Back at my room, I collapsed onto the bed, breathing hard. "He's going to know I took it."

Max's lips pulled to the side. "Maybe. But the excuse might have bought us some time."

"What if he reports the theft?"

"To who? The school? He sure as hell won't want those vultures on the council getting their hands on it."

"Well, he's not just going to lie down with someone stealing his book."

"Yeah."

His eyes locked with mine, and it was one of those moments I was glad to have a dimidium. For someone to feel the same fear, the same emotions I was struggling to put words to. "So we hurry," he said.

"So we hurry."

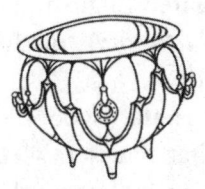

CHAPTER FORTY-ONE

The book was old, that much was clear. How old, though, was beyond either of our guesses. The cover was brown and soft, bound in vellum. It must have been repaired throughout the ages; the spine had been rebound in a worn leather, and there were pages appended to it that couldn't have been part of the original manuscript.

With two hands gently supporting the spine, I flipped the cover open.

The front cover had only two words: *Liber Autumnus*. The author was simply denoted as S.

I skimmed through the pages, written on a mixture of papyrus and parchment, marveling at the ink that hadn't faded, inhaling the scent of time spilling over and staining the pages.

"Maybe it's just a memento, a collector's text," Max said.

"If it was part of a collection, don't you think it would be in some kind of protective binding? Or in a museum? He had it hidden. He was using it."

The first section of the book, twenty pages of papyrus, were written entirely in symbols.

"Have a look at these," I said to Max.

"What are those? Alchemical?"

"Maybe." I ran a finger over them, "Maybe Magical, too."

The second portion, still papyrus, was written in a very fine, thin print of Ancient Greek. I looked dubiously at Max. "I can't possibly translate this . . ."

"We could take it to Vern," he said, though even with his encyclopedic knowledge of texts, I didn't think Vern was fluent in a dead language.

The last portion of the book, the appended pages, were written on soft parchment, this time in antiquated English.

"The following is a translation of *Liber Autumnus*, or the Book of Autumn." There was no date supplied.

The translating authority's writing—an ornate, swooping script—I realized now was the same hand that had scrawled tiny notes in the margins of the first twenty pages of symbols. Notes like: *Poison? Demon or God. Unequivocally the word for evil.*

"So the author is S, whoever that is, but who wrote this third portion? Who translated it?" Max asked.

"I don't know. From the look of this binding, it's probably gone through multiple translations. Probably Latin first. It must've been passed down for generations."

From what I could see from the translation in English, the Book of Autumn was written in the style of a diary. It was a firsthand account of the author, S. Possibly meant to be a letter of some kind?

Even with the translation, the antiquated English was hard to read, and even harder to understand. From what I could make out, the first page read something like this:

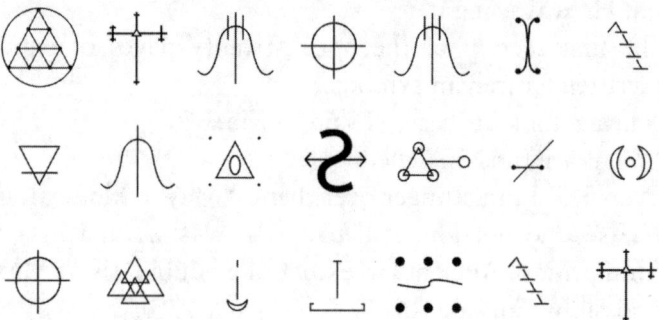

Note (Cella): The symbols go on for several pages, though pages are missing. Torn out intentionally or ripped by mistake?

The Book of Autumn

—S

The years pass, and I am an old man. My eyes falter by the candlelight with which I dictate these writings, and my fingers ache and bruise. But I must get my thoughts down. If I don't put them into words, then maybe no one will ever know they existed. None will know of these things I have found.

And you must know.

So I write this to you, dear reader, in hopes that you will accomplish more than what I have been able to do.

If I can ask one thing of you, first:

Apollonius knows not of the sacrifices I have made for him, of the ways I have ensured his safety in the event of my death. Do not torment him with the knowledge. He is young, and he has time left to take a wife and start a family. I have heard there are places yet where men can still freely discuss the world. Where the mystic arts and the world beyond ours is not such a feared subject. The lands of Crete and Babylon, where I traveled as a young scholar to decode the symbols at the beginning of this text. If you read this, send him there. Tell him to make a life for himself. Tell him to worry not, for birds will always fly east of the river, and there will always be a sun to shine.

I.

I was working as a scribe for Master Porphyr, copying stacks of texts, from the great alchemical findings of Assyria and the islands of Tyana, to star charts and navigation systems, to prayers, and stories of epic battles between gods and men. It was while I was at this task, copying letter upon letter in the dim light of a sweating tallow wick, that I came upon it. A stack of parchment, bound in twine. Twenty-one pages of alchemical and Magical symbols, authorship unknown, no hint or markings as to whence it came, nor any indication of what the symbols were in reference to.

I stared at the symbols until the wax ran thick and the light burned out, and when I closed my eyes, they were still ingrained there, burned against my eyelids. The next day, I asked Master Porphyr where they came from, but he was as baffled as I. "Cast it out," he told me. "I'm in the business of translation, I have no use for nonsense." But I couldn't bear to part with it. How could it be that a learned man like Porphyr did not see the beauty in it? The mystery? So I stole it away and hid it in my bedroll.

Night after night, I stared at the symbols, running my fingers over the ink, begging it to unleash its contents, to teach me the mysteries of the world. By day, I continued on as a scribe, though my work was poor, half of my attention elsewhere. At the end of the season, I said my goodbyes to Porphyr. After listening to my father relate in great detail how much an ungrateful fool I was, I set off to find a teacher to help me decode the symbols.

I spent years trying to find a teacher who could read the symbols. I traveled to Assyria, to the priests of Egypt, the Magi of Babylon, the <u>wise men</u> of Crete

[Translator's note: This word is unfamiliar to me. It may mean something like a sage, but more highly specialized in the mysteries and arcanum, more akin to a wizard.]

At last, my travels took me to Croton. It was here I joined a school, where I learned of the true nature of the universe, of the divine uttering of the One, and the whisperings therein. Though the symbols at the front of this text are but few, the message in full is much broader and deeper than I ever could have imagined. It is that which I attempt to explain, to show as fully as I can, in these pages.

Day 3 of Μεταρχιος waning
16 days past my arrival in Croton

There is a man here; a local merchant has told me to seek him out. He is said to be a master of the knowledge which I seek, but I am told he must understand the whole of a person's character and morality before he will accept you into his school. Admittance is only granted after a trial of some sort. Then there is a vow of silence for a time, not to be less than two years, before I am permitted to learn of anything. I suppose I have traveled this long and this far, so if he knows of what I need, I am prepared to at least speak with him. I will seek him out tomorrow. He lives at the top of the hill.

25 days past my arrival in Croton

I believe that He is the one who can decode these symbols, though His teaching is nearly as cryptic. His methods are strange to me. He subscribes to the theory that a clear mind is necessary for all things, that we should abstain from unnecessary food, any and all sexual relations, and communications with the uninitiated. Under no circumstances are we to share His *teachings with those outside our sacred community. Punishments for breaking His laws range from the mundane to the extreme, to include deprivation of sleep, piercing of needles through the eyes, isolation, excommunication and the erection of graves for the excommunicated, and fasting from food and drink for no less than two days.*

He believes that, through the study of mathematics, alchemy, geometry, and science, one can learn the true nature of things and perfect their soul so then it may be freed from this prison of endless migration into other bodies, and I am eager to learn all that He will teach me. I am eager to perfect my immortal soul. He insists I will learn the symbols in due time, and I do believe Him. Though I have not been here long, it is clear He is famed for his wisdom. Men and women come to him from great distances begging for His help, and He speaks to them in a calm, low voice. He is a very learned man. My father would be proud. Though first I must make it through my schooling. I fear it is this which brings me the most agitation.

I have seen those who have not been able to withstand the teachings. They have burned the bottoms of their feet with hot coals in their shame. They have thrust needles through their eyes and walked over the edge of the sea cliffs. I do not know what it is about Him that inspires such devotion; I only know that His students profess to love Him like a God. He has made it clear that He is not one.

One moon's rotation until the solstice
70 days past my arrival in Croton

As the solstice draws near, my mind becomes preoccupied with one thought. He has told me that, although He has accepted me into His school, there are levels of initiation. In order to progress, He has said that, on the fifth day unto the solstice, I must travel into the deepest caverns of Midi and stay for sixteen days. I have heard tales from the others, mere whisperings of this place. A stillness like no other, a darkness that forces you to wander into the depths of the mind. I fear ... I am ashamed to admit it, but I fear that in sixteen days of traversing the depths of my mind, I may lose myself entirely. But for me to delve further into my studies, it is necessary, and so it must be done.

c. 4 iota 16 - Recipe for a bloated bowel

One must praise Him in all that we do. Do not cut fire with a sword. For relief of a bloated bowel, it is necessary to travel thrice around a wood surrounding a bank, dip thy feet into the source, and say the words of the Three's incantation, which is found in c. iota 4. [Translator's note: Not found]

FIVE DAYS UNTIL THE SOLSTICE

I will enter the caverns at sundown, for it takes some time to reach the center, and will stay for sixteen days and nights. I fear that I may lose my mind in the depths, though He teaches that there is only One we will find there. I can only pray that He is right.

How silly my old fears seem now, how foolish I was for doubting Him and His teachings!

He was right, for if I had interpreted the symbols all at once, my brain may have been summarily overwhelmed by the knowledge transferred to me. I now know they are not meant to be read simply from left to right, nor from right to left. Each relays a vast amount of knowledge that is meant to be combined, intermingled, transposed, jumbled in every order, in whatever order one's imagination supposes, to derive the maximum transference of information.

How many doors I feel have been opened to me! For these symbols are the whisperings of knowledge hidden to me, now revealed.

Note (Cella): Though S seems to have learned the meanings of the symbols, it appears that his last attempts at decoding them took place before he entered the caves. If I were to guess, I would say that now that he has acquired whatever knowledge he found, he no longer feels a need to decode the symbols for anyone else—with the exception of one symbol. The very first in the book. The circle with a ten-dot triangle inside it.

I recognize it as the symbol in Dani's notebooks, the symbol inked on the bull skulls over the campus dormitories. The symbol that inspired in me the same feelings when I listened for the book in Basile's office as when I look at Dani. The feelings that are so very strange to me, yet somehow, inexplicably familiar.

I shall decode starting with the first, which is thus.

There is a presence here, not a man nor a god, not angel nor demon. I feel its coils wrap around me like a vine, drawing the strength from me, while beckoning me ever closer. It has a will of its own, that I know for certain, though I don't know if I would call it alive. My master says there are many names for it, in many different tongues, for it has existed long before man arrived on this earth.

It is what this symbol represents. It is what found me in the caverns of Midi.

We call it Magia. *It is that which encapsulates all else. It is the One.*

[Translator's note: Magic. This term was derived from the Greek *mageia*, transcribed here to the Latin *magia*. I kept it as the Latin *magia* here because I believe it likely that the true meaning of what S was trying to convey may have been lost to the centuries as the term "Magic" evolved. Whatever it once was, it meant something far greater than what we consider "Magic" today. A presence, not man nor god, but more powerful than either.]

In this text, I will relay the incantations, the recipes, the supplications, which I have learned both from the symbols and Him. Spells for luck, health, for an ill-sitting bowel, for a fever of the head, for a depressed wife, for urges unbecoming of a man loyal to his wife. To know which herbs may improve the taste of a goat's milk, to make larger the eggs laid by fowl, to increase the bounty of the sea, to make sweeter the grapes and fruit of the trees. To beseech his friends. To quiet his enemies. I have learned much in my workings with Him and the One. I admit, sometimes I am afraid of these things I can do. I know I am not the only initiate who feels this way. He tells us it is only once you lose something that you may find another.

Note (Cella): After this point, I have a difficult time understanding the text. There are a few recipes and incantations that I am able to wade through, though save for a few writings here and there, the rest is essentially gibberish. It seems as if as time continues on and S becomes more entrenched in the school, the writings become more dense and unwieldy, written by someone who either enjoys being particularly long-winded or someone who is slowly losing their mind. I admit, I am frustrated because here it is—I was convinced if I could just make sense of these pages, then we'd know what to do about Dani. But I can't for the life of me make sense of it, and it makes me want to scream.

One passage, for example, utter nonsense, starts with: "One thing one may do which seems profitable and tactful at times, though only certain times willing and only with an apt subject, or in this case another which has the same knowledge to do, holds a writing penned on parchment, tablet, or glass, and holds the words under water, moving water or stream is best, and under the full bright Moon, and the ink will be of sufficient to stay and not bleed in the water, can reflect the knowledge therein to a man whose hands are in that same stream, no matter the distance between them," before veering off into another nonsensical statement.

I should have expected this. Many of the earliest alchemists and Magicians obfuscated their work in this way, not only to hide it from those who might persecute them for what they might view as *goeteia* or another unsavory form of Magic, but also to disguise it from those they felt were undeserving of the knowledge. Shrouding it in coded and complex language was a way to guarantee it would only be understood by initiates or other expert Magicians.

A little more of what I am able to make out is transcribed below.

The order tonight has, at Melophorus's urging, swayed public opinion in the election. There has been much uproar as a result, and I cannot help the anger in my heart, for I urged him not do those writings. I fear public opinion will vastly sway against our favor as a result of our interference, but I suppose I have little choice in the matter. We are all rational men, and I just have to hope that logic and sense will win out in the end.

[Translator's Note: I cannot make this out. My best guess is this next entry takes place two months later, amid frantic scribblings.]

They have burned our headquarters. Infiltrated our ceremonial rooms and most precious spaces. Burned our writings. I watched with my own eyes as they ran Melophorus through with a long sword, his mouth falling open, a look of shock and pain printed in his eyes, which will be seared in mine for all my days. So now, we are running. I have escaped through an underground tunnel out of the city. We have all broken up, it is only through the grace of my uncle that I was able to get out at all.

Note (Cella): There were a few like these off and on throughout the year, and a pervading sense of ragged paranoia by S that he will be found. He moves back to Babylon and creates a new society with even more cryptic motives, praying to a mysterious god for fear of being found out. But few join, and eventually the movement fizzles out when the Roman army intercedes.
There is one last entry prior to what I believe was S's untimely end due to a poison, which he denotes the recipe for. "In aide of pains to the head." It includes nightshade.

CHAPTER FORTY-TWO

Max and I decided that, rather than reading over each other's shoulders, I would take the book first, while he continued scouring the forum for anything that might help. He sat with me all night until he couldn't keep his eyes open anymore. "You should get some sleep, too, Cel," he said. "We can take a look at it in the morning."

I nodded, barely taking notice of him, and continued reading.

The more I studied the book, the more frustrated I grew, but also the more I found to like about it. The author, S, was unfailingly honest and open in his accounts, spilling his innermost feelings and thoughts. How it made him feel small and unimportant when another initiate dismissed his findings, how sometimes he wasn't quite sure what he was doing in the world. It was refreshing to see someone speak his mind so openly, to bear his soul in an account to be read by a complete stranger thousands of years later.*

That night I had strange dreams. Of strange planetary alignments and moving through an empty house. Floating without speaking, without noise, without light. Symbols marred the

---

* I was invigorated by S's findings. It was perhaps the greatest case of Magical anthropology I'd ever studied, a man writing from centuries ago on his daily life, his Magic, his fears and dreams. It struck me all at once. Anthropology was nothing more and nothing less than the study of what it means to be human—and all the beauty and horror that it entails.

walls, but all I could do was feel them with my fingers. Running over them again and again, until I woke up.

I started carrying the Book of Autumn with me all the time. I slept with it on one side and my Greek dictionary on the other. Though no matter how much I set my will against it, parts of S's text continued to elude me.

The nights started to feel late even after the sun had barely left the sky, and I guzzled espresso after espresso to stay awake. It seemed as if the translator—whoever they were—hadn't translated only for the benefit of others, but also for themself. Specific passages by S were copied over and over again, as if they were trying to understand it, too, the same lines that had given me such trouble. At each turn, my head ached and vision blurred.

Sleepiness came, and then more coffee. I lost track of how many espressos I had, until I was so jittery I felt like I could've leaped off a building and made it to the next roof. I was determined: I would make sense of at least one of these rambling passages, just take it one sentence at a time, but it was no use. My eyes kept glazing over, and before I knew it, I'd been reading the same sentence for the last twenty minutes.

At one point, Max caught me dozing off at my desk.

"Cella . . . how long have you been awake?"

"A couple of days."

"What? Jesus, get some sleep. You can't stay up for days reading this book."

"I'm fine."

But it was clear to me now that this was, unequivocally, a book of Magic. And among the rambling notes and healing prayers, omens and instructions for gauging the Moon's patterns, practices for health and well-being that S had learned in his travels, was the spell Dani had undertaken.

And, I hoped, one to bring her back again.

FROM THE JOURNAL OF DANICA STEWART
March 12th [three weeks before the murder]

Nyktipoloi, bacchants, maenads, initiates in the mysteries. A fiery punishment awaits us, my dear, didn't you know? For, as Heraclitus says, initiation into the mysteries is unholy.

but we've always been unholy, you and I, haven't we? And what has happened once, happens again.

the chief of charlatans,

our fraudulent art

CHAPTER FORTY-THREE

"Found anything yet?" Max asked, sliding me a bottle of green tea.

He'd been gone more and more often. It was almost like he was afraid of the book, or afraid of how much time I spent studying it. Despite all we'd gone through to get it, he discounted the book at every turn, finding new suspects to chase down instead. He hunted down Strauss's students to question them, was trying to get info on Joselyn Hart's family after trying to use his charm on her and being summarily greeted by a brick wall.

I shook my head. "No, but there's Magic here. I can feel it." It wasn't something I could put into words as much as something I could feel coursing through my veins, its heady buzz drawing me closer, beckoning me over a ledge that stood above a dark chasm.

After looking at the symbols in the book, things had started to shift for me. I felt as much as saw the symbol for Magic, for the One. I felt it as S had described it, as if it were its own entity, a presence all its own. And I felt like I could feel its eyes on me, watching over my shoulder, never far from me. I could even picture its voice as if I'd heard it before: ancient, and deep as the earth. These thoughts had started invading my dreams, and Bear had woken me up on more than one occasion, paws on my chest, big eyes full of concern. Always this was after I'd woken up on the floor, my throat raw as if I'd been screaming.

Max nodded and turned to leave before hesitating, chewing on his lip. "Hey . . . you okay? It wouldn't kill you to leave it for a second. I can take over."

"I'm just a bit tired, is all."

Max reached for my hand. "Cel, it's more than that. I can see it all over your face. Maybe we should switch off now, and I could hold the book a while. I don't like what this book is doing to you. Let me help." 🪣

But how could I tell him that reading this book was the only time that I felt okay? That it distracted me from the stuff on the walls, from the words written in my shower, the shadows creeping up my dorm wall? And the gnawing feeling that maybe there really was something there, that I wasn't just imagining it. Something that I just kept missing, that stayed just outside my reach.

How could I tell him that losing myself in a centuries-old book was the only thing that made me feel better? If I could just figure out this problem, maybe everything else would be fine, too.

🪣 (Max): I didn't know what to do. I was terrified to think that all of this had been for nothing, that she was just leaving me behind again.

CHAPTER FORTY-FOUR

When the Winds Blow, Worship the Noise

When I woke the next morning, I turned on every light in the room and the volume on my headphones all the way up. Bear hadn't come back last night. Max had texted saying he couldn't get the stubborn dog out of his truck, that Bear didn't even want to come into the building. I'd filled a bowl up with treats and left it outside, in hopes maybe he'd smell it and come back.

I sat at my desk and opened the book to a passage.

For the waters of kind, although possessing of prolonged and proper nature, notwithstanding that which belongs to the Air . . .

The birds outside were chirping, and the sun was so warm out the window.

. . . the segments could only bend; rejoice, for the bearer only has but to call . . .

My eyelids drooped. My head started to ever so gently lean against the table . . .

. . . shattered will the gemstone and gathered luck flee if any stones are carried hence . . .

Right before I fell asleep, my eyes slammed open.

It's a spell.

It was a freaking spell.

That was why I couldn't understand the lines, why it kept putting me to sleep. It was draining my energy. My eyes flicked back to the open page.

A spell for gathering luck?

Though I hadn't attempted any of the spells or "recipes" that S listed throughout the Book of Autumn, it was understandable, given that it was a book literally chock-full of Magic, for some of the residual Magic to try to latch onto me through the text.

I would just have to be more careful. "I'll read in shorter segments," I murmured aloud. "Have less physical contact with the book." That meant no more sleeping with it, obviously.

The croak of my voice startled me. I'd started speaking to myself while I was in my dorm room since I'd been spending so much time in here lately. It made me feel a little more comfortable in a space that I didn't feel exactly at home in. And since Bear had been gone, it had made me feel less alone.

I closed the book and stowed it in the locked trunk beneath my bed.

S's Magic was some of the most advanced I'd ever seen. I started cataloguing the spells I found. Here were the things I understood so far:

Pages 47–56: An extremely long-winded description of the significance of numbers in the great mysteries of the world, starting with the monad and dyad, to the decad, thought to be an extremely significant number.

56–57: Astronomy, star maps, where and how to pull power from the stars.

I'd just started cataloguing a lengthy study on the Magical properties of plants that S's teacher had learned from Magi in

Egypt when Max knocked on the door. I could tell from his aura that he was annoyed.

He sat down on the bed beside me and tossed a balled-up piece of paper into the air. "Look out, world. Cella's ready to crack the case. Leaving that dunce of hers behind. Max who?"

My eyes narrowed. "Well, one of us has to actually work on it. Might as well be me."

He stared at me. "I don't like what this book is doing to you."

Heat crawled to my neck. My head ached, and my eyes were sore, and all I could feel was Dani's hot breath on my skin. "Of course you don't! Because you don't ever want me to be doing anything without you. Well, this time it's not about you, Max. This book is what's going to fix her, and I'm not sorry if I'm actually here trying to figure it out while you're off wasting time."

"I don't trust the book, Cella. I didn't say I didn't trust you," he said quietly.

Hot, angry splotches spread across my cheeks. My words came out breathless and sharp. I shoved the book at him. "Here, you want to help so bad, have at it. Swoop in to save the day, like you do every time."

On my way down the hallway, I could barely see straight. I nearly ran into a girl coming out of her room. My fingers clawed at the side of the wall. "Are you okay . . . ?" someone asked.

"I'm fine," I snapped, but they just kept coming down the hall. A whole group of them following doggedly after me like a group of devoted followers.

I reached the door of House Torlaine. I shoved it open out into bright, much too bright sunlight, and then—I was falling.

How did I—

I didn't reach for my Magic, but there it was. And another even stronger thread that pulled me silently along.

I felt myself drowning.

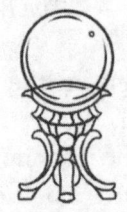

CHAPTER FORTY-FIVE

The sun was low when I opened my eyes. Though I was on my back, my mouth tasted like dirt and the metallic tang of blood. A figure stood over me. Two figures. I blinked in the low light and groaned when I realized who they were. Vern.

And Max.

"Easy," Vern said, as I scrambled to sit up.

"Ugh." I pressed my palms to my eyes. I felt like I'd gotten hit by a truck. "What happened?"

"You passed out just outside your dorm. Max saw you go down and ran to get me."

I winced, not wanting to meet Max's gaze, but all I felt radiating off him was guilt. He put a hand tentatively on my shoulder.

He looked down, his face in shadow under his hat. "I'm really sorry about earlier."

"No, it was my fault. I shouldn't have said that. I don't know what came over me."

"You did it, though." His mouth curved to a wry smile. "You cracked the case."

I shook my head. "What are you talking about?"

He handed me the book and laughed. "You even bookmarked the damn page."

I looked down; it was a page I had only really skimmed the contents of before dog-earing it and shoving the book at Max. I read the page now, and my mouth fell open.

It was barely noticeable, hidden between two spells to keep amulets from shattering. Another entry, a whole bit I'd missed while trying to wade through the nonsensical spells.

There is a belief among the others that Magia would be less treacherous if one were to perform his workings while wearing an amulet or talisman, in hopes that the excess power may be stored inside. There is certainly no denying that the toll the raw Magia takes on our bodies is not trivial. None of us speak it, but I know I am not the only one disheartened by the circumstances of Hermippus's death. Master said he died of a heart attack, that it was not related to the Magia he cast during the ritual, but he should have had at least fifteen years left of his life. Perhaps something like this will protect the rest of us, too. Something to bear the brunt of the Magia, much like a hot pan takes heat and we only wield the handle.

Update—

There is discourse among the others. Some of us believe these talismans of power make our workings less efficient, that it limits what we can do. Daelius complains that when he went to heal an ailing cousin, his dear cousin was pelted instead with bits of amethyst rock, and all his other spells are tinged purple.

Many of the others report similar problems. They say their charms do not work unless they are holding the talismans, that their Magia is now insufficient for their needs. They wish to rid themselves of their talismans. I confess I am conflicted as to one way or the other. I do not wish to end up like Hermippus, no matter how much it lessens my abilities. It pains me to say it, but I believe there are other initiates who do not fear this strange Magia as He has bid us to. They reach only for more.

Update—

Alas! In His ever-loving wisdom, He has discovered a way, a resolution to all our problems! I will add the full instructions below.

INSTRUCTIONS FOR UNBINDING FROM A TALISMAN OF POWER

Max frowned. "A talisman of power?"

"I think . . . an object.* It looks like S and his friends discovered objects, seemingly by accident. And when they didn't like the effects, they worked out a way to undo the process . . ."

We looked at each other, shocked.

"I didn't even know it was possible to become unbound once you've started casting with an object," he said.

"It looks like they found a way."

My fingers shook as it all swirled around me. It was unraveling, but it all felt so wrong all of a sudden and filled me with more questions than answers.

Our gaze traveled back down to the text.

Not everything has worked out as we had hoped. Thermoporo completed the Unbinding ritual and started his workings again. He called forth from the One wondrous, strange power. But he grew greedy, his thirst for Magia unquenched. The working went straight through him. The spell lifted him into the air and drained his body dry of power. He collapsed in front of us, nothing more than a lifeless corpse.

Daelius in his unbound state has become something strange and frightening. His wife and children report unusual behavior. They said he ate his food with the dogs and howled. He tore their pig's throat out with his teeth. He left messages in a script I have

---

* All my anthropological studies on ancient peoples and their Magic were coming back around. The folklore about wizards, with their wands and staffs, and the tales of witches and their familiars. In all the stories, Magicians had always used some type of objects. That was what these talismans were, and S and his friends seemed to know it.

never seen made of bizarre letters formed with circles. Our Master says this is more evidence that the One uses Daelius as a vessel, for the One only speaks in the old language.

Daelius came to us, the black toga and cloak of the initiates floating around him as if blown by wind and suspended in water, though no wind flowed and the rivers had long since dried. His eyes were pits of darkness glimmering as if from inside a long, deep well. The others feared him, afraid of the fierce power of the One. It was as if he was possessed by some nocturnal deity, but we had called forth no demon. Daelius had only called Magia to him, only the One.

When he sacrificed two young boys to the Underworld in order to summon the spirits of the dead, our Master put a stop to it.

"This is against our laws," He said, "Daelius must be stopped."

"But why is this happening?" we asked our teacher, for we were afraid and wanted to become bound again for the protection our talismans brought.

"The soul of Daelius is not yet perfected. This can only be done through an understanding of the world and of what is good. The One uses him as a puppet, a vessel, but not an equal. There is danger in what we have done."

We shut Daelius in a cavern in the mountain for fear that through him, the One would rip a hole through the world and walk through it at will. He, being the merciful, wise man that he was, worked for many days and nights to find something that could bind us again to protect us from the One. At last, He told us he had found a way to bind us again.

I have added the instructions below.

INSTRUCTIONS FOR BINDING TO A TALISMAN OF POWER.

"He did it," Max breathed. "The bastard found it. A way to fix them."

"If what Dani did was a spell to unbind her from her objects . . ." I began, thinking aloud, "then that—that *thing* that is tearing through her body, that made her kill Maya, and nearly throttled us, that's destroying her from the inside out, it's—"

"It's Magic. Or the One, as they call it," Max said. "Raw Magic, going straight through her. Just like Daelius. Because she had first bound to an object and then unbound from it, her Magic and body didn't know how to react. Without any objects to take the brunt of the Magic, her body is operating as the object instead. She's taking the full force of it."*

I paused, looked down at the book, running my fingers over the ink. A thought I didn't like wormed its way through me.

"But she's not casting any spells . . ." I said slowly. "I mean, she was unconscious before. Thermoporo had cast a spell that was too strong for him, but . . . Dani's not casting any spell."

He swallowed, his Adam's apple bobbing. "No . . . it looks like the Magic's doing it for her."

I was afraid, suddenly, of the power I'd felt under the soles of my shoes on campus, buzzing with a strange and steady hum. I hadn't realized before, but it sounded almost . . . louder now. Hissing and swirling and beating like a living, breathing thing.

"There's something else." My eyes scanned the last words on the page.

---

* This should not be confused with Britton Arcane's dismissal of objects entirely. Their students never bind to objects and so have never suffered these particular effects despite the fact that they don't use objects. However, one might say that because they don't use objects at all, the effects can be just as deadly, as when a student tries a spell that's too powerful for them.

Three talismans are required for the workings this time, instead of one. The brothers have sold everything for possession of the rare gems. So far, the spell has worked for two of the other initiates. After the ritual, they have scarcely parted with their talismans.

It has not worked for Daelius, who is still alive in the caverns. Sometimes, when we meditate or go for walks, I can hear him scream.

Master has done all he can. Once a person has been Magically unbound for one cycle of the moon, the Binding charm is no longer possible. Magia will take permanent ownership of the vessel.

Tonight, I think of Daelius and mourn, for the last of his water will surely run out soon.

Slowly, the realization dawned on us both.

"Oh, God."

I did a quick sum in my head. A month! If I'd arrived on the fourth day of Dani being possessed, that only left . . .

"One day, Max. We have one day until we can't turn her back. Until . . . 'Magic takes permanent ownership of the vessel.'"

FROM THE JOURNAL OF DANICA STEWART

April 2ⁿᵈ [the day after the murder]

Wouldst thou, great Jove, thou Father of Mankind
Reveal the Demon for that Task assign'd,
The wretched Race an End of woes would find.

And yet be bold, O Man, Divine thou art,
And of the Gods Celestial Essence Part.
Nor sacred Nature is from thee conceal'd,
But to thy Race her mystick Rules reveal'd.
These if to know thou happily attain,
Soon shalt thou perfect be in all that I ordain.
Thy wounded Soul to Health thou shalt restore,
And free from ev'ry Pain she felt before.

Abstain, I warn, from Meats unclean and foul,
So keep thy Body pure, so free thy Soul;
So rightly judge; thy Reason, so maintain;
Reason which Heav'n did for thy Guide ordain,
Let that best Reason ever hold the Rein.

CHAPTER FORTY-SIX

It was all unraveling, but it all felt so wrong all of a sudden. Passages from the text swirled over and over in my mind, and I found myself repeating snippets from S's account.

The One uses him as a puppet, a vessel, but not an equal. The One speaks in the old language.

And a memory, a thought, a *something*, pushed to the surface, as though long buried.

"*So be it,*" *whispered an ancient voice, as deep as the earth.*

With every moment, I became more aware of the thread of Magic tightening around me, as if just waiting for me to work it all out. It was that same feeling I felt when I was around Dani, that pull of deep, deep water.

Was it dragging me under, too?

I still had so many more questions, and I needed more from S than what he could give me. So I went back to the Dawn Underground.

Once again, I ended up on the author's page. I hovered over the link on the Order of Autumn.

A pagan mystery school of the Hellenistic period. Thought by some to be the original authors of the Book of Autumn.

A mystery school with strong political leanings that had to scatter and hide after their headquarters were burned. There was an entire section of the forum devoted to them, folders full of old newspaper clippings and from old scholarly journals. In his book *Alchemical Foundations for the Digital Age*, Elphabius Hobbs included a brutal recollection of their beheadings in the streets, of the ditches running red from their blood.

Then there was this essay from a philosophy textbook.

There is not much written about them. What we do have are fragments referenced in the works of later scholars, specifically in reference to "autumnus," while having no connection to nature or the seasons. In Iamblichus's text On the Mysteries of the Egyptians, Chaldeans, and Assyrians, *there is reference to the " . . . virtus dei autumnus."* The context of the passage discusses how people "marveled at their capacity for silence." The fragment is believed to be one of the most definitive references to the group, though symbols of them are decidedly more frequent, referenced by the number 191. The findings have given rise to the theory that the Order of Autumn were Pythagoreans who didn't disband as previously thought after the attack (it is unknown if Pythagoras survived the attack on his followers; some suggest he fled to Metapontum), but instead continued on in secret throughout the ages, their thoughts and beliefs evolving as the world did. It is believed they worshipped numbers as Pythagoras did, that they believed God himself was the number of numbers. Aristotle is said to have referenced the group in his two-book treatise on the Pythagoreans, though unfortunately those writings are lost to us.*†

Later, in an interview by the same author—

"If the Book of Autumn does in fact exist—and I'm not saying it does—that would make it perhaps one of the only surviving and legitimate accounts of the followers of Pythagoras or his teachings, as Pythagoras didn't write any of his teachings down because they were meant to be kept secret. It would be

---

* Virtues of autumn.

† Anthony Prescott Phillips, in *The Essays on Neoplatonists and Philosophers of the Alchemical Age* (Blackwell, 2003).

quite the discovery, an accounting of Pythagoras, one of the most controversial figures in history, a man whose legacy has ballooned through history to one of mythic proportions. The teachings are nearly impossible to separate from Platonic philosophy, for Plato was much influenced by the Pythagoreans, as evidenced in his dialogues *Phaedo* and *Timaeus*, which are decidedly of Pythagorean philosophy. The only teaching we know for certain belongs to Pythagoras was on the belief of the immortality of the soul, and of a soul's transmigration to a new body upon the death of the old."

Apparently, there was even a resurgence in 1993. The headline was ANCIENT GREEK MYSTERY SCHOOL PROVOKES INTRIGUE, OBSESSION.

A bunch of pamphlets had been released, along with a cryptic message: Whoever could decode the message on the pamphlet would be initiated into the order and inducted into their mysteries. For all of winter 1993, the forum was abuzz with people colluding to decode the symbols, to no avail. Eventually, the whole thing was dismissed as a hoax, though there were still some threads on the site of stalwart users insisting they'd used the wrong cipher, that everyone had just translated it wrong.

And it hit me all at once.

How had I not realized it sooner?

The Order of Autumn, with their political leanings, the headquarters that burned down. S had even detailed the nightmares he'd had after the beheadings in the streets, spoke of the smoke that clogged his throat from their headquarters burning.

The Order of Autumn was the mystery school that S was a member of.

And if Basile had the book . . . If it was sitting in his office, of all places?

Well. I guess he wasn't lying when he said they were more than just some math group.

I looked at my phone and opened Basile's feeds one more time. My phone was blowing up with notifications—I'd set it to alert me when new content of his dropped—and I also had push notifications from the Discord server owned by "the Basilites," a group of avid Reality Paradox and Basile Samir fans. They were going off, rapid-fire messages mixed with meme after meme.

> *sierraperez414: Did you see his new video????*
> *amateurPlato: OMGGGGGGG*
> *whatgoeskirdi: I knew it! I freaking knew it!! our boy is going to save the world. Things are really changing now. I can feel it.*
> *amateurPlato: Do you think he will take me with him?*

I opened Basile's page. He'd released two new videos and uploaded them to all of his socials. The first was a teaser video telling people to "watch this space" for exciting new content hours prior. It was strangely serene. He was dressed all in white against a white background.

The second was the same background, same clothes. In it, he seemed almost reverent, with his gaze reaching to the heavens. He laughed, then looked straight at the camera. "To all the nonbelievers, to all the people who have doubted me, I'm here to take my theory one step further. Not only can I prove the existence of a parallel world, but I can also get to it."

Then the video feed cut off.

I looked over at Max, the skepticism plain in his eyes. Sure, to some it might look like just another publicity stunt. But to me it rang true. Especially with all our research, everything I'd read of S and Basile's obsession with an invisible world living alongside ours, it was all starting to become clear.

I considered Basile's "search for truth," his Reality Paradox, his fixation on this parallel world, the world of Being. I started thinking of Basile's belief in reincarnation, his ever-driving desire to perfect his soul, and slowly, slowly, the pieces started to fit themselves together in my brain.

I looked at Max, the answer settling like a weight in my stomach. "Phi Kat is the Order of Autumn."

CHAPTER FORTY-SEVEN

"So what do we do?" Max asked. "Confront them? Get them to reverse what they did?"

But I knew what we had to do. I was more sure than I'd ever been about anything in my life. "We do the binding."

Max rocked back on his heels, mouth already flying open as a barrage of protests came forth. "You crazy? The last person who did this spell got themselves nearly killed in the process."

"Not exactly. If our theory is accurate, it was the brothers who did the spell."

Max threw up his hands, his hat flying off his head. "Semantics! It's dangerous, that's what we know."

"Of course it is." I stopped and looked at him. Dark half-moons shone under his eyes. The stubble had taken over his face, now coated in prickly black hairs. He was wearing the same shirt he'd worn yesterday and surrounded by empty paper coffee cups. Somehow through it all, he was still as handsome as the day we'd first met.

"What choice do we have? We're dimidiums, Max," I said more quietly. "It was always going to be us."

He looked down, rubbing a hand over his temples. He knew it, too. "'The Magic of both is stronger than any one,'" he said, reciting the old adage.

Even with everything we'd been through, I couldn't help but take comfort in having him here with me. Having someone here who knew exactly what I meant, exactly how scared I was, without having to explain myself.

"Fine. But we're not going in there without a plan."

I pulled the book out of the trunk and put it in a backpack. "There's no time."

"Cel, wait. Let's just think about this for a second—"

"There is no time, Max. Dani is getting worse by the minute. Luce, too."

He caught my arm. "What if the spell doesn't work? If we're right, that it's raw Magic ripping through Dani's body . . . and S's spell is meant to direct that Magic through something else, another object . . . If it doesn't work as planned, what happens to the excess Magic?"

I slowed, turned toward him, even though I had one foot already out the door. I knew what he was getting at. The excess Magic would look for other conduits instead, something else to pass through as an object.

"Us, Cella. It would pass through us. We're taking an enormous risk here."

"Do you think that's what happened to Luce?"

He blew out his cheeks, his eyes dark. "Maybe it's what his teacher warned of when he said the One would rip a hole through the earth and walk through at will."

"But if we could fix the excess Magic coming through Dani and put it back in her objects, maybe that would fix Luce, too. You don't have to come if you don't want to," I said. "I can try the spell on my own."

He picked up and dusted his hat off the ground, looking me dead in the eye. He stepped close to me, as close as he did the first day we met. Close enough so I could feel the heat radiate off his body, so I could see the sweat trickling down his neck, so I could feel the warmth of his aura. "Easy, there. You're not getting rid of me now. According to S, we still have until sunset tomorrow, so that's roughly twenty-four hours from now. That's enough time to see if this is even possible, right? Let's use the time to get prepared, make sure we can actually do this without killing ourselves. And then—then we do this thing."

I took a deep breath. I wasn't happy about the delay, but it would be harder, if not impossible, to do this without him.

"Fine. But if we don't figure it out by the morning, I'm going in, no matter what."

The window to my room was cracked, and air from outside drifted in. A whisper of something charred drifted on the wind. If a wildfire broke out now, this whole place would go up in smoke.

He gripped my hand tight, an anchor holding me steady. "If we don't figure it out by tomorrow morning, then both of us go in. No matter what."

S's spell was complicated. It required a large amount of strength to first grab hold of the extra energy siphoned from the target, to hold that thread taut, and then "push" it into the objects. I assumed S's brothers all completed the spell with him, though the instructions he left were sparse. It consisted of only a few lines.

> *Travel to that hollow place where your Magia lies, but be wary, do not step inside. For the One will pull you in.*

I couldn't stop thinking about what the results of this spell had done to people. Like Dr. Strauss. I'd seen him on a bench earlier in the day, head in his hands.

"Dr. Strauss? Are you alright?"

He'd looked right through me, like he didn't see me at all. He pulled out a small metal head the color of unpolished brass.

"It's your object, isn't it? The Newton statue you were trying to put back together?"

He nodded, clutching the disembodied head.*

---

* Most people didn't know that Newton was a Magician. It's funny. He's celebrated as this rational scientist, this bringer of the Enlightenment. Yet he would have never come up with his theory of gravity or his findings on light if not for his interest in alchemy and the occult. Historians buried that fact about him, though, and tried to explain it away.

"What happened?" I asked quietly.

He looked past me as if at some unseen horror. "I could see something was happening with Danica. I knew she was getting into dangerous Magic. If I'd known what she had planned . . ." He crushed bits of gold dust, watching the flakes dribble through his fist and to the ground. "Maya was the only one who did, but by then, it was too late."

"You tried to help her?"

He wiped his nose. "After I saw what became of her, I contacted colleagues at Britton. I was stupid, desperate to try and help. I performed an experimental spell and nearly got myself killed in the process. I probably would have been killed, if not for my object taking the brunt of the damage. And even then, I didn't go unscathed." He pulled down his sleeve, showing the marred skin and unnatural scarring that had crept up to his neck.

So that was why his object had become so badly damaged. Not by a hex, but by doing the very thing it was meant to do: protect him.

"That's why your skin looks like Dani's."

He nodded. "My body took an excess force of Magic. Experimental spells are not really what Seinford and Brown represents, so I was off the council. I lost more of myself than I thought trying to help her. I loved Dani, but not in the way that everyone thinks. She was like a daughter to me. I suppose that's why Dr. Robetresse said I was too close to it."

"I promise you, we will do everything we can to try and fix her."

It struck me in that moment that I'd forgotten how beautiful our connections could be to each other. How much Strauss cared for and looked out for Dani. I felt silly now for ever suspecting he had hurt her. Sometimes, all it took was one person who cared to make all the difference. And I started to think Vern was right. There was something I loved about humanity, about community, about my life here. Maybe I lost that somewhere along the way. All I knew was there was good in them, and good in her, and I was going to do my best to find it again.

But in order to do that, I had to make sure that what had happened to Strauss didn't happen to me.

I had to study this spell as much as I possibly could.

The spell at least told me that S also "traveled" somewhere, like Max and I did, when he did his Magic. I wonder where he ended up. Somewhere like his home, maybe, with olive trees and steep crests of rock.

Pronounce loudly and clearly, "I bind thee to three," and direct the excess Magia into the talismans.

First, we needed to practice the basics. Get accustomed to each other's Magic again and become familiar with Danica's telescope. We needed to see if it was even able to accept Magic.

Max and I sat across from each other in a field, overlooking the apple orchards and with a red mesa at our backs. Dark gray storm clouds gathered overhead, moving in from the east. Clusters of yellow grasses swayed, and I tried to not think about all the times we had lain in grass just like this, looking at the stars and making each other promises we could never keep.

He looked out at the storm clouds over the hills. "You know, lightning and thunder mean danger in cattle country. Those clouds would've had the cattle on edge, restless."

"We should have an hour or two before the storm hits."

Dani's telescope was on the ground between us. I set my objects in front of me. First, the jar of water, then the leather cord, then the mug. Max did the same with his.

I closed my eyes, breathing in slowly through my mouth, and touched the glass jar.

I was submerged like an anchor dropped in water. For a moment, my heart seized in my chest. The water was pitch-black and freezing, and I watched myself hurtle toward the bottom. My throat choked on garbled words.

I was drowning.

I should've known better, should've practiced my Magic more before now, should've—

But then Max's voice sounded in my ear. *Kick.*

My feet kicked out, shins and thighs pumping furiously. My arms scrabbled for the surface, eyes focused on the circle of light at the crest of the salty water. I reached the surface, and my lungs heaved a gulp of air. The waves crashed against me, but I was holding.

I could do this.

"Good," he whispered.

The sea was stormy, but I treaded water, bobbing along with the current, letting the water sweep me away. Letting the Magic flow over me. Outside of this, my hand languidly touched my second object.

The leather was warm in my palm, and in the distance—the familiar sound of horses.

"I'm coming."

Max's horses were running. I could smell the heat on the back of their necks, the pant of the horses' breath. They were coming fast. I heard the whip and tap of rope at Max's side, as if readying to wrangle a runaway colt.

I was treading water in an ocean with no land in sight, but he was coming. He was running to me.

"Max," I whispered. Our connection was faint, nowhere near as strong as it used to be. We needed more practice—years more practice to do S's spell—but I pushed the doubt away. There was no room for doubt. No room for a lack of concentration because losing concentration when you're holding this much water means I really would plummet to the bottom. It may not have been literal water that I would sink into, but it was clear as day in S's warning. If I lost my concentration during his spell, I would be lost to this world—lost somewhere in the Magic.

My head bobbed above water, my limbs tiring when gentle drops of rain fell on my head, warming me to my core.

Max.

No matter where I was, he always found me. In that shadow-space of Magic, he brought the light streaming in, a single beam of sunlight bursting through gray storm clouds.

I'm here.

Down came the walls between us, and without them, he was exposed and vulnerable. I held onto a timid hesitation, too. But below that, an eagerness, a hunger.

I'd missed this.

Together, our Magic tangled up in each other, strong, pulsing with electricity. "Let's try to funnel Magic toward the telescope," I said. "Just enough to test."

Dani's telescope wasn't radiating Magic. It felt cold and lifeless. But it hadn't always been that way. Just days ago, I'd heard the steady beat of its pulse, the notes swirling around it like some twisting melody only it could play. It had Magic still in its veins. It just needed to be reminded of that fact. Reminded of what it had once had.

"A thread," Max agreed faintly.

Together, we reached a hesitant thread out to it. I concentrated on pushing the cord toward the telescope, threading it like a string through a needle. It was hard work, and the cord of power shook and vibrated as the power weighed on our limbs, drawing our strength.

"Cel," Max said beside me, voice strained.

"Just a second longer. You can do this."

The telescope still felt cold, but the closer the cord got to it, the more I sensed something. A flicker of life in there, still. It might accept the power, if we could just hold the thread for a second longer. Push just a little farther—

But the cord of power bobbed up and down violently now, and the ocean below me was sucking up into a whirlpool, as if going down a giant drain.

"I can't," Max groaned, and with one long last thrum, like a finger on a guitar string, the thread of Magic fell to the ground and dissipated.

I opened my eyes.

"We've got to hold it longer than that."

Max was on the ground, sweat pouring down his forehead. "I don't know if I can. How are you able to hold it?"

Suddenly, I felt a tick of anger replace the cold chill of the Magic. How were we going to save Dani if he refused to help? I could hold it just fine—it shouldn't have been any more difficult for him.

But, of course, I already knew the answer. It was because, in his heart, Max still was afraid of Dani. He still believed that she was a cold-blooded murderer.

"That's why we're practicing. Please, we have to try again," I begged. "We're so close."

"Okay." He got up off the ground and wiped the sweat off his brow with the lip of his shirt. "If you think we can do it without killing ourselves."

"I know we can. Just trust me." I reached for his hand and gave it a squeeze.

He looked up at me, his eyes a liquid, brilliant blue. "Of course I do."

My heart fluttered at the touch. Doing Magic like this brought on the craziest runner's high. Suddenly, I was aware of how close we were, of the way his shirt stretched across his chest, his hair falling in his eyes. The way his stare warmed and steadied me. I became very conscious of my own body. Of how badly I wanted to reach for him, pull his lips to me, feel his body crushed against mine.

"Marcella . . ." His voice was strained, a husky growl. He ran his tongue over his lips. "We need to . . . focus."

But his hands weren't obeying because they were already running up my thighs. And we were already so close. Our chests practically touched. The only thing that separated us were our objects bumping up against our knees.

I closed my eyes and again plunged into the water.

This time, I was in a room in a dark house. Water spilled from a drainpipe in the corner. The place seemed familiar somehow—it was somewhere I'd been before, only different. The walls were dark, and though there was a window in the corner, no light came in. As I spun back around, I noticed the water was already up to my knees. It filled the room quickly, pressing me back against the wall.

"Okay," I breathed. With my leather cord, I could make a plug for the pipe to stop the water.

Again, I could hear the gallop of horses, felt a warm spring rain on my shoulders. Sun streamed through the windows. Satisfied the water had stopped, I nodded. "One thread to the telescope."

"Wait," Max said suddenly, and I blinked lazily, still halfway in the Magic. "How are you doing that?"

"I'm just concentrating," I answered.

"No I mean, how are you doing that? You're not touching your leather cord. How are you conjuring leather?"

I looked down. He was right. I wasn't touching any of my objects. "Oh, I—I don't know." Memories flooded through me, of another time I'd cast something without the use of my objects. Dr. Perez yanking me aside, the smoke from the fire still choking my throat.

"How did you do that?"

"What are you talking about?" I cried, too dazed to focus on anything except the rage, except all the feelings swirling around like a chasm that I couldn't control. I looked at my reflection in a car window and barely recognized myself, my hair a vicious tangle around me. Dark ink blotted out my irises like a stain.

"The fire, Cella," Perez said, his eyes wide, and . . . frightened. "How the hell are you conjuring fire?"

Now, in the field with Max, I shook my head, embarrassed. Quickly, I put a hand on the leather cord. "Let's just keep going." I looked out at the horizon. "We're running out of time."

Max eyed me warily for a moment, then nodded.

I closed my eyes, back once again in that strange house. In my mind's eye, I imagined the telescope in the room across from me.

"Got it," Max said.

Gently, we eased the Magic to the telescope. Water dripped from the pipe. "It's working," I said. "Keep going."

The cord of power circled the base of the telescope, creating a gentle spiral that wrapped around it, waiting to be let in.

But the stopper I'd weaved around the pipe went shooting out. Water rushed out faster than ever. In seconds, it was at my waist. Then my chest.

Tendrils of power reached out to the telescope, ready to pierce through. I held my breath as the water rose past my head and steadily inched toward the ceiling.

It was then I realized that I had been in this house before.

This was where Dani had been in my nightmares. In all my visions with her, she was always here.

A flicker of movement happened in the next room. A strand of blond hair next to the telescope.

"Dani?" I whispered, though the water went streaming into my throat.

This was it. She was here.

"Push, Max!"

The water plunged down my throat, stars burst in my eyes, but there she was. A hand, running a slender finger down the telescope, the Magic encircling it like a viper.

"Cella," came a choked warning, though it was far away. Too far away and—

I was submerged in darkness.

I could feel Dani here. Even if I couldn't see the pale strands of hair or the shadow over the floorboards, I knew it, felt it in that same inexplicable draw I had to her ever since I first saw her in Maritza's cottage. And somewhere, in the haze inside my mind, I realized I wasn't drawn to her because she reminded me of my brother, or because she was lost and needed my help.

I was drawn to her because she reminded me of . . . me.

The same thread of Magic that had its grip around her tightened its coils around me.

As if something had been knocked loose, memories flashed through me more quickly than I could keep up.

In my mind's eye, a weak, hollow-eyed Cella standing in the bathroom. Bear, barking at me to wake up, to snap out of it. And my eyes, unfocused, running over the 1's all over the shower door. The 1's that my fingers were still tracing over the door.

In another—black paint stained my hands as I fled flashlights scouring the dry campus grounds, sending a panicked glance back at my work on the skulls without truly seeing. Without realizing what I'd done at all.

And memories of a voice that sounded like Basile's, but wasn't. A soft smile, an outstretched hand. "Join us."

I opened my eyes, gasping for breath.

Max was on his back. He stared at the sky, breathing hard. "Jesus, do you have a death wish?!" He slammed upright. "When we're tied together, we feel the same things. *And I like breathing.*"

But I could barely hear him.

FIVE YEARS AGO

Jamie had found me in the library again and asked if I wanted to tag along to one of their lectures.

"What do you even see in those guys?" Max asked.

"They're nice." But it was more than that. They were ... different than most people on campus. They took walks together every morning; they practiced group meditation on Tuesdays and ate a (vegetarian) lunch together most days of the week. They valued silence over saying the first thing that came to mind. They were some of the most thoughtful, disciplined group of people I'd ever met. "They're philosophical. Sort of like an academic club. They prize their minds more than anything. It's refreshing. Really, you should come to a meeting. Get to know them. Aaron introduced me. He says they're pretty cool."

"No, thanks. I've had enough Elon Musk fanboys to last me a lifetime."

"They're not like that. You'd give them a chance if you saw what they were working on." It really was groundbreaking stuff. Some of it . . . a little experimental, but I'd never met another group of people as driven to discover things about Magic, who were so dedicated to mastering their craft. I thought, at last, I'd found my people.

I knew Max would change his mind about them if he met them. So I knocked on his door one morning before a meeting, intent on dragging him to it.

He didn't come when I knocked, but I could hear him in there, stumbling around. I could already imagine the whiskey smell on his breath. Must have been some night.

He finally came to the door in boxers and no shirt. "You're not supposed to be in the boy's hall," he said, eyes widening. He angled himself in front of the door and made to close it behind him.

I shrugged. "It's fine, Jamie let me in." There was a rustling from inside his room. I frowned. "What's that?"

He moved to close the door behind him, but I reached out my hand. "It's nothing," he mumbled. "I'm busy this morning. Rain check?"

More rustling, and a distinct utterance of "shit" from inside.

"There's someone in there."

"Cel, this isn't the best time." There was a strange look that passed across his face, panic and shock and . . . guilt?

My voice rose unusually high. "Who's in there, Max?" I shoved open the door.

A girl, her bottom half covered by sheets, top half only clothed in a bra, tapping the screen on her phone with bright pink nails. I stared at her stupidly, my thoughts sluggish and hazy.

"Did you sleep in here last night?" I asked. For all the books I read, I still said the stupidest fucking things.

But when she looked up, my brain started working again. I recognized the long sweep of black hair across her shoulders, those pretty brown eyes that didn't miss an inch, and the oh-so-familiar look of disdain. My stomach heaved.

"You—you slept with Luce?"

Max's eyes darted frantically around the space as if an exit might just appear in the wall.

Luce started gathering up her things, and all I could do was stand there, staring at the book still sitting outside the door. Feeling so stupid for leaving it there the night before, because of course he hadn't read it. He was fucking Luce, right there in the bed that I'd slept with him in.

I couldn't take it. Everything was too much, too bright, and Luce was mumbling some bland apologies or excuses, and something about getting off her shirt because I was standing on it.

My footsteps carried me down the hall, until I was all-out sprinting. All I heard at my back was Max, calling my name.

In the blinding days that followed, I fervently ignored my phone. I found a new spot in the library and paid an underclassman to cast an illusion charm so Max wouldn't find me. I searched for any escape—anything to occupy my mind and keep me from thinking about him and the smell in that room, sticky sweet like body spray and sweat. I found solace in books, in my old routines of obsessive study of Magic.

But now there was a problem. All my methods of casting were with Max. Though I ordered myself to hate him every chance I got, my Magic felt his absence like an aching chill. My fingers itched for him. Magic had always been the only thing that had been there for me, so big it blocked out all other thoughts until I could only see, breathe, and live in the Magic. Now it had been tainted by the person who'd hurt me the most.

So I went to talk to Jamie. They'd been bringing it up casually to me for weeks now, something they'd found in an old book. "It's just experimental," they'd said. "Something to advance the science." And I'd thought about it off and on, but never had the courage to pull the trigger. Until now.

"I want to do it."

Jamie had told me about this spell that could unbind you from anything that had fractured your soul. As a dimidium, my Magical soul was in two pieces, so it was theoretically a way to no longer be a dimidium. A way to stand on my own two feet, on my own accomplishments, to never need anyone else again.

"You're sure?" he asked, but Jamie was already beckoning me closer.

"My Magical soul is broken in half, right? Well, let's put it back together again."

"It should be . . . relatively uncomplicated," Jamie explained. "As a dimidium, you have one foot in the world of Being already. You can access the aura of another person and sense their emotions and power. You can read their Magic almost like the pages of a book. We just have to find the right materials for the unbinding. Unfortunately, the spell is not as detailed as I'd like."

Over the course of a week, we experimented with all types of materials to get the Magic to unbind from my objects and from Max: glass, cloth, under solar eclipses and full moons, rare minerals, steel, iron, gold, silver, but the thing that seemed to have the greatest potential were bones.

Bones, charred and blackened by fire. It seemed the Magic was readily able to attach to them; the threads flowed straight to it—but only for a moment. Almost like it wanted to jump into a person. But once the Magic found the bones were dead and lifeless, they jumped back into the next living thing, me, and we were back where we started.

For weeks, we worked at it, when finally . . . It was an ordinary Wednesday, and unbearably hot.

They had me standing inside a circle of bones lit by fire so that the bones burned as we cast the spell. The flames soon grew out of control. They flickered dangerously close to my clothes.

I reached for my Magic to cool the fire. But when I reached for it, the darkness I plunged into was so much darker than normal.

I could still feel the heat pricking at the edges of my consciousness. Dark water enveloped me, but there was something else there, too. Something all-encompassing; foreign, yet intimately familiar.

What have you done?

Even now as I recall its voice, I cannot remember the sound of it. I only remember how it made me feel. Like a minuscule drop in the ocean, a mere ant in its grandness. Ancient and immovable, like rushing water or shifting earth, wind through creaking bark, the hiss of air through a gap in stones.

It felt as old as the Earth itself, like I was speaking to its bones, but edged with something wrong, something dark. Something humans should never have disturbed.

Give me more, I said. *I need it.*

I was familiar with the Magic, had felt it before when I cast, but this was something different. A more . . . direct line, as if I were accessing a god, or some powerful deity of the sea, beseeching myself at its feet.

Only now did I sense the threads of power running through the Earth, could practically see the lines running from people, see the way their power was transposed through objects. Magic was everywhere, always was waiting to be called to, to be let in.

Why?

In that one word, an entirety of emotion, thoughts—measured in years, decades, millennia. It didn't care about me. Didn't care about my response or my thoughts. Whatever I said would be forgotten seconds after our interaction. But for now, for this one moment, a spark of curiosity. *What do you want from me, and why do you want it?*

That one question—*Why?*—caused me to think all kinds of things—some petty, some not, some fundamental to me as a person.

But at the heart of it, the staunch desire to make my own way in the world.

I wanted to be my own person, to stand on my own two feet, not have to be tied to the great Maximilian Middlemore. Dependent on him no matter how much I fought it, always and forever sinking into his inescapable shadow. My achievements forever assumed to be the product of his genius. Forever relegated to the role of girlfriend, not peer. Not colleague. Just the latest idiot to fall in love with someone who could never care quite as much as you did. I didn't want to be connected for all my life to someone who had hurt me. Didn't want to feel his presence with every nerve in my body, didn't want to feel his heartbeat across the room, to always know how he was feeling.

I didn't want to be a dimidium anymore. Didn't want to be one half of a Magical soul. I wanted to be one full, unified soul that was all my own.

I didn't have to say all this to the Magic, of course.

It was in everything I did, in every breath I took, entwined in the veins in my wrists, wrapped around my lungs. It knew; it just wanted to make sure I knew, that I was sure.

And I was.

I held my breath as I awaited its reply, felt it breathe around me, as old as the Earth itself. Its reply rattled my bones.

So be it.

CHAPTER FORTY-EIGHT

"Max," I said now, my heart racing as I lay beneath the steadily darkening sky. "I think I know why I can cast without my objects."

As I explained to him what happened that final year before I left, more memories that had been tamped down—by the Magic?—rose to the surface.

"So all that stuff you were doing with Jamie and his friends . . . you were unbound?"

I swallowed. As the realization dawned on him, his eyes lost all their blue. They took on a hue as gray as the sky.

"Looks like it. And that's why I could sense Dani when you couldn't, in her Magic. When we pushed the Magic, she was there instead to take it, like a black pit or something. Just a void."

"But why aren't you like Dani then? Levitating and out of control, and skin all scarred up?"

I chewed my lip. "Well, from what I remember, Jamie and the others hadn't had much success before with the spell. It was still an experiment, something they were curious about but not sure could work. Jamie and the others, that must've been the foundations of Phi Kat, they must have been the founding members, before it was officially a frat on campus." I shook my head, still dazed. "I think that must be why Basile and the brothers are so enamored with me, why they try so hard to get me to talk to them. I'm the first successful case of unbinding they know about, and I think, because I was the first one, the Magic wasn't that powerful yet. I only opened the door, and it waited, festering and growing in power, until they were able to do it again."

Max looked down, and I could feel the hurt swirling in his aura. He could barely look at me. "I knew something was up, I just didn't know what."

"I think everything just boiled over at once, with Aaron, and you, and it was—yeah."

Each memory that came flashing back caused searing pain in my head. My eyes watered from the strength of it. "There's something else, too. They have something to do with Aaron. Jamie, and I think maybe Basile, too."

"What do you mean?"

"I don't know. I just remember Aaron was the one who first introduced me to the guys. And Basile mentioned him a few times, though I don't know how they could have met. He said something like 'he believed in the Magic, too.'"

"Maybe Jamie and Aaron talked. Do you have Aaron's phone? Maybe they texted each other?"

I didn't have his phone, but I did still have a login to some of Aaron's old accounts that I'd used after his death to close them out. In the months after his death, it was a tiny piece of him I could still hold onto. Now I pulled out my phone and logged into his email account. I did a search for "Jamie," for "Basile," for "the One," for "Magic."

And there, three hits. Email drafts to Robetresse and to his advisor:

To Whom It May Concern:

I have begun to suspect a group I've been spending time with is conducting experimental spells on students. I have reason to believe at least one of the people they tried it on died. I believe they should be shut down. The names of the individuals are as follows—

Max and I looked at each other, agape.

"It was never sent."

I held my Christmas mug clenched around my fingers, my eyes growing hot. "What the fuck did they do to my brother?"

Max wrapped his arms around me. "Hey, hey," he whispered. "You can't fall apart on me now. I need you, champ," he said, wiping my tears away with his fingers.

He paused, looking at me thoughtfully. "Do you think . . . you could use you being unbound to save Dani?"

"I'm not sure," I said, my teeth chattering. "Maybe. But I still need your help."

He nodded. "Then we need that third object. It was too much Magic for me, and too much for the telescope to take on its own. And I don't know how to access the North Star."

"She doesn't have a third object. That's what Dr. Strauss said."

"She had to have at least another in order to summon this much power."

"There was nothing in the records. I checked."

"Maybe they went back through and deleted it? Or maybe she kept it a secret. But I'll bet you if anybody knows, it's the people who did the spell on her."

"They're not going to tell us anything."

"Then we go look for ourselves. You remember what Jack said, right? That they do some fucked-up shit up in the canyon." He turned around to the red hills behind us. "If I wanted to hide something somewhere it wouldn't be found, that might be where I'd start."

An hour later, we were hot, exhausted, and no closer to finding Dani's third object. We'd headed due south from the brothers' house toward the mountains. The clouds inched closer, a dark charcoal stain marring the sky.

"Over there." Max pointed. "See how the grass is all tamped down? It's got to be a trail. Someone's been out here."

Things kept resurfacing in my memories as we walked. In the days after completing Jamie's spell, I felt my life sinking from me, control of my body and mind slipping away from me little by little. I was afraid of what was happening to me, taken in by the One while at the same time being drowned by it. I began to think only in symbols and left myself a cryptic trail, one that only I would understand, to save myself. Part of me broke through, but I was still not fully conscious of what I was doing. Like when I carved HELL IS HERE into my headboard. Or when I'd blacked out and drawn the number 1 all over my shower. It was only now I realized it was a way of telling myself that the One had taken me.

The One had used me as it pleased that final year at school, drawing from Max's and my strength. When I set Luce's car on fire, I was so numb I could barely feel anything. I shouldn't have been able to set her car on fire—my objects were composed of water, leather, and porcelain. But while unbound, I was just a vessel for Magic. Magic took my anger toward her and turned it into intense, flaming power.

And the One was clever. After I left, it took me far from my dimidium, who the spell hadn't disconnected me from after all, as we were not each other's objects. But it wasn't clever enough, because the only thing that saved me from drowning steadily from the drain of Magic was coming back here to begin with, to investigate how it took someone else. In the end, it was Dani who broke through.

The pages hold the truth, and the truth will set you free. She sent me to the source of it all, to the Book of Autumn.

But now? I could feel the foreign presence of the One twisting through me, as if it were peering right over my shoulder, entwined around my veins, as it had been all along.

We followed the trail down to an alcove and reached an outcropping of cliffs, but it was a steep drop to the bottom. Max slid his palm down the rocks.

"Is there another way down?" I asked.

"I don't think so."

He kicked a rock at the top. It was a long way down, and

I didn't think either of us had the energy to make it in one piece right now.

"I don't suppose you have any belaying equipment lying around," I said.

Suddenly, he grabbed my wrist and pulled me behind him. "Someone's coming."

We crouched behind the rocks and listened. About twenty yards away were voices.

"Can you see who it is?" I whispered.

He shook his head, leading us around the corner so we weren't spotted. "We should go. We can come back at night."

I hesitated. If there were people here, that meant there had to be something out here to find, right? I wanted to follow them. I inched closer, crouching down in the rust-colored dirt.

The voices sounded closer now. In the distance, I could make out black outfits of some sort. Black leather sandals and black cloaks, and a low, whispered murmur like a chant.

Max's voice took on a sharp edge. "Cella, come on. We can come back at night."

I bit my lip. "We're so close," I whispered, but something about the low voices, like some demented Gregorian chant, sent gooseflesh raising on my arms.

"It's them. It's the brothers, the Order of Autumn, please, Max, we've got to—"

Max pulled me back. "All the more reason to come back when we're not outnumbered twelve to two. Come on," he said, heading back up the trail.

CHAPTER FORTY-NINE

Receive Not a Swallow in Your House

The clouds had moved overhead at last, pregnant with moisture, such a dark gray they were nearly black. Returning to campus, I felt shaky and unsteady, like I was standing over the precipice of a steep drop.

"You shouldn't have stopped me," I said, anger shaking my voice. "We could've followed them and seen where they were hiding it. Now what? We go back and just hope we find the spot again in the entire canyon?"

Max shook his head. "Don't do this, Cel. Not now."

"They did something to Aaron, Max! Intimidated him, scared him, God knows what else." I shut my eyes tight. I couldn't let myself imagine what else.

I was terrified and frustrated. A million other emotions were all swirling around me, and I couldn't keep them bottled up anymore. "We could have had them."

"And what if they found us?" he said. "We were outnumbered. Even with Magic, we would've never gotten out of there. I suppose you'd like to go and leave me behind again, but guess what, Cel? Even if you don't think you need me or anyone else, sometimes you do need people. Especially if you want to take on a whole group—"

But something was at a breaking point. I'd swallowed my feelings this entire time here with him, shoved them into this tight little box to not dredge up things better left buried. Now

I was sick of holding them all in. And with the revelation that I was unbound, neither of us knew where we stood. We were afraid, and I could feel it all, swirling around us.

Tears seeped from my eyes. He turned toward me, his eyes widening. "Cel?" Suddenly, we were too close. The heat of his hands was on my face, cupping my chin, holding me all together.

And I felt so stupid and embarrassed at the tears sliding down my cheeks, but I just couldn't do it any longer.

"Of course, I fucking need you," I half-laughed and half-sobbed. "I need you every second of every day. But I'm terrified to need you. I don't want to need you, but I do all the same."

And I guess that was all he needed to hear because then his warm lips were on my freezing mouth. His hands tangled in my hair and clutched my waist like I might fly away if he didn't hold me tightly enough. I leaned into him, hands running up his chest, drinking him in.

Tears rained down my cheeks, but for the first time in what felt like forever, something actually felt like it made sense. Our Magic hummed together, reunited at last, and I felt so safe, so warm, so right.

Then he pulled away. "I can't."

What? "We're two halves of a freaking Magical soul, Max. We're meant to be together."

He shook his head and walked toward the cliff at the edge of the parking lot. Behind the clouds, the sun was setting over the horizon, and it lit up the canyon with flecks of gold. But all I felt were the coming shadows and the chill from the storm clouds overhead.

"I spent so long wanting you, Cella, and now you pick this moment? You left without a word. Hell, you tried everything you could to tear yourself away from me. You didn't give a shit then, so what makes it different now?"

Was it really some great mystery to him why I'd left? I walked over to him and put my hands against the metal railing. "You slept with someone else."

He kicked the ground. Rocks scattered and clattered down into the canyon below. "I seem to remember quite clearly you telling me we should just be friends, that getting closer would 'interfere' with the Magic. Mind you, this was after we'd slept together three times. How do you think that made me feel?"

"Well, I—"

"I was in love with you, Cel. You have to know that. And then you just left me behind. Vanished. Poof, like that. You're always leaving me behind. And, you know, I think I finally understand why it all feels so goddamn familiar, why you care so much about saving Dani. The similarities are so blinding I don't know why I didn't see it before. The unbinding, all that time you spent with Jamie and the others. You hated being a dimidium so much that you were in exactly the same place as Dani—willing to try whatever experimental spell, in whatever book you could get your hands on, to separate yourself from me. I can't help but think you'd be right here in Dani's shoes if you were at school now."

"I wanted to separate myself from your Magic," I said quietly. "Not from you."

He shook his head. "I see no difference. You had to know how it would've made me feel, or you wouldn't have been doing it in secret. Jesus, I was in love with a girl who hated being my dimidium so much that she nearly killed herself to get rid of me. Can you imagine how pathetic that feels?"

"I'm sorry," I said. Tears stung my eyes, and I wiped them with the back of my hand. "But is it so wrong to want something on my own for once? I was sick of living in the shadow of the great Max Middlemore, of having every one of my accomplishments tied to you. Especially when you didn't give a shit about Magic to begin with."

"Of course I cared about Magic! Why would I have studied it for years and years? But whatever you could use to justify moving a thousand miles away without a thought as to what it'd do to me, you did. You didn't give a shit about how it would affect me when you took my Magic away, too. All I ever had was Magic. I didn't know how else to help my family, and you went and took it away. Dad can't work anymore, and Mama's sick to death taking care of him all the time."

"They only ever needed you, Max, not your Magic." I took a breath. "And I didn't want to be your dimidium, but that didn't mean I didn't care for you because I did. I do."

My voice broke, and the sky opened up at last. Rain drenched our clothes, our hair. It washed all the sweat and makeup from my skin.

"I wanted you, Cella. Every messy, gritty, wonderful part of you. And I've been beating my brains out this whole time trying to make you believe that I'm not some anchor tying you down, holding you back from uncovering the mysteries of the world. I didn't want to be the anchor, I wanted to be right there on that ship with you. Can you really say you wanted that, too? Have you ever wanted that?"

"I don't know," I said, and the rain and my tears were mixing in my eyes. For a second, my vision blurred as my contact slid out of place, and I could barely see him. Maybe that was good; it all hurt too much.

"I was young and hurt," I said. "I was stupid."

I was supposed to be like Ellendale, with a score of books published under my name, the next great Magical theorem discovered, spells and research and accolades. But after Aaron died, I couldn't even look at myself anymore without thinking of all the things I'd missed as I tried to become great. After he died, I ran so far from Magic that I could barely feel it anymore. Since I'd left, my life had been a study in shades of gray.

And now I was back here, where life was a burst of red, the cherry-red of Max's cheeks when he laughed too hard, the rust-colored hills, the apples in the orchard, the clay and sand and dust over the buttes and mesas. The colors all melding together like the blood of the earth, and the Magic underneath its warm, beating heart.

"You've never been stupid in your life, Cel," he murmured.

And I knew he was right, that I'd made this decision. I'd

made it years ago and had stuck by it every day since. As we looked at each other, we both knew it.

There was no Magic to make us work, to fix all the things that were broken between us.

I opened my mouth once, twice, and he waited for my reply, always waiting on me, but that was it. His eyes left mine. I saw it in the way his shoulders turned away from me. He was tired of waiting.

He opened the door to his truck and turned the ignition, and I slid down to the ground and held myself, trying to keep it all in. Trying to hold myself like a bandage so I didn't fall apart.

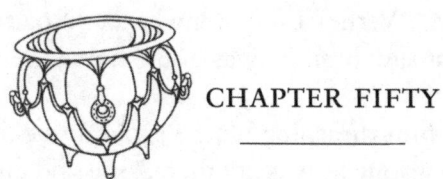

CHAPTER FIFTY

I don't know how long I sat there at the edge of the cliff, trying to hold it all in. The rain had soaked me to the bone, leaving me shivering and drenched.

A group of girls got out of their car and crossed the lot whispering among themselves. One of them hit the other when she saw me. I didn't want anyone seeing me like this. I just wanted to get back to my room, curl up in a blanket, and never come out again.

I was close to the door of House Torlaine when a voice yelled my name. For a second, I considered pretending I didn't hear it. My nerves felt like exposed live wires, ready to hit the nearest passersby with an electric jolt.

"Cella!" the voice called, more anxious this time. Footsteps pounded the ground behind me.

I turned and saw Maritza, face pale. "Maritza? What's wrong? You look like you've seen a ghost."

She swallowed hard. "They've found another one. Another person like Dani and Luce."

Another? My stomach dropped. I thought I had more time for the binding spell—more time to confront the brothers. Hell, I thought I'd at least have until morning. "Who's the student?"

Maritza averted her eyes. "I just want you to know that he's stable, for now. The worst of the thrashing seems to have stopped, but there are some concerns about his heart, given his age—"

My stomach clenched violently. "Maritza, who was it?"

"The librarian, Mr. Fernara. They found him outside the cafeteria. His spine—they've given him a powerful muscle relaxant to stop the contortions, but it's only been a few hours. We aren't sure how much worse it will get."

My blood ran cold. "Vern?" I shook my head. "No, it can't be Vern. He, no, I just saw him, he was going home the other night, and—"

"A student found him thrashing on the ground this morning. We don't know how long he was out there," she said quietly.

A thread knotted in my stomach. I felt like I was going to be sick. "Where is he? Oh God, what about his wife? Has anyone told her?"

She nodded. "They've taken him to a secure wing of the hospital. Sonia is with him there. I have to go. I just thought you'd want to hear it from me personally."

"Thank you," I said, barely able to concentrate on what she was saying.

She squeezed my arm. "Try not to panic. He's sedated right now. From what we can tell, he has about two hours until the worst of it kicks in and he starts to levitate."

She hurried away, and I squeezed my eyes shut, trying to not let the world collapse all around me.

Magic had its foothold in, and unless I could stop it at its source, bind Dani to her objects, it would get stronger. It would find more and more conduits, more ways into this world, and tear them apart until there was nothing left. Until it swallowed us all.

I threw open the door to House Torlaine and tore down the hall. I pulled out the Book of Autumn and reread the instructions for binding.

What had I done? "Vern. Please, God, I'm so sorry."

This was all my fault.

Max was gone because of me. This had happened to Vern because of me. Because I wasn't good enough. Because I couldn't figure it out before it was too late. Because I tampered with things I had no business dealing with.

I glanced back at the spell. Even with Max, S's spell would be difficult. Without him, it could kill me.

This was no simple charm. This was dealing with one of the strongest, most destructive forces on earth. This was trying to tear a hole through an ocean and hold back the water with the palm of your hand. But I had no choice. It was Vern. I wasn't just going to let him die.

Out of some form of self-preservation, I pulled out my phone to call Max. He didn't answer, so I started typing out a text.

Max, I know you hate me right now, and I deserve that. I probably deserve a thousand more things, but—

Delete, delete, delete.

Vern is a vessel. Need to do the binding spell. Pls call me back.

I hit send. Then I held the phone in my hand, begging the screen to light up again.

"Come on!"

I stood, legs shaking. I needed a plan. Plans were how you moved forward. Plans were good. Smart.

I tore the spell out of the book, tucked it in my jeans, and started gathering the ingredients, dumping all my objects into my backpack.

"Two hours, Max. Then I'm doing this spell . . . whether you're here or not."

Two hours for the worst of the convulsions to set in, for Vern's body to levitate, for the Magic to start to whittle its way at his skin. Two hours and no longer.

Max, or no Max, I would do this spell.

I wondered vaguely, as I filled a water pack, if Odysseus made a plan before he went to the Underworld, if Hercules did before he captured Kerberos. I wondered if they had any tips for summoning courage.

I unrolled a pair of wool socks Max's mom had knitted for me years ago and pulled them on. She'd used yellow and black yarn and embroidered them with little bees. Then I strapped a mounted flashlight to my head and steeled my nerves. I'd never been comfortable with any kind of darkness. The darkness in the desert was one that felt so alien to anywhere else, but it wasn't just that. Things found me in the dark. Magic. Dani. In every one of my dreams, she was in a dark room, a hallway, a shadowy corner of some long-forgotten place. And it terrified me.

I rubbed my finger over my leather cord, felt the familiar weight of the Christmas mug in my backpack. Then I headed back toward the spot where we'd gone the other day, before we'd decided to turn back. There was something there; I just knew it.

I was praying to anything listening that it was Dani's third object, because Max or no Max, I still needed that object if I was to do the spell.

I snuck out past the Phi Kat house, keeping low. I hoisted my legs over the old barbed-wire fence, the faint smell of fire catching on the breeze. A wildfire? Or another one of the brothers' bonfires?

My nerves were on edge. I jumped at every sound of the wind blowing through the creosote bushes and each snap of a twig.

I squinted in the low light, flinching at every movement in the grass, terrified that someone or something would jump out of the bushes. The moon cast just enough light that every shadow of a rock looked a little like a figure looming in the dark, and the distant coyote bray sounded like a scream.

What if the brothers were still out there? I couldn't run away this time. I sent another text to Max. *Going into the canyon. If I'm not back by dawn, tell Robetresse. Tell everyone.*

But I'd already gone too far to get a signal. I turned off my phone to conserve the battery.

It took me longer than I thought to reach the spot again, a rough crag of red rock down a weathered cliffside. I dug my foot in, testing my weight, then climbed onto it. Suddenly, I realized climbing in the dark wasn't one of my brighter ideas, but something told me this was it. I just needed to get down there.

I moved steadily down.

Below me was only a chasm of blackness, and though I wasn't that high up—it couldn't have been more than twenty-five feet—my stomach swooped violently. A bird echoed in my ears, screeching like a nighthawk about to take its prey. My eyes swiveled wildly, and I fumbled for the headlight to shine on the bird and scare it off, but the light slipped off my forehead and clattered to the rocks below.

The smell of burning filled my nose. When I shut my eyes, images were burned behind my eyelids. Symbols on the cattle skulls, symbols that *I* had drawn as a warning, as a reminder, as yet another one of my plans that hadn't worked out as I'd imagined. Dani's face, over and over again. A pale hand, a strand of blond hair plastered against her forehead.

Concentrate, Cella. You can do this, I ordered myself.

My foot stretched for the next foothold. As my hand reached out for a rock, it slid off a sharp edge, slicing my palm down the center. I cried out at the pain and clung with my other hand to the rock.

Shit shit shit.

"I'm so sorry, Vern," I whispered to the sky. How the hell was I going to climb down with only one hand?

I remembered the last thing he'd said to me. I was leaving the library for the day, and he looked at me. "Just keep moving forward," he said quietly. Vern believed in me. He thought I could do this. For him, I had to. I would.

I went over the facts in my head, tried to keep them straight, repeating them like a mantra.

But the symbols just kept burrowing in my eyes, and the birds sounded closer now. My eyes yearned for light, and my heart thumped erratically in my chest.

The flap of wings sounded near my ears, and a wild screech filled the air. The bird was going in for the kill.

Wings beat furiously; beaks pierced my neck, my face. I

swung my arms to keep them all off me, shoving away razor-sharp talons. My foot slipped, and my remaining grip on the rock fell away.

A scream ripped apart the air—mine, I realized—and then I was falling.

FROM THE JOURNAL OF DANICA STEWART

April 2ⁿᴰ [the day after the murder]

Then if this mortal Body thou forsake,
And thy glad Flight to the pure Æther take,
Among the Gods exalted shalt thou shine,
Immortal, Incorruptible, Divine:
The Tyrant Death securely shalt thou brave,
And scorn the dark Dominion of the Grave.

—
—

A man must be made good, then a God.

CHAPTER FIFTY-ONE

12 Hours Until Sunset —

When I woke up, I was freezing. There was something wet near my ear. My hands groped the ground and returned only fistfuls of dirt. The first rays of sunlight peeked out of the sky.

Had I been out here all night?

Vern.

I looked around for my flashlight, wincing at the pain in my leg, but it was nowhere to be found.

What if Vern had gotten worse? What if his heart couldn't take the Magic? What if a million things and here I was, too far away to do anything about it. I didn't even have the objects I needed for the spell.

I scrambled to stand, tentatively testing my weight on what I realized was a sprained ankle. That's when I stepped back and stifled a scream.

Crouched a few yards ahead of me, digging through my pack, was a man.

I scrambled for my phone. Mercifully, it hadn't fallen out of my pocket when I fell. Turn on, come on, *turn on*. I bit my lip hard.

I wanted to scream. No service.

My objects were in that bag, so that put Magic out of the question. I dug around in my pocket for something—anything to defend myself.

I gripped my keys hard between my two fingers, ready to jab for his throat or sternum. I waited for him to turn around and steadied my voice, praying with everything I had that it sounded braver than I felt.

"My friends know where I am."

The man laughed. "Yeah, and you're goddamn lucky, too. I had to pinpoint your last location from your phone." He turned around, and my shoulders sagged with relief. "What were you thinking, Cel?"

"Jesus, Max! You scared me half to death."

"I scared *you*? What gave you the bright idea of going down into a ravine in the middle of the night? I thought you were dead."

I held my stomach. My head swam, my ankle ached, and I tasted bile on my tongue. "I thought if I could find her third object, I could do the spell on my own, in case you . . ."

He looked down. "I was always going to come back. I just had to take care of a few things, in case we were going to . . . well, you know."

"In case we died, you mean." We both winced. That was me. Always so eloquent.

"Yeah." The silence stretched taut around us. He ran his fingers through his hair, quickly. "Well, did you at least find anything?"

"No." I looked around, but everything looked so much different in the daylight. I realized this wasn't the place at all that we'd seen the people chanting. I sighed, shoulders tugging down. "I didn't even make it back to the place where we were."

"Think again," he said, pointing to the shelf of rock above us, a short distance from where I'd climbed down. "That's the rock we hid behind the other day."

He bent down to study the dirt, and my eyes widened.

Hidden in the outcropping of rock, barely visible except for its movement in the stiff breeze, was a rope ladder. It was on the other side of the rock face, across from where I'd climbed down. If it had been daylight, I might have even seen it while I was climbing.

My eyes followed the line of the ladder and stopped at the

mouth of a small cave. It was nearly hidden from three sides, the perfect cover for doing something you didn't want other people to see.

Max chuckled, clapping me on the back. "Shall we?" He offered me his hand, and I frowned. My hand wasn't bloody anymore.

"I wrapped it to stop the bleeding," he explained, "but you're going to need stitches when we get back."

"Thank you," I said, leaning on his forearm to take some of the weight off my ankle. I held my breath at the precipice of the cave, a cool draft of air drifting past the opening.

The walls of the cave sloped to a dark dome, and the floor was damp. On the ground were white quilts and towels I recognized from the dorms. Candles had been mounted along the wall. A table in the center had been draped in loose black fabric. There was a tattered black cloak in the corner, along with other personal effects: loose sheets of paper, women's clothing, mismatched shoes, a hair comb, and a tarnished ring with a small red gemstone. The brothers had clearly been using this place for some time.

"They were down here, that's for sure," Max said.

I picked up a white Converse and one red heel. One was size seven and the other size nine. "These things belong to more than one girl."

The ring was, without a doubt, an object, though I wasn't sure whose. I could hear the faintest of murmurs from it, only a glimmer, indicating that Magic had once passed through here, but no more. This was the object of someone who was now dead. "This is where they did it."

I kept walking, keeping an eye out for anything that looked like it belonged to Aaron, too, and ended up kicking something with the toe of my shoe. A bone, like the others back on campus. This one was thin, spindly, only about the size of my forearm, and cracked at one end. It had been beside a bowl with some foul-smelling liquid inside.

I sniffed the bowl once, then backed away. "The bone must

have been wiped down with the bleach." I turned the bone in my hands. "But why would they bleach a cow's—?"

I dropped the bone with a clatter, feeling bile rising to the back of my throat. "Oh."

Max's mouth twisted. "My guess, the shin."

I swallowed, fighting against waves of nausea. Quietly, I said, "If this is here, then where's the rest?"

As we searched, I half-prayed we wouldn't find anything. I'd hoped they'd just robbed a grave. Anything other than killed someone. But then Max called to me from outside the cave, his voice low. "We should get out of here," he said, trying to direct me away from the drop, a shallow shelf of rock just large enough for a body, but I saw it. The glimpse of hair was enough. The bile in my stomach turned acidic, and I threw up against the wall.

He rubbed my back in small circles. "We've got to get out of here and let the school know."

I was terrified. All I wanted was to do what he said, to race back to campus and tell the council, and have all the brothers arrested. But that would still leave Dani, Luce, and Vern without our help. "I'm not leaving without Dani's object."

I turned back to the cave. If it was anywhere, it had to be here.

I walked toward the women's clothing and other items, which I realized now likely belonged to the girl at the bottom of the ravine. Someone had written their initials on the inside of a sweatshirt. EG.

"Emma Garcia." My heart sank.

"Those fucking bastards," Max said.

I picked up the small comb. Small pearls decorated the top, yellowing with age. The handle was mother-of-pearl. "This one's different." I ran a hand over it lovingly. It felt familiar to me somehow, and like something I should protect, should treasure. It was Dani's, I just knew it.

"A gift from Dani's mother, maybe? Or an aunt?" It had the same faint flicker as the telescope. Reticent, removed, but this one was so full of warmth, too. "A family heirloom, I think," I said.

But Max wasn't as excited about my discovery. He looked like he was about to retch. "Let's grab it and get out of here."

I nodded. I gathered the other objects, too—the ring and the notebook and even the shoes—and stowed them in my backpack. There was no power in them anymore, but these things were important to the girl out there once. Mementos of a life, things that linked her to the people she loved and the people who loved her. It seemed wrong that they should be out here all alone, that she should be out here all alone. When they came back for Emma's body, I would give them to her family.

As we walked back, me limping and leaning heavily on Max for support, I noticed he was wearing a different hat. A black one with silver braiding. "Why the change in attire?"

"I figure I'll save them the trouble of dressing me for the funeral."

"How considerate of you." My laugh rang hollow. We both knew there was more truth to the statement than we liked.

We reached the other side of campus in a cool ten minutes. When we walked up to the door of Maritza's cottage, Max grabbed my hand, his thumb tracing down my palm like he used to. "Last chance to run," he said, his dimple just poking out of a sad half-smile. "We could hitch a ride to Mexico. Me, you, and Bear. Unless you'd rather go it alone again."

The smell of dried red chiles hanging from the porch wafted under my nose.

I squeezed his hand. "No, and no."

He looked in my eyes for one long moment. "Well, if I die . . ." He faltered, seeming to want to say something, then shook his head.

"We won't," I said.

I took a deep breath and walked up to the cottage, tying back the Wall with a hairband. "Ready?"

"As I'll ever be."

We stepped inside.

CHAPTER FIFTY-TWO

9 Hours Until Sunset

When we got inside, Basile, Robetresse, and the other council members were already inside the room, along with Vern, Luce, and Dani in cots. Their arms were bound at their sides and connected to IV drips. Vern's head sagged on his chest.

I frowned. "What is this?"

Dr. Robetresse cleared her throat. "We might ask the same of you."

"Yes, Cella," Basile said, an elegant hand running across his collar, "care to tell us what you're doing here with a book of experimental spells tucked beneath your arm?"

My eyes darted across the room. Luce's eyes were shut, but her upper body twisted in the restraints, head whipping from side to side. Magic pounded the ground with such intensity that I could feel it in my spine.

"They shouldn't all be in here." Max's eyes darted toward me; he felt it, too.

The Magic had grown even more powerful with Luce and now Vern being taken. Three conduits generated three times as much power. And we'd just walked into it. We'd submerged ourselves into a pool with a dozen live wires hissing at its surface.

"Why not, Cella? Will it ruin the spell that you're attempting to do outside the council's knowledge?" Basile said, the line of his jaw long and sharp. There it was, the only indication of the real Basile, hiding behind the cold stare reserved just for me. His dark eyes glittered, daring me to challenge him.

"You're one to talk," I shot back. I might've laughed at the irony. All along we thought the monster was Dani, and here was the real one in front of us the entire time.

Dr. Robetresse and the other council members stared. "Basile has recommended we keep the three of them together. He has something he's been working on that he believes can help."

"He is the one responsible for all of this. You can't trust a word he says."

He cocked a brow and lowered his voice so only I could hear him. "What's wrong, Cella? Disillusioned with us already?"

"How about you tell me what the hell you did to my brother?"

Basile waved his hand in dismissal of the accusation. "She's lying."

Robetresse's lips drew into a thin line. "If what you say is true, why not tell us before now of your suspicions? Basile has only ever been up-front with us, and you've never indicated any distrust of him before. You're saying now he's a suspect?"

"It certainly looks suspicious, you only bringing this up now," Dr. Nguyen agreed. The red spool of thread behind her pointed at me accusingly.

My stomach sank. Of all the scenarios I'd anticipated, I hadn't expected this—that they would be here already, suspicions whispered into their ears by Basile. But the stark truth stared me right in the face. I'd been gone from the school for too long, had been out of Dr. Robetresse's confidence. While I was worrying about trusting her and everyone else on the council, I'd never given thought to whether *she trusted me*. Basile had had plenty of time to work these people, to make friendships. Now I was just an outsider, blaming one of their own.

"That's because we didn't know until now. At least, we weren't sure. But I have proof."

"Please, let's not waste time with ridiculous claims," Basile said, his smooth voice cutting over mine. "The only involvement I've had in this investigation has been trying to find the culprit. And here she is. Just have a look at what Cella is carrying under her arm."

My fingers scrambled for my phone. I opened the picture of the cave where they did the ritual, and the ravine below it. "We found a body."

Max stepped forward. "Saw it with my own eyes."

Robetresse's eyes darted from Basile to us, no longer sure who to believe. She was clearly unhappy with me springing this on her, but there was no way she could ignore this. I looked at the other council members. Ellendale ran his hand over his chin and took a step closer to Basile. I wasn't going to win him over to my side anytime soon.

"You think I'm responsible for a *body?* What evidence do you have to make such an outrageous claim?"

I pointed to Luce, Vern, and Dani. "The same evidence I have that shows you're responsible for all of this. The body we found was outside a cave that I believe the brothers have been occupying to cast spells in this book. I believe the body is that of a local girl, Emma Garcia, and that she died in a failed attempt at Basile's Reality Paradox. Basile and the brothers have been experimenting on students, attempting to unbind people from their objects to send them to some other world, all in order to perfect the spell for themselves."

Basile shook his head and laughed. "Wow."

I ignored him and continued. "When Dani became unbound, she was left unprotected from Magic, and so it walked straight through her. She had no control over herself when she killed Maya, and she has no control over herself now. Through this spell, the brothers opened a door to the other world. What they didn't know was the door went both ways. And now they can't control it."

Max nodded. "The entire student body is at risk because of what Basile and the brothers have done. The Magic is too strong to control. It stepped right through Luce and Vern, taking over them, too."

Basile started clapping. "While I applaud the lofty

conclusions you two have jumped to here, you're still missing a key ingredient. Proof. Where is the proof you have for all these wild accusations?" He turned to the others. "I hope you will all think twice before believing our colleague here on word alone. It's obvious the case has done a number on her. Just look at her."

Dr. Robetresse's footsteps wavered. The other council members looked on, unsure of who to believe.

I bit hard into my cheek. "And I suppose it's just coincidence that you released a video saying you proved the Reality Paradox and could send someone to the next world on the same day we discover another person like Dani. What happened to Luce, Basile?"

He laughed. "While I'm flattered you've taken an interest in my work, clearly someone failed to teach you not to believe everything you see on the internet. Last I checked, there's no crime against drumming up publicity. Particularly when doing so raises desperately needed funds for children's summer camps."

More murmurs from the other council members. Dr. Nguyen's thread twisted anxiously behind her. With a sinking feeling, I realized we might be losing this.

"We're running out of time," said Max. "The only way to save the others is to bind them back to their objects. The longer we spend arguing with the guy responsible for all of this, the stronger they get. The stronger the Magic gets."

"Basile's entire Reality Paradox is about getting to another world," I said. "This mystical 'world of Being.' He told me himself that you can get there by living a 'good life,' according to his group's laws."

"Yes," Basile scoffed, "surely there's no crime in having spiritual beliefs. I fail to see where she's going with this."

I looked over at Max, who carefully positioned himself between Basile and the door. He looked at me, eyes blazing. *You can do this.*

Basile was a snake. Just like the Magic that had curled

around them all and sunk in its teeth. But I was done letting people manipulate me, and I was done doubting myself and my own power. Who cared if I didn't have a big following? So what if I couldn't charm a crowd? There were people here who believed in me just as much as in him. There were people in this room who'd traveled the country just to get me to return. I wasn't some little insignificant thing: I was Marcella P. Gibbons. And I was done being ignored.

I turned to the council members and steadied my voice.

"Basile is a smooth talker, and he knows just what to say to make you want to believe him. I—I admit, I believed it myself at first. I was taken in by the allure of it, by the idea of it. But this little club of his is a cult, and he'll say anything to deflect from it."

I held up the drawing Vern had made of his office. "Tell them about the book, Basile. The book that has the very spell Dani underwent to become what she is now. Go ahead, explain away how it came to be in your office. Or maybe you can explain how Luce Montgomery's field journal indicates the Phi Kat house was the last place she went before turning into this? No? How about why Emma Garcia's friends said she was terrified after what happened at a Phi Kat party and then she was never seen again. Explain why her belongings are sitting in a cave close to the Phi Kat house." I swallowed. "Explain what happened to my brother."

Fiery-red splotches crept up Basile's neck as he fought the contemptuous look on his face.

I faced him head-on, jaw set. "Explain to them what you told me. That if someone lived a 'good life,' they'd become divine, able to control and shape every thought and idea in this world for all of time. It's how you get people to follow you, isn't it? You promise them control. It's how you get your friends to go along with you while you kill people."

The last dregs of his self-control melted away. His face contorted in rage. "I didn't kill her," he shouted. "I set her free!"

The council members took a step back, shocked by his

admission. Dr. Perez's eyes widened. Quietly, Dr. Robetresse said, "Someone get Esoteric Medicine. I want confirmation on Emma Garcia's remains. And for God's sake," she said, voice breaking, "cover the poor thing."🖋

"That's not what I meant, I—" Basile said, trying to backpedal.

His eyes scanned the cottage, looking for a sympathetic face and finding none. Even Dr. de Vries edged away from him.

I couldn't help it. My face broke into a triumphant smile.

Then I watched as Basile carefully walked over to Dr. Robetresse, a million emotions flashing across his face, and his anger slipped away, replaced by a controlled, easy charm.

"Dr. Robetresse," he said, his voice turning liquid and melodic. More softly, "Thea. Aren't you sick of scouring the country for professors willing to teach at Seinford and Brown? Aren't you sick of the measly funds coming in that barely keep the buildings from collapsing around us? Picture it: students flocking in from all over the world, begging you to teach them, begging you to help them make their mark on history. Imagine the most influential Magicians all over the world calling you, begging for a teaching position. Begging *the* Thea Robetresse."

He turned to Ellendale, standing stiffly in the corner.

"Ellendale, it's what you've always wanted, isn't it? What you thought was merely theoretical but couldn't stop yourself from dreaming of all the same. I can show you how to surpass even your own reputation."

"And, Cella," he said, turning toward me as I opened my mouth in protest. The anger in his eyes was gone, replaced by smooth charm, the same charm that had gotten thousands of people to follow him, to tune into his posts, his videos, his math proofs. He cast a sidelong glance at Max. "You were sick of living in someone else's shadow, sick of being overlooked. People told you that you couldn't do it, that there was no way

---

🖋 (Robetresse): I was trying to stay calm, but I could scarcely believe it. Someone had died here, under my very nose.

someone like you could do it. Here's your chance to prove them wrong." He stroked his fingers down the side of my face. "Come with me."

I smacked his hand away.

He grinned, and the shape took readily to his mouth. With a sinking feeling, I realized I should have never fought him on his own turf. He was made for this. He was made for eloquent speeches, tailor-made to pull people over to his side. "Most Greeks believed that, upon death, you would live a shadowy and bleak existence in the underworld. Then when our teacher came, He taught that the soul was immortal, and that you could be reborn into a life similar to the one you left. He brought hope to the Greeks. And through His teachings, we are doing the same for people today, people who feel powerless, who feel lost. Just imagine. When you die, your soul will have all the control you lacked in this life. You could correct all those horrible things you saw in this world but never had the power to do anything about. Can you honestly look me in the eye and tell me that's not something any of you want?"

He turned his sculpted chin to the light, took an elegant hand and gestured all around us. "Why fight the power that we could reach out and take? Magic has always been there, pushed to the side, belittled and scorned. Attacked and mocked by a religion that feared the threat to its power. But we were the ones who had the power all along. We hide like rats when we could be kings."

I backpedaled, looking at Dr. Robetresse and the others, afraid they were falling for it. Ellendale stroked his chin, considering what Basile said. Dr. Nguyen's spool of thread tangled faster and faster behind her. "He's manipulating you," I pleaded.

Dr. Robetresse shook her head, eyes hardening. "Why? Why unbind people from their objects? Why all of this just to get to some other world?"

"Not just some other world, *the* other world. The world of Being, where your soul could live on forever, influencing every action of this world for all of time. Objects fracture the soul when it needs unification to be pure for the One. Removing those limitations by unbinding is the fastest, most direct way to get to the world of Being."

Dr. Robetresse clenched and unclenched her hands to stop their shaking, her usual calm authority knocked off balance. "You're with Britton, then. They set you up to this? Did they want to see me fail so badly they sent some cult leader to defy me?"

"My dear, Britton could never," he said. "We are our own. We have existed before that silly little school was even a thought, was even a murmur. We have existed before time itself. Our one purpose is to keep safe the Book, to carry on His word. To purify the souls of the world through mathematics and His teachings." He looked to me.

"We have kept the Book safe for centuries, and we will not stop now." The door to the cottage swung open, showing the brothers lined up outside the door. At least thirty of them, and more still coming, all clad in black robes. A chill shot down my spine.

They drew the shape of a **Y** across their brows and started a low chant.

The Pythagorean Letter two ways spread,
Shows the two paths in which Man's life is led.

One of them tipped his hood back so I could see him and grinned. Grant. I looked at Max, frowning, when the realization dropped like a stone in my stomach.

Of course.

The gruesome meme he'd posted of Maya, standing before two paths. The curling snake symbol of snakes formed into a Y I'd seen in Basile's office. S joining a mystery school thousands of years ago run by a man "famed for his wisdom," who had all these rules for initiation and prized mathematics and an understanding of the world and all its mysteries. And the interview on the Dawn Underground, the mention of Pythagoras's belief in "immortality of the soul" and its transmigration into a new body upon death.

"S's teacher was Pythagoras?" I nearly whispered it, but Basile looked at me, a cold glaze over his eyes, before turning to the crowd to address them.

"Brothers! Today, you are all Mathematici! Let us not stop now, when everything we want is within reach. Danica has done it. She has ascended to the realm of immortals. And we can, too. Think of it, my brothers! To be immortal. Never forgotten. Never discounted. Never ignored." He raised his arms in the air.

"Don't you want them to hear you?"

They chanted in unison. "*Kathari psychi!*"*

He spread his arms wide, lovingly, as if embracing them all. "Danica accepted that if she died in the process, we have still given her a great gift. We have united her soul so she may live on in the beyond forever."

"A gift?" I spat. "You've nearly killed her."

Basile's face was set in a firm line. "Dani isn't just some poor, overlooked, under-loved girl anymore. I made her matter. I made her a god." He turned to the crowd again. "And I can do the same for any of you. Power is there for all of us, if only we reach out and take it. Remember, my Mathematici, a man must be made good, then a god."

Screams came from outside the cottage as the group tussled with students. Grant cast a spell that threw a girl across the yard. A freshman was surrounded by three of them, sporting a bloody nose. Dr. Robetresse looked to the other council members and closed her eyes, summoning her Magic. "Perez, de Vries, Nguyen, with me." Dr. Robetresse and the council members rushed into the crowd, clashing with the brothers. Max tackled a brother trying to rush into the room.

---

* Pure of soul.

Besides the conduits, Basile and I were the only ones left in the room. I positioned myself between them and him.

"It's over, Basile. You're not getting away with this."

He smiled, and the curl of it reminded me of smoke. "You can't stop us. Even Aaron believed in us. The poor thing was so desperate for any type of belonging, we barely had to offer more than an outstretched hand. He drank up our teachings almost as readily as you did. Unfortunately, unlike you, he didn't take as easily to the spell." He reached a hand beneath my chin and whispered, "It's a shame that he wasn't as strong as you. Didn't have the stamina."

My voice quivered. "You're lying."

"We couldn't have him ratting us out, could we? Poor thing, the Magic was too much for him. I imagine it drove him to the untimely end you witnessed. Terrible waste."

"I'll kill you," I whispered, my hands shaking with rage. I closed my eyes and called my Magic to me.

But before I could, something slammed into my side. Searing pain flashed against the side of my head, and the last thing I saw was Basile, looking down at me.

CHAPTER FIFTY-THREE

7 Hours Until Sunset

When I opened my eyes, Basile wasn't in the cottage anymore. Students and teachers were fighting. Many of them had broken noses or lips split with blood.

A horde of the Order of Autumn stood behind Basile, ominous in black cloaks and black leather sandals. Their heads were bowed as they chanted low and quiet, their own sonorous chant.

"*Our Father*," they chanted, "*who art in the ground. Hallowed be thy name Pythagoras—*"

Max ran back inside and heaved a wooden bar against the door. "Cella," he panted, "this is it. We've got to do the binding."

"Okay," I said, scrambling for my book bag. I pulled out the objects, still glancing out the window at the commotion outside.

Behind me, Max took a step backward. "Cella . . ."

"One sec, I'm just getting my stuff."

"Cella," Max said, more forcefully this time.

I looked up. Vern still dozed in his bed, head sagging on his chest. Luce was slightly more animated, neck whipping from side to side. But Dani wasn't in her binds anymore. And she wasn't in her cot.

She stood across the table from us—barely two arm's breadths away from me. And unlike all the other times, when she had been fading in and out of consciousness, this time, she wasn't just awake. She wasn't just alert. She was staring right at me. And she was smiling.

Heavy purple circles ringed eyes that were so dark they were almost black. Her lips were bone white. And her hair was no longer plastered to her head from sweat, but flying about her like she flowed with an electricity all her own. She crouched, and a small voice inside my head screamed:

Run.

But I was frozen in place. All I could think was how frail her body had been before, so thin and ragged and weak. She shouldn't have been able to stand. She shouldn't have been able to move. Now she watched me like an animal, while my heart hammered in my chest.

"The objects, Cella!" Max yelled, and I remembered all too late what we had practiced. He already had the telescope planted on the ground. The comb hummed in my pocket.

I put it on the table, ready to grab my own objects and cast, but it was too late. Dani's face twisted into a gruesome rage. She lunged for me.

She knocked me back. Her fingernails gouged at my skin, my eyes, twisted around my neck. Her breath was rancid and hot on my cheek. Adrenaline pumped through my veins.

"Max!"

Before the scream ripped from my mouth, he'd pulled her off me. She snarled, then darted across the room. All of our eyes locked on the door.

"Max, now," I screamed.

I held my strip of leather in one palm and reached for the mug with the other, willing the Magic forward, harder and faster than ever before.

Come, I nearly screamed to it.

My Magic, however timid it might have acted in the past, crashed into me like a wave breaking on the shore. It hit me in three bone-crushing waves, rushing over me until I was suspended in water. For a moment, I couldn't breathe.

And then a single "Kick!" boomed in my ears. I kicked to the surface, and the water subsided.

My eyes shot to Dani. Her lip had curled into an ugly snarl. She rushed to Max, who in the moment's distraction had clamped one of her wrists in a restraint on the bed. I rushed over to help, staying clear of her fingernails and snapping jaws. Already, I had a deep gouge on the back of my hand from one of her dirty fingernails. We managed to get the other restraint on.

Dani writhed, her blond hair whipping from side to side in a rage. It shook the bed so much, the cottage rattled in the sandy dirt. Rocks and pebbles rolled from corners; bits of dust shook loose from the wooden rafters.

I opened the book and started S's incantations when Dani's gaze turned on me, and all the shaking and writhing stopped.

For one long, quiet moment, everything was still. Dani smiled at me.

Then I was drowning.

CHAPTER FIFTY-FOUR

6 Hours Until Sunset

As I fell through water, watching as the surface drifted farther away and the water got deeper and darker the farther I fell, I remembered that this was what I was afraid of. Drowning just like that man on the beach. Slipping under the surface, with no one to see or hear or care. Sliding alone into the darkness.

The water crushed me under its weight. My ribs squeezed, and my head felt woozy and light. It felt as if there were hundreds of pounds on top of me. Three hundred pounds. Four hundred. I felt my ribs fracture, the bones jabbing into me, sharp and splintering. Pain filled my chest, puncturing my organs and my lungs. Blood filled my mouth. And water, so much water, and I felt myself, falling, falling . . .

And then with startling clarity, there was Max's voice.

Kick, Cella. Kick. You can do this.

I heard the *thump thump thump* of horses and the sound of cicadas chirping, felt the cool kiss of summer rain, smelled grass and the sweet scent of summer blossoms, felt the flutter of moths on my face, and the coarse fibers of the saddle blanket Max kept in the back of his truck. His hair brushed my cheek; as I looked into his eyes, all I saw was blue, blue, blue.

"Cella, stay here, stay with me," he said, and his lips were on mine, then off again. Each time, I felt a stab of pain as they left me once more.

His mouth formed quick words. "I bind thee into three

objects." He chanted it over and over again, more forcefully each time.

"I bind thee into three. *I bind thee!*"

The water was receding all around me in large, sucking swells like someone had pulled the plunger on a drain. All of a sudden, the room was in sight again. A light glowed at the surface. I reached for it, stretching with everything in me.

I opened my eyes.

I was back in the room with Max.

He was straining from the force of doing the spell on his own. The veins in his neck and arms bulged. The wind bit at my eyes. When did it get so windy? Hot red clay swept in from under the door, cutting my cheeks, swirling around the room, stinging my skin. Crosses shook against the walls and fell to the floor.

The wooden piece we'd used to bar the door shook and popped off. In stormed the brothers, led by Basile.

Dani looked at me, and things grew hazy again. I felt myself flying under the water again, simultaneously yanked deeper under a Magic I could no longer control, while Max worked to pull me back to the surface. Back to the farm, to his horses, to the dry, grassy space that encompassed him when he cast.

I didn't know how long I wrestled beneath the waves, simultaneously drowning and sucking in the scent of evening air. Life became a single pinprick of blue, of darkness, of a call to infinite, inexpressible power, a chasm that I was so foolish to think I could hold onto.

And then there was Max, brown and warm and green and coarse and creaking. Callused hands, warm lips, rough stubble on his cheeks grazing my face, but I held onto his voice. It was what I focused on, rather than slipping into this deep, dark trench.

"Cella, come back to me. Come back," he was saying. My memories blended with the present until I couldn't tell where or when or who I was. We were back in his truck, and he was kissing my lips and my neck and willing me back to him, the call to my dimidium powerful in its own right, but I was so weak. I murmured for more.

His face appeared in front of me, larger than life. Sweat dripped from the tip of his nose; his hair was damp against his forehead. His lips pulled away from mine. Then he was yelling, shoving at something behind him as hands pulled him away from me.

4 Hours Until Sunset

I opened my eyes. I was no longer in Maritza's cottage. I was in some sort of dark space—a cell maybe? No. As my eyes adjusted to the low lighting, I realized it wasn't a cell at all, but a cave. One like the cave we'd found in the canyon that the brothers had used. A sliver of light shone on a flat rock in the center, and there, sitting on it, was Luce Montgomery.

"Luce? What are you doing in here? Are you okay?"

Luce took one look at me and threw up. She ducked her head between her knees and moaned.

"No," she said drily. "I'm dying, and apparently, I get to do it stuck here with you. *Wonderful.*" She retched again.

"What is this place?"

"I don't know," she admitted. "All I know is Basile knocked me out as soon as I went to talk to him about what I found in the canyon. After that, I remember a few hazy lights, and then . . . nothing. For a while, I thought I'd died and woken up in Hell. Actually, now that you're here, it's looking like more of a possibility."

I looked around. "I don't know what Basile did to you, but outside of this, you're not doing so well."

"Outside of this? What do you mean?"

"Last I saw, you were, um . . . possessed? By the Magic." She retched again. "Oh, that absolute ass."

And I realized, all at once: Basile's livestream. The brothers must have done this spell on Luce, let her become a vessel to the One to show they could send someone to the other world.

"Maybe that's what we're in," I said. "Maybe this is the world of Being."

"Well, great, I'm part of his little experiment. But why would the brothers want to get here? For all Basile's talked it up, it looks like a prison."

"I guess no one's exactly made it back to tell them." I shivered.

Luce keeled over and vomited black bile. I put my hand on her back and rubbed in small circles the way my mom used to. She whimpered and put her head on my knee.

She sat up at last, wiping bile from her lips, a thin streak of blood smearing across her hand.

"There's got to be a way out." I stood up, sticking my hands out in front of me to feel my way toward the entrance. As soon as I reached the opening of the cave, black iron bars appeared across it. I took one of them in hand—

"Ow!" I cried. An angry welt appeared on the inside of my palm.

"Yeah, they burn," Luce said. I looked toward the opposite end of the cave. "Nothing back there, either," she said. "It only goes back about six feet past here, then stops."

I sat down on the ground. "What about—"

"Magic doesn't work either."

When I tried to reach for my Magic, there was . . . nothing. Just static, like there was some block in the way.

"Looks like you're right about the prison thing," I admitted.

Luce looked at the bars thoughtfully. "We're taught that Magic is always around, right? Just waiting to be let in? What if this is the same place Magic is trapped until someone lets it into our world?"

"Then we're trapped here."

I lay down on the cool ground and stared out into the darkness. Time seemed to move at some unknown pace here.

With no sun and no difference in the lighting of the cave, hours could've passed already, or even days.

I'd been so stupid to not tell Max how I felt about him before we went to see Dani. And now it was too late, and I might never see him again.

A story flashed into my mind. Something Jamie had told me. That when Pythagoras had discovered the Pythagorean theorem, he sacrificed a hundred cattle in his joy. This was despite the fact that his teachings were explicitly against the sacrifice of animals. "It's an allegorical story, of course, like most of his teachings," Jamie explained, "not meant to be taken literally. It meant that Pythagoras's love of numbers was so great, he would do such a crazy thing to celebrate the discovery. Like strip off your clothes and run through the streets."

"I see," I'd said.

"It's why we took the bull skull as our group's symbol," Jamie said. "A symbol for how easily myth and mistruth spreads in the absence of fact. It's also why Pythagoras's teachings weren't shared widely to begin with, why they weren't written down. It's hard to trust the public to consider nuance. Pythagoras preached *Receive not a swallow in your house.* Meaning don't accept a loud, bombastic person into the teachings because they won't be able to keep the knowledge a secret."

Cut not fire with a sword . . . *When the wind blows, worship the noise.* All these Pythagorean teachings* that had been in Dani's notebook, in the note from the party. Hints that I would have known if I'd just remembered.

Another memory. Of me, drawing the sign for the One referenced in the Book of Autumn on top of the bull skulls around campus: the ten-dot triangle inside a circle, adopted

---

* And Orphic beliefs (which served as the basis for many of Pythagoras's religious beliefs).

from the tetractys.* It was the same symbol the brothers had taken for their Order of Autumn. I guess I thought if I drew it there, it would be clear to me. *The One has infiltrated the Pythagoreans. Don't trust them.* But this too turned to a muddy pool in my head.

Because how could I know that the One would take me over so fully, and bury me so deep that I wouldn't remember any of it afterward?

2 Hours Until Sunset

Luce ran her hand down a slick crevice in the rock. "Look, it's an oyster mushroom. I didn't even notice it before." She smiled. "You know, some people are afraid of fungi because they don't understand them, but there's so much good they can do."

I squinted in the low light. I could barely see my hand in front of me, so I didn't know how she could see it. I moved closer to her, focusing on movement in the dark. Her finger was stroking the mushroom. The thing seemed to respond in kind, bobbing slightly in contentment.

"I used to be so angry and dejected," she said. "Like I didn't sign up for this shit, why do I have to dredge through endless days of bullshit and everything being so hard all the time? But when I got into mycology, I realized something. Even in the soil beneath you, there are millions of fungi. The world is not this cold, dark place. It is so, so alive."

I nodded. "There's a lot of beauty in the things we overlook."

---

* The tetractys was a ten-dot triangle that stood on its own. It was the same symbol inked on Dean Morren's wrist. That was why I couldn't find anything linking him to Phi Kat, because the ten-dot triangle wasn't the symbol for the Order of Autumn. It was a symbol in Pythagoraeanism. It really was just "a math thing." I felt like I could finally see through the cloud I'd been under for so long.

She keeled over again, and I held her hair back. She squeezed my hand as she heaved, her body racked in a cold sweat. "Like you. I never expected to be glad Cella Gibbons was with me in my bleakest moment, but here I am. I'm sorry for being such a bitch to you all these years."

"It's okay," I said, squinting at my shoes in the dark. "I'm sorry I set your car on fire."

"Eh, the insurance took care of it. Besides, I probably deserved it."

"No, you absolutely did not."

I could hear the grin in her voice. "We're not going to do that thing where we hug and make up and give each other friendship bracelets."

I looked up at her and smiled. "Matching ones with our names in little beads shaped like hearts."

She chuckled. "Tempting. So tempting."

Luce stroked another mushroom in the corner of the cave, in a moist crevice where water dripped down.

I leaned my head back. "You ever wonder what else you missed because you weren't looking?"

I thought back to the scars on my brother's arms. The need for belonging so strong that it drove him right into the arms of a cult. And my own obsessive need to learn more, to master more Magic, which nearly drove me to the same point. The signs that had been there; I just hadn't seen them. My mother's warm, cracked hands wrapping around me, landing a gentle kiss on my forehead. Her hair, now gray, tickling my cheek. The love that was there, even if she didn't quite know how to show it. I thought of Vern, leaving cups of tea out for me, pulling a blanket over me after I'd fallen asleep in the library. Dr. Perez, telling me there was always a spot in his department for me, even after all these years. He'd been in my corner this whole time, and I hadn't seen it. Even Luce, the girl who was so much more than some petty rival, who was brilliant and full of wonder and a force all her own. I just wished I'd noticed it all sooner.

Luce smiled. "God, all the time."

She looked down at the mushroom and cocked her head. "Hold on a second . . . there are more here." She stood up, followed some invisible line of fungi weaving around the stones of the cave. "Oh my God," she breathed, "you see these little red streaks in the gills? These are the fruiting bodies of the fungus I've been looking for! This place—"

Her footsteps hurried as she continued tracing the line of mushrooms through the cave; then she was moving too quickly toward the bars.

"Wait Luce, you'll hit them—!"

She turned back abruptly, flashing me a feral smile. She wiped blood off her lips with the back of her hand.

"If I don't make it back, give Basile a kick to the balls for me."

Her laughter traveled out of the cave, and her footsteps receded. I couldn't see her anymore.

"Luce?" I called after her. "Luce!"

30 Minutes Until Sunset

I sat there for a long time, peering at the bars in front of the cave, trying to find a gap underneath or between them that Luce had slipped out of. But every time I got closer for a better look, I got burned. I stood back, frowning.

After a long time, footsteps sounded in the gloom. I perked up. "Luce? Is that you?"

No answer.

"Luce? Who's out there?"

Wind whistled through the cave, rushing all around me. Then I felt the water trickling over my feet. And I realized it wasn't footsteps, but the familiar *thump thump thump* of horses. I looked up, and I wasn't in the cave at all, but on a moonlit beach, my feet in the water. Sparkling stars shone overhead beside a waxing crescent moon.

"Cella?" At first, I could only feel his aura, but then I concentrated on his voice. "Max? Max!"

And then he was there. He closed his eyes and held me, his lips to my forehead. "Max? How are you here? How do we get out of here?"

"We're in the Magic," he breathed. "It has control of you."

"Can you get me out?" I asked, but he wouldn't look down. He held me even tighter. And it hit me—in all my time of doing Magic, I'd never brought anything out again. He didn't know how. Neither of us did.

I looked up at him, my voice going quiet. "How long can you stay?"

He kissed my head, and I could feel the tears on his eyelashes brush against my skin. "For as long as I can hold it. You know I'd go into Hell itself to save you, don't you? I'd give it all up for you, Magic, every single bit of it."

You ever wonder what else you missed because you weren't looking?

It was Max, always Max. How we lost each other. How we found each other. Max willing to get lost in the Magic forever to save me. Max throwing away his life to bring me back to mine. Max helping me in a hundred ways, always putting me above himself. That was love. Pure, unrelenting love. I wondered if that was what it meant to be a part of someone, to never truly be apart from them, no matter how far away you went.

"I love you," I said. "I've always loved you. I'm sorry it took me so long to say it."

He tilted my chin up and kissed me, and for one brutally blissful moment, it didn't matter where I was.

"Is this our goodbye, then?" I asked. "I guess I finally got what I wanted. Only to find out it's not what I wanted in the first place."

"You'll always be a part of me, Cella. No matter where you

go, how far, what . . . plane, what world. I will find you in all of them and bring you back to me."

We stood there in the Magic, holding each other in the moonlight. We held each other until the waves lapped at my feet and the moon dimmed in the sky, and at last when I opened my eyes, I knew I was alone.

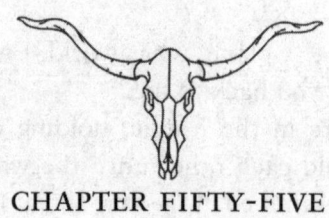

CHAPTER FIFTY-FIVE

10 Minutes Until Sunset

A million things went through my head. A million memories, a million echoes, like my life was passing before my eyes.

Kick, Cella!
Come on, kick to the surface.
Breathe.
Live.
Kick.

Standing on that windy beach that lived in a perpetual state of twilight, my objects fluttered around me. The cup from my brother, spinning in the air, HOLLY JOLLY spinning so fast I could only make out the first two letters.

The leather strap twisting and turning in the air, and the jar of water from the lake Aaron and I had swam in as children. Back when things were simpler, when my life consisted of summer camp and family trips to the lake, playing tag and sleepovers with friends, and, encased in all this, home. The idea of home, which I seemed to have lost over the years. Wasn't Seinford and Brown its own kind of home? After all, it was where my colleagues and friends were—Perez and Vern and Robetresse and Luce and Max and Maritza and the rest of the council. My family just down the road. All these people, and the love of my life, all here, waiting for me to return.

Every memory with Max fluttered to the surface. Every

time he'd been there for me, as strong and secure and safe as an object. And yeah, we hadn't been perfect. But love wasn't perfect. Life wasn't perfect. It was messy and complicated and sometimes sad, but it was so *alive*. It was filled to the brim with new beginnings and, sometimes, old beginnings, too.

My objects floated in front of me, clear and crystalline as glass.

Kick, Cella!
Come on, kick to the surface.
Breathe.
Live.
Kick.

I didn't want to stay here. This wasn't the place where I belonged. I belonged in Marble County, New Mexico. I belonged at home. Whatever that word meant, whether it was in his arms or my mother's, or with my friends, or with any number of the people who'd believed in me when I didn't believe in myself.

I reached out for my objects.
I opened my eyes.
And I kicked for the surface.

CHAPTER FIFTY-SIX

"Cella, thank God!" Max was in front of me, his hair drenched with sweat. Behind him, Vern and Luce leaned in to get a better look. Even my mother was there. She broke down in tears when she saw I was okay and wrapped me in a sweater that smelled like her.

"Alright now, let's give her some space," Robetresse said.

I sat up from the ground, still dazed. We were still in Maritza's cottage. My boots scraped the ground. "How—how did you . . . ?"

Vern's wife, Sonia, screamed and hurried over. "Cella's awake!" She hugged my shoulders, while Vern chuckled, removing his glasses and wiping his eyes.

"Vern!" I hugged him tight. "I'm so glad you're okay."

"I could say the same about you," he said with a chuckle. "We thought we'd lost you there."

The room was filled with staff and students, all in various states of exhaustion. Some people sagged against the cots. Many were sitting on the ground or on the doorstep, drinking bottles of water and breathing hard. One student looked like he might have passed out at one point. Maritza kneeled over him, dabbing a wet washcloth over his forehead. He sat up, coughing.

"We did the spell, Cella," Max said. "All of us. Well, most of us." He cast a pointed look at Basile and Alex, who were outside, surrounded by the remaining council members and Dr. Strauss. "The Magic took so many people that we needed more objects and . . . we each threw in one of our objects. And"— he appeared astonished as he looked around the room. "And it worked, Cel. It worked. We were able to bind Dani again, and—and you, too, so the Magic won't have control of you all ever again."

Objects were on the ground, turned to ash or shattered into pieces. A girl cradled the torn pages of an aged storybook, holding the soft cover now in pieces in her palm. A boy tried to tape back on the wing of a model airplane. Another boy stuck a cracked phone in a bowl of rice. Dr. Oswold peered sadly at her splintered Etch-a-Sketch.

"You each gave up an object to save me? You didn't have to do that. I didn't ask for that, I didn't want—"

These people had sacrificed an object each to try and contain the overwhelming surge of Magic. In doing so, they had willingly diminished their own Magical abilities. And not only that, but a part of them, items they'd treasured and held dear, things that were inextricably part of who they were.

I closed my eyes, picturing the loss each of them must have felt. I imagined how I would feel if the Christmas mug that my brother had given me shattered, how I would feel willingly throwing the leather cord from his journal into a fire to be burned to ash. "I'm so, so sorry."

I hadn't trusted people in a long time, but here was this community I'd all but given up on, that I'd thought had forgotten about me a long time ago. And it had now banded together to save me. They all had sacrificed parts of themselves just to save me. It left me at a loss for words.

Dr. Perez handed me a bottle of water. "We did it to save all of you. Vern came out first. He was the easiest. Luce came out by herself, said she 'followed the mycelial network,' whatever that means."

Luce shrugged and looked at her hand, "Turns out having part of me be mushroom comes in handy. It helped me find my way back."

"It's a good thing she pulled herself out, too. I don't know if we would have had enough strength to bring you all out. Then, next after Luce was, well . . ."

Perez stepped aside, so the solitary girl standing behind him was in view. She tucked a wisp of blond hair behind her ear. "Hi, Cella," she said shyly.

Her cheeks and lips had regained their color. Even her blackened teeth had turned a normal shade. She had a gentleness about her, an angelic sweetness to her smile.

"Dani?" I closed my eyes and hugged her. "I feel like I know you."

She laughed, her fragile bones shaking against mine. "Same here."

I wanted to talk more, make sure she was fully okay, but my mother swept me away, harping about needing my rest. "It's my job to make sure *you* are okay," she said.

Maritza seemed to agree that everyone could do with a good lie-down, so they all scattered, ordered back to their dormitories to sleep and eat and try to regain some strength.

Dr. Robetresse scooped the Book of Autumn into her arms. "I'm going to put this in a secure location. Somewhere no one can ever use it for harm again."

I thanked everyone once again for everything they'd done for me, my words falling short of adequately thanking them for the sacrifice they'd made and what it meant to me. "The sacrifice is one I will never forget," I said.

In my exhaustion, I let my mother take me away to my childhood bedroom. She tucked me into the soft quilt she'd embroidered years ago, the sheets she'd cleaned just anticipating me coming to stay, all the pictures and photographs and mementos from my youth. I let her crack open the window so I could hear the birds outside, feel the gentle breeze. She tucked in the blankets around me once more and kissed me on the head before turning out the light.

I slept more peacefully than I had in a long, long time.

CHAPTER FIFTY-SEVEN

"Dear old world," Anne murmured, *"you are very lovely and I am happy to be alive in you."*

—L. M. Montgomery, *Anne of Green Gables*

THREE MONTHS LATER

I was just leaving Dr. Perez's lab. "Cella, when do you think you'll have the notes on object personalization done?"

I smiled and handed him a manila folder. "Last night."*

He shook his head. "This is not what I meant when I said we'd return to work gradually."

I grinned. "You can thank me later! I'm off for the weekend."

"Say hi to Max, and take a break this time—I mean it. Oh, and if his mother has some of that red pepper jelly?"

"I'll grab some. See ya Monday!"

Dr. Perez's lab shared an adjoining wall with the Ecology lab and the newly created Mycoforestry Department.

Luce popped her head over and made a series of smooching noises. "Bring me some too, if his mom has extra!" she yelled.

"You got it. See y'all Monday!"

I raced out of the building, a trail of mushrooms following me as I went—Luce's Magic, sending me off. It turned out

---

* I was more than happy to be working on what had drawn me to Dr. Perez's research from the very beginning. Determining if Magic of the dead could be retained or passed to loved ones through the objects they treasured. I no longer grappled with the desperate anguish I'd felt around Aaron's death, but I knew something like this was a way to help other grieving people.

that not only had she found the fungi she needed in the world of Being, but she came out changed somehow. There was a glimmer to her eye that wasn't there before, a new brown-gold shimmer in her eye, in the exact shape of a mushroom's cap.

I kicked up red clay with my boots as I ran, tying my hair back with a sunflower ribbon, and stopped to take a long look at the sun setting over the canyon. The burst of red and orange and purple lighting up the sky felt like a gift, one I wasn't going to squander.

Max, in his truck, pulled up beside me and did a wolf whistle. Bear popped his head out the window and barked happily. "Wooh-wee, now where would a pretty lady like you be heading on a Friday night?"

"Oh, you know, just spending a romantic weekend with my boyfriend."

He grinned. "Must be some guy."

I climbed into the car, and we shared a kiss. "Must be."

The aftermath of everything wasn't clean or tidy. Basile and a few of his most loyal followers, Paul excluded, had disappeared. Dr. Robetresse was with the Arbiters trying to find them. Paul and a few of the other brothers worked on a rehabilitation program at the school in which people learned to cast with only two objects. A lot of the people involved in the spell had given up their Magic entirely. What they'd seen had scared them off it for good. But others kept at it, keeping in mind what they knew could happen.

We entered a new age of appreciation for Magic—part fear, part respect, but always careful practice. Rumors of what happened even convinced Britton Arcane to start a Three Arts program, for students who were interested in learning a safer form of practice. If there ever really could be a safe way to perform Magic.

And many of the people found new objects to replace the ones they had lost, as they made new memories, forged new bonds and relationships with people. Letters, a cherished memento from an experience or time together. Kind moments sprung up new objects, new things to love, and our relationship with Magic grew into something different, something more respectful and more inclusive of our own boundaries.

I worked on the farm with Max all that summer, mucking out the horse stalls and brushing the horses, and for a while, we ignored Magic. We did small tasks around the house, restitching his mother's quilt, caring for his father's tomato plants, working at his family's farmer's market stand. We harvested the honey from the bees and placed it into jars. We made candles from the beeswax. There was so much Magic in those memories we made, in those little things.

I visited Vern and Sonia often, bringing a beeswax candle or a jar of red pepper jelly. I went to pottery class with my mom. I left flowers at my brother's grave. I spoke to him daily, about all the things I'd noticed now, the simple gestures that brought me so much joy. The time I spent with Max. Even my newfound friendship with Luce. There was so much to appreciate about this world, I told him. It was so, so alive.

Max drove to a far spot on the farm overlooking the lake, where the grass was long and the sun was warm, and pulled out a couple of beers and a blanket.

In time, the Magic began to find us again. It latched onto little objects that we found near and dear; a piece of fence that we'd built over the summer splintered off and became something Max carried with him everywhere. A horseshoe from my favorite mare in the barn became something I carried for luck. A hairclip, a torn piece of a blanket we shared at night. A million little things, a million little memories that we made.

Max lay down on the blanket and patted the spot beside him. Bear gave me several slobbery kisses before running off into the grass.

We camped out beneath the stars so many nights that

summer, tangled up in each other. Our lips kissing all those pieces of us that had always belonged to each other, finding their way back once more.

He ran a finger over my dress and down to my thigh, and I playfully slapped it away. I threw the dress over my head and ran toward the water.

"Woman, you're gonna kill me," he yelled. "Where are you going?"

I looked out at the swaying grasses, the sun beating down on the backs of my legs, the sweet smell of honeysuckle in the air and the cicadas buzzing in the grass. And all I could think was: *I wish you were here, Aaron. You would've loved it.*

And I remembered there was one thing in all of this that I'd nearly forgotten. Anthropology wasn't just the study of humanity; it was the study of what it means to be human. And maybe, sometimes, disillusionment is a part of that. Maybe it's natural to doubt, to take a step back, to retreat. To heal. What matters is coming back.

Because it's easy to lose your faith in people. It's easy to see the bad when we miss plans or we lie or hurt each other. What's harder is to hold on. To see the good, to remember what we can do. But if you look, it's there. And if you're lucky, there will be a community of people who will help show it to you, who won't give up on you, even when you give up on yourself. Who will remind you that humanity isn't perfect, that people aren't perfect, but, goddamn, are they something special.*

---

* Some places never let go of you. My greatest wish for you, dear reader of this record, is that it's because the people who live there have dug their hooks so far into you, you don't want to live another second of your life without them.

Author's Note

While this novel was a work of fiction, I referenced several real-world grimoires and all the historical records I could find involving Pythagoras. Most of note here is the excerpt from *The Golden Verses of Pythagoras* in Danica's journals. I used Nicholas Rowe's translation from André Dacier's French. Another text of note was William Bridgman's translations from the Greek, viz. *The Pythagoric Symbols, with the Explanations of Iamblichus*, which includes many of the alleged Pythagorean sayings referenced in the novel. I'll leave it up to the reader to decide if the writings are actually from Pythagoras.

Acknowledgments

Thank you to my brilliant editors, Alex Sunshine and Shannon Plackis who saw something in this book and took a chance on me. This book is so much better because of both of your insights and sharp eyes, and I am so grateful for the chance to work with you. Thank you also to Jackie Dinas, Steve Zacharius, Adam Zacharius, Robin Cook, copyeditor Pat Fogarty, Madeline Brown, and everyone at Kensington Books. I came into publishing not knowing what to expect, and I have been nothing but blown away by the kindness and excellence of this team every step of the way.

Thank you to my agent, Samantha Fabien, AKA pitching extraordinaire, for your kindness and support over the years. I am so glad to have you as part of my team.

Thank you to my lovely friends and beta readers Gwenyth Reitz, Genoveva Dimova, the Codex Writing Group, and especially its Novel Contest. Thank you to Francesca May for being the first person to see something in my writing. I learned so much in Author Mentor Match; hopefully one day Scarlet will make her return. Shout-out to the 2025 debut group, I feel so privileged to find myself among such a supportive, thoughtful, and kind group of writers.

Thank you to #TeamSamantha. I love how supportive we are and I cannot wait to continue to fill my shelves with all of your amazing books. To De Elizabeth, Alysha Rameera, Katie M. Wilson, and Dana Choe-Murray Draper, for the support, beta reads, and commiseration through this crazy journey. I can't wait to hold all of your books in my hands.

Thank you to my family, my mother-in-law Sandy, and to my dad, who has read every story I've ever written, every school essay, every book, who was at every practice, every tournament, and every game. And who always said to me, "Hey Molly, you should write a story about that." Well, Daddy, I did. Thank you for always believing in me.

Thank you to my angels, Aubrey and Rosie, who are the reason I write stories about girls fighting for their place in the world.

To Clarence Knight, for being a great friend. I'm not saying you inspired Vern. . . but I'm also not NOT saying that. Sorry for missing your calls a lot, hopefully this at least kind of makes up for it. *Runs*

Thank you to my husband, Chris. Undoubtedly, without you, this book wouldn't exist. I could write a thousand novels and never quite express how much you mean to me and how much of a difference you've made on my life. I always kind of think of my life in two parts, the one before you, that was gray and shadowy and dark and sad, and the one after meeting you, which is anything but.

And to my bubba, Royce, who was the first person who read my very first book and chuckled at my character's name—I still smile when I think of that memory. I wish I could show you this book. There are so many things I wish you could be here to see. There's no grave for you, no marker that I can talk to, but I hope you've found some peace on the beach I imagine you at, with a Mai Tai in one hand, and a comic book in the other, and not a care in the world.